CHARLOTTE STREET

Also by Danny Wallace

Friends Like These
Yes Man
Join Me

CHARLOTTE STREET

DANNY WALLACE

wm

WILLIAM MORROW
An Imprint of HarperCollins*Publishers*

CHARLOTTE STREET. Copyright © 2011 by Danny Wallace. All rights reserved. Printed in the United States of America. No part of this book may be used or reproduced in any manner whatsoever without written permission except in the case of brief quotations embodied in critical articles and reviews. For information address HarperCollins Publishers, 10 East 53rd Street, New York, NY 10022.

HarperCollins books may be purchased for educational, business, or sales promotional use. For information please write: Special Markets Department, HarperCollins Publishers, 10 East 53rd Street, New York, NY 10022.

This book was originally published in 2011 by HarperCollins Publishers Ltd., London.

FIRST U.S. EDITION

Library of Congress Cataloging-in-Publication Data
Wallace, Danny.
    Charlotte street : a novel / Danny Wallace. —1st ed.
        p.   cm.
    ISBN 978-0-06-219056-7 (pbk.: acid-free paper) — ISBN 978-0-06-219058-1 (ebook)
    I. Title.
    PR6123.A454C47   2012
    823'.92—dc23   2012027414

12 13 14 15 16 OV/RRD 10 9 8 7 6 5 4 3 2 1

9246

There's nothin' like the humdrum
Of life and love in London
Chasin' girls out of the sticks
Changing worlds with twelve quick clicks

—"Girl in a Photo," The Kicks

As good things go . . . she went.

—"Ex," Hovis Presley

For Elliot

BEFORE

It happened on a Tuesday.

I suppose the noise it would make in a film would be *boom*, but there was no boom with this.

No boom, no bang, no tap, crack, or snap.

Just a flash of glass, a moment in flight, a flicker of shooting star through a history lesson, and all the colder for it.

Things like this aren't supposed to happen on Tuesdays. It's history, then art; it's not *this*.

I shivered the second I saw him, but the strange thing is that I also noticed the weather; this weak gray veil of rain beyond the chipped old railings, beyond the thin scarred trees.

It was like the moment in a dream where you see something happening, something bad, something that should never be, and your bones become heavy and your feet hard to raise, as whatever warning you try to call out through the fog of it all becomes too slurred and too blurred to be useful.

It would have been better, had it been a dream.

What would you call him? A gunman? Seems dramatic, especially this early in the story, but a gunman he was. There, on the other side of the street, maybe nine stories up, pleased with his first shot, now cocking the rifle and snapping it back, reloading, finding his aim.

Gunman will do.

"Right. *Up*. Let's go."

Calm. Short words. Quickly.

"*Now*, please."

I'm suddenly in the middle of the room. It feels like I can do most good here, but really, what *can* I do? I turn and scan the flats again, find him.

He's *laughing*. His mate is, too.

"What? Where to?" said someone, maybe Jaideep, or maybe the one with the hair whose name I could never remember. You know the one—the one the teachers call Superfly. Instinctively I stood in front of him, his paid protector, like he'd made himself a target just by asking sir a question.

"Hall" was the best I could manage, the back of my neck expecting attack, my faked calm fighting my fight or flight. "Up."

"Hey..." said someone else. "Hey...," and I looked at them, and right across their face was the terror I felt, as they struggled to understand what they were seeing, what it meant.

"Okay, *now* please, Anna. Please."

"Sir..."

The waver in the voice, the fear; it would spread, and fast.

"Out the DOOR."

They moved, shocked, and quickly now, as quick as the news spread through the school. As quick as the police arrived, with their own guns, their cars and their dogs, their helmets and shields. The kids found their confidence again then, pressed up against windows, peeping through buckled Venetians, as eight or ten armed coppers made a heavy path up the stairwell of Alma Rose House while the others, tense and furrow-browed, stared the place out, willing our shooter to try something.

The kids applauded as they dragged him out. Applause was the first sign it was over. They applauded the vans, shouted jokes at the coppers, and cooed at the chopper . . . but the kids hadn't seen what I'd seen.

I was last out of 3Gc, I'd tell Sarah, later. She'd stopped at the offie for an eight-pack of Stella and a bottle of Rioja—the only medicine she had a license to give—but she'd rushed home to be with me, her arm on mine, her head against my shoulder. The kids had been safe, I told her, and I'd stayed with them while Anna Lincoln and Ben Powell ran to Mrs. Abercrombie's office to get help, though Ranjit had already dialed 999 by then, and probably posted on Twitter, too.

But I'd stayed in that room just a second or two longer, just to work out whether this could be real, whether he could actually be doing what he was doing, whether I was making a mistake raising this alarm.

And that's when he'd laughed again. And taken aim again.

I'd never felt more alone. Never more aware of myself. What I was, what I wasn't, what I wanted.

And another glimpse of shooting star flit its path inches from my face, to bounce against a wall behind and scutter and scuttle and skip on the floor.

And that, Doctor, is when the damage was done.

ONE

Or "(She) Got Me Bad"

I wonder if we should start with the introductions.

I know who you are. You're the person reading this. For whatever reason, and in whatever place, that's you, and soon we'll be friends, and you'll never ever convince me otherwise.

But me?

I'm Jason Priestley.

And I know what you're thinking. You're thinking: Goodness! Are you the same Jason Priestley, born in Canada in 1969, famous for his portrayal of Brandon Walsh, the moral center of the hit American television series *Beverly Hills 90210*?

And the surprising answer to your very sensible question is no. No, I'm not. I'm the other one. I'm the thirty-two-year-old Jason Priestley who lives on the Caledonian Road, above a videogame shop between a Polish newsagents and that place that everyone *thought* was a brothel, but wasn't. The Jason Priestley who gave up his job as a deputy head of department in a bad North London school to chase a dream of being a journalist after his girlfriend left him but who's ended up single and going to cheap restaurants and awful films so's he can write about them in that free newspaper they give you on the tube that you take but don't read.

Yeah. *That* Jason Priestley.

I'm also the Jason Priestley with a problem.

You see, just in front of me—right here, on this table, just in front of me—is a small plastic box. A small plastic box I've come to regard as a small plastic box that could *change* things. Or, at least, make them *different*.

And right now, I'd take different.

I don't know what's in this small plastic box, and I don't know if I ever will. *That's* the problem. I *could* know; I could have it open within the hour, and I could pore over its contents, and I could know once and for all whether there was any... *hope* in there.

But if I do, and it turns out there *is* hope in there, what if that's all it is? Just a bit of hope? And what if that hope turns to nothing?

Because the one thing I hate about hope—the one thing I *despise* about it, that no one ever seems to *admit* about it—is that suddenly having hope is the easiest route to sudden hope-lessness there is.

And yet that hope is already within me. Somehow, without my inviting it in or expecting it in any way, it's there, and based on what? Nothing. Nothing apart from the glance she gave me and the fleeting glimpse I got of... *something*.

I'd been standing on the corner of Charlotte Street when it happened.

It was maybe six o'clock, and a girl—because yeah, you and I both *knew* there was going to be a girl; there *had* to be a girl; there's *always* a girl—was struggling with the door of the black cab and the packages in her hands. She had a blue coat and nice shoes, and white bags with names I'd never seen before on them, and boxes, and even, I think, a cactus poking out the top of a Heal's bag.

I was ready to walk past, because that's what you do in London, and to be honest, I nearly did . . . but then she nearly dropped the cactus. And the other packages all shifted about, and she had to stoop to keep them all up, and for a moment there was something sweet and small and helpless about her.

And then she uttered a few choice words I won't tell you here in case your nan comes round and finds this page.

I stifled a smile, and then looked at the cabbie, but he was doing nothing, just listening to TalkSport and smoking, and so—and I don't know why, because like I say, this is *London*— I asked if I could help.

And she smiled at me. This incredible smile. And suddenly I felt all manly and confident, like a handyman who knows *just* which nail to buy, and now I'm holding her packages and some of her bags, and she's shoveling new ones that seem to have appeared from nowhere into the cab, and she's saying, "*Thank* you, this is *so* kind of you," and then there's that moment. The glance, the fleeting glimpse of that *something* I mentioned. And it felt like a beginning. But the cabbie was impatient and the night air cold, and I suppose we were just too British to say anything else and then it was, "*Thanks*," and that smile again.

She closed the door, and I watched the cab move off, tail-lights fading into the city, hope trailing and clattering on the ground behind it.

And then—just as the moment seemed over—I looked down.

I had something in my hands.

A small plastic box.

I read the words on the front.

Single-Use 35mm Disposable Camera.

I wanted to shout at the cab—hold the camera up and make sure she knew she'd left something behind. And for a second I was filled with ideas—maybe when she came running back, I'd suggest a coffee, and then agree when she said what she *really* needed was a huge glass of wine, and then we'd get a bottle, because it made better financial sense to get a bottle, and then we'd agree we shouldn't be drinking on empty stomachs, and then we'd jack in our jobs and buy a boat and start making cheese in the country.

But nothing happened.

No screech of car tire, no pause then crunch of gears, no reverse lights, no running, smiling girl in nice shoes and a blue coat.

Just a new taxi stopping, so a fat man could get out at a cashpoint.

You see what I mean about hope?

"Now, before we go any further whatsoever," said Dev, holding up the cartridge and tapping it very gently with his finger. "Let's talk about the name. 'Altered Beast.'"

I was staring at Dev in what I like to imagine was quite a blank manner. It didn't matter. In all the years I've known him I doubt he's seen many looks from me, other than my blank one. He probably thinks I've looked like this since university.

"Now, it conjures up not only mysticism, of course, but also *intrigue*, meshing as it does both Roman culture *and* Greek mythology."

I turned and looked at Pawel, who seemed mildly traumatized.

"Now, the interesting thing about the sound effects—" said Dev, and he pressed a button on his keyring and out came a tinny, distorted noise that sounded as if it *might* be trying to say, "*Wise fwom your gwaaave!*"

I put my hand up.

"Yes, Jase, you've got a question?"

"Why've you got that noise on your keyring?"

Dev sighed, and made quite a show of it. "Oh, I'm sorry, Jason, but I'm *trying* to tell Pawel here about the early development of Sega Mega Drive games in the late 1980s and early 1990s. I'm sorry we're not covering your personal passion of the work of American musical duo Hall & Oates, but that's not why Pawel is here, is it?"

Pawel just smiled.

Pawel does a lot of smiling when he visits the shop. It's usually to collect money Dev owes him for his lunchtime snacks. I sometimes watch his face as he wanders around the floor, taking in ancient, faded posters of *Sonic 2* or *Out Run*, picking up chipped carts or battered copies of old magazines, flicking through the reviews of long-dead platformers or shoot-'em-ups that look like they were drawn by toddlers now. Dev let him borrow a Master System and a copy of *Shinobi* the other day. Turns out you didn't really get many Master Systems in mid-'80s Eastern Europe, and even less ninjas. We're not going to let him borrow the Xbox, because Dev says his eyes might explode.

"Anyway," said Dev. "The name of this very shop—Power Up!—owes its existence to—"

And I start to realize what Dev's doing. He's trying to *bore* Pawel out of here. Dominate the conversation. Bully him into leaving, the way men with useless knowledge often do. Throw in phrases like, "Oh, didn't you *know* that?" or "Of course, you'll *already* be aware . . ." in order to patronize and thwart and win.

He can't have enough cash on him for lunch.

"How much does he owe you, Pawel?" I asked, fishing for a fiver in my pocket.

Dev shot me a smile.

* * *

I love London.

I love everything about it. I love its palaces and its museums and its galleries, sure. But also, I love its filth, and damp, and stink. Okay, well, I don't mean *love*, exactly. But I don't mind it. Not anymore. Not now I'm used to it. You don't mind anything once you're used to it. Not the graffiti you find on your door the week after you painted over it, or the chicken bones and cider cans you have to move before you can sit down for your damp and muddy picnic. Not the ever-changing fast-food joints—AbraKebabra to Pizza the Action to Really Fried Chicken—and all on a high street that despite its three new names a week never seems to look any different. Its tawdriness can be comforting, its willfulness inspiring. It's the London I see every day. I mean, tourists: they see the Dorchester. They see Harrods, and they see men in bearskins and Carnaby Street. They very rarely see the Happy Shopper on the Mile End Road, or a drab Peckham disco. They head for Buckingham Palace, and see waving above it the red, white, and blue, while the rest of us order dansak from the Tandoori Palace, and see Simply Red, White Lightning, and Duncan from Blue.

But we should be proud of that, too.

Or, at least, get used to it.

You could find a little bit of Poland on one end of the Caledonian Road these days, the way you could find Portugal in Stockwell, or Turkey all through Haringey. Since the shops came, Dev has used his lunchtimes to explore an entirely new culture. He was like that at university when he met a Bolivian girl at Leicester's number one nightclub, Boomboom. I was studying English, and for a month or so, Dev was studying Bolivian. Each night he'd dial up Internet and wait ten minutes for a single page to load, before printing it off and committing stock Spanish phrases to memory, hoping once again to bump into her, but never, ever managing it.

"Fate!" he'd say. "Ah, fate."

Now it was all about Poland. He gorges himself on *z szynka* cheese, proclaiming it to be the finest cheese he's ever tasted, ignoring the fact it's processed and in little plastic packets and tastes *exactly* like Dairylea. He buys *krokiety* and *krupnik* and more cheese, with bright pink synthetic ham pebble-dashed across each bland jaundiced slab. Once he bought a beetroot, but he didn't eat it. Plus, if it's the end of the day he'll make sure whatever customer happens to still be there sees him with a couple of *paczki* and a goblet of *jezynowka*. And once he's made it obvious enough and they've asked what on *earth* he's got in his hands, he'll say, "Oh, they're brilliant. Haven't you ever *had paczki?*," and then look all international and pleased with himself for a bit.

But he's not doing it to show off. Not really. He's got a good heart, and I think he thinks he's being welcoming and informative. It's still the laziest form of tourism there is, though. No one else I know simply sits there, playing videogames, and waiting for the countries to come to him, with each new wave of what he likes to call the "Newbies." He wants to see the world, he'll tell you—but he prefers to see it all from the window of his shop.

Men come from everywhere to shop here. Men trying to recapture their youth, or complete a collection, or find that one game they used to be brilliant at. There's new stuff, sure—but that's just to survive. That's not why people come. And when they do, sometimes they get the Power Up! reference. After that, it's only a matter of moments before Dev mentions Makoto Uchida, and that's usually enough to establish his superiority and scare them off, maybe having bought a £2 copy of *Decap Attack* or *Mr. Nutz*, but probably not.

Dev sells next to nothing, but next to nothing seems to be just enough. His dad owns a few restaurants on Brick Lane and keeps the basics paid, and what little extra there is keeps Dev in ham-flecked *z szynka*, at any rate. Plus he's been good to me, so I shouldn't judge him. I lost a girlfriend and a flat but gained a flatmate and virtually no rent in return for a few afternoon shifts and a weekly supply of *krokiety*.

Talking of which . . .

"Right, we've got Żubr or Żywiec—take your pick!" said Dev, holding up the bottles. I wasn't sure I could pronounce either of them so pointed at the one with the least letters.

"Or I think I've got some Lech somewhere," he said, pronouncing it "Letch" and then giggling. Dev knows it's pronounced "Leck," because he asked Pawel, but he prefers saying "Letch" because it means he can giggle afterward.

"Żubr is fine," I said—something I'd never said before— and he flipped the lid and passed it over.

I caught sight of myself in the mirror behind him.

I looked tired.

Sometimes I look at myself and think, Is this it?, and then I think, Yes, it is. This is literally the best you will ever look. Tomorrow, you will look just a little bit worse, and this is how it will go, forever. You should definitely buy some Berocca.

I have the haircut of the mid-thirties man. Until recently, I wore cool, ironic T-shirts, until I realized the real irony was they made me look less cool.

I'm too old to experiment with my hair, see, but too young to have found the style I'll take to the grave. You know the one I mean—the one we're all headed for, if we're lucky enough to have any left by then. Flat and dulled and sitting on every man in an oversized shirt at an all-inclusive holiday resort breakfast buffet, surrounded by unpleasant children and a passive-aggressive wife who have worked together in single-minded unity to quash his ambitions the way they have quashed his hairstyle.

I say that like I'm any better, or that my ambitions are heroic and worthy. I am a man between styles, is all, and there are millions of me. I'm at that awkward stage between the man of his twenties and the man of his forties. A stage I have come to call "the man in his thirties."

I sometimes wonder what the caption at the bottom of my *Vanity Fair* shoot would say, the day I wrote the cover story and they decided to make a big deal of me:

> *Hair by Angela at Toni & Guy, near Angel tube, even though her fingers smell of nicotine and she says "ax" instead of "ask."*
> *Smell: Lynx Africa (for men). £2.76, Tesco Metro, Charing Cross.*
> *Watch: Swatch. ("It was an impulse buy at Geneva airport," he confides, laughing lightly, and picking at his salade Niçoise. "Our plane was three hours delayed and I'd already bought a Toblerone!")*
> *Clothes: Model's own (with thanks to Topman VIP 10% discount card, available free to literally everyone in the world).*

But I'm not that bad. A Spanish model I met at a Spanish bar on Hanway Street and once even had a passable date with said I looked "very English," which I took to mean like Errol Flynn, even though later I found out he was Australian.

"What. A. Day," said Dev, sighing a little too heavily for a man who can't really have had that much of a day. "You? Yours?"

"Yeah," I said. "You know, not bad," by which I meant the opposite.

It had been bad from the moment I'd got up this morning. The milk had been off, but how's that different from normal, and the postman had slammed and clattered our letterbox, but the real kicker was when, with a grim tightening of my stomach, I'd flicked my laptop on, and headed for Facebook, and even though I *knew* something like this would eventually happen, I saw those words, the words I *knew* would come.

. . . is having the time of her life.

Seven words.

A status update.

And next to it, Sarah's name, so easily clickable.

And so I'd clicked it. And there she was. Having the time of her life.

Stop, I'd thought. Enough now. Get up, have a shower.

So I'd clicked on her photos.

She was in Andorra. With Gary. Having the time of her fucking life.

I'd snapped the laptop shut.

Didn't she care that I'd see this? Didn't she realize that this would go straight to my screen, straight to my stomach? These photos . . . these snapshots . . . taken from the point of view and angle *I* used to see her from. But now it's not *me* behind the camera. It's not *me* capturing the moment. These memories aren't *mine*. So I don't want them. I don't *want* to see her, tanned and happy and sleeveless. I don't *want* to see her across a table with a cocktail and a look of joy and love and laughter on her face. I don't *want* to search for and take in the tiny, pointless, hurtful details—they'd shared a Margherita, the curls of her hair had lightened in the sun, she'd stopped wearing the necklace I gave her—I didn't want *any* of it. But I'd opened up the laptop again and I'd looked again anyway, pored over them, took in *everything*. I hadn't been able to help it. Sarah was having the time of her life, and I was . . . well. What?

I'd looked to see what *my* last update had been.

Jason Priestley is . . . *eating some soup*.

Jesus. What a catch. Hey, Sarah, I know you're off having the time of your life and all, but let's not forget that only last Wednesday I was eating some soup.

Why didn't I just delete her? Take her out of the equation? Make the Internet safe again? Same reason there was still a picture of her in my wallet. The one of her on her first day at work—all big blue eyes and Louis Vuitton. I'd not been strong enough to rip it up or bin it. It seemed so . . . final. Like giving up, or something. But here's the thing: deep down, I knew one day *she'd* delete *me*. And then that really would be it, and it wouldn't be my decision, and then I'd be screwed. Part of me hoped that she wouldn't—that somewhere, in that bag of hers, the one full of makeup and *Grazia* and Kleenex, somewhere in that bag would be a photo of *me* . . .

And yeah, there's that hope again.

But then one day it'll be cruelly and casually crushed and I'll be forgotten, probably just before she decides that she and Gary should move in together, or she and Gary should get hitched, or she and Gary should make another, tiny Gary, which they'll call Gary, and who'll look exactly like bloody Gary.

I'll probably be sitting there, on my own, when she finally deletes me. In a gray room with a Paddington duvet above a videogame shop next to that place that everyone *thought* was a brothel, but wasn't. A momentary afterthought, if that. Staring at a screen that informs me I can no longer obsess over her life. That I'm no longer deemed worthy of seeing her photos, seeing who her friends are, finding out when she's hungover, or sleepy, or late for work. That *she's* no longer interested in finding out when *I'm* eating soup.

My life.

Deleted.

Misery.

Still. Could be worse.

We could have run out of Żubr.

An hour later, and we'd run out of Żubr.

Dev had suggested the Den—a tiny Irish pub next to the tool hire shop, halfway down to King's Cross—and I'd said yeah, why not. You never know. I might have the time of my life.

"Ah, listen," said Dev, waving one hand in the air. "Who wants to go to Andorra anyway? What's so good about Andorra?"

The Pogues were on and we were now a little drunk.

"The scenery. The tax-free shopping. The fact that it has two heads of state, those being the King of France and a Spanish bishop."

A pause.

"You've been on Wikipedia, haven't you?"

I nodded.

"*Is* there a King of France?" asked Dev.

"President, then, I can't remember. All I know is it's some-where you go and have the time of your life. With a man called Gary, just before you have a pride of little Garys—all of whom will look like tiny thuggish babies—and then you buy a boat and make cheese in the country."

"What are you *talking* about?" said Dev.

"Sarah."

"Is she having tiny thuggish babies?"

"Probably," I slurred. "Probably right now she's just popped another one out. They'll take over the world, her thuggish babies.

They'll spread and multiply, like in *Arachnophobia*. They'll stick to people's faces and pound them with their little fists."

Dev considered my wise words.

"You didn't used to be like this," he said. "Where did you go? Who's this grumpy man?"

"It is me," I said. "I am Mr. Grumpy. I called home last week and Mum was like, 'You never come back to Durham, why do you never come home to Durham?'"

"So why do you never go back to Durham?"

"Because it's a reminder, isn't it? Of going backward. Anyway, Sarah doesn't have that problem. She's gonna have tiny thuggish babies."

"I don't think she'll have thuggish babies. I thought Gary was, like, an investment banker?"

"Doesn't mean he's not gonna have thuggish babies," I said, pointing my finger in the air to show I would not accept any form of contradiction on this. "He's *exactly* the type of man to have a thuggish baby. A little skinhead one. Who's always shouting."

"But that's just a *baby*," said Dev.

"Whatever," I said. "Just don't feed one of them after midnight."

There was a brief silence. An AC/DC track came on. My favorite. "Back in Black"—the finest rock song of its time. I was momentarily cheered.

"Let's have another pint," I said. "A Żubr! Or a Zyborg!"

But Dev was looking at me, very seriously now.

"You should delete her," he said, flatly. "Just delete her. Be done with it. Leave Mr. Grumpy behind, because Mr. Grumpy is in danger of becoming Mr. Dick. I'm no expert, but I'm sure that's what they'd say on *This Morning*, if you phoned up and asked one of those old women who solve problems."

I nodded.

"I know," I said, sadly.

* * *

"These are 2,000 calories!" said Dev. "2,000! I read about it in the paper!"

"You read about it in *my* paper," I said. After several pints in the Den, we'd had the "one we came for" and stopped at Oz's for a kebab on the way home. "I'm the one who showed it to you and said, 'Read this! It says kebabs are 2,000 calories!'"

"Wherever I read it, I'm just saying, 2,000 calories is a lot of calories for a kebab. But they're good for you, too."

"How are they *good* for you?"

"They line your stomach with fat, so that when the apocalypse comes, you are better prepared. We'll survive longer. Tubby people will inherit the earth!"

Dev made a little "yahoo!" sound, but then started coughing on his chili sauce. He's a little obsessed with the apocalypse, through years of roaming postapocalyptic landscapes, scavenging for objects and fighting giant beetles in videogames, which he genuinely regards as his "important training."

Right now, he was having trouble getting the key into the door. You'd lose points for that in an apocalypse. You'd also lose points for wearing glasses, but they're an important part of Dev. He has an IQ of around 146 according not just to a psychiatrist when he was four but also to some interactive quiz he did on the telly, which makes me proud of him when I'm drunk, though you'd never think it was anywhere *close* to 146 to speak to him. He has applied for four of the however-many-seasons of *The Apprentice* there've been, but for some reason they are yet to reply satisfactorily to this part-owner of a very minor secondhand videogame shop on the Caledonian Road, which I would find funny, if I didn't know this actually broke his heart.

It'd be easy to argue that Dev was defined at fourteen. His interests, his way with girls, even his look. See, when Dev was fourteen, his grandfather died, and that had a huge impact on his life. Not because it was emotionally traumatic, though of course it was, but because Dev's dad doesn't like to see money wasted. And the year before, Dev had started to notice he wasn't like the other kids. Just small things—not being able to see a sign, not being able to read a clock, and persistently and with great flair falling out of his bed. He was short-sighted.

His dad is a businessman. His dad thought, why pay for frames, when a pair of frames was clearly so nearly ready and available for no money whatsoever?

And so Dev had been given his granddad's frames. His *granddad's*. Literally three days after the funeral. Relensed, obviously, but by his dad's mate, on the Whitechapel Road, and with cheap, scuffable plastic. Dev went through the next four years ridiculed by all and sundry for having a young boy's face and an old man's pair of specs, like a toddler wearing his mum's sunglasses. He tried to grow a mustache to compensate, but that just made him look like a miniature military dictator.

And he'd never bought a new pair. Why should he? He'd found his look. And these days, it was working to his advantage. At university, at least at first, it had been considered odd, these thick black frames on a weird new kid, but they were a comfort blanket in year one, an eccentricity or quirk in year two, and, he hoped, a chick magnet in year three.

(They weren't.)

But later, when you added them to the hair he couldn't be bothered to get cut and the T-shirts he either got for free or bought from eBay for a pound and a penny, these glasses screamed confidence. These glasses screamed . . . well, they screamed "Dev."

Foreign girls, who couldn't understand him but liked bright jackets, thought he looked cool.

"Come on!" he said, finally through the door and slamming the banister with his fist as we stumbled upstairs. "I know what'll cheer you up."

In the flat, Dev threw his kebab onto the table and made for the kitchen, where he started to go through cupboards and loudly shift stuff about.

I wandered into my bedroom and picked up my laptop and made a determined face.

Maybe I *should* do it, I thought. Just delete her. Move on. Forget about things. Be the grown-up. It'd be easy. And then I could turn on my computer without that low, dull ache. That anticipation of maybe seeing something bad. I could get on with my life.

I heard Dev shout, "Aha!" as I fired up the Internet.

"Found it, Jase! Prime bottle of *jezynowka*! Blackberry brandy! How's about we hook up the N64 and drink *jezynowka* and play *GoldenEye* till dawn?"

But I wasn't listening. Not really. I was only guessing at what he was saying. He could have been knocking over vases and composing racist songs for all I knew, because I was transfixed, and shocked, and I don't know what else, by what I saw on the screen.

One word this time.

One word that kicked me in the teeth and stamped on my hope and made fun of my family.

"Jase?" said Dev, suddenly there, in my doorway. "D'you want to be James Bond or Natalia?"

But I didn't look round.

My eyes were pricked with tears and I could feel every hair on my body, because all I could see were the words "Sarah Bennett is . . ." and then that last one, that killer, that complete and absolute *bastard* of a word.

TWO

Or "Some Things Are Better Left Unsaid"

Engaged.

That was the word, since you ask.

Engaged.

Sarah was engaged to Gary. Gary was engaged to Sarah. Sarah and Gary were engaged to *each other*.

I didn't stay up till dawn playing *GoldenEye* with Dev after that. I just sat there, numbed by shock and *jezynowka*, in a cold room that now reeked of blackberry, and clicked refresh and refresh and refresh as the congratulations poured in.

Hurray! wrote Steve, which is *typical* of Steve, and *Yahoo!* wrote Jess, which is *just* like her, and *About time!* wrote Anna.

Really, Anna? About time, is it? They've been together *six months*, Anna. I was with Sarah for *four years*. But you never thought *we* should get married, did you? What was it about me you didn't like? Was it my clothes? Was it my job? Was it that time I spilled red wine all over your table and some of it got on your shoes and you called me a twat and then I was sick?

Yes, it was probably that.

Couldn't happen to a nicer couple! wrote Ben, and that one really hurt, because Ben was *my* friend, Sarah, not yours. You got custody, of course—you ended up with all of them—but only because I was too ashamed and scared to look any of them in the eye anymore.

I swigged the brandy from the bottle and read on, each yelp of excitement and each congratulatory pronouncement and each *OH MY GOD* and extra, unnecessary exclamation mark a jab in the heart and a poke in the eye.

What about me? I wanted to shout. Is no one thinking of me? How come when Sarah writes that she's engaged you all go mental, but when *I* eat some *soup* suddenly no one's got *anything* to say?

I knew then I had to delete her. Make a statement. Let her know this was not good, *not* okay.

But doing it now would look churlish, childish, immature.

And besides, then I wouldn't be able to look at her photos.

Oh, Christ. There it is. The ring.

He must've proposed right there, at that table, after a couple of cocktails on a sleeveless Andorran night with a bad Margherita.

Margherita! Not even a Meat Feast! What, I suppose you guys are doing healthy eating now, are you? Going to Pilates classes and drinking vitamin-enhanced smoothies? Yeah, I bet you are.

I wouldn't have proposed like that, Gary. I'd have made it *special*. I'd have hidden the ring in a champagne flute, or—you know—abseiled out of a hot-air balloon and into a football stadium, and proposed right there and then, down on bended knee and broadcast on a big screen for all to see. Because I've got class, Gary. And yes, Gary, I *was* going to propose to her, actually. I didn't, but I was going to. One day. I had it all planned. Or, not planned exactly, but I'd *planned* to make plans. Plans were very much part of my plan. And even though I never did, and even though I now never can, let me tell you this with no reservations whatsoever, Gary: my plans would *not* have involved a boring pizza and a bright blue cocktail.

Oh, God. She looks so happy.

I swigged at my blackberry brandy and made a V-sign at the screen.

And then I got up and rattled about in the kitchen and found another bottle.

It was far too early and I tasted of blackberries.

But something was buzzing near my face, and it wouldn't stop.

I forced my eyes open and found the phone, looked at it.

It took a moment to register the name. Or not the name. But *why* the name.

SARAH.

What time was it? Seven? Eight?

I couldn't. Not now. I'm not prepared. I needed coffee, and maybe a series of notes and things to say that would make me seem diffident and unaffected. I pressed divert and stared at the ceiling. That'd send her a message, I thought. Let her know she can't rely on me to just answer whenever she . . .

It was buzzing again. I held it up.

Maybe something's happened. Maybe Gary's dumped her. Maybe I should be there for her at this time of need. Show her how sensitive and brilliant I can be.

ACCEPT.

"Hello?"

Wow, my voice was low.

"Jase?"

"Hey."

And *croaky*. Low and croaky.

"How are you?"

"Fine."

She didn't sound upset. She sounded cold. Stern. She sounded like Sarah.

I realized she probably didn't know I knew.

Okay, I decided. Just tell me you're engaged.

"Rough night?" she said.

Yes, as it happens, Sarah, a very rough night indeed. Now how about you tell me you're engaged and I can act surprised and mature.

"Just a . . . I just had a couple of drinks with Dev, and—"

"Why are you such a dick, Jase?"

I frowned. That wasn't in the script. And anyway, it's *Mr.* Dick to you.

A second passed.

"I'm . . . what do you . . ."

"You could at least be happy for me, Jason. You can't blame me for any of this. We both made choices, and . . ."

Not this. Not this conversation again.

"Happy about what?" I said, innocently.

"You *know* what."

How did she know I knew what? What?

"Sarah—"

"I'm engaged, Jason. Are you happy now I've said it like that?"

"I . . . well, that's good news!" I said. "*Good* for you."

"That's not what you said last night."

I blinked a couple of times. Had I called her? Had she called me? I glanced over at the table in the corner. A streak of blackberry brandy had made its way down one leg, and there, next to it, the messenger: my laptop, my betrayer, still on, still proudly displaying a bright and colorful photo of a very happy Sarah.

"Last night," she said, "you seemed to think it was a bad move."

"No, I'd never."

"You said it was a bad move and that all my friends were bad friends for not stopping me making the greatest mistake any woman has ever made in sacrificing any chance of getting back together with you for a life of Margherita pizzas and stupid days."

"Stupid *days*?"

"Gary's very upset. He's very sensitive. He feels you've humiliated him. You said he was the Margherita of Men. You said you were like a Meat Feast and he was like a Margherita."

"I probably meant he's popular, and I'm not to everyone's taste, especially if they're health-conscious, and—"

"That's not what you meant, is it?"

There was something else behind the coldness, now. Anger? No. What was it? It was resignation. It was like she just couldn't be bothered anymore.

"Grow up, Jason," she said. "Find someone else. Anyone else. Move out of that rancid flat—it's next to a brothel for God's sake—and move on."

"It's not—"

"Don't call me."

Click.

I listened to the silence for a moment, and then sat up.

"It's not a brothel," I said.

My head had started to pound, and I checked my phone for dialed calls. I hadn't made any. I hadn't phoned her at all. I knew it.

Hey, maybe she was mental. Maybe Gary had turned her mental. That'd be great, if Gary had turned her mental. Then who'd be right? Me, or her friends? Those same friends writing with such casual abandon about how happy they are for them both, about what a great bloke Gary is, about how well suited and perfectly matched they are, about . . .

I stopped.

The faintest glimmer of a hint of a rumor of a memory.

No.

Please, no.

I made it out of bed and stumbled to the laptop. I could see it already.

Whoops.

"'Whoops' doesn't seem to quite cut it," said Dev, wisely.

He was wearing his *Earthworm Jim* T-shirt and tucking into a full English and a foreign Coke at the café down the road.

"Nope," he said, shaking his head and smiling. "'Whoops' is not in any way the appropriate response in this situation."

He was right. I thought about what I'd done.

I'd carefully and passionately annotated around fourteen online engagement photographs in all, each of which was, in my drunken state, presumably of Wildean splendor and Fry-like wit. I'd presumably thought I sounded sharp, incisive, and intelligent. I now realized, in the cold light of day, I sounded more like a tramp banging on the window of Currys.

"Ah, look," said Dev. "How many people would've seen it? Really?"

"Everyone. Everyone who looked at their pictures. Her friends, my friends, *our* friends."

Dev nodded thoughtfully and shrugged it off.

"Her family. Her many and various colleagues."

He looked a little more concerned now.

"*Gary's* friends. *Gary's* family. *Gary's* many and various colleagues."

"Right . . ."

"Distant relatives. People they haven't seen in twenty-five years but sat next to in maths. Randoms. Michael Fish."

"Michael Fish? The weatherman?"

"Michael Fish the weatherman, yeah. He plays golf with Gary's dad."

"Well, let's not worry about Michael Fish the weatherman. I'm sure Michael Fish the weatherman wouldn't think twice about it."

I had a sudden flashback and felt my ego shrink to the size of a peanut.

Gary's face. Gary's beaming face, so full of joy, so delighted that the woman of his dreams had said yes, the happiest picture he'd ever taken, and underneath it, my name and a picture of me with two thumbs up, next to the words: *HI! I GARY, STUPID MAN'D FACE WHO LIKE A BAD n BORING PIZZA . . . WILL YOU MARRY AND WE CAN ATE PIZZA BUT BAD ONE!!????*

Christ.

Stupid Man'd Face?

I shuddered, and took a sip of tea. Dev's eyes lit up. Not because I was sipping tea—he's seen me do that before and not even commented—but because the waitress was here. The same waitress he tries to impress *every* time we're here. Because yes— as we've established—there's *always* a girl.

"*Dobranoc!*" he shouted, suddenly. "*Jak si masz?*"

The waitress gave him a half-smile and said something back, quietly, and waited for an answer, but Dev didn't have one, so just stared at her.

Unlikely as it seems, she wandered off again.

"This is good," I said. "Eventually, you'll build up to an actual exchange."

"Shouldn't have worn this T-shirt," said Dev, kicking himself. "Should've worn the *Street Fighter* one."

He watched her walk away.

"Whoops," I said.

* * *

Here's the thing.

I've got absolutely nothing against Gary. He is a perfectly nice, perfectly ordinary man. And I can say that, having met him. An awkward and unexpected encounter at a mutual friend's birthday, during which I'd behaved impeccably, even made a joke or two, but we could see in each other's eyes we weren't supposed to be talking; this wasn't natural.

If I was still a teacher, I guess I'd mark him like this:

> *Appearance: Average.*
> *Conversation: Average.*
> *Overall: Gary is a very pleasant pupil not weighed down by ambition or thought. You will always know exactly where you are with him. And that is Stevenage.*

You see? Nice guy. Perfectly nice, perfectly good.

But that's what annoyed me, I guess. This idea that "He's okay, he's good enough, he'll do." There was no spark, no light. No stand-out trait. And as I stood there at that party, and looked at him, and at Sarah, over his shoulder, pretending she hadn't noticed that we were talking and that this was a perfectly normal thing for twenty-first-century grown-ups to deal with, I thought: Where's the magic?

The magic had been there when *we* met, Sarah.

The bar neither of us had been to before. The walk down the South Bank under an almost-full moon. The old lady on the nightbus who asked how long we'd been married. The number you gave me on your doorstep, the call five minutes later from the phonebox at the end of your street, the cheese on toast and wine in your kitchen, the kiss, the next kiss, the promise we made that one day we'd track down that mad old woman and invite her to our wedding.

Okay. Maybe not real magic. Maybe the moon could have been more full, and we could have found something other than cheese on toast, and maybe our teeth shouldn't have clashed the second time we kissed, but magic enough for me, Sarah. And I thought magic enough for you. That's a real start to a relationship. A story. What have you and Gary got?

You met at a company away day. You were in the same team-building exercise. You got drunk in a Hilton near a motorway. Two months later, due to corporate restructuring, Gary was relocated from Stevenage. You met at seven, you were both on time, and you went to an All Bar One and then a Pizza Express. The next day, Gary helped you get a better deal on a second-hand Golf. Now you're engaged.

Well, good God, Sarah, I hope you sold the film rights.

But no. That's all fine. And yes. I'm being an idiot.

But I wanted the beginning to be strong enough to get us to the end, Sarah, and you should have wanted that, too. Neither of us should have to settle for a Margherita.

And so, to work.

London Now is the freesheet I told you about earlier—a kind of *Metro* or *London Paper*, but this one packed to the brim with reviews of things you can do NOW! or TONIGHT! or TOMORROW! It's aimed at people who just don't know what to do with themselves, or who like to impress other people on the tube by turning to the Live In London section and circling avant-garde Mexican jazz fusion gigs they'll never go to, and would mispronounce anyway.

There's the usual mix of other stuff: news straight from our inbox, horoscopes bought in from some mental with a fax machine in the country, pap pics of pop stars and comics stumbling out of the Groucho or Century, there are On This Days, and Did You Knows, and I Saw Yous, and other ways to start a sentence no one will ever want to hear you finish.

It's also doomed. We all know it, but there's only so much a vanity project can do in a market like this. They'd managed a successful launch in Manchester and simply thought they could add a little London content and start a whole new paper in the capital. It was a little swagger in a knee-deep recession, a bold move with a bit of Russian money behind it, but it was Zoe and the team who now had to deal with it day to day.

And God, I just listened to myself. I sound ungrateful. And I think I may be giving you a picture of myself I'm not entirely comfortable with. I enjoy the job when there's enough of it, I have my savings, and being freelance means I have to turn my hand to anything, but that's also kind of the problem. I have no speciality. I am not *London Now*'s resident *anything*. I'm just a general reviewer, giving general thoughts to the general public about things in general.

Well, I say "general thoughts." That's not quite true. These thoughts aren't my general thoughts. They're extreme versions. Because you have to have an opinion. Last week, I went to a Persian in Bayswater called Sinbad. I suppose if I was still a teacher, I'd have marked it like this:

Starter: Yep, fine, absolutely fine, nothing special, but okay.
Main: Not bad, I ate it all, so yeah.
Overall: This place is okay, so if you're in the area, and you are hungry, and you like Persian food, give it a go, or not. I'm not fussed.

But now I can't get away with that. Now I have to say things like:

Starter: Bland, turgid, ironically a nonstarter.
Main: Insult to possible internal injury.
Overall: Irritatingly forgettable. If it were a name refer-ring to its food, Sinbad could not be made up of two more apt syllables.

You see? Ha ha. I am clever.

More barbed, more cynical, more knowing. And all from a man who once gave himself food poisoning cooking chips.

Zoe loved it. She loves all this kind of stuff. And I guess I do it to impress her a bit. Partly because it means she'll give me more work, but partly also because it's nice to impress a girl.

I suppose if I were still a teacher, I would mark her like this:

Appearance: Zoe Alice Harper is neat and tidy with an eye for the latest fashions, as evidenced by the very many ASOS bags that litter the area around her desk. Her hair, once a long chestnut mane, is now cut into a bob, which is the type of thing that can happen when you have a "long lunch" and are feeling unnaturally gregarious in the stylist's chair. Zoe would do well to remember this in future.
Attitude: Zoe is a girl with ambition and drive, whose work is consistent and above average, although her greatest dream, I think, if I can break character for just a moment, is to work on one of those I Hate Everything columns. You know the ones. The ones that tell you everything is appalling. Every new TV show or story in the news has some terrible downside to it that is a complete affront to the person writ-ing it, furious that they could have spent their time doing other, more important things, like microwaving some pasta, or staring. That they could have done a better job, even

*though they'd never make it past the first wave of interviews.
That everything would be better if they were in charge.
Problem is, I don't think she's really like that. It's just the
trend. A way to get noticed. A shortcut to humor, like those
people at dinner parties who mistake cynicism for wit, or
bile for interesting opinion.*

Still. It's her own time she's wasting.

(© The Teacher's Bumper Book of Handy Phrases)
*Overall: I applaud her confidence and like her new hair
and predict great things.*

I'm as guilty of faux cynicism as anyone, by the way. Although
I'd hope it was for a forgivable set of reasons. When Sarah
and I were splitting up, I described almost every album I was
given for review as trashy or slipshod or synthetic (I know nothing about music, unless you count Hall & Oates). I started writing "whom" instead of "who." When she finally left me, I
vented by scowling through screenings and crucifying directors
(I know nothing about films, either, apart from *The Shawshank
Redemption*, which I *love*, and I quite like Pedro Almodovar,
too, but I don't tell anyone because it makes me sound
pompous). The simple truth is, I did not care. Life dictated
those reviews, not me.

And today, a hungover day after a horrible night, I guess
someone's in for it.

But whom?

"Abrizzi's," said Zoe.

She was wearing a black polo neck and those glasses she
doesn't really need but that make her look like she's some kind
of commissioning editor on a metropolitan newspaper. Which
she likes to remind me she sort of is. I think secretly she doesn't

like the fact that I knew her at university, when she was all Long-pigs T-shirts and 20/20, a doe-eyed Winona Ryder in Converse.

We'd been close at uni. Talked earnestly about the future and our places in it. Then she'd gone her way, which had earned her a desk and those glasses, and I'd gone mine, which had earned me some bags under my eyes.

"New Italian place, for the New In Town section. Should be nice for you. You used to say breadsticks were just vegetarian Peperami. Remember those days? When you used to get outraged in the Pizza Hut on Haymarket because you thought that them putting out breadsticks was a conspiracy to fill you up and stop you gorging on the rest of the free buffet?"

I am amazed I never became a celebrity chef.

"You look dreadful, by the way. And what's that smell?"

"It might be blackberries," I said, "or nerd. I've just had breakfast with a nerd."

"It's not blackberries," she said. "Must be nerd. How *is* Dev?"

"More like Dev than ever," I said, looking at the printout she'd given me. "A restaurant, then. Another restaurant."

She just smiled. She'd been good to me, throwing work my way, and I was grateful. One night, when things had been going wrong with Sarah, I'd poured my heart out to my old friend, told her the mistakes I'd made in life, been far too honest and drunk and lost. Told her if only I could start again; if only I had something of my own to shape and shift and mold. Despite everything that had happened since, despite the distance that was now between us, I wanted to do right by her, as she was doing by me.

She'd loved the last review, I could see that, because something about it had appealed to the world-weary woman this girl wanted to be. But instantly I had it again: this crystal-clear vision I've been having. The head chef at Sinbad, eagerly awaiting the return of one of his waiters, because he's heard the restaurant's finally been reviewed, and he can't wait to see what they thought. "A food critic!" he'll be thinking. "At last! A well-traveled and knowledgeable urban connoisseur! What delights await me? How do my wonders translate to the written word?" And then, as the waiter dashes in from the tube holding a rain-spattered copy of *London Now* over his head, his stomach will sink and his eyes sting as the words "irritatingly forgettable" are forever branded onto his heart. And as his ventricles smolder, and his eyes cloud over, it won't occur to him that really, that phrase makes no sense, because why would you be irritated by something you can't even be bothered to remember? And yet it'll all be fine. Tomorrow night, there will be as many people in Sinbad as there are tonight. No one else even cares. Even I only cared for about half an hour, and then I watched *The Weakest Link*. But Mr. Sinbad? Mr. Sinbad will carry those words with him to the grave, feeling a little less of a chef on the way. And all thanks to a man who can't even remember what it was he ordered.

I shook the image away.

"Where is it?" I asked.

Somewhere central, please. Not Harrow, or Uxbridge, or Mudchute. The last thing I want is an hour's trip to Mudchute to eat on my own at a bad Chinese.

"Charlotte Street," she said, brightly.

Charlotte Street. I was just there. Just yesterday.

Blue coat. Nice shoes. The smile.

What if I'd talked to her last night? *Properly* talked to her?

"It's a six o'clock reservation."

"Six? You must know some people in some pretty high places."

She smirked. I thought back to our uni days. When did we change? Were we still pretending to be grown-ups, more jaded and jaundiced than we were? I'm not sure who we were trying to impress: the world, or each other.

"Whenever you can file is good," she said. "Ask them what they recommend, order whatever it is, keep your receipt, don't go mad, and pay for your own booze. Also, keep Thursday night free."

"Why?"

"Gallery opening."

"But I don't know anything about art."

"I'm giving you work," she said. "I thought that's what you wanted."

I spent the journey home looking at the albums and DVDs she'd given me for review, trying to work out how I could make fun of their titles.

When I got back to the flat, I knew there would be e-mails. Ones I wouldn't really want to read. Ones telling me what a fool I'd made of myself, how I should just grow up, and others full of concern for my mental health and saying things like, *Hey, pal, if you ever want to talk.*

So I checked them anyway.

Jase, wrote Ben. *Do you want to meet up for a coffee? Might be good to chat.*

Delete.

Jason, it's Anna, wrote Sarah's best friend, who'd been just waiting for this engagement to be announced so she could run around town organizing horrible hen nights and buying pink fairy wings for everyone to wear as they crash and whoop and blunder their way into every Pitcher & Piano in Islington and beyond. *I just think you need to take a long, hard look at yourself and maybe rein in the drinking because it's not healthy, all this drinking, Jason. A pint does not solve anything, and you also need to let Sarah and Gareth live their lives because you had your chance and you need to be a grown-up about it.*

There were another nine paragraphs below it.

Delete.

And then . . . uh oh.

Gary.

Jason. Listen, fella . . .

I cringed. He was using "fella." He was going to be matey. Worse, he was going to be *understanding*.

Sarah doesn't know I'm writing this, so best keep it on the down-low.

Of course she knows, Gary. Because you told her and she said it didn't sound like a good idea, but you decided to be the bigger man about it, and she probably said, "God, that's why I love you. It's so amazing to be with an actual grown-up," and then she stood there and read over your shoulder as you typed.

But I saw your messages and I just want to say I know how you must be feeling. I wouldn't want to lose Sarah either. And the way it happened means I guess there are unresolved issues. If you ever want to talk . . .

And that's where I had to stop reading.

I fired back a quick, *Thanks, Gary, that's really good of you*, and I wandered downstairs to get Dev to shut up shop and come for a pint.

Because actually, Anna, sometimes a pint solves *everything*.

There can be nothing worse than sitting in a restaurant on your own, people who don't often sit in restaurants on their own will tell you. But I don't mind it. I get to think.

My afternoon with Dev Ranjit Sandananda Patel had ended at Postman's Park. We seemed to end up at Postman's Park, nestled between Little Britain and Angel Street, a lot these days. It's the tiles we love.

I'll explain.

In 1887, George Frederic Watts, the son of a humble piano maker, wrote to *The Times* with a brave new idea. An idea that would commemorate for all time the heroism shown by normal, everyday people. It would mark Queen Victoria's Golden Jubilee, and stand as testament to ordinary lives given out of extraordinary good. It was a beautiful idea.

Dev and I would make a point of swinging by whenever we were near—and since the offices of *London Now* were just a few minutes away, that was often—and today, our pub crawl had taken us closer and closer. We didn't have to say where we were going. We just knew.

Anyway, Watts's letter to *The Times* did nothing. No one backed him. No one believed in him. So he did it anyway. And now, along one wall of an old church garden in the middle of the City of London, yards from what used to be the General Post Office, are dozens and dozens of glazed Royal Doulton tiles, each one commemorating another act of selfless, singular bravery.

We'd stood in front of one, and Dev had rolled a cigarette.

GEORGE STEPHEN FUNNELL, police constable, December 22 1899.

In a fire at the Elephant and Castle, Wick Road, Hackney Wick, after rescuing two lives, went back into the flames, saving a barmaid at the risk of his own life.

It was the silences after reading I most enjoyed.

"Maybe," said Dev, at one point, "it's because we're not heroes. Maybe we don't feel worthwhile because we've never done anything heroic."

"I didn't say I didn't feel worthwhile."

"You do, though, don't you?" he said. "*I* do."

I turned back, and read another.

ALICE AYRES, daughter of a bricklayer's laborer, who by intrepid conduct saved three children from a burning house in Union Street, Borough, at the cost of her own young life.

"I mean, we go about our daily lives," said Dev. "You write your reviews and I sell my games, and sometimes you sell my games and I write your reviews."

I smiled, but Dev didn't.

"We feel like we're doing things," he said. "But what are we really doing? What will we be able to say we've ever done?"

I thought about it.

"I had some soup last Wednesday."

Dev lit his fag and shook his head.

"I'm serious, Jase. What if life's about the moments? And what if you don't take that moment? What if you don't take that moment and another moment never comes? You could be remembered as a hero, or you could just be another person who quietly lived right up until the day they quietly died."

He pointed at another tile.

"George Lee," he said. "At a fire in Clerkenwell, carried an unconscious girl to the escape, falling six times, and died of his injuries. July 26, 1876."

He paused.

"He used the moment," he said.

"So what do you recommend?" I asked the waiter.

Abrizzi's was fine. It had nice, functional decor (which I'll have to call boring), efficient staff (Cold? No, robotic. Robotic is better), and, well, I don't really know what else. What else do restaurant critics look out for? There was cutlery. Enough cutlery for me, certainly, although I didn't know how to turn that into a negative. And bread—there was a small basket of bread. I guess it could have been slightly bigger.

"The penne is excellent, we have very good veal," said the waiter, who moments before had split his sides laughing when he realized the reservation wasn't for *that* Jason Priestley. I laughed along, too, even though, now that I was thirty-two, the joke was just beginning to wear a little thin.

"We also have pizzas, of course, the very best in town."

"Cool. What type of pizza?"

"My favorite is a thin crust, with fresh tomato, plus a little basil, and mozzarella."

"A Margherita?"

"Well . . . an Abrizzi's."

A Margherita seemed fitting.

"I'll have an Abrizzi's."

The waiter—whose name I then noticed was Herman, so I don't think he's got much right to laugh at others—wandered off with my menu, and I sipped at my drink. I was at a table for two, and I was facing the window, watching the evening crowd leaving work, hailing taxis, heading for the pub. Meeting friends, meeting partners, having fun.

I snapped a breadstick in two.

But hey. This wasn't so bad. Perhaps I looked mysterious to the people around me: this lone, dangerous man staring out onto Charlotte Street. Perhaps I looked like a trained killer, and everyone was craning their necks to see what a trained killer would order, and then be disappointed when it was a Margherita and some Appletiser.

And then something remarkable happened.

Something that made me put my breadsticks down and sit right up. And then get right up. And then leave my Margherita far behind, before it had even arrived.

I saw her.

THREE

Or "The Woman Comes and Goes"

"So what happened?" said Dev, excited. "To the pizza, I mean?"

He took a slug of his Polo-Cockta and did a little burp.

"Are you serious?"

"Did you just leave it? Had you paid?"

"I don't know what happened to the pizza. I presume they brought it out and then took it away again. Maybe they wove it into the curtains. That's not really the thrust of this story."

"I wonder if someone else took it. That'd be great, if every time you went to a restaurant you could just pilfer other people's pizzas. Mind you, I suppose you *were* getting it free, so—"

"Dev...the girl. The girl, Dev."

"Yes. Sorry. Go on. The girl."

Because *that's* the point. The girl.

She'd come out of nowhere.

One moment I'd been staring at my own reflection in the window, wondering if I could pass for a trained assassin, and the next, there was a small movement somewhere in the dark. As small as a flinch a mile away, but enough to shift my focus on what lay outside.

She was walking out of Snappy Snaps—same blue coat, different shoes, I think—and she was looking around.

For what? For me?

Of course not. But for something.

I stood up, almost involuntarily, hoping to catch her eye, all lit up in an Italian, maybe exchange a wave, but she couldn't see me, and even if she did, she wouldn't remember me. How odd it would be if she did.

"Hi, I'm the fella who—"

"You held some bags for me once."

"Yes!"

"Okay, bye!"

And then, with a jolt, I remembered.

"My jacket, can I get my jacket?" I asked a waitress.

"You're finished?"

"No, I just need something—I need my jacket."

She pointed me toward the concierge desk, but the lady there was dealing with someone else, and I tried to make her see me, but she wouldn't look round. I grabbed someone else, a man with a tray.

"Hi, could I get my jacket?"

But he just smiled and said hello, and carried on walking.

I looked out the window. She was still there, still looking about.

Should I run out? Should I say, "Hi, you don't know me, except you kind of do, but wait there for a second and I'll bring you something"?

"Yes, sir, how can I help you?"

At last. It had only been a matter of seconds, but *at last*.

"I need my jacket, please! I'm on table . . . I don't know what table, that one there with the breadstick and the Appletiser."

She glanced round and for a second I lost the girl, but there she was, slightly farther up the street, still looking around. I could *do* this.

"Table 9. Mr. Priestley?"

"Yes."

"Jason Priestley!" She laughed. "A celebrity!"

"Yes, I know. *Please*, can I have my jacket?"

I'd lost sight of her now, but she couldn't be far away, she'd be on the corner of Goodge Street at worst, but now Herman was taking his time fishing my jacket out of the cloakroom, and I started clicking my fingers and saying "Come on" a lot, which didn't really endear me to anyone. Finally, it arrived.

Was it still there? Still in my inside pocket? I patted to see.

Yes.

Now I was half jogging down Charlotte Street, looking out for her, scanning both pavements...

There!

She was looking my way. Smiling. *That* smile. Arm in the air, waving.

I stopped in my tracks. She looked *lovely*.

And then the taxi she'd been looking for crept past me and slowed to a halt.

This was my chance. This was it.

"So did you?" asked Dev, wide-eyed. "Did you use the moment?"

I paused.

"No."

And I hadn't. I'd frozen, for whatever reason. The camera was in my pocket—right there in my pocket. I could've held it up, and shouted, "Stop!," and run over and handed it to her. And maybe then we could've got chatting, and she'd have suggested that wine, and I'd have suggested some dinner, and then, who knows? Maybe I'd have helped her get a better deal on a secondhand Golf.

Because for the second time in two days, this felt like a beginning. And for the second time in two days, it had not begun.

"Why?" said Dev. "Why oh why oh why?"

He'd drained his Polo-Cockta and tossed it in the bin. He opened another one.

"What *is* that, anyway?" I said.

"You never had a Polo-Cockta? Oh, they're brilliant. Bit like Coke, but a little more metallic."

He took a swig and winced. I considered his question.

Why?

Why hadn't I done something, said something? Because here's the killer bit. As she climbed into the cab—unassisted this time—she'd seen me. I knew it. It was subtle, but it was there. The briefest of reactions, a tiny sliver of something, but something nonetheless. A quizzical glance, a tiny nose scrunch, something that told me she sort of thought she knew me. A pause of a millisecond, nothing more, and then into the cab, door shut, gone.

"Or maybe," said Dev, "she was looking at you because you were a man, at night, standing perfectly still, staring straight at her, with one hand inside your jacket pocket."

Maybe.

Still. At least I finally looked like an assassin.

"And this thing, this—"

"Single-Use 35mm Disposable Camera," I said, turning it round in my hands.

"Yeah. What are you going to do with that? Just hang around Charlotte Street, hoping she'll turn up again so you can hand it to her?"

"Twice in two days I've seen her on Charlotte Street. Both

times near Snappy Snaps—once *in* it. She's clearly into photography."

"Or maybe someone keeps nicking her cameras. And who uses disposables, anyway? She sounds like an oddball. So what are you going to do?"

I shrugged.

"Nothing."

"*Nothing?* Come on."

"What can I do? And anyway, what do you mean, 'What are you going to do?' Do about what?"

Dev took another swig, and just looked at me for a few seconds.

"There are some good pubs around Charlotte Street," he said.

I dashed off my Abrizzi's review that afternoon.

A magical slice of pizza heaven, I wrote, and then some other things that were complimentary, like how I'd been given *just* enough bread, and how the waiting staff were really *excellent*. Well, they knew my name now. That's the problem with sharing your name with an early-'90s icon. People remember you. It's something to talk about on a dull day. Imagine if you worked in a shoe shop and you sold some Birkenstocks to a Shaquille O'Neal. You'd tell everyone. You'd text your friends and say, *I've just served a bloke called Shaquille O'Neal!* And they'd text back with stories of namesakes they went to school with: Rip Van Winkle and Toby Anstis and that kid in 4B who went to medical school and became Dr. Dre.

Plus, Herman would remember I'd run off without paying for my Appletiser, and that I'd never even come *near* one of their pizzas. I'd been too embarrassed to go back in, too distracted to sit there and eat. They'd be sure to ring the office and tell them—unless the review was good.

Zoe had written a short e-mail back.

Er, thanks for that. Must have been bloody incredible to get that kind of praise from you. Strange, I'd been told it was terrible. Is everything okay?

How sad, I thought. People asking if you're okay when you're nice about something. Still. Imagine Herman's happy face when he reads that.

I like pizza, is all, I replied, and closed my laptop.

It was just before six, and we were standing outside number 16 Charlotte Street. The Fitzroy Tavern. Corner of Windmill Street.

"This is stupid," I said.

"Dylan Thomas used to drink here!" said Dev. "I wonder why he stopped."

"This is stupid," I said, again. "Let's go somewhere else."

"Didn't you hear me? Dylan Thomas used to drink here! Where do you want to go? A Wetherspoons? Great—we might see Natalie Pinkham from *The Wright Stuff*."

"You're not going to see Dylan Thomas! And since when did this become about 'seeing' someone?"

"You know who we're here to see," said Dev.

Both times I'd seen this girl it'd been around six. Maybe she worked around Fitzrovia, I thought. Fitzrovia, named after this pub, in turn named after a man named Fitzroy. I admire any area that takes its name from a pub. There were others in London, of course. Angel. Manor House. Royal Oak. Swiss Cottage. Plus Elephant & Castle, which only ever made sense to me as a name when I realized that . . . let's just say it remains incredibly fortunate that the pub wasn't called the Vicar & Boobs or something, seeing as that's the kind of thing that's often been known to affect house prices.

And Dev was right about Dylan Thomas. The first time we

came here, a toothy man in tweed down from Bristol for the day had told us it'd been a hub for artists and intellectuals and bohemians in the '20s and '30s and '40s. They'd crowd each corner, he'd said, swapping ideas, arguing drunkenly, fighting and loving, until the pub came to define the whole area. George Orwell drank here. Augustus John. Now it was people like me and Dev. You couldn't help but think that if a pub could look disappointed, it would be looking just a little disappointed right now.

But what did that mean as far as the girl was concerned? Media? Or waitress? Designer? Charlotte Street had changed, even in the time I'd been in London. Once, it was all photography and fashion. Then advertising. For a while, TV and the odd bit of radio. Now—restaurants and bars. Only the Fitzroy Tavern seemed to have seen it all through, like the old man fighting off progress, stubbornly refusing to give up his place at the bar, even when they bring in a karaoke machine.

I kind of wanted to talk about her to Dev, but I'd been passing this off as just a silly thing to do; another excuse to go for a pint. Treating it like Dev's idea, and one I would indulge him this once. I was playing it cool and changing the conversation whenever he brought her up, appalled at myself for actually wanting to bring her up myself.

"Maybe her name's Charlotte," he said, and I pretended to find my shoes suddenly fascinating. "Maybe her name is Charlotte Street. 'Miss Charlotte Street.' Sounds like advice for a tourist."

"Tourists love Charlotte Street," I said, avoiding his eye.

And they do. Or, not tourists, exactly. Businesspeople. American businesspeople. There go some, right now, watches catching the evening sun, as they skip down the stairs of the Charlotte Street Hotel in its Farrow & Ball green, all smart suits and cleanshaven skin, silver Mercs arriving to pick them up for dinner at, I dunno ... The Ivy, probably.

They glide by, and Dev and I watch them go.

"It'd be nice to be American," said Dev.

"They're not all like that," I said. "Some of them are Hulk Hogan."

Dev's eyes darted up and down Charlotte Street, taking in the Londoners spilling out of the bars, laughing their way out of restaurants. There's a holiday vibe to Charlotte Street. Something other. Something happy. It was obvious that Dev was looking out for the girl. I couldn't help it. I did the same.

And then I stopped myself. I felt weird. Weird for being here, weird for being a hair away from stalking, but weird also because, what if? What if she turned up? Walked by? My stomach flipped slightly, the way it flipped the night I waited for Sarah in that Thai place off Piccadilly on our second proper date.

I kicked myself. This is not a date. This is stalking.

And then Dev's eyes widened. He was looking at something. Something—or someone—just over my shoulder.

"Her!" he half whispered, face perfectly still. "Is that her?"

I froze.

"I don't know," I said, eyes wide.

"Blue coat?"

I nodded.

"Shoes?"

"Of *course* shoes."

I turned, slowly.

"No," I said, looking at the figure striding quickly by in a blue coat and shoes. "That's a tall black man."

Dev started laughing. Sometimes he is an idiot.

"Well, I don't know, do I? I've never seen this girl. What color hair does she have?"

"Sort of blond."

"Sort of?"

"Well, blond*ish*."

"Eyes?"

"Definitely."

"What *color* eyes?"

"That you'd have to ask her."

"You need to up your game, stalking-wise. My round!"

Dev walked inside, and I smiled, and shook my head and laughed. Because really, this was all so stupid. Stupid, but fun. If I'd come on my own, well—*that* would have been weird. And also, it would never have happened. But with Dev, it felt like, well, a bit of an adventure, somehow. Like stumbling across a signpost, and following it, just to see where it leads. And I wasn't taking it seriously. Not really. I mean, this girl could be anyone. She could be a Nazi. And have a boyfriend. Who is also a Nazi. Perhaps they've just bought a Nazi dog, and in their spare time go Nazi dancing. There are more than one billion reasons why this complete and perfect stranger may be utterly unsuitable for . . .

Well, for what? What did I really expect to happen here? I mean, let's say she turned up tonight? What then? What do I say that doesn't sound odd, or creepy, or mental? Do I act casual? Do I tell her I saw her last night, as well, and that I had her camera, but that I didn't give it to her in time? That I could've, but chose not to?

I looked at my watch. Five past six. This was pretty much the time. I glanced up the street, toward Snappy Snaps on the corner. A few people were milling about. A rowdy bunch was wandering toward Zilli's. But no sign of The Girl. Not yet.

"Here you go," said Dev, handing me my pint. "Seen her

yet? She's got to work round here. You've always seen her leaving, haven't you? Never arriving?"

I nodded.

"Yeah, she must work round here. Lot of high-class escorts in this area. And traffic wardens, too. She's probably one or the other. Which way does she go?"

"Well—and again, I've only seen her twice—she tends to go this way. Both times she's caught a cab."

"Interesting. Probably a local journey. The tube's only up there. So we can safely say she works round here, and lives not far away. Unless she's meeting a client."

"She's not a high-class escort," I said. "Or a traffic warden."

"Would explain the camera, if she was a traffic warden. They take pictures nowadays."

"Not on a disposable. Anyway, she'd have had a hat on."

We were both staring up the street now.

But she wasn't there. It was ten past, and she still wasn't there. Dev looked at me and stuck his bottom lip out, and rocked on his heels.

I felt awkward again. The excuse didn't seem to hold water anymore. Yeah, so there was a thin veil of "fun" attached to this, but it was getting thinner. Dev clicked his tongue a few times and sniffed.

Oh, what were we doing?

"Listen, let's go," I said.

"You must be joking!" said Dev. "I want to hear what you say to her!"

Suddenly it didn't feel fun anymore.

"No, I feel weird," I said. "Let's go home. Play *GoldenEye*. Or *FIFA*."

That usually worked a treat.

"Let's wait it out," said Dev, and we both stood in silence, and turned our eyes toward Charlotte Street.

We didn't see her.

Of course we didn't see her.

We've all been places two days in a row. That doesn't make it *tradition*.

We stood outside with the rest of the pub, Dev rolling his cigarettes, the evening sun low in the sky, the street a warmed amber.

At seven thirty, or maybe seven thirty-five, we'd exhausted our conversation.

"Shall we have the one we came for?" said Dev with a shrug, and I said, "Not here."

So we walked up Charlotte Street, toward the tube, and then, just on the corner, right outside Snappy Snaps, Dev stopped me.

"This thing with Sarah," he said, touching my arm. "It must be difficult."

I made a face and said, "No, no, God, no," but he was still looking at me.

"I mean, yeah, it's kind of tough when it's out of the blue and everything, but you know how things were, and . . . what are you doing?"

He'd made a small darting movement toward my jacket.

"What was that?" I said, but then I realized: he'd nicked something out of my pocket.

He held it up.

The camera.

"If you can stop banging on about Sarah for two seconds," he said, "come on! They close in half an hour!"

He jogged off, opened the door, and walked into Snappy Snaps.

FOUR

Or "London, Luck, and Love"

Dev had opted for the SuperXpress 24-hour processing, which sounds deeply impressive, until you remember that only flying to the moon in twenty-four hours could really be considered SuperXpress these days.

We would meet back here, he said, outside Snappy Snaps, the following evening. It seemed an unnecessary pronouncement, seeing as we'd probably travel in together.

And I know what you're thinking: you're thinking we shouldn't have done that. It's a gross invasion of someone else's privacy. Two grown men developing the private photographs of a woman neither of us know. Because who knows *what* could be on there? Or *who*? And who knows what that who could be doing on there?

And you're right.

Dev, though, had been reassuring. He said she would never find out. And if she did, it would only be because those photos had led us to her. Led me to her.

I'm not sure how Dev thought these might lead me to her. He doesn't own a camera. Perhaps he thinks people who do often take pictures of themselves holding up pieces of paper with their contact details on them. Maybe he thinks we all pose by street signs, and point to which house we live in, just in case a stranger finds our camera and might like to pop round. And let's say that somehow, his wildest dream came true, and there *was* a picture like that in it—what then?"

I go round, do I? I knock on the door, and say, "Hello! My friend and I developed your private photos and then studied them carefully so that we could come round your house and see you!" She would never have her picture taken again.

"What kind of saint are you?" he said.

"I'm not a saint," I said. "It's just—"

"What? You're not interested? You'd rather never know?"

"It's just . . . this could be seen as creepy."

Dev pressed his keyring. *Wiiise fwom your gwaaave.*

"How's that relevant?" I said.

"I just mean, 'get on with it.' Sorry, I thought that'd be more powerful than it was. Anyway, who's going to know? You don't have to write about it in the paper. We can have a cheeky look and then chuck them away if we need to. Besides, it's a disposable, they're likely to be all blurry and rubbish. She's probably one of those quirky students who take pictures of pigeons and lost gloves sitting all lonely on a fence and then write pretentious captions underneath, like 'Verisimilitude' or 'The Mind Is Its Own Compass.'"

I nodded. Dev was right. There was always the outside chance she might be an idiot.

But I knew she wasn't. And, already, I wanted to do right by her. It sounds weird, and it sounds strange, but I felt I owed her something. She wasn't strictly a stranger anymore; she'd smiled at me.

And then, and then and then . . . I also knew I'd done this before. Felt like this before. At school, for sure. College, too, maybe. A couple of times in my life, anyway, when I'd got an idea into my head about someone, allowed it to run free and develop.

There was Emily Pye at school. One year below me, and pretty; she'd smiled at me once as she walked past with her friends near the gates. At least, that's how it'd felt. I realize now, she'd simply been smiling as she'd walked past. There was no "at me" about it. Our eyes had met midsmile, though, and she'd looked away quickly.

But that smile came to obsess my afternoon, and then my week, and then the last term of school. Emily Pye had smiled at me! Which meant . . . she *liked* me. Suddenly, from being a pretty girl in the year below, she'd become everything and anything I had ever wanted or desired in a life partner. She was perfect—and she liked me! Oh, Emily Pye, what times we would have! We would travel, and then we would settle down and have a living room with big sun-streaming windows and shelves full of books, and then we would keep a small apartment in New York, or perhaps Paris if we've had a child and don't have enough frequent-flier miles to upgrade to business. I would excel at my job, and you would have one, too, because I am modern and encourage that kind of thing, and perhaps when we get a bit older you would start wearing little oblong glasses and long cardigans and we would still hold hands and walk in the park, and get takeaways, too, because just because we were old doesn't mean we couldn't still be cool.

Emily was even a year younger than me, which everyone knows is precisely the right age a girlfriend should be. I was twisting almost any fact to make it fit, make it fate. All I'd wanted was to run into her somehow, and so I'd excuse myself from lessons just in case she'd done the same and we might pass each other in the corridors. I'd ride my bike near her house, wearing my mirrored Aviators, and I'd imagine stopping a robbery or saving a small child's life just to get her attention. Emily Pye went from someone I'd never thought twice about to becoming someone I couldn't *stop* thinking about, and only because she now seemed *achievable*. She'd *noticed* me. There was something there! I was in with a shot!

And so I'd written her a love letter. Well, not a love letter, really. A short note, saying *I think we should meet up!*, basically chickening out of talking to her properly and putting the ball in her court, but under a cloak of mystery and grown-up cool. And one night, after discussing it at great length with my very bored friend Ed, I thought, Yes, I'm going to do it, because I genuinely believed, in my stupid youthful head, that she'd been waiting for this. Waiting for my move. Waiting for this moment.

So I posted it through her door and then cycled away very very quickly. And, a day or two later...

Bzzzzz.

Hang on.

I was jolted from all thoughts of Emily Pye by a text. I stopped walking, and Dev did, too.

"What's up?" he said.

Sorry about going off on one yesterday. I still value you, Jase. Maybe we should talk. Got a lot to say.

"You-know-who," I said, and Dev made an "Ah" face.

I stared at the text. Oh, just let me be embarrassed and go home and sit in my room. And never has the phrase "got a lot to say" been less appealing. "Got a lot to say" means "Got a lot to say to you" and "Got a lot to say to you" means "I would like you to sit perfectly still while I tell you precisely what I think of you." And I couldn't face that. Not yet. Yeah, so I'd have to see her again eventually, because as much as anything we were still friends, kind of. Friends is always what we'd been best at. I guess it's the reason we could never be anything more.

I put the phone back in my pocket and half-smiled at Dev.

Anyway, I heard back from Emily Pye a day or two later, via one of her network of friends. As did everyone at school, most of whom then also saw my letter. Turns out she had absolutely no idea who I was. Not a vague idea, not an "oh, yeah, what, *that* guy?" No idea whatsoever.

And once more I present to you: hope. Ta-*dah!*

I decided, there and then, not to pick up the photos.

Mum and Dad were in town that night, down from Durham.

They were seeing *Billy Elliot* for the fourth time with Jan and Erik from over the road and were staying at their normal hotel in Bayswater. They haven't worked out that the £12 a night they save by staying there is a little less than the £20 it costs them in taxis to the theater and back.

"Seems like we're always coming to you!" Mum said, mock-jokey, as soon as I saw her. We were at the usual Hungarian, the Gay Hussar at the top of Greek Street. We always eat here, because Dad likes looking at the cartoons on the wall—the ones of Michael Howard and John Cole—so he can pretend he spent his life at the center of government, when in fact he mainly spent it at the center of Bryant & Hawesworth Cladding & Ceiling Services Ltd. Mum likes the chilled wild-cherry soup, though I think she likes saying she likes it more than I think she *likes it* likes it. She certainly never made it for our tea.

Since Sarah and I split, I always got the impression they weren't as pleased to see me. Paranoia, of course, but I also knew I was no longer quite the draw I once was. I was just Jason again; just Jason like I'd always been. I felt like I'd been a tower the world was finally happy with. I'd taken years to build and no one ever expected me to be finished. And now, just when the last few bricks were in sight, everyone's grand project had toppled and crumbled and was in dusty pieces scattered across the ground, and everyone *knew* they'd have to rebuild me, but couldn't be arsed to start straightaway.

"Why?" they wanted to wail. "Why did you take our Sarah away from us?"

But they were loyal. They'd always love me. I always felt the distant accusation, though: that somehow, I'd wasted their time. It turned me back into a teenager.

"Yeah, well, you only come down here to see *Billy Elliot*," I said, finally.

"We come down here to see you," said Dad. "*Billy Elliot* is just a bonus."

"So how are things?" asked Mum, moving things on, just like she was trained to. "How's the 'writing'?"

I ignored the speech marks.

"Going well, yeah," I said. "Got a few commissions I have to get done tonight, so I'll have to . . ."

I could see her face fall slightly.

"Otherwise, you know. It's a tough market. There's a recession."

"Well, you're well out of teaching," she said, nodding to herself. "Though, of course, it's an option, isn't it? But you're well out of it. Aren't you?"

"Yes," I said, studying a sausage.

I guess we should talk about Stephen. But I left this jaundiced spotlight on me for just another triumphant second before I said, "And how's Stephen?"

"He's doing well!" they said, almost in unison.

My brother, Stephen, was always doing well. But this isn't one of those tales of sibling rivalry. I didn't envy his life. That's not to say it wasn't good; it was terrific, if you like that sort of thing. He was head of operations at MalayTel now, his kids were tanned and healthy, his wife funny and feisty and waist-deep in plans for their brand-new azure-blue swimming pool. They'd be back at Christmas, Mum said, and I suddenly realized I'd be getting pep talks this year instead of just presents.

But no, I envied Stephen not his life but his direction. He'd only ever been on one path. From university to his first job in Singapore, to meeting Amy his first week at the company and starting a family, to moving his way up the company with solemn predictability. It was like he'd been given all his five-year plans at once and simply popped them all in the same Excel document, ready to gradually tick them all off one by one. I was happy for him, but frustrated, too: he was happy, but I had my own brand of middle-class disappointment. One where you know you can't blame your life on anyone but yourself.

"And . . . have you seen Sarah lately?" asked Mum, daringly, with just the faintest hint of hope in her eyes.

"Yes!" I wanted to say. "Yes, I forgot to say! We sorted everything out! We met up and had a milkshake and it turned out the whole thing was just a misunderstanding and we're fine!"

I wanted to say that for her. I think I wanted to say that for me.

"She's engaged," I said, and I nodded, and under the table, my dad squeezed my mum's hand, hard.

I had work to do.

These reviews. An '80s Best of . . . (easy—name a few tracks, pretend we're all so much cooler these days, make a lazy '80s reference or two). An American import by a folk band with beards (find a few quotes that sound like they know what they're on about and reword them). And a documentary that did well at Sundance about animals who can paint (and which I would actually have to watch).

But this, of course, was why I'd left teaching. Or at least, it was what I'd left teaching to do; dashing off articles and being welcomed and celebrated by London's literati: the new golden boy with potential and opinions to boot.

I'd said my good-byes and made my speech at the leaving do they threw for me at Chiquita's on the high street. They gave me a miniature trophy, engraved with my name and "Most Likely to Succeed" underneath, and I drank tequila and toasted seven happy years. And then Mrs. Haman, head of humanities, had a dizzy spell and knocked over a potted plant, and that felt like the right time to go. We'd been spotted leaving by Michael Shearing and his gang, hoods up, some of them on bikes, congregating around a can of lager someone had left near a bin.

"Oi! Sir!" he'd shouted. "You pissed?"

"It's not 'sir' anymore," I shouted back.

"What is it then?"

I struggled with a comeback.

"Lord!" I tried. He didn't get the joke. If it wasn't on YouTube, and didn't have a man falling over, Michael Shearing never got the joke.

"Lord?" he said, and then one of his mates—Dave Harford, maybe?—muttered, "*Gay*lord," and they all laughed. I let them have that one. Because I was finally free of them all.

Free. Free to sit here, in this room, enjoying my dream: a cup of milky coffee in a Codemasters mug on a rickety table in a room above a videogame shop next door to a place that everyone thought was a brothel, but wasn't, watching a film on a scuffed MacBook about animals that can paint.

Who's laughing now, Michael Shearing?

Still, I know what you're thinking. The money, right? The money makes it better? Well, no. The money's appalling. I might as well take over Dave Harford's paper round. It would certainly be a firmer footing in the media. Certainly more likely to be welcomed and celebrated by London's literati. But this was a start. Sarah and I had always had big plans, and we'd saved accordingly and well. As things began to crumble, and though we'd deny it to each other's face, I think each of us had secretly had our eye on our half. Another good thing about living practically: hope fades, but at least savings get interest.

So I had a decent bank account, I paid no rent, and I was building toward something bigger. Features writing, maybe, or travel. Some kind of speciality. *London Now* for now, *Vanity Fair* or *Condé Naste Traveller* or *GQ* for later. Gone would be the days I was offering opinions I didn't have to people who didn't care.

Only the PRs really cared. And the artists, of course. They cared the most. But there were PRs between me and them, and editors between me and PRs, so I didn't let it affect my journalistic integrity, of which, of course, it sometimes seemed I had little. Just enough to watch *Paw Prints: The Wilder Side of Art.*

I pressed play.

"How was that film?" said Dev.

It was the next morning and Dev had toothpaste round his mouth.

"Brilliant," I said, leaning on the counter. "Did you know sea lions sometimes paint in orange when they're having an off day?"

"Serious?" he said.

"Apparently."

I'd watched it from start to finish, as a cat sat at an easel slapping paint about the place with its paws. Then there was an impressionist elephant, carelessly slapping blue paint across a huge canvas with his fat trunk while a woman in a hat made astonished noises.

I could do better than that, I'd thought, but then realized that yes, of course I could, because I am not an elephant.

"What's happening today?" I said.

"There's a bloke bringing in a limited-edition Sega sound track. Blue vinyl. Theme tunes from *Golden Axe*, *Out Run*, the classics."

"You've not got a record player."

"Owning it is what matters. What about you? What you up to?"

"I'm going to swing by the office. See if there's anything going."

"Why don't you just e-mail them?"

He had a point. Most of our work was quite obviously done on e-mail. But I liked the idea of the office. I liked the interplay. The tradition. It was as close to a staff room as I got these days, and it was nice to talk to my fellow journos. And also, it got me out of Power Up! and away from Caledonian Road.

"What about tonight?" said Dev, smiling. "Am I just going to meet you there, or are we going in together?"

"To where?" I tried.

"Snappy Snaps," he said, wide-eyed and apparently offended. "Charlotte Street!"

"Oh, yeah—it's . . . I might have to go to this gallery thing. For the paper. It's in Whitechapel, and I dunno if it'll end in time, so . . ."

"Will the beautiful Zoe be there?"

"No, she won't be there."

"How often would you say Zoe's talked about me?"

"I would say it's in the single figures, overall."

"Ah, but you don't know how often she *thinks* about me."

"If it's possible, it's probably less than she talks about you. So anyway, I've got that to do, and I need to sit down and come up with some feature ideas to send to another mag, and—"

Dev just looked at me.

"Mate, are you not intrigued? *I'm* intrigued, and I've never *seen* this girl. For all I know, she doesn't exist and you've just bought a disposable. Come on!"

"She exists. But I'm busy. And it feels a bit...odd. Besides, what's the point? So we can perv over pictures of some girl?"

"Yes!" he said. "Yes!"

"No. There's no point. It would've been fine if we had developed them in an hour—"

"The place was closing!"

"I'm just saying, as part of a night out, we can get away with it. High spirits! Hijinks! But there's surely something... borderline illegal about going back the next day?"

"Bollocks!" said Dev, and then the little bell above the door rang.

"Distasteful, then!"

"Pawel!" said Dev. "Get in here!"

In stumbled Pawel, taking a moment to glance behind him to see what it was that had made him stumble. It was a piece of Lego. Dunno why I told you that.

"Hello, Jason. Dev, you owe me four pound for yesterday, and six pound for *jezynowka*."

"Pawel, riddle me this. Jase here"—he pointed at me—"was given some photos by a fit girl and now he doesn't want to develop them."

"What?" said Pawel. "Make them!"

"They weren't 'given' to me."

"She left them in his hands."

"That's not strictly true either."

"You stole a woman's photo?" asked Pawel.

"No!"

"She knows you have these?"

"Not exactly."

"She will find out?"

". . . no."

"*Make* them!" he said.

Dev made a satisfied face. Because he knew they were already pretty much developed.

I ate my lunch in Postman's Park. It made me feel like I had a proper job. Around me were city girls and city men, smart and tailored in white fitted shirts and pinstripe suits and A-line skirts. The camaraderie of work is the first thing you notice has gone when your office is your bedroom. Don't get me wrong, I liked waking up late, and getting my news from *The Wright Stuff*, my first port of call whenever I needed to copy an opinion on global events from Anton du Beke to pass off as my own. I liked making my own lunch, with *Loose Women* on in the background, and then sitting down to think up ideas that might take me further at *London Now*. But it was moments like this, moments spent watching other people's colleagues sitting down together, spooning out their M&S salads and coleslaws, making their in-jokes, swapping snide gossip and who-does-she-think-she-is's and half-meant promises to meet Friday at Bar 18. I liked the smokers huddled outside the buildings, laughing and wheezing in a fug of friendship. I liked it when people nodded their hello to the security guard on the way in, and ignored them on their six o'clock run for freedom.

It's not the teaching I missed. I'd never had grand ideas about being an educator. It's not as easy as it looks. And it's not as if I was some kind of intellectual. I guess if I was one of my old teachers, this is what I'd say:

Attitude: Yes.

Aptitude: No.

Overall: Maybe.

It was the kids, mainly. The job was fine, the kids weren't. And although I tried at first, it wasn't long before I stopped trying.

Here's an actual honest-to-goodness conversation I overheard just last week. I'd been standing on the platform at Essex Road, and from somewhere to my right I heard a voice I recognized. It was Matthew Fowler, a kid I'd taught my first year at St. John's. He was gone in the blink of an eye, off to make his mark on the world, but not before he'd made it at St. John's, nearly blinding a kid in the year below with a compass.

And now here he was, on his mobile, hood up, tracksuit bottoms pulled up high, nasty bruise on his arm. I instinctively turned away from him, and pulled my newspaper to my face— a day-old copy of *Metro*, since you ask, but don't tell Zoe; that's a sacking offense. I'm not sure why I hid. He'd never have recognized me. As a teacher, I'd made far less of an impression on him than he'd made on me.

Then, suddenly, another voice, this one unknown. Some kind of family friend.

"Maffew!" she shouted. "Haven't seen you in fucking ages! How's your mum?"

"Okay," he said.

"You married, then?"

"Nah." He shrugged.

"Not married? How old are ya?"

"Twenty-one."

"Twenty-one?" she said, in disbelief. "You must have a *baby*, though?"

"Yeah," he said. "Ten months."

"Bloody hell!" she said, relieved. "I was gonna *say*...!"

Somehow it was hard to get Matthew Fowler interested in soil erosion. But this sounds cruel, and patronizing, and empty.

There were clearly extenuating circumstances, you'd say. Broken home, maybe. Abuse. Nope. Matthew Fowler just couldn't care less. Simple as that. And when it came to teaching, I was never cut out to be Michelle Pfeiffer, turning geography into rap, inspiring and uniting through belief in myself, belief in the *kids*. No. I wanted to review bad bands and stay up late and watch films about animal art instead. Actually, maybe it was me who couldn't care less.

I finished my ham and mustard sandwich and scrunched up the plastic, standing to read the plaque opposite.

JOHN CRANMER, CAMBRIDGE, AGED 23. A clerk in the London County Council who was drowned near Ostend whilst saving the life of a stranger and a foreigner. August 8 1901.

I looked at the people on their benches, with their salads and their smoothies. Did they read these? Do they make them feel the same? Like . . . useless?

I downed the rest of my Polo-Cockta, and chucked it in the bin.

"You know you can just e-mail us this stuff," said Zoe.

I'd already plugged in the memory stick, and sort of mumbled my excuse.

"I was passing."

"You're always passing. Where are you always on your way to?"

"Here and there," I said. "I am a very mysterious man."

"Nothing about you is very mysterious, Jason," she said. "You're an open book. And I've read you a few times and I'm bored. So are you good to go to this gallery tonight?"

"Thanks, Zoe. Yeah, seven, yeah."

"The bloke's supposed to be a genius. Not that I want to compromise your opinions."

"Do you know him?"

"He's my cousin's fiancé."

"Ah. I'll be kind."

I transferred the files to Zoe's computer, which meant I had to lean close to her, which meant she had to move her chair back a bit, but she could only move it as far as the wall and for a second or three we were quite close. We didn't say anything. It would've been awkward, so we just listened to the tap-tap and whirr of her desktop. But she smelled nice. Like coffee and mints. For a second I wondered about us.

"I'll give them to Rob," she said, as I stood.

Rob's the reviews editor. I don't really know what that means. It's Zo that hands everything out.

"Great. So."

I stood there and blinked a couple of times.

"So . . . ?" said Zoe.

"So, I'll be going, unless . . ."

"Unless?"

Sigh.

"Got any more work?"

Zoe smiled, weirdly. Not disappointed, exactly, but like maybe she'd thought I wasn't going to just—you know—ask for more work. A strange thing happens to an old friendship when suddenly there's money at stake. But then, enough things had happened over the years to put strain on this friendship. It was remarkable we were still holding on, somehow. Jason and Zo.

"Talking of work, as we mainly do these days," she said, now a little more sternly, "your Abrizzi's review ran this morning."

Oh. Shit.

"Did it?"

"Yeah."

Shit shit shit. Why was she bringing this up?

"They phoned up. Wanted to speak to you."

"Did they?"

Shit.

"Yeah. Spoke to me instead."

Busted. *Royally* busted.

"They want to use your quote."

"What? Which quote?"

" 'A happy slice of silly pizza,' or something."

"Oh. Right. Is that what they said?"

"It'd be a weird thing for me to make up."

"So what did you say?"

"Well, publisher's keen to get our name in more places. Said so last week. Wants us to become a 'London Recommender.' And now that we've heralded them as the savior of Italian food, Abrizzi's are going to take out an ad. Everyone's a winner."

Phew.

"Well, tell them I said yes, then."

"Lucky, seeing as it's not your decision. Not ours, actually, either. Anyway, they're doing it. They're sending round a voucher for you, too. A thank-you. I said it wasn't really allowed, but then I remembered we're not the bloody BBC, so it's free meals for you and . . . whoever else you might want to take with you."

"Dev, probably."

Zoe looked at me, with what I hoped was admiration and respect for taking someone like Dev almost *anywhere*, but was, in actual fact, pity.

"I'm going to have to check it out, too, sometime," she said. "Check out this magic pizza."

"Yep. So. Any more work?"

She held up a ticket.

"Rob's called in sick. Again. I'm starting to believe him. There's a screening at four. Fancy it?"

* * *

In a small screening room somewhere round the back of China-town, the film had begun.

There was me, someone from *Time Out*, and a bloke with a beard from Radio 1, who laughed like a nitwit throughout. Somewhere at the back, the film critic who used to be on the *News of the World* sat, motionless and silent, his pen never once lifted, his eyes dull and bored. I've sat in the screenings like this before with him. He doesn't seem to like anything he sees. And yet it's his name you'll see flash by on buses, underneath words like "HILARIOUS!!!" (with three exclams) or "A LAUGH RIOT!!" (with two) or "THE MOST IMPORTANT FILM OF THE DECADE!" (with a sober and important one).

Which would be fine, if any or all of those applied to *Super Troopers*.

Today's offering was a teen comedy, in which lots of people fell over in a mall. There were hot girls, and geeky boys, and a scene in which a food fight broke out in a canteen, and halfway through they cut to a fat lad under a table shoveling discarded hamburgers into his mouth. That was the only time the man from the *Mirror* laughed, which woke the guy from the *Mail*.

I stopped paying attention roughly halfway through. Some-where along the line I got to thinking about the evening that lay ahead. Subtly, I took the gallery flyer out of my pocket. I could sense a PR somewhere in a darkened corner looking round at me to ensure my attention was still on the action on the screen. I folded the flyer up again, as if somehow getting it out had been a mistake, but when they turned back, stole a glance.

Enigmash-up: A Journey Through the Ego to the Id via You, Me & They.

Christ.

The main picture they'd used looked terrifying. Jesus on the cross holding a Pot Noodle in one hand and a copy of *Heat* in the other. I knew how the evening would go. Warm white wine in plastic cups and canapés bought from Lidl. Considered silences standing before canvases that look like mistakes. And I'd be on my own. There'd be a list, of course, and once they knew I was press, I'd be engaged in overfriendly chitchat I'd never remember with someone I'd never see again. And then I'd get on the tube, and go home, and write it up, and maybe watch the news at ten, and go to bed.

What an evening.

"I like your name," said the PR, an hour and a half later, as I made it to the door. "It's like that other man's, isn't it? From the program."

"Jason Priestley."

"Yes."

"Yes."

"So what did you think?" she said, and this of course is why she'd stopped me.

"Oh, gosh, you know," I said. "They must have had such fun making it!"

"It's a *lot* of fun, isn't it?"

"Must've been," I said. You need to be nimble with these people. "My kids would *love* it."

This was an excellent technique.

"Would they?" she said. "How old are your kids?"

"Oh, they're, you know, young. Young kids."

"How young?"

"They're . . . four."

"Both of them?"

"Uh-huh."

"Twins?"

I tried to work it out.

"Yes."

"Well, it's an 18!"

"Ha, yes, but, you know, they'd probably like the . . . colors."

"Lovely, I'd love kids. What are their names?"

Oh, let me go, I've got an awful gallery to see.

"Alex," I tried, pulling the names out of thin air. "Alex is the . . . one of them. And Bob."

"Alex and Bob?" she said. "What? Like in the film?"

Eh?

I saw the poster over her shoulder and took in the film's name for the first time. *Alex & Bob Get F***ed Up.*

"Bye," I said.

When I got out, there was a text waiting.

Ready?

It was from Dev. I read on.

I'll be at the Fitzroy. You better be there.

I looked at my watch. He'd already be there. What if he'd picked up the photos? I still had the ticket, but he could be persuasive. What if I just swung by, just to make sure he wasn't up to any monkey business?

No. It's out of the question. I'm a professional. I'm working.

I looked again at the flyer for the gallery opening.

Enigmash-up: A Journey Through the Ego to the Id via You, Me & They.

Jesus and a Chicken & Mushroom Pot Noodle.

I tapped my lip.

"Bollocks!" said Dev. "She's married."

I looked at the photo in front of me.

There were others, of course, but this was the only one I really needed to see.

"She's married!" he said.

I don't know what I'd been expecting. I don't even know what I'd been hoping for.

We'd done it, of course. Picked up the photos. It had only taken the one we'd come for, and we were in Snappy Snaps like a flash.

And now, here she was. *The Girl.* There was a glow on her face, and that smile.

I kicked myself. Of *course* she was married.

"Mind you," said Dev, pointing at The Girl. "Doesn't look like a wedding dress. Who gets married in something like that?"

"Yeah, what *is* that?"

Whatever it was, and despite what she brought to it, it was hideous. Pretty much the only word applicable, though not one I'd use in her presence, obviously. It was a very odd green, and looked like it'd been designed by someone who'd never seen a girl. Or a dress.

"But that's definitely her boyfriend. Check the body language."

The man—handsome, urbane, probably good at skiing, owns a number of powerful motorcycles, can doubtless tell you the difference between red and white wine—had his arm around her, and she looked pleased. Really pleased. He looked pleased, too, and why not. She's stunning. Despite the dress. I found myself cursing his chunky watch and tan.

"Nice looking, isn't he?" said Dev. "Probably quite cultured, too. Probably calls them 'bosoms.' Still. I imagine it's for the best. You wouldn't want her turning up at the pub dressed like that."

"You're wearing a *Street Fighter* T-shirt."

"Just wearing it in. Planning on seeing Pamela soon."

"Who's Pamela?"

"That waitress. Pam-*eh*-la. That's how you say it in Poland."

I flicked through the photos, taking in each for a second or two, but what was the point? The Girl had a man with a chunky watch and powerful motorcycles putting his big tanned arm round her.

"Oh, that's a good one," said Dev.

She'd taken a photo of her shoes by accident. And one of the pavement. But the others . . . the others seemed to tell a story. A wedding, an old car, a cinema.

"We should leave the photos back at Snappy Snaps," he said. "Say there was a mistake. She probably bought the camera there, or maybe she meant to develop them. She might come back."

Yes. He was right. He was quite right.

I flicked through the last few, almost like a good-bye.

"You never know, if you leave your number, she might get in touch, and—"

But suddenly . . .

. . . suddenly, I wasn't listening.

I was hearing, but not listening.

Because something about this photo—this last photo—had caught my eye.

"Where now?" said Dev, draining his pint. "What shall we do?"

But I was still staring, still struggling to comprehend.

This photo . . . it was a photo taken in a café. There was a table in front of whoever took it, with a half-finished coffee and the remains of a slice of something, and a spoon to one side. The café looked warm, and welcoming, and through the window the bright yellow light of a black cab was just about visible. A waiter was clearing up, and there were checkered tablecloths and monochrome photos on the wall of minor celebrity diners, like Andy Crane and Suggs, and over to one side, cut in half by the framing and reading a copy of *London Now*, was a man.

In fact, over to one side and cut in half by the framing and reading a copy of *London Now* was *me*.

"One who refused advice was later seen bleeding."

—Traditional Shona Tribe proverb, Zimbabwe

Hello?

I hope there's someone out there. Is there a button I can push that will tell me?

Hello?

I will listen to my friends in future. If you're my friend, maybe you'll help me work through this. I will listen to your advice. So if you've got something to say to me, you just go right ahead and say it to me and I will listen, and it sounds as if that means I will not bleed, which is a good thing all round, isn't it? Especially if I'm at your house and you don't want me bleeding everywhere.

But I can see, listening is important.

Because the problem is—or at least it has been—sometimes you go deaf when what you can see is so overwhelming.

So yes. I'll listen.

Thank you in advance.

Thank you!

FIVE

Or "Everywhere I Look"

"That is mental," said Dev, as we walked toward the tube.

"I know," I said, and that's all I could say. My mind was racing.

I patted my pocket. The photos were still in there. They'd suddenly become precious, somehow, and I couldn't help but keep checking them.

"No, I mean that is mental. Absolutely *mental*. Do you have any idea how mental that is?"

"I know exactly how mental that is. It's mental."

"No, mate—it's *properly* mental. That's you. You, in the photo. In the photo she took just before you ended up with that photo in your hand. What if you'd never developed the film? Then you'd never know that—"

"What?"

"Well, it's fate, isn't it? It's got to be. It's destiny!"

I tried to ignore what Dev was saying, but it was difficult. It was me in that photo. Half of me, and not a particularly flattering half either, but me all the same. Sitting there, paper flattened down on the table, shoveling a sausage into my mouth. And it's not like this was a regular haunt of mine, Café Roma. It's not like anyone taking a photo in there at just before six on a weeknight would be statistically likely to catch me wolfing down a Roman sausage. I'd been there maybe twice before, both times after a lonely visit to the cinema on Tottenham Court Road, and this time I'd only popped in because it was kind of familiar, and I was nearby, and I was hungry.

And yet there I was.

"You've got a connection now," said Dev, eyes ablaze. "If she's a hippie, you might be able to trick her into thinking it's the universe guiding you together. If she's not, you might be able to appeal to her anecdotal side. It'd be a great 'how we met' story for dinner parties. She looks like she goes to dinner parties. I wonder what it must be like to go to dinner parties."

"Are you still talking?" I said, but we both knew I was trying to be casual. Thing is, I was kind of excited. I had no reason to be, rationally speaking. I'm probably in lots of strangers' photos. Right now, there's probably a family in Osaka doing an extended slide show of their trip to London, and there I am, squeezing a Calippo and blinking in the background near the traffic at Trafalgar Square. I'm probably in the background of a thousand others, too, late for work, hungover or harassed, drinking cans of Coke near Westminster or looking at girls on the Heath, captured and immortalized forever in someone else's memories, over someone else's shoulders.

The only strange thing is that I should ever see one.

I wondered if The Girl had noticed me in there. I hadn't seen her. I'd been too preoccupied with reading my latest stuff in *London Now*, seething as I asked myself why the subs had insisted on changing almost everything I did so that it was no longer as pithy or perfect as I'd wanted. I'd had mash with my sausage, and a cup of sugary tea, and I'd studied the listings to see what was on telly that night. But at no point had I noticed The Girl, and at no point had I heard a click or seen a flash. If she'd noticed me, if I'd been promoted from a mere extra in her life to a dayplayer, she hadn't let on when I'd helped her with her packages. Maybe that was a bad sign. I'd never even entered her radar. But then, she's got a boyfriend. One with a chunky watch. Why should I have entered her radar? I wear a Swatch.

But what if . . . ? What if there *was* a connection?

The next morning, I tried to convince myself that, hey, as weird as it is, these things happen. So what? She'd been finishing off her film before taking it to be processed, I'd happened to be nearby when it happened. After all, it was only because I was nearby in the first place that I'd even seen her that night. What seemed like a huge coincidence was now just a conversation-starter. An icebreaker at best. A "hey, here's the funniest thing."

But Dev wasn't fooled. And he was still hugely impressed by what he saw as the startling global ramifications of it all.

"Dude, people have *kids* for less of a reason!"

"When did you start saying 'dude'? And is that what you think I should tell her if I see her again? 'Hi, you don't know me, but I was in the background of a picture you once took. Hey, let's have a child!'"

"Jase, you're forgetting everything else. The fact you ended up with the camera in your hand."

"That's down to my ineptitude," I tried.

"You saw her again in the same place!"

"Yeah, probably looking for her camera."

"Mate! Come on! This is a moment! Yeah? Use it!"

Truth was, I wanted to. I'd stayed up late last night, flicking through the photos, looking for I'm-not-sure-what. You and I both know I knew nothing about this girl, and yet more and more, somehow I felt I knew *something*.

Here's what I thought I knew.

Her favorite season was spring, because yellow was her favorite color, and daffodils are yellow. She liked daffodils, because maybe she'd grown up on a farm somewhere, and as little as I know about farms I imagine sometimes they're quite near daffodils. She liked animals, of course, because of the whole farm thing, and also it's hard to like a girl who hates animals; it messes with the order of things. But her small flat in London with the shabby chic furniture she'd bought from a weekend flea market and painstakingly painted and restored herself when she'd moved down to London from—where? Wales, maybe, where she'd also left her childhood sweetheart, the only boy she'd ever kissed? Well, it was just too small for a dog or a cat and so she'd just pet them when she passed them in the street, and engage their owners in long, sweet conversations. Cats! It was cats she loved most! And she rode a bike for sure, even though both times I'd seen her she'd been in a taxi, and the blue coat she wore was her favorite, and she wore it everywhere, whatever the weather.

I knew it was stupid. I knew the picture I was painting was just of a girl I *wanted* to know, no matter how clichéd the love of animals or the battered old bike or the blue coat she took everywhere or the fresh daffodils from the stallholder she greeted every day on her way to work were.

And then there was work. What did she do? Again, the ideas were probably better than the reality. In my mind, she was maybe a book publicist, working on quiet but important texts and making sure professors got their sandwiches before the lady from *New Scientist* turned up, or the fella from the World Service dropped by to record an interview on an ancient, scuffed Marantz. Or maybe an art student, with a free, cartwheeling mind and painted rainbow toenails and a rabbit called Renoir.

Or just French. I honestly wouldn't mind if she was just French.

The truth, of course, was that she was probably in sales. For a window fitting company that broke several EU environmental safety guidelines in the late 1990s and was on *Watchdog*. That blue jacket was all she could find that day. She didn't care about animals. She couldn't spell "daffodils." She smoked Marlboro Reds and couldn't stand kids and had never been to Waterstones. And if she *did* have a bike, it wouldn't be an old battered one with a basket on the front and plastic flowers on the wheel, it'd be a slick and soulless titanium one she'd bought off her wastrel brother and never really used and made her flat look awful, all propped up against the hallway wall and unused and ignored.

Because it doesn't matter how someone seems inside a photo; it's what's on the outside that counts.

And that was what kept my mind from flying out the window, my heart and my hope exactly where they were, and my feet in a videogame shop on the Caledonian Road.

I put the kettle on, and Dev flicked the CLOSED sign to OPEN. An instant later the door swung open.

"Hello, Dev. Hello, Jason."

"Hey, Pawel."

"Dev, you owe me four pound. And also, six for *jezynowka*."

"Absolutely!" said Dev. "But first, I need your advice."

"Why?"

"I aim to woo one of your kind."

Pawel looked a little blank.

"A girl called Pamela. Pam-*eh*-la. I need some dialogue. Interesting things to say. Pointers."

Pawel nodded gravely.

"From café?"

"That's her!" said Dev. "Pretty. Brown hair with big yellow streaks."

"Yes. You will need much help. She is maybe the most boring woman in world."

Dev looked confused.

"She seems enigmatic."

"No, no. Very boring. A very boring woman."

I decided to leave Pawel and a stunned Dev to it, and wandered upstairs.

Work. No, coffee. First coffee, then work. Real coffee, though. None of Dev's instant. Not because I don't like instant. I just don't like Dev's instant. It was Sarah who got me onto real coffee. I think it was mostly showing off. Look at me, with my cafetière, and my proper coffee cups, and my fair-trade beans. I had a mental image of her and Gary, suddenly, sipping homemade lattes, sitting crosslegged and barefoot on polished floorboards in white linen trousers in rooms with fresh flowers and breaking croissants in two and listening to Coldplay and smugly quoting Charlie Brooker's column at each other and laughing about how rubbish everything is.

I took the photos out of my pocket and threw them down on the table, the green-and-yellow Snappy Snaps packet now creased and crumpled. I thought about opening them up again, just to have another quick look at someone else's life, but shoved them in a drawer instead.

I found the smudged side of A5 I'd pressed down into the very bottom of my pockets, and brought it out.

Film, it said. *Two lads. Alex and ???*

I wasn't sure how much use this would be.

Director: Peter Donaldson. Funny bit with an owl.

I thought back. That *had* been funny.

Somehow, I had to make this last 250 words.

Alex & Bob Get F***ed Up, I wrote.

Word count: 6.

I sat back in my chair and stared at my work so far. I liked it. I had a sip of coffee and leaned forward again.

. . . is a film directed by Peter Donaldson.

Word count: 13.

I drummed my fingers on the table.

Don't get distracted, I thought. Concentrate.

I turned the radio on and then turned it off again.

Take two guys, I wrote. *One called Alex, one called Bob.*

Word count: 22.

I added *and* after Alex. 23.

I drummed my fingers again and looked out of the window. A truck was delivering vegetables to the grocer's on the corner. The man who ran the Ethiopian restaurant was putting out the bottles.

I looked at my drawer. Opened it. Saw the pictures lying there, in their packet.

"Jason!" shouted Dev, from downstairs. "Favor!"

"What?" I shouted.

"Can you look after the shop for a bit? Pawel's going to teach me a Polish love song!"

I closed the drawer and looked again at the word count.

23.

Yeah, not bad.

Dev had been gone maybe fifteen minutes, maybe twenty. He'd left the theme tune to *Golden Axe* running in the shop, which I turned off the moment the door clicked shut and replaced with Magic FM.

I know next to nothing about games. There are facts I can

regurgitate, and there are things I can say, but knowing about them—that's different. It makes interaction with those few brave souls who enter Power Up! a tricky affair. I bluff sometimes, if they look like the sort of person I can bluff, but more often than not I have to hold my hands up and admit there and then, I'm looking after the shop. Sometimes they'll look relieved. That means they've heard about Dev. *Retro Gamer* magazine ran an interview with him recently, calling him "the UK's last bastion of high-street retrogaming quality." He had it printed up on business cards, and then framed the article behind the counter, next to a signed picture of Dave "the Unstoppable Games Animal" Perry, a joypad that had once belonged to Big Boy Barry, and a photo of Danny Curley, European Games Playing Champion 1992, who he thought had once come into the shop but had been too shy to talk to.

The DJ on Magic had just finished making a joke about the weather when the little bell above the door went. I looked up and froze, slightly.

It was Matthew Fowler, the kid I used to teach. Well, not teach, exactly. The kid who'd sit there while I just sat there. The one who nearly blinded someone. The father of a ten-month-old, who itself couldn't be more than ten months away from shouting at someone on *Jeremy Kyle* or *Trisha*.

He was wearing his hood down and there was the tinny *tik-tik-tik* of an MP3 player somewhere in his tracksuit bottoms.

His eyes flicked toward me and then away again, and he started to go through a box of secondhand carts and CDs.

He hadn't recognized me.

I relaxed a little, and started to pretend to be tidying up the counter, but I couldn't help keep looking over at him, through fascination, I must add, not suspicion. What had he been up to since leaving St. John's? Why was he in here? It was a bit like spotting a celebrity, though one you're a little afraid might beat you up.

The *tik-tik-tik* stopped, and he cast another look my way. I felt guilty for watching, and so turned away and started to pile things that didn't need to be put into little piles into little piles.

And then he was at the counter.

"Hullo, sir."

Oh.

"Hello . . . Matthew. Matt."

"You work here, do you?"

It would be weird if I didn't.

Hang on—I don't.

"No. Just looking after the place. For a friend."

He nodded, and glanced about the shop.

"Yeah, what's his name again? I been in here a few times. Quite nervous, that fella, isn't he?"

That'll be the hood.

"You still at St. John's, then?" he said.

He was talking to me, but looking anywhere but.

"No, I'm a journalist now. Sort of. A sort-of journalist."

"Yeah, I seen your name in the paper. Didn't know if it was you or the other one."

"The bloke from *90210*?"

"Reasoned it probably wasn't."

I smiled.

"You all right then, sir?"

Now he was looking at me, shyly.

"You don't have to call me 'sir.'"

"What then?"

"I dunno. Mr. Priestley?"

I suddenly felt ludicrous. I was a man standing in front of a

Sonic the Hedgehog poster demanding a customer address me as Mr. Priestley.

"Or Jason. Just call me Jason."

Matthew sniffed and scratched his face.

"I'll call you Mr. Priestley. You're all right, though, yeah?"

There was an awkward moment. I didn't know what else to say. I tried to think what Dev would say.

"Yeah. Did you find everything you need?"

"Just looking."

"How's your kid?"

It was instinct. But now he'd wonder how I knew. He smiled.

"I saw you that day, too. At the station. Thought you wouldn't recognize me."

"What's his name? Or her?"

"Elgar."

Elgar? Elgar the baby?

"Elgar is a wonderful name for a . . . baby."

"I haven't got a baby," he said, smiling. "That woman you saw, she's always on at everyone about babies. Better she thinks I've got one and I might be able to get something done with my days."

I laughed. Elgar seemed a weird reference for him, but one I liked.

"How've you been?"

He shrugged.

"School wasn't for me. Dunno what is."

"Where are you working?"

"Garage off Chapel Market."

And then, from somewhere in his trousers, Akon started singing. Either it was Matt's ringtone, or Akon really needs to start looking for new gigs.

He stared at the name on the screen.

"I gotta go. Cheers, sir. Nice to see you. Glad you're all right."

"See you again—" I started to say, but his back was turned and he was already halfway out the shop.

I watched him jog across Caledonian Road toward a scuffed-up mountain bike chained to a lamppost.

School wasn't for him. I knew how he felt.

And then, the small tinkle of the bell above the door again, and in walked another customer. I flashed a half-smile at him and turned away, not really taking him in, and not trying to either. I wasn't done thinking about Matt yet. But there'd been something familiar about the shape of the man, about his tan and his neat hair, and I turned back, and there he was, still in the doorway, smiling a small smile and raising two thin eyebrows.

"Hello, buddy," he said, with something approaching sadness in his voice, like I was a kitten coming out of anesthetic, and he was a vet with a hammer in his pocket.

SIX

Or "The Sky Is Falling"

"I know you still love her, buddy."

Oh, please, no, not buddy. Who says buddy who's not from America or the 1950s? Gary's thirty-four and from Hertfordshire.

I'd closed the shop—Dev would understand—and reluctantly agreed to a "quick coffee . . . just a catch-up . . . just a chippity-chat."

I'd already spent ten minutes staring at Gary's mouth while words came out. Big, round words, meaningless and foggy. And then, like coming out of a long tunnel and realizing you're still tuned to the radio, he was there.

". . . how hard it must be for you that she's with someone else," he said, and I snapped myself to attention. "But at some point, you're going to have to take responsibility for your actions. Put your hands up. Say, 'I messed up,' and move on. Otherwise your life just won't be worth living."

From anyone else, this last line could have been intimidating. A warning shot fired across the bow. From Gary it came across like something from a weaker episode of *Dr. Phil*.

I tried to stop him.

"It's not that I still love her," I said, staring into my coffee, but he ignored me and just carried on.

"We've all been there," he said, and I noticed his fleece. *Dubai Desert Classic 2004* and a small Emirates logo. No bobbles, no fluff. This was a fleece he took care of. "I mean, you have someone, you lose someone. But this is the way of the world. Life's too short."

I suddenly realized what Gary was. Gary was someone who said things like "Life's too short" as if he'd just come up with it himself. He probably thought he was a genius, coming up with something as profound as "Life's too short." I bet one day he'll see it on a bumper sticker and think someone's ripped him off.

"You need to use every day as if it's your last," he said, at least pretending to find this awkward and fixing his eyes on a stain on the tablecloth. "And if you're hung up on someone—"

"I'm honestly not hung up on Sarah," I said. "I was drunk, and in front of a computer, and yeah, I agree I made mistakes— I made one *huge* mistake—and you can pat yourself on the back because you've never made a mistake like it, but people make mistakes, Gary."

Oh, God. I just said "People make mistakes." I'm worse than Gary.

"It's no use living in the past," he said.

Then again . . .

This was embarrassing. Like being told off by a grown-up. A real man. Someone who's perfectly able to take a relationship in his stride. And that, I think, is why he was enjoying it so much. He wasn't doing this out of pity, or concern. He was doing this to say, "Look at me. Look at what I can do. Not only can I make it work with Sarah, I'm big enough to be able to tell you where you've gone wrong, why you're a failure, and yet still make it seem like I'm doing you a favor. I should really be wearing a top hat."

"Gary, listen, I'd better be going," I said, snapping out of it and doing my best to swig half a cup of coffee in one. I inched my chair backward to show I was serious.

"Dev'll wonder why I've shut up shop. He's learning a Polish song. And Tuesdays between three and four are our busiest time. His busiest. I don't work there."

Gary panicked.

"Before you go, mate," he said. "Look, it's not my place to say it, but..."

But what?

He paused, and seemed to love it. Usually, I love pauses, too. I can pause for anything up to a minute; it's like a gift. Sarah used to say life happens in the pauses; that some pauses are great pauses; comforting pauses. The pause a taxi driver gives you the second after you name a street, the second before the nod that confirms they know the way. The pause between the ads at the cinema, when the music and the visuals and the noise disappear all at once, and all you're left with is the glow of a mobile being switched off or the slow self-conscious rustle of a sweet wrapper. But this pause...this wasn't a good pause. There was no comfort to be taken from this pause.

"Forget it."

"What?"

"No, it's not my place."

"What, Gary?"

A final, decisive pause. A quick one, this time, but no nicer.

"No."

And with that, he threw a fiver down on the table, smiled, and inched his chair back, too.

"Righty-ho."

Gary had insisted on walking me back into the shop. I'd tried to show him how busy I was by splitting the little unnecessary pile I'd piled up earlier into two, but to be honest, it still didn't make me look particularly busy. It just made me look like a man with piles.

You know what I mean.

Gary had picked up a few games and read their descriptions out to me. Gary's one of those people who read things out.

"Two for one!" he'd said, in a jaunty voice, as we'd passed the Esso garage. "Fresh rolls!" There's very little you can say in response to "Fresh rolls!," let alone "Caledonian Food & Wine!"

And excellent: now he'd found the photos. I'd not had time to put them away.

"These yours?" he said, and I had to stop myself from visibly squirming.

"Yeah. No. A friend's."

I held my hand out, tried to get him to relinquish them, but he was fascinated.

"Who is she?"

"She's . . . like I say, she's a mate. A chum."

A *chum*?

He allowed himself another moment to study her. His eyes flicked around the first one. I knew what he was doing. He was comparing her to Sarah, weighing up who the winner was.

"That's good, Jason," he said, eventually, and fanning the photos out in front of him. "It's good to have friends."

I nodded. Well, what was the harm? If Gary thought I was hanging out with pretty blond girls with lively eyes, perhaps he'd tell Sarah. Although, of course, he wouldn't. That would make me seem far too attractive. No, Gary would tell Sarah I was working in the videogame shop and was wearing a jumper with a sailor on it.

"Whitby," he said, wistfully.

"Hmm?"

"That's Whitby, isn't it? I recognize the abbey."

He pointed at one of the photos. She—whoever she is—was wearing a red scarf, and laughing at something someone off camera was saying. It was one of my favorites. You couldn't see the wind, but you could almost feel it. Brisk and cold and sweeping away the cobwebs, fresh and clean. In the background, high on a cliff, was the building Gary now had his finger all over.

I did my best to subtly move them away. These were mine. You can't have them, Gary.

"I used to go there as a kid. Not on my own, obviously. Dad had a caravan and liked it up there. When were you in Whitby?"

I managed to nod and shake my head at the same time. Gary took this in whatever way he took it.

"Well, good luck, Jason."

And I would've watched him go, except I had the picture in my hands, and I didn't want to look away.

Dev was back an hour later and humming a strange tune.

"It's 'Bo jesteś Ty' by Krzysztof Krawczyk," he said, before adding, "I have no idea what I just said."

"What's it about?"

"Love. Endless, yearning, aching love. The kind of love only a man in a videogame shop can have for a Polish waitress called Pamela. What you been up to?"

"Gary came round."

Dev's face fell. But secretly, he loves stuff like this.

"What did he want?"

"To sort things out. Make sure there's no bad blood. Call me buddy."

"He's *brilliant*, is Gary. Enigmatic."

"But also—I think—to unnerve me."

"How so?"

"He paused."

"He paused?"

"He paused. On purpose. Started to tell me something. Then paused. Then didn't tell me."

"Sometimes people pause. Sometimes I pause."

"You *press* pause. And this wasn't just a pause. It was a notable pause."

"Sometimes I pause notably. I paused notably just the other night. People took note as I paused. I wouldn't worry about it."

"I just think—"

"Don't think. If you think, you'll never truly get over her. Thinking just extends things."

So I decided not to think.

Upstairs, I finished my *Alex & Bob* review (3 out of 5) and stared at the screen.

Enigmash-up: A Journey Through the Ego to the Id via You, Me & They.

The cursor blinked at me, as surprised by the sentence as I'd been.

What the hell was I going to write about?

I studied the leaflet. Lots of inappropriate words were in bold and there were too many exclamation marks.

"Kaiko Kakamara is one of Britain's **most** surprising new artists!! His **vision** and tenacity have set the scene on **fire**, and his fans **include**..."

I suddenly lost the will to live and exhaled, heavily. Art is subjective, no? So my opinion is valid whatever. But is it valid even if I haven't seen the exhibition?

Yes, I think it is. I began to type.

With fans including...

And ten minutes later, I e-mailed it off.

I sat back in my chair and thought about Gary. Why had he paused? And what would he have thought if he'd known I'd had a stranger's photos?

And then my phone rang. It was Zoe.

"Hello, dickhead. How are the words coming on?"

"E-mailed them off a moment ago."

"What did you think?"

"You'll find out!"

"Of the exhibition, I mean."

I picked up the leaflet.

"Oh, you know. Surprising. Full of vision, and . . . tenacity."

"Gosh, it sounds amazing. And there was me, never taking you for an arty one."

"Well, it turns out I am."

"Do you remember at uni when we were in that house on Narborough Road with that French art girl and Dev and she asked you to do that life modeling thing and you nearly moved out because you thought she meant naked?"

I laughed.

"She just wanted you to sit on a bench and hold an apple!"

Now she was laughing, that familiar, smoky laugh. We'd come close to being together, me and Zo, if you know what I mean. Just once at uni, after one of those fashionable School Disco parties. Her cousin had been in town and was being violently ill in her room so she'd snuck into mine and we'd watched *The Goonies* till dawn. So I knew she'd liked me once. Maybe she still did. Maybe that suited me, after everything.

"So anyway, I didn't see you there."

"Hmm?"

"I didn't see you at the gallery."

I froze. Was she joking?

"What do you mean?"

"At the exhibition. I went along in the end."

Was this a bluff? Or had I been found out?

"You were there, were you?" I said, with what I hoped was a light and jokey undertone, but which may very well have sounded like fear.

"I was. I thought I'd stop by. Whereabouts were you?"

"I must've been . . . in the other part."

"Which other part?"

"The part just off the main part."

"There was no other part. There was hardly even a *main* part."

"Well, I only popped in, and it was so busy, so I just—"

"It was half-empty. You didn't pop in."

In the background, I heard her computer ping. Shit. My e-mail. My e-mail had arrived.

"I popped in! I popped my head round the door!"

Please believe me. Please believe me.

"Jason," she said, and now I was starting to sweat, because I could hear her using her mouse, clicking on something, opening an attachment. "Have you submitted a review of something without having seen it?"

Was that her clever trick? Remind me of the old days, catch me off guard?

"No . . . I'm . . . I went, but maybe you didn't see—"

" 'With fans including Evan Dando and Carl Barat,' " she said, and my stomach flipped, because that was how my review started. " 'Kaiko Kakamara is an artist of surprising vision' . . . Well, I must say, Jason, I'm surprised at *your* vision."

"Zoe, I'm sorry, I can explain—"

"Did you see that film? Or did you make that up, too?"

"I saw it. I can describe it in painful detail, but the exhibition . . . I was late, and the trains were—"

"How about that restaurant? Did you even go there?"

"I did! I ordered the Margherita!"

Factually correct.

"Knowing what you've done makes this phone call a lot harder."

Oh, God. Oh, Christ. Come on. No.

"I'm going to need you to come into the office."

What? Why? If you're going to sack me, just sack me.

"Rob's still off sick and he's just phoned to say he'll need a few weeks. Some kind of operation. So I need someone to fill in."

"Rob the . . . ?"

"Rob the reviews editor."

"So . . . you want me to be reviews editor?"

"No, I want you to fill in for the reviews editor."

"So I'd—"

"You wouldn't even have to go anywhere. Just tell other people to. It'd mean office work."

"I don't mind! I mean, I'd love to!"

There was a pause.

"Zoe, you're not doing this because . . ."

"What?"

"I want you to know you don't owe me anything."

"I'm doing this because I need someone to fill in and Jennifer's booked her holiday, Sam's away Monday, and Lauren said no. So Monday, yeah? We get in for ten, but I reckon you should probably pick up some croissants and put the coffee on and be there for nine."

And that was that.

Jason Priestley. Reviews editor. *London Now*.

It was on a napkin, but if I squinted a bit it looked like it could nearly be a business card.

Dev had bought me a celebratory pint and set it down on the table.

"I've noticed that the mainstream press tends to sideline videogames," he said. "But in 'Game On,' *London Now* would have a window into this brave new world. I would review fearlessly, and from the heart, combining—"

"I'll check with Zoe," I said. "I'm not sure how many decisions I can make."

He seemed satisfied with that.

"Will it be weird, though, working with Zoe?"

I shrugged. Then so did he. I guess neither of us knew.

I let the silence hang in the air. Tried to turn a pause into a notable one. And then . . .

"What do you know about Whitby, Dev?"

"Whitby?"

"Whitby."

"I know almost nothing about Whitby, other than its name. Why?"

"The Girl. The photos. Turns out one of them was taken in Whitby."

"Aha!" he said, clicking his fingers then pointing one of them at me. "I knew it!"

"Knew what?"

"I knew it! You! You love her!"

"I don't love her! I just know she was in Whitby once. I know you were in Asda earlier—doesn't mean I love you."

"How do you know one of them was taken in Whitby?"

"Gary."

"So Gary knows?"

"He knows about Whitby, not about The Girl. He used to go there on holiday."

"Hey, check it out," he said, suddenly, and pointed across the street. "Pamela."

He started humming that weird song again.

"When are you doing it?"

"The wooing? Dunno. Tomorrow, maybe."

We watched in silence as Pamela jogged to the bus stop, and continued to watch as she jogged on, toward a car that was pulling up on the side of the road. It was a blue Viva, dented and chipped, but that didn't seem to matter, because she looked delighted to see it. There was a man driving, and he looked delighted, too, and I was way ahead of Dev here, so made sure I was in the middle of a large gulp of lager as Pamela got in, leaned over, and kissed the man, her hand stroking the back of his head.

"Oh, come on!" said Dev, and I winced, and nodded my sympathies. "Oh, come *on*!"

And then I got a call. And I was asked how I was, and I moved away from Dev and I told her, and I mentioned Gary had been by, and she said she knew, and she said sorry about that, and I said it was fine, no problem, and then she said we needed to talk, and could we meet up, because this would be better face-to-face, and just to show how busy I am these days I churlishly said no let's just talk now, and so we talked, and I listened, and she told me why she'd rung today.

And the clouds may as well have darkened and the rain begun to fall, because the sky came crashing to the ground.

SEVEN

Or "A Lot of Changes Coming"

Look, it was good news.

Technically, it was good news.

"I'm pregnant," she'd said.

She hadn't known how to tell me, apparently, especially after what had happened, but it was true, and she was delighted.

She'd had her twelve-week scan. They'd gone away to celebrate. He'd proposed. They'd told their friends. It was terrifically grown-up.

"I'd rather have told you face-to-face," she'd said, and I'd said something back, which was positive, and encouraging, but which I can't for the life of me remember, because all I could think of was, What do I do now?

And now I knew what Gary's pause had meant.

"I suppose you could say it was a *pregnant* pause!" said Dev, and then I stared at him, and he stopped laughing and sipped at his pint.

Because it wasn't just a pause about Sarah. It was a pause that summed up me and him. A pause in which he'd managed to convey the fact he had special knowledge, knowledge he could choose to hit me with if he wanted, but that he wouldn't, because he's too decent, too trustworthy, too honest, but that *he* still *wins*.

We were back in the Den, next to the van rental place, and we were somber.

So that's it, then. That's that period of my life over. Properly over. Sarah's going to be a mum. And I'll always just be the ex-boyfriend. Then one day just "an" ex-boyfriend. Then one day, sooner than you'd think, I'd be nothing at all.

And yeah, I know it sounds like I'm hung up on her, and yeah, I know you've amassed enough evidence to prove it—for Christ's sake I've even written it down for you—but this is something else, this. This isn't about her. It's not my past. It's about my future. Because when one person moves on so quickly, and all the other one really has is what *was*, thinking about what *will* be is difficult.

Maybe I should feel relieved. I'm out of limbo. I'm somewhere, rather than who-knows-where. The decision has been made for me: "Jason & Sarah" can never work again; they'll absolutely, undeniably never share a letterhead—and now I don't have to worry anymore.

But that's just it, isn't it? The fact that my happiness is so reliant on other people's whims and fancies.

I need to stop being decided for. I need to start *deciding*.

"We need to do something," said Dev, tapping his finger on the bar to show he was serious. "Get away. We are men disturbed by women. You, with your now engaged-and-pregnant ex-girlfriend that you're *totally* over, and me with my Polish wife-to-be kissing another man in London's only remaining Vauxhall Viva."

He looked me in the eye, very seriously.

"What are your thoughts on EuroDisney?" he said.

"I am not going to EuroDisney with you."

"Come on. We could go to EuroDisney. You and me."

"I am *not* going to EuroDisney with you."

"We could treat it like some kind of perverse stag weekend."

"You're asking me to go on a perverse weekend to Euro-Disney with you?"

"I just mean we could treat it like a lads' adventure. Show the women of the world we have no need of their ways and means. We could drink lager and burp in public."

"At EuroDisney?"

"Fine. Bruges, then. Amsterdam."

"I've a job to start on Monday."

"Dublin."

"I need to be fresh."

"Okay, let's sit about in our pants watching Phillip Schofield and his magic cube. We could just watch *Come Dine with Me* all of Sunday and not even speak."

I bloody love *Come Dine with Me.*

"Let's eat bad food and mope about and pop cans of awful lager!" he said, more passionate with each word. "Or...let's use the moment. Turn something bad into something good! A trip! An experience! You and me!"

And with each pint, it actually sounded a little bit better.

It was early—far too early—and I was struggling to stay asleep. There was a whine outside. A high, throaty whine, like a man strangling a van.

I stumbled out of bed and winced as I pulled up the blind. I recognized the noise already. It was Dev's Nissan Cherry. It was the noise it made every time he tried to use it, after which he'd inevitably give up the second he saw a bus coming, and slam down the hood to leg it across the road instead. It was eight o'clock. What the hell was Dev doing attacking his car at eight o'clock on a Saturday morning?

Maybe he'd seen Pamela coming and wanted to look manly. He'd probably made sure he was carrying a wrench, and had agonized over exactly how much oil to smear on his face. This is the best thing about being manly: it's so easy to fake. Smear some oil on your face, or nod and say "Aaah" near mechanics.

I was about to close the blind again, but then...then I noticed something. The man under the bonnet was wearing baggy jeans. Dev doesn't wear baggy jeans. He wears jeans either slightly too tight and far too short or slacks with elasticated waists he gets for nine quid out of a catalog. And was that a hoodie? The car whined again and I suddenly realized...I was witnessing a theft! There was a robbery in progress! Someone was trying to nick Dev's car! Well, fix it first, but *then* nick it.

"Dev!" I yelled, falling backward onto the bed with the sheer shock and excitement of it all. "Dev!"

But there was no answer. I needed a weapon, and I needed one urgently. The odd thing is, I own very little weaponry. I have no nunchakas, all our knives are blunt, and a badminton racket lacks that certain menace. So I grabbed a hairbrush from the little table in the hall and was surprised for a moment because I didn't know we had a hairbrush, and I banged on Dev's door as I ran past.

"Someone's nicking your car!" I shouted, bounding down the stairs, my grip tight on my hairbrush, my mind racing as I tried to decide which end of it looked the most threatening.

I heard the whine again as I reached the door and I panicked. Where the hell was Dev? I needed backup! The Nissan was screaming for help, and it needed that help in a hurry! The thief was surely just a few short hours from making it work!

"Dev!" I shouted. "Bring more weapons!"

I pulled the door open, and was suddenly there, right in front of the Cherry, blinking in the morning sun, a man in his pants with a hairbrush he obviously hadn't used yet.

And there—there he was. The thief. My enemy. Still under the hood, still fiddling about, still completely oblivious of the terrible danger he was in. I couldn't work out if I should just strike him with the brush, or shout some kind of warning. But what's a good warning? And what should I say afterward? "Why are you fixing this terrible car?" was the only thing that seemed to make sense, so instead, I raised my hairbrush and just said, "Hey!"

The whining stopped. I tightened my grip on the brush.

"Morning, sir," said the man.

Oh.

It was Matthew Fowler.

What was Matthew Fowler doing fixing Dev's car?

"Matt?" I said. And then I realized I was still in my pants, brandishing a hairbrush. A bus went by, giving me enough time to think up a brilliant excuse.

"I was just brushing my hair."

Well, an excuse, anyway.

"Oi, oi!" said a voice to my left. It was Dev, striding toward us, carrying coffees and small brown bags. He threw one at me and I crushed it to my chest. It was warm, and oily, and wet.

"Oz did us some bacon sarnies," he said. "You wanted a Fanta, yeah, Matt?"

Matt gave him a thumbs-up, then pointed at the car.

"Chipped flywheel," he said.

Dev and I both nodded and said, "Aaah."

"I can sort it."

* * *

"How come Matt's fixing the car?" I said, pulling some jeans on.

"Well, we couldn't go in a broken one."

"No, I mean, how come Matt? And what do you mean 'go'? Go where?"

"We're going on our trip! Our trip to send a message to the women of the world! We planned it last night!"

I was pretty sure we hadn't. But what if we had?

"I tried to get the thing going, and Matt was passing, and he asked if I knew you, and at first I said no in case it was some kind of contract killing, and then he mentioned he worked in a garage, and that was that."

I walked to the window. Well, well. Matt Fowler coming in handy.

I took another bite of my bacon sandwich as the whine outside turned to a low growl.

"Wheels rolling in ten," said Dev, delighted.

"But where are we going?"

"We discussed this!" he said, clapping his hands together, and he jogged down the stairs.

I shoved a spare T-shirt in a Tesco bag and grabbed my wallet. Well, why not? A trip might be fun. But I had an uneasy feeling that I already knew what Dev had planned.

I made my way downstairs, and saw something odd.

"Oh, are *you* coming, Matt?"

He was in the backseat, swigging his Fanta. Maybe we were dropping him somewhere.

"I invited Matt along for the trip," said Dev, finishing his sandwich. "He fixed the car. He's already done more to earn it than we have."

I balked slightly. This was weird. We can't do this. There's hardly a day goes by you don't see a story in the *Daily Mail* about some teacher who's gone on the run with a former pupil. They're usually blond, though, and hardly ever slightly thuggish-looking men with access to a pipe wrench.

"And, does Matt know where we're going?"

"Yeah," said Matt. "Whitby."

"*Whitby?*" I said, surprised. Dev smiled. Of course he smiled. We hadn't talked about going to Whitby last night. I'd mentioned Whitby, and he'd talked of a trip, but at no point had anyone said, "Let's get up really early and go on a trip to Whitby." This was Dev's plan, not ours.

"So Whitby's in Yorkshire or something?" said Matt. "Never been."

"But you're happy to go? I mean, don't you have things to be—"

"Not really been out of London," he said. "Got an auntie moved to Swindon so seen that. And Bosworth."

"Bosworth?"

"Yeah. With you, sir."

God, yeah. We'd been to Bosworth. A school trip I'd tried to blank out. Matt had stolen twelve rubbers from the gift shop, and Neil Collins had peed in a bin. This, though, this was different. This was recreational. And it was Whitby. I didn't want to go to Whitby.

"Thing is, today's quite a bad day for this," I tried. "I just got an e-mail, saying—"

"Your computer was off. I saw it."

"Much earlier, I mean—"

"You were asleep."

"Look," I said with a sigh. "Are we sure we want to go to Whitby? What about Alton Towers? Or . . . Snaresbrook? There's a big hill in Snaresbrook."

"A big hill!" said Dev. "Would you like to see a big hill, Matt?"

Matt shrugged.

I stared at Dev. I couldn't go into it much further, not into the whole Whitby thing, not in front of Matt. I couldn't face explaining. Plus, it'd be approximately fifteen minutes before every single kid I'd ever taught and every single kid they'd ever met knew about it. I tried a different tack.

"It's . . . quite a long way to Whitby."

He shrugged, and nodded. This was all a little odd.

The car was running and Dev scrunched up his brown paper bag.

"Right!" he said. "It's a five-hour drive! Let's see what this baby can do!"

I looked at the car. I didn't have to get in. I could go back inside, wait for Phillip Schofield and his talking cube, maybe grab a kebab from Oz's, or pop down to the Den.

I thought about it.

We roared off through Caledonian Road at very nearly four miles an hour.

"No matter how thoroughly a crow may wash, it remains ever black."

—Traditional Shona Tribe proverb, Zimbabwe

I love the Internet almost as much as I love London.

I'm not sure London loves me in quite the same way, but it's a relationship we're working on.

There are six people following this blog now, even though so far all I've written are three embarrassingly whiny boo-hoo entries, including one terrifically self-pitying thing about listening to my friends in the future, which of course I won't, because I'm not that type of girl. Also, I shall try not to drink and blog in the future. Sorry about that.

So I suppose I'd better welcome all six of you, however you found me, to whatever you think this is.

Hello, Martin in Malaysia.

Hello, Captain Stinkjet.

Hello, Maureen.

Hello, FrrrrrrrrrrrBeep.

Hello, DownAndOutInPowysAndLuton.

And hello to the sixth person, whoever you are, because somehow you've managed to remain anonymous.

As shall I, for now, unless Captain Stinkjet can come up with a name to rival his?

You're probably wondering about the last entry. I wrote it on a bad day. It was a day I lost something. Two things, actually, neither of which I've found again. One was love, and that's probably the main one, I suppose, because not many poets write wonderful poems about the loss of a disposable camera, which was the other thing. No great paintings or operas feature a bright yellow Kodak that I'm aware of. But then I don't know much about art. I went to a gallery once, but everything looked like those paintings you see elephants doing on the news, so I went to Café Roma instead.

Strangely, I'm not sure what to miss more: the relationship, or the camera.

See, a relationship you can deal with. It hurts, and for a while it hurts so badly it's like your lungs collapse and your heart contracts every time you realize it's gone. But in the long term, for me at the very least, it's what's left in a heap on the floor that helps get you through. That little heap of evidence helps you to heal, is the idea I've got.

For me it was the photos, which I'd taken with me in my bag to Fitzrovia. I wasn't sure if I would and I wasn't sure if I wouldn't, but I had to sit in that café again then walk past that bright yellow photo place about three hundred times while I decided.

If I was strong enough, I would develop them.

If I was stronger still, I would not.

But now I never can and I feel robbed of the chance to move on. To see those moments once more, to tell myself the story all over again, to decide how I should move forward and when. Maybe that's what this is.

There must be a thousand blogs like this out there and I apologize. So many girls and so many boys thinking the world is interested in their story. I'd tell my friends, but they're back home where it's safe and besides: I'm not sure I want them to know. Here's me, in London, alone, sad, living the dream.

So I will stop for now, because Come Dine with Me *is on, and really, that takes precedence. So I'll simply wish all six of you a very pleasant evening indeed.*

Sx

PS. There's a stock phrase I'm used to hearing on soaps or in bars, if I'm eavesdropping. One person looks at the other and says, all serious like, "Things change. People change."

They'll accentuate the "people" so that we know they're talking about "people" and then they'll leave a pause after they've said it so you can see just how very serious they are.

I think things do change, of course. But in my experience, I think often things change because people don't.

EIGHT

Or "Getaway Car"

"Hey, Matt," said Dev, turning down the radio. "Just so you know, Jason's ex-girlfriend is now engaged and pregnant."

A pause.

I shot Dev a look that said thank you.

"Congratulations," said Matt. "Or...whatever."

We were somewhere past Barnet, on the A1. You didn't need to know that.

"Plus," said Dev, "my one's just copped off with a fella in a Vauxhall."

Well, this was awkward.

"Hence this trip. We are striking a blow for men everywhere."

"We're not striking a blow," I said. "I doubt the women of the world even know about this."

"Subconsciously, they do," said Dev. "Subconsciously, they feel very bad about it. Are you with us, Matt? Anything you need to let the women of the world know?"

"So what's so good about Whitby?" said Matt, staring out the window. "Good clubs, or what?"

I bristled.

Don't, Dev. Just don't.

"Jason wanted to go, didn't you, Jason?"

"Mmm," I said, looking away. "Whitby."

"Jason knows someone who went to Whitby once, y'see."

"Right," said Matt. As a reason for a five-hour drive, it was somewhat lacking.

"A girl," said Dev, enjoying the moment.

"I don't actually know the girl," I said, hoping that would make things clearer, but realizing that actually, it didn't. "It's kind of a joke."

"It's not a joke," said Dev. "Check this out: Jason saw this girl he liked, ended up with her camera, developed the photos and found out he was in one. Now he's found out one of the pictures was taken in Whitby and so we're going there."

"That's not why we're going there," I said, flatly.

Dev just looked at me.

"Mate, it's exactly why we're going there."

I turned to try to explain more to Matt but he had a slightly horrified look on his face.

"What if she's not still there?" he said. "Just 'cause she's there in a photo doesn't mean she'll still be there today."

It was true. That's not generally how photos work.

"That's not why we're going, Matt—"

"Okay . . ." said Dev. "We're going there to get away. To *do* something. But who knows—we might pick up a few clues."

"What's this girl look like?" said Matt.

"It doesn't matter," I said.

"Check the glovebox," said Dev. "The photos are in there."

"You brought the photos!" I said.

"Course!"

"Let's see," said Matt, now interested.

"It's weird," said Matt, still holding the photo of The Girl. "It's like, fate, and that."

It had been a long, long journey. We were leaving a Little Chef outside Worksop and Dev and Matt had been talking about, like, fate and that for the last two hours. I'd had little choice but to join in. I'd also had a horrible sausage.

"Like, if you met her again, what would you say? Or if you saw her for the first time again, what would you say different? I mean, would you take her camera this time?"

"How do you mean?"

"Would you take her camera again, or would you hope you realized sooner and then tell her before she got into the cab?"

"Why?"

"What he means," said Dev, "is given the chance, would you rather not have these photos in your possession?"

I shrugged.

"I dunno."

But of course I'd rather have them. They were exciting. Something new. A connection I was yet to make, if I was ever to make it at all.

"If you didn't want them, you'd have chucked them out, I reckon," said Matt. "But you didn't. You kept them. And now here we are—"

"Outside a Little Chef near Worksop that does horrible sausages."

"Exactly!" said Matt. "Exactly!"

I'd warmed to Matt over the last few hours. He was more articulate than I remembered, and certainly more curious. There was something more sensitive about him, and he was more rounded, too. By which I mean he had less edge, not that he was perfectly spherical.

We got back in the car, pointed it at Whitby, and continued to drive.

* * *

"Right," said Dev. "I've said we're a family, so try to look like one."

I stared at him.

"You've said we're a what?"

"A family. They did us a family rate. Thirty quid."

"But we're not a family. We don't look like a family. If we're a family, who's Matt?"

"We'll say he's our son."

"Oh, good plan! So, what, did you and I have a medical breakthrough when we were *nine*? Also, he's not half Asian and we're both men."

"We don't have to pretend we're a *traditional* family. We'll say we're from London—they'll understand."

He knocked on the door of the B&B. A moment or two later, it opened. A dumpy lady in a pink velour tracksuit stared at us.

"Hello!" said Dev, loudly. "We're a family from London!"

She took a bite of a Mars bar.

I was having fun.

I could try to be cool, and I could try to be cynical, but I was having fun.

In the past couple of hours, we'd played mini golf, drunk G&Ts from a can, visited a fairground, pulled Dev away from the arcades, pointed at a goth, and seen the first six items in the Words & Wool exhibition of poetry and textiles.

Whatever this was, it was . . . *good*. Lads' Weekend? Not really. Dev and I make rubbish lads, and the Words & Wool exhibition had been Matt's suggestion. No, this was more random. More instinctive. More fun.

"So what now?" said Dev.

We were down by the quayside, after Dev said he'd felt sick

on too much Orangina and needed to see the sea. We'd been talking to an old man about Captain Cook, and read a leaflet about Dracula. Dev had found a leaflet with Kermit the Frog on it, offering the bearer entry to a marvelous-sounding night-club called Cadillacs for just £1. From the look of the leaflet, it was hard to think that this might be a bargain.

"I'm starving," said Matt. "KFC?"

But I wasn't listening.

Over their shoulders, right there in the skyline, I could see it.

We were at a different angle, sure, and at a different distance, but that was it. High on a cliff, overlooking the quayside. Some kind of church . . . the church Gary had pointed out.

"What's that called?" I said to the old man, now on a bench.

"St. Hilda's," he said. "Up on the East Cliff. There's a path. 199 steps, mind."

But I wasn't bothered about going up a path. I didn't need to see the abbey close up. I wanted to see it as I'd seen it. From the angle I'd seen it. The distance I'd seen it. The way *she'd* seen it.

Suddenly, something had clicked. It was a strange moment. Maybe it was the boy in me—the collector—but I was looking at the same view as The Girl had seen, and I wanted to save it somehow. To prove I'd been here, too. A souvenir, or some-thing to show.

"Boys, that's the—"

But Dev was already smiling. He knew. I realized he'd only had one Orangina.

He pulled something out of his pocket and held it at me.

It was a box.

A small plastic box.

A small plastic box with *35mm Disposable Camera* written down the side.

* * *

"Bit more to your left, man," said Matt. "Now bit more to your right."

He was studying the photo very closely and attempting to replicate it exactly. The viewfinder on the new disposable was tiny and scratched—Dev had bought it for a quid from a Happy Shopper—but although the sky was darker today, and the wind higher, this was the same place.

She'd been near a blue post on that day, and maybe twenty feet from a bin, and we'd found both, it seemed. But getting the angle right, getting the placing just so . . .

. . . that was where the art was.

"There!" said Matt. "Thassit!"

I froze.

"All right, ready?" said Dev.

"Hang on, hang on."

What kind of face should I pull? I mean, I'm in front of two men, having my picture taken. Etiquette dictates I should do something imaginative. Pull a face, maybe, or wave madly. But this isn't *my* photo. This is someone *else's* photo. It's *hers*. I'm gate-crashing it, in some way. I don't know what the rules are here. Should I be more respectful? Maybe I should comb my hair. Or . . .

Click.

"Great. Nice one, Matt," said Dev.

"Hang on," I said. "I was . . . just looking."

"It was perfect. You looked moody and romantic. It was like the cover of a Westlife single."

"But I was just *looking*!"

"I really am properly starving, boys," said Matt, putting the camera away.

"Wait! One more!"

"Sounds like you care," said Dev, smiling.

A pause.

"Think we passed a chicken shop round the corner," I said.

I can't remember what it was called, so let's just call the place Captain Terrible's Palace of Harmful Chicken. Matt was thrilled they were doing bargain buckets for under a fiver, and the man behind the counter—Iranian, maybe?—seemed to like us.

"Where you boys from?" he asked.

"London," I said.

"Holiday?"

"Sort of," I said. It'd be a bloody weird *business* trip.

"You know what I reckon would be a great job?" said Dev, at the table. "Door-to-door door salesman."

We were lit by a jaundicing strip light. It was like dining in Superdrug.

"There's no such thing as a door-to-door door salesman," I said.

"I'm just saying. You'd go from door to door trying to sell doors, and once you'd knocked on one, you'd already know they had one, so you could just go home. Take the day off."

"What are you talking about?"

"I'm just saying. That's not a bad gig."

"They might need doors inside," said Matt. "If they answered, you could be there all day. That's a shit job."

I nibbled on a corncob and turned to Matt.

"Are you happy with yours?" I asked. "At the garage?"

Matt shrugged.

"S'all right."

"But is that what you want to do?"

He shrugged again.

"I mean, forever. Some people seem to find they're born to do the things they do. Others need to be born again," I told him, self-righteously.

"Is this like a Christian thing?" said Matt, suddenly horrified. "Is that why we're here? Taking pictures of churches? Is that why we told that fat bird in pink we're a family?"

"It was an abbey, and she was only a bit dumpy. And no."

"So what's wrong with my job?"

"Nothing. No, that's not what I meant. I just meant, y'know . . . what are your ambitions?"

"Fighter pilot?" said Dev. "Drag racer?"

"He's not seven."

"I wanna *make* something," said Matt, quietly.

"Teapots!" said Dev. "Of course!"

"Yeah, okay. Look, what I really want to do," said Matt, "is go to the pub."

"Workwise, though," I said.

"I don't mind what I'm doing."

"Is that enough?"

"What, like teaching was enough for you?"

I sighed.

"I was a rubbish teacher," I said.

"Nah," said Matt. "You was weak, yeah. But you let us do what we wanted to do."

"I'm not sure that's exactly the job description," said Dev, and Matt sat up.

"I don't mean that. I mean you let us be. You didn't try to change us. You were all right. Just maybe, your heart wasn't in it, is all."

I felt bad. I know he was right, and you know he was right. I just didn't know he knew he was right. It was like I'd been found out. Like he knew that whatever I'd been up against—

DANNY WALLACE · 115

the kids, their parents, the school—I just hadn't particularly wanted to be there. I'm not going to go all dark-night-of-the-soul on you. I'm just saying maybe I thought I'd got away with it. Maybe I'd convinced myself that I was meant for something else, without actually trying to do what I was there to do. Maybe I never actually try. I decided to try now.

"What do you want to do with your life?"

"I dunno," he said, embarrassed.

"That's okay," I said. "Sometimes people don't know for years. I didn't."

"I wanna make something."

"Okay," I said. "That's good. What are you interested in?"

"Football. Music."

"What kind of music?"

"Just music. Whatever music."

"Is that why you called your baby Elgar?" I said, and he smiled like it wasn't, but of course it was. "You should do a course or something, y'know? Work out what you want to do and find the right course. It's all out there. The world is there for the taking!"

Matt looked at me. I knew what he was thinking.

"Pub, then," I said.

Four pints in at the Jolly Sailor and we were absolute geniuses.

"Spain!" shouted Dev.

"Spain is not the capital of Spain," I said.

The machine had so far robbed us of eight quid, and some-how Chris Tarrant's recorded sympathies weren't as welcome as you'd think.

"Madrid," said Matt, and I turned, impressed. And then that felt patronizing and teacherly so I turned back and pressed C.

"Real Madrid, innit," said Matt. "Pro Evo—"

"You play *Pro Evolution Soccer*?" said Dev, shaking his head. "Bit commercial for me."

"What do you play?"

"Sony *World Tour Soccer*."

"That's shit."

"It's not, it's brilliant."

"Dev!" I said, desperately. "In what year was *Sim City 2000* first released on PlayStation?"

Surely this, of all questions, Dev would get?

"What are the options?" he said, urgently.

"Dev! Open your eyes!"

"I'm thinking!"

"A: 1990. B: 1993. C: 1999. D: 2000."

Dev opened his eyes and looked at the screen, blankly. The timer started to count down. Chris Tarrant rocked on his heels, looking smug.

"Dev? Quick! We stand to win a quid!"

"Well, this is interesting . . ."

Ten seconds to go. Dev stroked his chin and said, "Hmm."

"*Dev!*"

"I need more time!"

"We've got no lifelines!"

Five seconds.

Matt slammed his hand down.

"'93!"

An agonizing moment.

Ding.

"*That's the* right *answer!*"

Chris Tarrant looked absolutely *delighted*. We high-fived and grinned in one another's faces.

A pound coin skittered about in the tray below.

"Crisps on me, then," said Matt.

"Or . . . ," said Dev, and we looked at him. He pulled something out of his pocket and unfolded it.

Turns out places that offer a £1 entry fee don't then spend that money on decor.

Cadillacs was horrible. Properly horrible. Cheap, battered, and tacked to the side of a ropey hotel. It stank, too, of a decade of lager spilled on carpets and worked in by stilettos and Nikes. The walls were sticky—the *walls*!—and there was something else in the air, too. Aggression, maybe, or at least the smell of disappointed men who've drunk too much and eaten too little on a Saturday night in a small place. Their uniforms were on: Ben Sherman shirts, smart belts, shoes with silver buckles or trainers with puffy laces.

"We should get some Cristal!" said Dev, and this, I believe, is probably the only time a sentence like this may have been said in Cadillacs. It was certainly the first time Dev had said it. "We should get some Cristal, and then talk to some women we can later refer to as bitches!"

"I'm not sure that'll work in Whitby."

"We could call them 'ladies,' then."

"There will be no Cristal tonight," I said.

"A fancy cocktail, then!" said Dev, delighted.

Somewhere nearby, someone started a fight.

We sat with three manly lagers in a corner near the dance floor. Dev stared at women and Matt got his phone out.

"Texting home," he said. "Little brother."

In the corner of the room there were three other men, in Slipknot T-shirts and ponytails, keeping their heads down, Snakebites in hand, the only three Kerrangutans in Whitby, sticking together for safety and solace.

Then, suddenly, Dev said, "Oh my *God*, look at *her*!"

There was a girl—a feisty-looking girl with a quiff and a bottle of something blue—and Dev was now pointing at her.

"Don't point!" I said. "Just observe, if you have to."

"It's all right for you," he said, turning to me. "You're sorted! You've got destiny on your side! You've got this girl in a photo! What've I got? I've got a disinterested Pole with a boyfriend!"

"I wouldn't say I was sorted, Dev," I said. "And I wouldn't say I had destiny on my side. I've got Snappy Snaps on my side. They are very different things."

"You've got destiny! And you've been promoted—"

"Promoted?" said Matt, looking up. "What, has he put you in charge of the till?"

"Not at the shop. At *London Now*," I said, calmly. "I am acting reviews editor starting Monday."

"Yeah?" said Matt. "Sweet."

"Back to me," said Dev. "You've got a girl in a photo. Matt's got a family. It's only me who's . . ."

"Free?" said Matt.

"Precisely!" said Dev. "Free!"

But I'm not sure that's what Matt had meant.

"Therefore, if I wish to point at a girl—"

"What was you pointing at?" said a voice, somewhere to our side.

We looked up. The girl with the quiff and the bottle of something blue was standing before us, staring. She had a burly friend in a denim miniskirt either side.

Oh, God, I thought. There are three of them. And three of us. What if they bully us into relationships?

"No," said Dev, clearly terrified, pushing his glasses up as far as they would go. "I was pointing at another thing."

Thing?

"Person. Another person," said Dev. "Who *was* here. But is now gone."

"Who are you?"

Who? Not "What's your name?"

"I'm Dev," said Dev. "And this . . . is my family."

He cast me a panicked look. Maybe he thought the woman from the B&B had spies everywhere.

All three girls looked at Matt. Not one of them looked at me.

"All right?" said the main one.

"All right," said Matt.

They still weren't looking at me. I was slightly offended.

"What's your name?" she said.

"Matt," said Matt.

"These your dad?" she said.

Are these your dad?

"My mates," he said, and I felt quite warm inside. Mates. Not "They're my old teacher and his flatmate." *Mates.*

"Who's this?" said a man, suddenly there. He was wearing a Ben Sherman shirt and shoes with little silver buckles on, but then you'd probably guessed that.

"No one," said the burly girl, seemingly quite pleased by the interest.

"Paul's got you a lager," he said, trying to guide her back to the dance floor.

"Don't want a lager," she said.

Uh-oh.

"Paul. Has. Got. You. A. *Lager*," he said, slowly and deliberately, staring straight at her.

"Didn't ask for a lager," she said, turning away from him. "Budge up."

Oh God. She wanted to sit next to Matt.

I cast a frightened look at Dev, but he wasn't looking at me. He just looked delighted. Matt stared into his drink. I didn't know what to do. She'd asked me to budge up. Me. What are you supposed to do when a burly girl asks you to budge up? I mean, Paul had bought her a lager, whoever Paul is. He was probably waiting for her. And this man—this man with his muscles and knuckles and buckles—he was still there, still towering over us. Who was he? Her boyfriend? Her brother? She inched toward me, waving at me to move up, and I caved.

Down she sat, momentarily puffing the small sofa up at my end, and raising me up by an inch, which, if I'm honest, made me feel a little less masculine than I'd like.

Her burly friends drifted off, taking the man with them, but not before he'd drilled deep into the back of my head with his eyes.

"It's not me!" I wanted to shout. "I'm just a *budgee*!"

But shouting you're a budgee in a nightclub in Whitby is just one of four ways I know to guarantee you'll get beaten up.

"Where you from?" said the girl, and before Matt could even answer, Dev had shifted closer in his seat.

"London," Dev said. "North London. Near Angel?"

She ignored him.

"Just down for the night, are you?"

She took a swig of her blue whatever-it-was and Matt just nodded.

There was an awkward pause.

"You know, if there's one thing I just can't get off my chest"—Dev paused—"it's my nipples!"

He beamed, delighted at this joke, his joke, the joke he's been telling strangers for years, but the girl just looked at him, and then at where her nipples would be. I gave Dev an encouraging smile, which actually may have looked more like a grimace, and looked away.

On the other side of the club, the girl's friends were sitting blank-faced and ignored, sipping at their drinks, while the man and two friends sat forward on their seats, staring at us.

We stayed maybe ten minutes longer, the girl eventually finding her way back to her lager and whoever Paul, her most generous benefactor, was.

"So this girl in the photo, then," said Matt, eating his chips. "You gonna find her, or what?"

We were on a bench, the end of the night upon us, and I laughed.

"Do you think I should find her?"

"Tonight should be the night we decide on something!" slurred Dev. "It's in the air! We've already won a pound from a quiz machine and been to an exhibition about wool. It's perfect timing!"

We stood, and began our walk to the B&B.

"Decide about what?" said Matt.

"I dunno! Jase should find this girl! I will make Pamela my own! And you...you can, well, what do you want to do?"

"I dunno," said Matt.

"Well, we'll find something for you. Something important and life-changing and good."

"I'd like to be happy," said Matt, and Dev and I stopped walking.

But Matt didn't.

Matt just kept going.

"Back in a sec," he said, jogging over to a shop doorway. Dev and I started to walk again.

"He's a top lad," said Dev.

"He is. He is."

"What was he like at school?"

"Not *exactly* like that."

"He likes you."

"This is not a blind date."

"No, I just mean, he looks up to you. Must be weird for him, hanging out with an old teacher."

"Little weird for me, too."

We rounded a corner. A group of lads on a bench outside Millets started laughing between them. One of them kicked a can, and it skittered against a shopfront.

It is not good being another man in this situation. It is worse being two men. Two men is a group. A rival group. Even when one of them's in slacks, and the other still smells of that fried chicken from earlier.

The group laughed again, and I immediately started to look anywhere but at them, but I know there are three of them at least, and I know they're the type of men to kick cans at shops. But I allowed myself a glance, and—shit.

It's *those* guys.

The guys from *earlier*.

I started to puff my chest up, and walk in a more deliberate and masculine manner, because that's what men on document-aries tell you to do. Be big. Be brave. Be confident. Be beaten up five minutes later. It's a walk I've perfected on countless nights down the Caledonian Road, as I scurry past Pentonville Prison, absolutely certain that every man I pass is about to strike me down with that baguette he's eating, or stab me with his chips.

And then it happens.

"*Oi.*"

Keep walking. Just keep walking.

"*Oi!*" said the voice, closer this time, and I turned, and the bigger one, the ringleader, is striding toward me.

"You called my name," he said.

Breathe.

"Eh? No, I didn't."

"You called me a twat, then."

What?! Oh, God, this is how it starts. This is how it starts in the playground, and this is how it starts at night, in a strange town, near phoneboxes and scratched cashpoints and men who've run out of booze.

"Honestly, mate, I didn't say a word."

"Does your name sound like twat?" asked Dev, half-smiling.

"What did you say?"

"I just mean maybe you misheard, or—"

"Look," I said. "Honestly, there's no problem here. We're just on our way home, and—"

"Where's home?"

"We're at a B&B."

"No, where's *home*?"

"London," said Dev.

Wrong answer.

"Just *outside* London," I said. "Quite a way outside London, actually."

Christ, why was this happening? Why, in Whitby, of all places?

"Where's your pal?" said the fella at the back.

"He's"—I turned, looked—"I dunno."

The main guy was getting very close to me, now. I could smell his breath. Cider, definitely. Maybe a whiskey on top? Fags, too.

No, that was the other one. The wiry one next to him, smiling, and bouncing on his heels, too excited to take a drag. Paul, maybe? He looked like a Paul. And there's always one like him. Too small to fight, but so full of aggression, like a little dog feeding off the power of his mate, and dangerous, because he'll do anything, absolutely *anything* for his master, his eyes bright and excited, his chest rising quickly.

"Look," I tried. "Everything's cool."

But they didn't seem to think everything was cool. They seemed to think everything was anything but cool, for whatever imagined slight they were so bruised by, and for a very real second I remembered Mr. Waterhouse in Year Two telling us the best thing to do in a fight was to curl up in a little ball, but how was I going to tell Dev to curl up, too, and then what would happen, because we'd be two curled-up little balls of London, and what if . . .

Boom.

From somewhere to our right, a boom, or not a boom, exactly, but something: a huge, buckling, shatter of a noise. I froze, and Dev flinched, and there it was again. The men raised their arms to their heads instinctively, and turned, and there he was.

Matt had found something—a short length of pipe, some kind of metal bar, who knows what—and he was smashing a phonebox to pieces.

Smashing. It. To. *Pieces.*

He'd pulled his hood over his head, and didn't once look round, just kept smashing, and *smashing*, splinters of glass flicking through the air, and just that noise, again and again—something pained and guttural and frightening.

"Fuck . . . ," said the little dog, backing off, but we remained quiet and in our places, not because we were brave, but because we were just as frightened.

And then Matt threw the metal bar to the ground, and it clattered about violently from the force, and he was panting, and walking straight toward us, and that was enough for the fellas—they were off.

And then, the strangest thing.

Matt stopped in his tracks, got the disposable camera out, took a picture of the men as they pounded down the street, then put it away again.

Dev and I kept our distance, not sure if he'd flipped for real, not sure if he wouldn't now get us in headlocks, or push us through a window, or take a picture of us running away as he swung another metal bar about. I mean, what was I supposed to do? Revert to teacher mode? Shout, "Matthew Fowler, stop that at once"? We were on our own, past midnight, in a strange place, and a boy who'd once nearly blinded a kid had just smashed up a phonebox at the merest sniff of a hint of violence.

I braced myself as he got closer, ready for whatever might be, ready to try to defend myself, but instead, he lowered his hood, and clapped his hands together, and said, "All right?"

"That was *amazing*!" said Dev, as we walked up the street. We were full of adrenaline and relief and life, lit every few seconds by another streetlight, like we were in a very slow disco. "That was like something out of *Grand Theft Auto*!"

"You saved our arses tonight," I said, a little giddily.

"Just barked at 'em," said Matt. "Just scared 'em."

"No, I mean on the quiz machine. No way we'd have won that quid."

And I put my arms around them both as we walked, and gave them a little man hug, and then we heard a distant police siren and decided to jog.

* * *

We spent the night in the Nissan Cherry, outside our thirty-quid B&B. Dev had managed to lose the key, of course, and the lady in the pink velour tracksuit seemed quite strict about the ten o'clock curfew.

"Disgusting," Dev had said. "Kicking a family out on the street like this."

But it didn't matter. It was better, somehow. Because we laughed, and we swapped stories, and although I think you could say we'd bonded already, there's nothing like bonding in a Nissan Cherry.

And as we giggled like little women, I thought about what had happened to bring me here, in a small car, having fun. The breakup? Her engagement? The pregnancy? Yeah.

But no. Not really.

Not when you think about where we'd gone, and why that place particularly, and what Dev had planned.

I kind of sort of owed it to The Girl.

Maybe I'd been right earlier, when I'd thought I should stop being decided for. That I should start deciding.

"Check it out," I said, as dawn broke, and Dev stirred.

There, in the distance, was the top of St. Hilda's, the sun catching its weathered stones, smudging them into soft amber.

"Hungry," he yawned.

But I kept staring.

At the Little Chef, just outside Worksop, we clambered—hungover, messy-haired, and aching—back into the car.

Matt had waited in the car. He'd been a little quiet this morning. Dev said he must just be hungover. I decided to agree.

I polished off the last of my horrible sausage as we entered the motorway.

"That was a bloody great trip," said Dev. "Violence! Gambling! Girls! It was like Vegas, or something!"

"We nearly got our heads kicked in, won a pound, and were *ignored* by girls. It was like *Whitby*."

Dev laughed, but Matt didn't.

I turned round, to make sure he was okay, but he was lost in something. In his lap were the photos; he'd only seen the abbey shot before, and so he'd been in the glovebox while we'd fetched coffees and food, and now he had them all right in front of him.

"Matt?" I said.

He looked up, mouth open, and held out one shot in particular for us to see.

NINE

Or "Next Step"

On the bus in, I picked up a discarded *Metro*.

A BRITISH man has married a 28-year-old woman after dreaming of her phone number and then sending her a text.

Nick Bremen, 29, said he woke up one morning with the same number repeatedly running through his mind. His best friend, Michael Simms, urged him to send a text, reading, simply: Do I know you?

Random recipient Jo Logan was cautious at first, but eventually replied. Before long, the couple started exchanging more messages. After a month, they met and fell in love.

A love-struck Bremen said: "I still can't believe how random this seems. But something was telling me to give it a go. I guess I found my lucky number!"

The couple married on Monday, in Logan's hometown of York.

I didn't know what to buy so I bought a little of everything.

Croissants. Pain-au-chocolat. Pain-au-raisin. Six pretzels and a bag of nuts.

I felt like a worker for the first time in ages, and lowered Rob's office chair to make it feel a little more like my own, before clearing a little space in his debris for me to work in.

Zoe would be in soon, and then the others: Clem, the features editor; Anthony, the art editor—all ready to piece together the next edition from the bulk Manchester sends us and the scraps we find ourselves, each of us ignoring the metaphorical ticking clock we imagined above us. I didn't want to imagine it. I was just happy to be here, a small piece of even the worst business plan, in a room so beige it looked like it'd been dipped in tea, with scuffed walls, Macs, ironic posters, and lonely, ignored PR gifts. A giant Guinness hat with *Happy St. Paddy's Day!* scrawled across it lay by a bin under a desk, used and used once, next to a fat cotton cat with suckers for hands dropped off by courier to "Celebrate the much-anticipated release of *Garfield* on DVD and Blu-ray!"

Dev would love this stuff. He'd save it; savor it. He'd look forward to wearing his Guinness hat each March, and doubtless would use the fat cotton cat in the Nissan, hoping it might be a conversation starter at traffic lights. I made a note to bring him something back soon as a token of appreciation. He knew I needed to get away. So he'd got me away.

I looked around the office and spotted them. Two giant yellow Hulk Hogan wearable foam fists and a *Hogan Knows Best* DVD.

They were Dev's. Soon, I mean. Once I'd been here a bit. Once I'd *earned* them.

I sat quietly, like the new boy, not daring to do much else in case I got into trouble, somehow. Yeah, so my name had been a regular fixture in the paper for the past year or so, but I wasn't one of them. Not yet. I was one of the others. The people drafted in to fill space. The people who usually had some special little section to work on and file. Like the property girl, who'd write stories either about how property was getting more expensive, or about how property was getting a bit cheaper. The showbiz guru (sample story—and this was an exclusive: *Sienna Miller says she'd love to turn her hand to singing, but she is also happy to concentrate on acting for now*). The weekly gadget roundup (*Kettles are in!*). Motoring. Sport. An uninforming Celebrity Questionnaire (sample question: *If you were a type of fruit, what type of fruit would you be?*). Health. Wealth. And Reviews. *My* section. All of it designed to be read, half-digested, and discarded in the time the marketing people had decided was the same as the average tube journey through London: twenty minutes.

I decided to get to work, starting with Rob's in-tray. There were releases already opened, for film premieres and cocktail parties and album launches. Exciting. Maybe I should throw myself into the scene, become like one of those women you see in films. I could change my outfit every few minutes and buy new shoes and be fabulous as I saunter around Manhattan eating canapés and catching cabs. Except this is Britain. And more specifically, this is Britain on a weeknight. Over here on a Monday, Carrie Bradshaw would have to make do with just changing her cagoule every few minutes, and being fabulous as she saunters around Westfields eating warm sushi and catching colds. Still, I thought, as I opened more mail, where else could she be invited to attend the launch of a new Ryman's on Kentish Town Road? What was Carrie Bradshaw doing on the sixth of next month? Was she going to the upstairs room of a pub in South West London to watch a bad band called Ogre Face kick off their six-date regional tour of upstairs rooms in pubs? No. But it looked like I would be.

I slit open a slim package. Another CD from another band. The Kicks.

Might as well start.

I pressed play on the stereo while I opened more mail. The people at Jaffa Cakes had sent a box of Jaffa Cakes and a note all about the future of Jaffa Cakes, and about how popular Jaffa Cakes not only were but are and will be. They were using the words "Jaffa Cakes" quite a lot.

Hey, I thought, flipping round the cover of the CD. This isn't bad. I studied it.

The Kicks: "Uh-Oh."

It was...good. I mean, I'm no muso. I know the difference between 6Music and Classic; I bought *Melody Maker* when I was at college; I know who Steve Lamacq is and I once sat quite near Zane Lowe in a pub with copper tables, but I'm not one of those guys who can hear a band and immediately cite their influences and probable heroes. There are guys like that out there. Play them the first drumbeat and they'll start banging on about Led Zeppelin or Limp Bizkit or how everything can be traced back to the man who wrote "The Birdie Song." Dev can do it with videogames. He can take one look at a game and tell you what it's trying to be, where it got the idea, what it's been crossed with, and how well it's done, but I just can't. Because I'm the other sort of person. A Type 2. One that judges everything on its own merits. Not because it's the right and just and fair thing to do, but because there's something about me that doesn't quite have that passion. That need for peripheral knowledge. I like a little of everything; I don't need it all. It can make conversations with the Type 1s a little strained. A Type 1 will have all his opinions ready to go and probably alphabetized before he even gets near you. A Type 2 will then shrink behind his sandwich.

Maybe reviews editor will suit me, I think. Maybe my speciality is not having a speciality. Though I do know quite a bit about Hall & Oates.

(Where it all started? *"(She) Got Me Bad."* Best song? *"Las Vegas Turnaround."* Best album? *Big Bam Boom.* Best member? *Hall. Or Oates, if you prefer him.* Best—.)

"The hell's this?" said a voice, suddenly there. I spun round in my chair—Rob's chair, whatever—and turned the music down. It was Zoe.

"The Kicks," I said, trying to sound as instantly knowledge-able and insightful as John Peel. "Brighton band, gigging around, this is 'Uh-Oh.'"

"The single or the album?"

Tsk. I'd have to look. John Peel wouldn't have had to look. Distract her.

"Hey, I brought croissants like you said. And some other stuff."

"Jaffa Cakes, too?"

"They're from . . . well, they're from Jaffa Cakes."

And it was with this inspiring and profound exchange of words that I, Jason Priestley, began my tenure as reviews editor of *London Now*.

I'll tell you what. I'll tell you as little as possible about my working day for now. You don't need to know. Not really you don't. You don't need to know that I had a Toffee Crisp and an apple at eleven, that I popped back out to Pret at just gone one where I bought myself a crayfish wrap and a Coke. You don't need to know that Clem was twenty minutes late, or that Zoe said Clem was *always* twenty minutes late, and you certainly don't need to know that after I'd sorted out exactly what reviews should go to exactly what reviewers, I played a game of *Castle Defense* and ate a Twix.

All you need to know is that I was happy. This is what I'd wanted when I'd left St. John's. An office. Somewhere to sit, people to sit with, lunch hours where I'd buy crayfish wraps and Cokes. A little bubble of security and company.

I'd had company at the school, of course. In the staff room. The place we suddenly weren't teachers anymore, the place we didn't have to be moral arbiters in. It was pretty easy to be cynical there. It was encouraged, if anything. When you're spending all day telling people how to behave and what not to say, that staff room is a little beacon of beige joy. A release. A glorious place in which the pressure lifts from your shoulders the second you find your mug and pile your instant coffee and sugars in it and you're suddenly locked in a battle to see who can say the most inappropriate thing about a child. The time it takes the kettle to boil is the time in which you and your colleagues have already put down most of the kids you've ever met, and when I say "put down" I think you know what some of them *wish* they meant. They say only those who've seen warfare can ever truly understand one another. It's much the same with playground duty. And then there was the grim inevitability of the assemblies. Public speaking is not and never will be my thing. I'd managed to sneak out of assembly duty all but once and I'd vowed never to do it again. There is nothing more dispiriting than giving a motivational speech to the terminally unmotivatable. It's very demotivating. Especially when no one in the room—you, least of all—believes in what you're saying.

But despite it all—despite the kids, and despite their parents, who could never quite see what the point of teachers was, who seemed to confuse school with daycare—I carried on. I would probably never have left. Not if it weren't for Dylan Bale.

I shuddered, and put his angry little face out of my head.

Because it was six o'clock, and I didn't want to think about kids like Dylan Bale.

And anyway. I had somewhere to be.

* * *

Charlotte Street was awash with people like me. Good, honest workers, done for the day, with their manbags and gladrags, spilling out of the Fitzroy and packing the Northumberland, and each of them looking very happy indeed. I'd walked straight past them all. I was round the corner, tucked away in the tiniest pub on Rathbone Street, not feeling I'd quite earned my place among the high achievers with their branded satchels and limited-edition Converse. There were students and men in Chelsea shirts outside the Newman Arms, pointing at the sign that says Percy Passage and laughing, their Peronis and Fosters slopping out of their glasses and slapping onto the pavement every time they did. That was the thing about Fitzrovia. Plenty of side streets and passages; the curse of a bunch of minor landowners, each having their say and doing their own unordered thing with their puny part of London, with never a thought to the future. Marylebone or Bloomsbury next door wouldn't have a Percy Passage. They'd have a Percy Square, or a Percy Buildings.

That's why Fitzrovia wins.

I kept an eye out for the boys. They'd be here in a minute, with their research.

Matt had been amazed when he'd seen it. He'd just pointed at it, and said, "Look!" And then he'd pointed at it some more, because we were looking—really looking—but all we could see was a car. Turns out it wasn't just a car to Matt.

"Ha!"

I turned. Dev had wandered in. He was pointing behind him.

"Percy Passage!"

I could sense the barman tensing. I wondered how many times he'd heard that today. I wondered after how many years exactly it had lost its charm.

"How was your first day at big school?" said Dev, sitting down.

"It was good."

"Did you tell them about the Level Up section?"

"I thought you were calling it Game Over?"

"Level Up is far more powerful. Game Over sounds like something kids would read."

"Well, I've not mentioned it. I didn't want to come in and start proposing new features just yet."

"You should! Prove your worth! Put ideas forward! People love that! Our jobs *revolve* around ideas."

"You work in a videogame shop."

"Dreams, Jase! I deal in dreams! I can make you a pilot. A tank commander. A superhero. I can make you a little blue hedgehog. I am like a wizard, or a dreamweaver, or a more masculine version of that girl out of *Bewitched*. Just this morning I made someone into Daley Thompson."

He sipped at his pint and made an important face, like not just anyone in North London could make someone into Daley Thompson.

"I was right" were the words I heard next. "The car."

Matt sat down heavily beside us.

"It's rare. *Really* rare."

He looked excited, and brought the photo out from his pocket. His fingers were oily and I was annoyed to register his hands were far more manly than mine.

"Bryn from work reckons only twelve were ever made but he thought it was a Facel Vega Excellence. It's actually not."

"Well, that helps."

"It's a Facel Vega *something*, though, and it's from the '60s," said Matt, maybe pleased to be teaching *me* something. "Only eleven hundred made. Dunno how many are left."

I looked again at the photo. The car was green, and well-looked-after, and other than that there wasn't much I could tell you. It had some wheels. But in the foreground, there she was, looking delighted. A delighted girl, under a bruised sky, near a green car. This was like Cluedo for oddballs.

"I'm not really sure where this is getting me," I said.

"You could find her, man! It's another clue! Like Whitby! Find the car, find The Girl!"

"She's only standing near it. And not even *very* near it. It's over her shoulder. And it's not like we have access to police files, is it?"

"It's a clue, man!"

He laughed, incredulously, and a moment later, Dev did, too, but then he shrugged at me.

"I dunno, maybe there's a classic cars club where this is registered," said Dev. "Maybe it belongs to a neighbor of hers. Or her . . . friend."

Yeah. The chunky watch tan man. Of course he'd have a classic car. One of only twelve. That was *just* like this man I didn't know.

I picked up the photo again.

"I *suppose* it's a clue," I said.

"Of course it's a clue!" said Dev. "Look, this car might be a red herring, but it's something. It's—"

"A fish," I said, reminded of something. "It's a fish."

There was an awkward moment.

"Look," I said, quietly, pointing at something I'd just noticed in the photo. There was a building behind them. A huge white building, at the very end of the road they were on. And, just near the top, you could make out half a word. The bottom half.

"Alaska," said Dev, taking it from me.

"Can't be—that's a right-hand-drive car. British made. S'pose import's an option, but—"

"It's not *in* Alaska," I said. "It must just be the name of the building. What is it, a factory? Maybe it's a factory. Maybe she works at the factory."

"What would they make there?" said Dev. "No one makes Alaskans. They're just . . . Alaskans."

"I dunno," I said, because suddenly my mind was racing, and I picked up the other photos and started riffling through them, too, and an odd thought occurred to me: I'd learned how to see.

I read this book once, called *Your Inner Fish*. It was about a scientist who became obsessed with finding a 375-million-year-old fossil of a fish he reckoned we all came from. It was halfway between the journey from speck of dust to chest-thumping monkey, and it was a fish with a neck, and the beginnings of wrists. It was the fish that made it out of the confusion of the water, and into the vast unknown of the world. And without that fish, that world would always *remain* unknown. We'd *have* no world. No things to do or places to be. No girls in cabs, no Percy Passage, no straight, no gay, no soup of the day, no nothing. This man, he ended up in the Canadian Arctic, with a bunch of other scientists, all also looking for the same fossils, and he spent weeks following them about, despairing every time they spotted one and he didn't. What did other people have that he didn't? What was missing?

And then one day, it hit him. He hadn't been focusing properly. His priorities were out. He didn't know what to look for. He didn't know how to see. And the second he did—the very *second* he saw that first fish—the ground lit up for miles around with the glint of fossils in the morning sun. I'm paraphrasing, slightly, maybe even romanticizing it a bit, but that's how it sounded to me. Suddenly, as soon as he realized, as soon as he opened up those eyes, those fossils were everywhere, winking at him, waving at him, congratulating him for finally being able to see, and sparkling like diamonds in the ground. That's what it felt like. These photos were packed with diamonds in the ground.

Maybe I had found my inner fish.

I was impressed. It had taken that other bloke nine years and hundreds of pages.

Whenever I'd looked at the photos, I'd only really looked at The Girl. Not even when I was standing in the place one of them was taken had it truly hit me that all these photos must have actually been taken somewhere. It sounds crazy, but because they weren't mine, the places didn't seem like *real* places. Real places I could go to, or might have walked past, or—in the case of Café Roma—might even have been in.

"What we need to do," said Dev, trying to take the photos from me, "is establish a link. A common theme."

I scrunched my nose up.

"That's not how photos work, is it?" I said. "You don't take them by theme. You just take them."

"Yes," said Dev. "Agreed. But that's with digital stuff. We are talking about the psychology of the disposable."

"Why can't it just be chaos?" said Matt, and I felt proud, like a teacher again.

"Because disposable pictures are actually anything but," said Dev, sounding like he'd rehearsed this.

He made a wise face and sat back in his chair. Me and Matt leaned toward him, but then realized our faces were a bit close, so sat back again.

"The thing about disposables is, they're special pictures. You delete pictures normally, because you know you can, so you fire them off with no thought or regard to quality or timing. You take one look, and you decide you look too drunk or puffy or tired and you take another, using your special picture face. But these—"

He picked them up, and waved the packet in the air.

"*These* are proper snapshots. Snapshots of life. Happy moments, or special ones, and you have to *decide* to take them. You have to *plan* them. Because you're running out of moments. You're *always* running out of moments."

"What're you on about?" said Matt, but now I *did* lean in, because I *got* what Dev was saying.

Lately, that's just how I'd felt. Like I was running out of moments.

"You have twelve exposures," he said. "Twelve moments to capture. It's finite. So every time you capture one in that little box, you've got one less to spare. By the time you get to that last one, you better be sure that moment is special, because what if the next one comes along and you've got to let it go?"

What a terrible thing, I thought, to let a moment go.

"With a disposable, you want to complete your little story. End on an ending. Or a new beginning. A dot-dot-dot to take you into the next roll."

This is where Dev's theory started to falter a little for me.

"Hang on. That last shot was of me."

And Dev just smiled.

"That's just the thing," he said. "You're already part of her story. Now you get to make her part of yours."

And he reached into his pocket, and he slid the new blue disposable across the table.

I looked at it.

I picked it up, and put it in a pocket of my own.

And as we sat there, and drank some more, and the excitement built as we pointed out new clues from previously unseen backgrounds or foregrounds or bent and ripped corners, I started to wonder if I should tell them. Tell them what I'd already done today. That no matter how inspiring this moment was for me, I'd already created a little moment of my own.

After the crayfish wrap, after the *Castle Defense* and the Twix, the thing I'd done that I'd tried to avoid telling you by blaming boring work and assuring you it held no interest.

Because I'd already done one thing today to bring me and The Girl one step closer.

TEN

Or "She's Pretty"

Thursday, 8 a.m. I sat on the number 91 to King's Cross with something approaching nervous excitement in my stomach.

Since I'd decided to do this—to crawl out of the water, try to catch that moment before it faded entirely, become my inner fish—I'd begun to feel eerily comfortable with it. That I deserved this. That you never know, it might lead me somewhere. Dev mentioned destiny. I used to believe in destiny. Until destiny tripped me up and pushed me into a flat with Dev. That my destiny could be living in a flat with a man who talks a lot about destiny seems too cruel to be feasible as a concept.

I looked up and saw the yellow-jacketed men and women, standing outside the station, stamping their feet to keep warm, trying to shift as many complimentary copies of *London Now* as they could before the rush was over.

"Complimentary" is what they're trained to call them, by the way, not "free"; same way some men are trained to call themselves "sharpshooters," not "snipers." They both mean the same, of course, but I know which one I'd rather sit next to at a dinner party.

So I grabbed my complimentary copy of *London Now* and made a point of thanking the man who gave it to me, thinking this might make his day, but he was on to the next person already and so I kept my head down and walked into the ticket hall, then down into the depths of London, below everyone and everything and everywhere else, and where I could read my paper without anyone knowing.

On the back carriage of a shuddering, jolting Northern Liner, I opened it, and flicked to page thirty-eight. The page you read as you approach the end of your very average twenty minutes.

The I Saw You section.

Clem had been out of the office for a couple of days with a chest infection so I'd used his computer. I'd had to be quick, had to make it happen while Sam was out having a fag, but I'd made it work. My own little moment of effort. Something to make me feel that, well, I'd tried, and even if the story ended here, today, then hey, I'd given it a go.

I'd been subtle and sensible in my approach. Nothing too full-on. That was the mistake some of these people made. Many's the time Dev and I have sat around in the flat, reading them aloud and wondering what the other person must be thinking, as they realize the bloke who'd been staring at them on the train platform probably wasn't just smitten, but also has a selection of sharp knives and a copy of *The Catcher in the Rye*.

So I'd learned the right way to do things. Picked them up, as others tumbled around me. There'd be no *I think I love you!* (June 18), and no *You're the most beautiful thing I ever saw!* (June 23), and absolutely no *I must see you again we must meet I like to TOUCH YOUR FACE* (September 4–9).

Nope. Just a good, honest, matter-of-fact thirty-word wonder.

I Saw You was popular, though mostly secretly. A third of a page of love gained and lost in a second, of moments gone untaken, of dread and angst and most of all . . . hope. Thirty words is all you've got to plead your case. To tell the girl or boy you've never met that you'd love to meet them. To assure them you're not a murderer or a thug or a born-again Christian. To suggest a coffee or a meal or a walk on the Heath. To convince them that the moment you shared must mean as much to them as it did to you.

And then you have to hope they see it. And that's some hope. Thirty printed words on page thirty-eight of one edition of a freesheet in a city of seven million. It feels like speaking thirty words out loud in the Arctic, and praying the wind might take them to the one person in the world you wanted to hear them. From the Arctic to the second carriage of a Central Line train. And all because you saw them, once.

And yet it works. Sometimes, it works. You hear about it all the time, usually in things like *London Now*. Stories that begin with sentences like, *Commuter Darren Howe, 32, knew at once he'd seen the love of his life in Julie Draper, 33, as he boarded his train home to Tottenham one night. Problem was, Julie was getting off!*, and end up with details of their wedding and what their colleagues thought.

And these small successes, these tiny triumphs, give every other single person being buffeted about a carriage on another Groundhog Day something more to hope about.

I hope she reads it. I hope she feels the same.

I hope someone saw me. *I hope* we'll *meet again.*

My eyes scanned down the page.

I saw you. On the 182 past Neasden Shopping Centre this Monday. I looked at you but you were looking out the window. Coffee sometime?

Yeah, good luck with that one, mate.

I saw you. Fetish party, Covent Garden. You were the giant nun slapping a small Asian boy. I was appalled.

As was I.

I read on, now no longer just scanning, but actually taking them in, understanding their hope, but hoping equally that I wasn't like them. Because surely *my* moment was *special*. Unique. Deserving of resolution.

London Now gets sixty appeals a day. As many from men as from women. And each appeal gets maybe twelve replies. People desperate to be seen. To be chosen. To be The One. *Anyone's* One.

As I read, I realized, with sickening excitement, that part of me was hoping—expecting—to find myself in there. The mysterious man on Charlotte Street. *You held my bags, you kept my heart*, that kind of thing. That would be right. Romantic. Maybe I was the kind of guy who'd get noticed. Maybe I didn't have to dress as a nun and slap little Asian boys to be worth a second glance.

I kept reading, quicker now.

I saw you and I see you every day. I greet you every day. Can you read my eyes? I miss you every day. I love you every day.

What was this guy's story? Doorman? Bus driver? Receptionist? Who's the girl? Has she noticed him? Is he anyone to her, or just the fella behind the counter at Benji's?

Why doesn't he *say* something to her?

But I knew why. Because there's the creeping fear that these moments don't actually exist outside your own head. No eyes meet across a crowded room, no two people think precisely the same thing, and if only one person actually has that moment, is it even really a moment at all?

We know this, so we say nothing. We avert our eyes, or pretend to be looking for change, we hope the other person will take the initiative, because we don't want to risk losing this feeling of excitement and possibilities and lust. It's too perfect. That little second of hope is *worth* something, possibly forever, as we lie on our deathbeds, surrounded by our children, and our grandchildren, and our great-grandchildren, and we can't help but quickly give one last selfish, dying thought to what could have happened if we'd actually said hello to that girl in the Uggs selling CDs outside Nando's seventy-four years earlier.

It's the what if? The what then? And we know that if we go for it, if we risk it, we immediately stand to lose it. But weirdly, some part of us believes the feeling is two-way, because it *must* be; it's too special not to be. We believe that something's been shared, even if the evidence we have is...what? A look that lasted a breath longer than we're used to? A second glance, when the glance could easily have been to check whether there are any cabs coming, or whether the jacket we're wearing that's caught their eye would look good on their boyfriend, or why it is we seem to be staring at them.

I saw you. You don't use overhead handles on the train. Hoped it would jolt and you would fall to me. But no.

I smiled. These small moments, never said out loud, as formed and perfect as sweet little haikus, romance and longing carved out in the dust of a grubby city.

And finally, there was mine.

I read it.

I saw you. Charlotte Street. You were climbing into a cab. Think I still have something of yours. Get in touch if you want me to give it back to you.

There.

Practical. Not astonishing, not mind-blowing, probably not something we'd read out at our wedding, but *fine*.

It was my stop.

I read one more I Saw You...

I saw and kissed you near Chelsea Bridge. It felt like a moment forever. I had to run but left you my number. Maybe you lost it?

. . . and then folded the paper.

I stood, leaving someone else's hope on the seat next to me, but taking with me a little of my own.

As I arrived at the office weighed down by coffees and crois-sants (a little more streamlined now . . . Clem's on a diet and Sam makes her own crumbly muffins), I felt my phone vibrate in my jacket.

A text from Sarah.

Thanks, Jase . . . a lovely gesture. Drink soon? (nonalcoholic of course) x

I smiled a small smile. The other thing I'd done yesterday, while pootling around on the Internet pretending to research, was send Sarah some flowers. Nothing too fancy. Just a standard bouquet with a tiny card congratulating her and—of course— Gary on their news. There was no point feeling slighted by a pregnancy. The minute babies start getting the better of you it's time to give up the fight.

I'm not suggesting you should fight babies.

I replied.

No prob. Congrats again. Sorry about . . . everything. Coffee would be nice.

I pressed send and stared at the screen for a second. It had been the right thing to do. But I still didn't think I could meet her. Not yet. Maybe when her baby was . . . what? Eighteen? Starting university? Still too soon.

Maybe when it retired.

As I got in, Zoe was just sitting down.

"Who were you texting?" she said, smiling. "Walked straight past you, outside. You seemed engrossed."

"Just, you know ..." I stalled. "Sarah."

"Sarah?" said Zoe, and there was a flash of something I couldn't quite place. "So you guys ...?"

"No."

"You're not ...?"

"Nope."

A pause.

"Shame."

I flipped the lid of my coffee and sat down at my desk.

"You guys were good together," she said, pretending to find logging on more difficult than it is. "It's a shame you ... you know, couldn't work it out."

And there it was. The familiar pang of guilt and regret, but stronger this time. Stronger because all this was coming from Zoe.

"Yeah. Well," I said, brilliantly, demonstrating this was the end of the conversation. I stared at my screen and made a mental list of things to do.

Clem was next into the office, noisily clattering the door against the wall, all black slacks under a flood of gut, having used his few days in bed to experiment with an underbeard, it seemed.

"Morning!" said Sam. "Coffee?"

"Yes, I am a little *coughy*, actually!" he said, beaming. "This bloody chest infection!"

I had slowly discovered that Clem wasn't the quiet, self-effacing man I'd considered him to be when merely popping into the office. Here was a man who hadn't made it into his forties without being very proud of his powers of punnery, observation, and topical satire. I'd go so far as to say too proud.

"Trains were late again," he said, sighing. "*That* was a big surprise."

He left a pause where he considered the laughter should have gone, and then said, "Bring back British Rail, that's what I say!"

I made a polite "heh" sound. But then he turned to face me fully. Now he'd found his target.

"You know what I call First Great Western, Jase, when I travel with them? *Worst* Great Western. And then I'm like, well, I'd hate to be on *Second* Great Western!"

He stared at me, willing my response, but all I could manage was another weak "heh" noise. But this was cool. Maybe he'd exhausted his First Great Western material. And then he tried some First *Hate* Western stuff that seems to be work-in-progress, but didn't seem to mind when I simply stopped looking, and swiveled back round.

I had press releases all around me, and a couple of reviews I fancied doing myself. The new Jim Jarmusch, for a start. I liked Jim Jarmusch. Or rather, I liked his name. Made me feel I knew about films, just saying it. Made me feel I was the kind of guy who'd buy obscure Colombian coffees instead of Maxwell House, because I "can't *abide* instant." Made me feel like someone at a dinner party boasting that "we don't even *own* a television, actually; we can't *abide* the thing."

Made me feel *impressive*.

Maybe I'd just find out what other people had written about his new film; get a sense for the general reception. No sense standing out on my first few days.

I headed for Google, and as I typed "Jim Jarmusch," I couldn't help but notice that that wasn't what was appearing in the little search box. Because I hadn't typed those words. I'd typed:

"Alaska Building London."

I checked no one was watching.

I clicked search.

"Erm . . . 'scuse I?" said Clem, swiveling round on his chair, a moment later. "Someone been using my computer?"

I froze.

"Not me," I said.

"Not you, Jason? Then why is your name in my log-in box? Unless, of course, it was not you and was instead the actor from the 1990s television program *Beverly Hills 90210*. But I have not seen him in the office so methinks it must be you! But it seems strange your name should be in my log-in box if you've not, you know, *logged in* in it."

All right, Clem.

"Ha. 'Logged in in it.' Logged in, *innit*. That is after all the purpose of a log-in box. To log in. Innit?"

Fine, yes, okay.

"Is there a log-in fairy I don't know about? A wee sprite, who logs in at random, wherever hence they do wish?"

All right.

"It was me, Clem. I logged in once while you were off. I just remembered. My computer froze. I needed to log in somewhere else."

Clem looked satisfied.

"Mystery solved, methinks!"

He looked delighted, like a man who'd worked out that just by saying "methinks" at the end of a sentence, you turn it into a joke.

"So let's see what you did on here," he said, turning back to the screen.

"What?"

"Let's check the computer history. I can see every move you made. Hope it wasn't kiddie porn, Jason. There's a law against that now, and quite right I say."

He chuckled, and started to click around, and a prickly, embarrassed heat began to burn my neck.

"Mate, I was checking my e-mail."

"Hmm . . . let's see."

"Clem . . ."

He was enjoying this, now, and scrolling through God knows what. I was instantly, sickeningly nervous. What was I going to say if he found out? If he announced it out loud? I Saw You is an office joke, a space for weary sneering and easy cynicism, a space for *look-at-the-state-of-these-people!*, which is an irony, considering the amount of meals-for-one this place goes through, but still, I'd be hung out to dry. I'd be the new boy at school, the one everyone is desperate to slip up, even just once, so that they've got a nickname they can use on him for all eternity.

"Clem, so help me God, I was checking my e-mail. Come on."

"Little touchy there, Jason. Mind if I keep looking?"

"Clem, there's nothing—"

"I'll be the judge of that, Jason! It's my computer, methinks!"

And then I lost it. I don't know what it was. The raised eyebrow? The patronizing territorialism? The innocent jokey stumbling into someone else's life? I needed to stop him.

"Clem, you are the least funny man I have ever met, so why not stop fucking around with your shitty little jokes and do some fucking work?"

He sat stiffly in his chair.

You know those moments where you say something terrible that you didn't know you were going to say and you've maybe three or four seconds in which to work out how to make it all seem a lot more lighthearted than you intended? Well, I blew my three or four seconds thinking about that.

"Jason, shall we have a chat?"

Zoe was standing next to me.

I nodded, and stood up. Clem still hadn't turned round. I looked at his screen. It remained at the log-in page.

"Couldn't have done it even if I wanted to, Jason, which I didn't, because I value people's privacy," he said, quietly.

Sam arrived, razor-burned and carrying a terrible muffin.

"So I think we need to talk about you and Sarah and all that that entails," said Zoe, in the Starbucks round the corner.

"I'm not sure I'm comfortable talking about personal things like that with my boss."

She smiled. But it was a good out; she knew that. My heart sank when I saw she wasn't giving up.

"It's understandable, you being down . . . especially after all you guys *went* through."

She made a pained face.

"And—"

"We don't need to talk about this, Zo. And I'm not upset about Sarah. It knocked me about for a bit, but the best thing to do is just push forward. Find the next moment to look forward to."

"Come on, Jase. You get a text from her. Five minutes later you're blowing up at poor Clem."

"The man's a berk."

"Yes, he's a berk, but he's a *nice* berk," she said. "Methinks."

I smiled.

"Do you fancy a bite tonight?" she said. "It'd be good to catch up. Hang out, like old times?"

"I can't tonight. I'm down to see a gig."

"Send someone else. You have that enormous power now."

"I'd like to do it myself. It's a band. Happen to be playing in South London, so I thought I'd swing by."

" 'Happen' to be in South London? Why are you going to be in South London?"

"I've . . . something to do. See. Something to see," I said.

She looked at me, curious.

"Do me good," I said, nodding at myself, like I'd considered it and maybe she was right, and actually, this might be the best thing for me. Like it was her idea.

She cocked her head.

Flats.

The Alaska Building in Bermondsey is flats. Flats tucked away from South London, and hidden behind the old gates of the converted factory, but flats all the same.

Maybe she lived here.

In, well, an old seal fur factory. I'm not sure I'm usually drawn to people who live in old seal fur factories. Or any place formerly packed with blubberers and fleshers and dyers. The clue was on the brick gates, with a dark and damp carving of an Alaskan seal. There was a pub opposite—the Final Furlong—which was checkered and blue but closed down and boarded up. No one on the streets, though. And no sign of life from the factory.

But still. Maybe she did live here. Or near here. Maybe she drank in the Final Furlong.

Actually, if she drank in the Final Furlong, this was never going to work.

I had the photo on me. My great idea was that perhaps I could ask someone. Keep things as lo-fi and natural as that. "Have you seen this girl?" People do it all the time. They do it for cats, for God's sake. And it's not like I'm in Bermondsey all the time. It's not like I'll get a reputation for it.

I walked a little farther down the street, until I saw the only real sign of life, in a kebab shop. I looked at the photo again.

This girl didn't look like a girl who ate kebabs. She looked like a girl who probably bought an M&S salad for lunch, along with a Milky Way if she was feeling naughty. I liked that about her. She seemed . . . *healthy*. There was a glow. But that didn't take away from the truth that is universally acknowledged, that once in a while, even Mr. Motivator needs a kebab.

"Hi," I said, when the man behind the counter finally turned around. "Listen, this'll sound a bit odd, but does this girl ever come in here?"

He frowned, moved some chili sauce out of the way, and took the photo from me.

"This girl?" he said. "Missing?"

"Missing? No, she's . . . I'm just trying to find her. We've lost touch."

Now didn't seem the right time to explain the camera.

"Wife?"

"No. A friend."

"Why you lose touch?"

"Just, you know."

"You fight?"

"Nope. So, does she come in here?"

"No," he said, still looking at it. And then: "You can put in window."

"Eh?"

"Yes. Make copy, put in window. Maybe she come past. Why do you think she come here? She like kebab?"

He laughed for quite a long time.

"Well, the photo was taken just over there, and—"

"Make copy. Come, look."

"No, it's okay. It's probably a bit—"

"Yes, make copy! Come!"

"It's fine!"

But he was hanging on to the photo. And then he was shouting. Shouting for someone upstairs to come downstairs. A young lad—seventeen, maybe, and in an ancient LA Lakers T-shirt—poked his head through a side door and the man, who was now talking to him in the way only a dad could, barked some instructions. The lad took the photo and closed the door, looking at it.

"He make copy. Canon. Printer does copy. Canon."

He nodded, and I made an impressed face, and said, "Canon."

I wasn't sure of the etiquette here. This man was doing me a favor of sorts. Helping me find my old friend who I'd lost touch with by sticking a photo of her in his kebab shop window. I suppose that meant I should buy a kebab.

"Um . . . while I'm here, I'd like a kebab, please."

"Chili sauce?" he said, delighted.

Minutes later the door opened again and out came the lad, holding a sheet of A4 paper with a bad printout of the photo. He'd left space above and below for a message, and he'd brought a selection of colorful pens.

"Go," said the man. "Write!"

"Oh . . . okay," I said.

This was awkward. I'd told the man we'd been friends. Who'd lost touch. How was I going to word this without it making me look mental?

I grabbed a green pen, and then remembered hearing something once about only psychopaths writing in green pen, so I picked up a red one instead.

Are You This Girl? I wrote, the man watching me the whole time, as he shook a fryer full of chips. *If so, get in touch!*

I looked at it. I decided it needed more exclamation marks.

So I added a couple in. Then changed pens and added more. And then I realized psychopaths probably did that, too.

The man seemed pleased with my efforts, and so I put my number at the bottom, and handed it to him.

"Good luck!" he said, sliding my kebab across the counter. "Hope she call."

I nodded, and popped a quid in his Poppy Appeal tin.

Outside, on a dark street, I stood for a moment and watched the man and his son argue for a second, all lit up, like a private soap opera. The picture hung in the window, smudged and already ignored by a couple, huddled together and heads down, like a team against the night.

I looked at my watch. I was late.

The Kicks were playing in a small venue nearby—Camberwell's bright green Crown & Anchor on the corner of Rodney Place, next to the windscreen repair center, just opposite the estate.

They must have felt like they'd made it.

I did, though. Genuinely. Already, I felt like a proper music reviewer, representing my paper. My name would be on the door, I'd been told, saving me the £3 entry and making me feel important.

"Hi. My name's Jason Priestley," I said, and the girl on the door laughed.

I was used to this.

"Wow, you smell like kebab," she said. "Sorry to laugh."

"Oh, yes. I just . . . ate a kebab. I thought you were laughing at my name."

"Why would I laugh at your name?"

She quarter-smiled at me.

"Anyway, I'm from *London Now*," I explained.

"Yeah, I know," she said. "I thought it was one of those made-up names. You know, when a paper writes bad reviews of things then makes up a name so they don't get all the hassle. I've seen your reviews. You're not a happy man, are you?"

She was pretty, this girl, and smiling. Maybe early twenties. Straight black fringe. She was wearing what looked like a home-made T-shirt and neon-blue leggings. She was cool. I suddenly felt fifty.

"It's not that," I said. "I've just got . . . specific tastes."

"Well, go easy," she said, and then she reached out and gently took my hand in hers.

I didn't know what to say.

And then she stamped it.

The Kicks were good. They were *really* good. I mean, as I've explained, I'm no expert, but I'm paid to look like one, so I'm telling you, with my best expert face on, they were good. Plus, they had fans. Maybe only a dozen or so, but they'd all traveled down from Brighton to watch the band they'd usually watch in Brighton, so you can't knock their enthusiasm.

The guys—five of them—were all about nineteen, but they stomped about, and rocked out, and made casual, easygoing, mock world-weary jokes between songs. I recognized one or two tracks from the album, and made a few notes from the back of the room on a piece of tissue I found.

I never know how to act at gigs. I feel self-conscious and odd. I can't let myself go, and I don't trust my sense of rhythm, so I sort of half-frown and bob my head, and I feel it makes me look like I'm somewhere else, on a higher plain, observing it as a piece of art on a level far beyond everyone else. Holding a piece of paper empowers me, too. It means I don't have to commit. I'm not there as a fan, nor by accident. I'm there to

Do Something, and For a Reason. I sometimes wish I could just hold a piece of paper throughout life in general.

And then I caught her eye.

The girl from the door was looking at me and smiling. She seemed to love this tune, and did a little ironic devil horn's gesture at me, and I nodded and smiled back, and tried to do the devil's horn thing, but it looked more like I was hailing a cab. She turned back to the band, and so I did my important face again, and made a few more notes, most of which were just random words, like, "music" and "singing."

I checked again to see if she was looking at me, but no.

And then the gig was over.

I decided to hang around, finish my pint. I watched the girl hugging the band as they came off their tiny stage. They were sweaty, and already holding cans of Red Stripe, and I felt self-conscious, so I drained the rest of my pint and folded out a small tube map to help me work out how to get home.

But then she was there.

"Drink?" she said.

It was 1:38 in the morning and we were in the Phoenix on Charing Cross Road.

Abbey—because that's her name—me, The Kicks, and their fans were slurring now, but it was a nice kind of slur. A comfortable slur. I'd found out a lot already. Abbey was single, for a start, and she'd taken on the role of a kind of head promoter and booker for the boys. She was a student at Brighton University, doing performance and visual arts, which she wasn't as into as she'd hoped, but really I can't tell you much else, because, like I say, she'd already told me she was single and that was pretty much all I could focus on.

"So you thought they were good, yeah?" she said, a little

closer to me than I was used to. I think she had glitter on her cheeks.

"I did," I said. "I really did. Here—look at my notes."

I found the crumpled piece of tissue and began to read.

"Music. Singing. Speakers. Guitars."

She giggled and tried to snatch it from me, but I managed to keep hold.

"Different songs and lyrics," I said. "Good use of drums."

"They're Brighton's brightest," she said, and it stuck with me.

We were on the benches to the side, and The Kicks seemed to fit in. Leather jackets and messy hair and T-shirts with rock and roll references. The usual clientele here were theater people. Good-looking men and women fresh from that night's show, some still in makeup, some you'd swear hadn't changed from the stage. The Kicks brought a harder, younger edge with them. And I looked like their rock and roll accountant.

I'd talked to Mikey for a while—he'd seemed to think it was some kind of interview, and so I'd had to play along, asking serious questions and trying to look like I was taking it all in—and he'd told me where they got their name (a nod to Feargal Sharkey, which I didn't really get but pretended I did) and what they hoped to do next. And then I found myself giving them advice. Sage advice from a man with literally no experience of their world whatsoever. But they took it well, and toasted me, and I felt like I was part of a cool new gang.

Outside, we high-fived our good-byes, which they took to be ironic, and I found myself using the word "man" more than usual.

"Good to see you, man. Good luck with it!"

"So when will the review go in?" asked Abbey, suddenly there.

I hailed a black cab, unsteadily. The boys all clambered into theirs.

"Next few days," I said.

And she looked at me.

"Tell me something about yourself," she said.

It was out of the blue. What do you say to something like that? She already knew I lived in North London (but not next to a shop everyone thought was a brothel, but wasn't), that I was the reviews editor for *London Now* (but not that I'd been doing it for two days and only because someone else was sick), and that my name was Jason Priestley (her big sister had had posters of Brandon Walsh on her walls for years, she said).

But what else?

Make it cool, I thought. You're an older man. You have experience. You are urbane. You wear proper shoes. You carry a wallet. You only need one more stamp before you get a free latte at Costa.

But instead, I said, "My girlfriend left me and now she's engaged and pregnant."

A pause.

"Also, I found a camera recently."

There was a horrible moment of silence.

She stared at me for a second.

And then:

"What *kind* of camera?"

I laughed. Mikey stuck his head out of the window.

"Come on, Ab!"

She started to back away, and then said, "I'm back in a couple of weeks. We could have a kebab if you like?"

I gave her the devil's horns.

Properly, this time.

ELEVEN

Or "Lazyman"

When I got up, Dev was making breakfast.

I say "making breakfast"; he'd boiled the kettle.

"Make me one, too, will you?" he shouted from the living room, and I could hear the sweet early-morning sounds of *Modern Warfare 3* flutter my way.

I handed him his tea and slumped onto the sofa.

"*Dobranoc?*" he asked, not taking his eyes off the screen.

"I. Had. A. Great. Night."

"Did you? What happened?"

"Rock and roll, my friend," I said. "Rock and roll happened. I saw this band and then we went to the pub."

"Wow," he said. "You don't get much more rock and roll than that. A pub! How am I going to live up to that? You are certainly living the high life now."

"The Kicks, Dev. I met these guys, and they were supercool, and we just got on, you know? And there was a girl called Abbey who seemed to take a shine to me."

"Their promoter, yeah?"

I balked. Dev saw me balk. I don't know what I look like when I balk, but Dev seems to. Maybe I'm always balking.

"Wanted a good review, yeah?"

"No, it's . . . I happened to be there after the gig, and—"

"You seeing them again?"

"Maybe in a couple of weeks."

"After the review's out?"

"There are no firm plans right now, but—"

"Yeah. Not happening. Forget about Abbey. It's not about Abbey."

And then Dev threw his controller down.

"Oh!" he said. "I forgot to say! It was *genius*!"

"What?"

"I saw your message! For the girl!"

I blinked. What?

"I saw it!" he said, again.

"The kebab thing?"

"What? No. What kebab thing? I mean in *London Now*. Very funny. Very saucy."

"I didn't write anything funny. Or saucy. I kept it completely aboveboard. Almost like a business transaction. Very straightforward."

Dev smiled at me like I was a cheeky so-and-so, and then threw a copy of *London Now* at my chest.

I found the right page and read it.

I saw you. Charlotte Street. You were climbing into a cab. Think I still have something of yours. Get in touch if you want me to give it back to you.

"I couldn't believe it!" said Dev. "You didn't say you were going to do that. But it was resourceful of you. Use what you have around you. Go for it! I thought it was funny!"

But it wasn't supposed to be funny. It's hard to be funny in thirty words. Twenty-eight, actually. The words "I saw you" are "complimentary," and I'd made sure mine was twenty-eight words long exactly, showing a skill for concise communication and demonstrating my sensible side. Also, it brought with it deniability. If the man with the chunky watch was also, as I suspected he might be, highly trained as an instructor in various martial arts, I could quite plausibly say I never meant this romantically. But twenty-eight words . . . is that enough?

I started to count them up, mindlessly, as Dev blethered on, wondering whether there was even the remotest chance she might have seen it, too. Whether right now she also had a flat-mate annoying her about it over breakfast. Perhaps right now thousands of flatmates across London were mocking those they live with over these ads. And maybe, in a very few cases, they were eliciting excitement in living rooms, or on buses, tubes, or trains, as people recognized themselves, and maybe realized the moment they thought was theirs alone was actually one they were sharing, and . . .

Hang on.

I recounted. And counted again.

Twenty-seven.

"I mean," said Dev, "I thought it was forward, but some-times that's what women like, isn't it? Bit of risk-taking."

Twenty-seven?

And then it hit me.

Clem had been on his way back into the office, because he'd forgotten his lighter, and that must have been when I'd spun round, and finished my message with a flourish, because I remember as he walked in, I was already several feet away from his desk, but I didn't check what I'd written, because why would I need to, and now here in front of me a day later I could see it.

There was a word missing.

A word that changed my sensible message into the kind of message I was really rather hoping to avoid. I'd been reading what I thought I'd written, because I'd agonized over it.

What had been published, though, ended in a different way. What had been published ended in:

Get in touch if you want me to give it to you.

I closed my eyes, and then opened them and read it again.

Give it to you? No! Give it *back* to you! Get in touch if you want me to give it *back* to you!

Not *give* it to you! That was *rude*! It was *bawdy*!

This was the kind of message Dev and I had mocked. Witless. Graceless. The kind of last-ditch effort a drunk and sunburned man with inappropriate tattoos makes to a smart and sober lady trying to ignore him at closing time. Laced with goodwill, but all the while carrying with it something less honorable entirely.

That was not me.

And now I was sure—absolutely sure—that she would see it. She would see this message, and her mind would be made up, and then she'd probably walk past the kebab shop and see that, too, with the red and yellow and green and blue exclamation marks of a genuine, bona fide psychopath, and then she would flee the country and marry the man with the chunky watch.

Well done, Jason Priestley! You took a hopeless situation and just gave it your own unique spin to make it worse.

I closed the paper quietly. Then Dev remembered something.

"*What* kebab thing?"

The fourth call that morning happened as I stepped off the bus outside the office. The conversations thus far usually went like this:

Me: Hello?

Teenage boy: Yes, it is me, the girl of your dreams you are looking for.

Me: You're a teenage boy.

Teenage boy: No, I am the lady from the kebab shop poster.

Me: I'm pretty sure you're the teenage boy who's been calling me all morning.

Teenage boy: Why are you putting up posters for teenage boys then?

Me: Look, I've got your number now.

Teenage boy: So now you're taking the phone numbers of teenage boys?

Me: Good-bye.

(Muffled laughter, high-fives, someone in the background saying, "Call him again, call him again!")

And so the search, such as it was, could have been going better.

I crept into the office, slightly sheepishly, holding a tray of coffees and a tub of chocolate Mini Bites for Clem. Clem loves Mini Bites. These are the kind of details you pick up in an office.

"These are not just Mini Bites!" he said, gratefully and with raised, comedy eyebrows. "These are *M&S* Mini Bites!"

"Ha ha!" I said, though I should have tried harder. "Well, I know you like them. And I'm very sorry about yesterday."

"No biggie!" he said. "We all have our moments."

"You were just being funny," I said.

"I suppose I was being funny, wasn't I?" he said, thoughtfully. "You just suffered what is technically known as an SOHF. Sense of Humor Failure!"

"Ha ha!" I said, again, as if I had no idea how he made these things up and they were brilliant.

"You know Clem's signed up to do some stand-up next week?" said Zoe, staring at her screen, not wanting to make eye contact.

"You're kidding?" I said.

"Well, I *will* be!" said Clem, delighted with his joke. "Hopefully I *will* be kidding! Hey, Sam, did you hear that?"

Sam turned around, bleary-eyed.

"Jason said, 'Are you kidding?,' about me doing the stand-up comedy and I said, 'Well, I *will* be!'"

Sam turned back round.

"You should've seen your face!" he said, back on me. "You keep setting them up, son, I'll keep knocking them in!"

I gave him a thumbs-up and sat down.

Clem stared into space, his mouth reaching for something funny to say about thumbs.

I started to write my review.

"Brighton's Brightest," I called it.

I put a *lot* of effort in.

Lunchtime. Postman's Park. A crayfish wrap, a can of Coke, and an excited Dev.

"It hit me just after you left!" he said.

"What did?"

"You. The Girl. The potential. You have everything at your disposal to make this work!"

I stared at him and tried to subtly work out if I could smell *jezynowka*. We started to walk.

"Think about it," he said. "You have an audience. An audience you can utilize to find her!"

"What are you talking about?"

"There are things you can do. You've got the whole place at your disposal!"

"What place?"

"London."

"More specifically?"

"*London Now!*"

No. No, thanks, Dev. Not to say I hadn't considered it. A feature in the paper would have its effects, but it would be too exposing. Too embarrassing. Too needy and too desperate. I've seen those articles written by journos in which they immerse themselves in something, like speed dating or whatever, always written with that same knowing, ironic smirk, and I want no part of it.

"I don't think it's the way to go," I said. "I don't think she'd like it."

"How do you know?"

"Too much attention. Who knows what her situation is?"

"What? I'm not talking about some big exposé. I'm saying there are tools you can use. Those pictures, right? We agree they're full of clues. A background, a shop, a fancy car outside a big building marked Alaska."

I kept quiet about my trip to Bermondsey.

"You don't know what that place is so you ask the readers. Hidden London, call it. Offer a small prize. Can You Identify This Piece of Hidden London?"

I started to smile, despite myself. This wasn't bad.

"Why are you so keen?" I said.

"It gets you out of the flat," he said. "Or how about this? You don't know who she is so again you ask the readers. Print a photo, one where there are other people around, then pretend like it's a random shot and the random person circled wins a random prize. She rings up, and Bob's your uncle!"

"What if she doesn't see it?"

"Then someone she knows will see it! And they'll be like, Susan, or whatever her name is, Susan, you're in the paper and you've won five quid!"

I pretended I was thinking about it. But I already had, and

this could work. Plus, it was charming, somehow. Less stalky. More . . . imaginative.

We stopped walking.

"*London Now* isn't just *London Now*," he said. "It's *your* London. *Now*."

He looked pleased with himself.

"You should suggest that as a slogan."

Over his shoulder, I could just make out a tile.

Ernest Benning, compositor, aged 22. Upset from a boat one dark night off Pimlico Pier, grasped an oar with one hand supporting a woman with the other, but sank as she was rescued.

"Use the moment!" he said.

"Yeah, maybe," said Zoe. "It's a bit local newspaper, though."

"But we *are* a local newspaper," I said. "You know. London's just a place, isn't it? I know most of the paper's done up in Manchester, but the bits we do should be for the audience we have. Londoners. It's better than another bought-in quiz, y'know? And I don't mind sourcing the images."

"From?"

"Well, not a picture library, so there's a saving already! No, I'll just take some snaps. I'm trying to get to know London a bit better anyway. It'll do me good. Getting out there. Seeing things. Bit of fresh air."

She thought about it.

"We'll give it a go for a couple of weeks. Could always ask the readers to send stuff in, too."

"Great!" I said. "Right, so . . . I'll find a picture."

This was good. This was doing something. Something less weird than another hour staring at The Girl's photos and then driving off to Whitby or Bermondsey or wherever. And these snaps . . . these were largely London snaps. Or looked to be. Dev's idea had legs. I just had to choose the right shot and unleash an army of London-based researchers upon it.

I laid them out on my desk and quietly flicked through them. Most of them weren't suitable. A shot of the man with the chunky watch eating scallops in a restaurant, for example. That did nothing for me. But others did. There she was, walking through some kind of park, two stone doorways behind her with huge triangular pedestals above them, green leaves tickling the lip. We could just zoom in on the doorways. That was hidden London. Someone would know where that was. Or this one, the inside of a cinema. An old one, the kind you'd expect an organist to suddenly shoot through the floor of, playing "We'll Meet Again" just before the Saturday matinees kick in. She looks happy in this one. A bag of popcorn, a bottle of water, the glow of an evening about to begin. I wonder where this is. I wonder what was going on, that night. I wonder if . . .

"Scallops?"

I jolted, and tried to collect my photos together. *Her* photos. Not mine.

"Eh?"

"Scallops!" said Clem, picking the photo up. "Sounds rude when you say it like that, doesn't it? Who's this handsome fella?"

"That's . . ." Well, how did I explain it? How did I explain why I had a photo of a handsome man eating scallops? "That's my brother." I lied.

"Is it?"

Shit. Actually. Zoe. Where was Zoe? She knows I have a brother. Mind you, I'd kept the details scant, probably to make myself seem more special, more unique, less one-of-two. Everything else we'd discussed and dissected. Where we came from, where we hoped to be, how we saw our futures going, where ten years might take us. We'd talked about it too much, if anything.

I cast my eye quickly around the office. I was safe. Zoe was by the printer, swearing. Thank God for cheap refills. Thank God ten years had taken her to an office that wouldn't pay out for the good stuff.

"Don't see the resemblance," said Clem. "What does he do?"

"He is . . . an orthodontist."

Clem looked impressed.

"He has his own practice," I said. "In . . . Wandsworth. He is married to a lady called Lilian and they have no pets."

I couldn't stop.

"Lilian is an industrial engineer. She's got yellow hair."

Wish I had.

"Finchley Road," said Clem, distracted.

"What is?" I said.

He pointed at the photo, and smiled.

"That restaurant."

What? How did he know?

He leaned closer, and pointed at the menu in the handsome man's hands.

"Where are you taking me?" said Dev. "What's all this about scallops?"

"There," I said, as the cab passed Swiss Cottage.

We were headed to Prince Albert Street not far from St. John's Wood, and Dev's not used to being anywhere a Prince or a Saint might have been.

"I'm taking you *there*," I said, pointing at the tower block, when finally we pulled up.

"A tower block?"

"It's not just a tower block. There's a restaurant at the bottom. One you wouldn't know was there. Not unless you were Clem."

"So it's a scallop restaurant?"

"No. I mean, I don't know. Maybe. We're reviewing it. That's what they're expecting, anyway. In reality, we're casing the joint."

"You're getting into this," he said, delighted, taking the photo from my hand and now understanding. "She looks a little masculine in this photo, though."

"That's Chunk, as he will now be known."

"I know who Chunk is. So what if we bump into him?"

"It's very unlikely he'll be here. But we can see how the place suits us. Get a measure of it. And maybe ask the maître d' if he's seen The Girl."

"Look at you. Saying 'maître d'.' Will you be telling the maître d' about your cozy home in the spare room above a shop next to a place everyone thought was a brothel, but wasn't?"

"A professional maître d' has no interest in such matters," I said. "Come on."

Oslo Court is an old-fashioned kind of a restaurant, it turns out. Old-fashioned decor. Old-fashioned men in old-fashioned clothes wheeling old-fashioned dessert trolleys round to people who like things old-fashioned.

"This is a bit weird," said Dev, taking in the pink and frilly curtains. "Why would Chunk take her here? This is just some-one's flat on the ground floor of a council house."

"No, it's not. And maybe he didn't," I said. "Maybe—"

But I couldn't think of another reason why two people would have ended up here. Thing is, it didn't exactly scream "date." It screamed "entertaining a corporate client." So maybe that was it. Maybe The Girl was a corporate client. Or he was. And they'd simply decided to spend the entire week together, going on walks in parks and to bars and to places like Oslo Court. Because that's what platonic businesspeople do. Platonically.

"Have you decided what you'd like to eat?" asked a waiter.

"I'll have the scallops!" said Dev. "And so will my friend!"

"Actually, I'll—"

"Come on! We came here because of the scallops, didn't we?"

"Well..."

"It's *because* of the scallops we're here..."

I looked at my scallops with disdain, and I'd swear they did the same back. Dev got out the disposable and snapped a picture of me pretending to make one talk.

I'm not sure I should be a professional restaurant reviewer.

"So did you do it?" said Dev. "The Hidden London thing?"

"I did, sir."

"What shot?"

"This one."

I took the photos out of my inside pocket and found the right one. I bristled slightly as Dev watched me do it. I knew what he was thinking. He was thinking, Oh, he carries them round now, does he?

It was taken on a cold day, it seemed, this one. Her cheeks were red and her breath hung in the air.

"A Walk in the Park," said Dev. "That's what I'd call this photo if I were an important artist."

"See these doorways? We zoomed in on them. Just used a detail. They look pretty distinct."

"Be embarrassing if they weren't in London," said Dev. "Wouldn't set a good precedent for this whole Hidden London thing if someone went, 'Actually, that's Russell Watson's house in Plymouth.'"

"That's no one's house. That's . . . a park. A London park. You can tell, because it's wet."

We stared at each other.

Dev looked proud of me.

Hidden London ran in that week's paper. I suppose it was a bit cheeky, hijacking these few inches of the paper, thrusting it in Londoners' faces just because I could. To anyone else, of course, it would have meant nothing. A small box on a page of bought-in crosswords and sudoku and cartoons that never ever seemed to have a punch line, no matter how hard you looked.

But to me, well, it was a little Trojan horse. And hey, the £25 prize for the correct answer wasn't bad either. I mean, it's not like we were cheating the reader. They just needed the correct answer.

Only problem was, of course, that I didn't know the correct answer. And people would expect the correct answer. That's really the minimum requirement of a quiz like this: that there's actually an answer to get right.

Still. It'll be fine, I thought. Surely there'll be a consensus. Maybe by now, sixty or seventy avid *London Now* readers would've e-mailed in their correct answers, each of them certain and confident and right.

I logged in at the office.

Apparently not.

Well. It was only 7:30 a.m. I'd come in a little early today.

I clicked refresh and refresh and refresh, and then made a coffee.

* * *

By midday, there were three guesses.

I toasted myself with a cup of tea. I had just successfully launched *London Now*'s least-successful feature of all time.

Zoe laughed when I told her, and said to just use a picture of Big Ben next time, but I already knew what I'd be using next time. The cinema. The old and battered cinema with its velvet and popcorn and dark purple glow.

"Any of them get it right, at least?" asked Zoe, and I made a face that started off as "yes" and ended up as "no," because really, I hadn't worked out my approach on this yet.

I looked again at the guesses, and wondered whether any of them were right.

I guess I'd have to check and see.

London in the summer can't be beaten. It's like it comes out of hiding in the sun. The things you notice, the people you see, the instant calm that soothes the city and slows a lunchtime down.

I'd seen it in Soho Square already today, as I searched out Len from Greenwich's first guess at Hidden London (sorry, Len: way off). The workers and the homeless all, at the first real sign of sun, apparently taking a day off from their very different activities, basking in the heat, opening plastic sandwich boxes or bright red smoothies, or shuffling about by the bins finding dog-ends to crumble into rollies, depending on which group you were concentrating on. A large group of girls, head-to-toe in white and from the hairdressing college down the street, eyed the pub on the corner, wondering if they could sneak in a large rosé before curling class.

And the trees. I'd never noticed the trees in Soho Square before. Were they new? Had they always been there? Large and long and looping, perhaps the council wheel them out during heatwaves, or maybe it's only when you need the shade you start noticing its protection.

And now, here I was in Highgate: a place I'd only been once or twice to visit an old girlfriend who'd tell me of the vampires and ghouls that are said to roam the streets at night. There'd been some kind of nobleman, brought to England in his coffin sometime at the beginning of the eighteenth century, buried in Highgate Cemetery but later roused by Satanists, and who then became the King Vampire of the Undead. I suppose it is sad that some people only discover their true vocation when it's too late. Many people said that the right way to handle suddenly having a King Vampire move into the local area would be to dig him up, put a stake through him, behead him, and then burn him, but as others pointed out at the time, this was illegal and rude. This type of thing makes me feel warm about Britain. Even if it does mean we're overrun by Vampire Kings.

I walked through the gates of the cemetery and studied my map. Sam from Wealdstone had been quite adamant that he was correct on this one. I wandered through, past a giggling couple who stopped giggling when they saw me, and carried on together, hands clasped together, eyes fixed to the ground.

It's creepy, Highgate Cemetery, and for a second I wished that couple was going my way. Trees crowd the sun, and in the afternoon light the mausoleums, catacombs, and vaults seem uneasy, like they're waiting for the coming night, like they're tolerating you for now, as you thread your way through. The East Cemetery is fine by me. I like the shade of the oaks, and the beaten-down paths, and pretty clearings. It's the West Cemetery I'm not so keen on. The ivy's taken over, wrapping itself around whatever it can, strangling the graves and hiding the Gothic monuments and statues, sometimes leaving just a bare stone hand or set of eyes clear, as if they're grasping for the light, as if they're fighting the death all around them.

I strode on, down a small hill, past ramshackle graves at all angles, like badly hit nails, and on toward Sam from Wealdstone's very confident guess.

Sam from Wealdstone was right to be confident.

There it was. The strange archway, the leaves tickling its top lip. The same place The Girl had been standing, healthy, and glowing, and happy, smiling broadly at the camera, smiling, for now, at me.

The entrance to Egyptian Avenue.

I stood there a second and took it in.

"So what did you do?" asked Dev, later. "Ask around? Put up a poster?"

"I'm not sure the poster campaign was such a good idea," I said, stirring my tea and thinking of the other two messages I'd received that afternoon from teenage boys in the Bermondsey area. "And no, I didn't ask around. I didn't know who to ask. Or what."

"So you just stood there?"

"I took a picture," I said, holding up my disposable. "And I had a think."

"Oh," said Dev. "Well, I'm sure that'll all come in handy. What did you think about?"

"I wondered what she was doing at Highgate Cemetery. Why she took the picture. One day she's outside a fur factory, next day she's eating scallops in a restaurant. Date three: a gothic cemetery! It's just random."

"Of course it's not random. There has to be a link. It's a disposable. One photo leads to another, I'm telling you."

"I don't buy it. Not everything is linked!"

Dev threw his hands up and gave me an I-told-you-all-this-already face.

"Those. Photos. Are. *Linked*. If this were a videogame, you'd be on, like, level six, 'The Graveyard,' and things would be starting to make sense. Although you'd probably have met an old professor in the woods and he would've given you some clues."

He stared at me.

"You didn't—"

"No, I didn't meet an old professor in the woods who gave me some clues. Just the Vampire King and a giggly couple."

Dev looked at me, strangely.

"Listen," I said. "Sometimes life is just life. Things happen, then some other things happen, and often there are no extra things in the middle connecting them. She went to a restaurant, she went to a graveyard—"

"A specific *part* of a graveyard."

"—and that's all we know."

I said that last part finally, so that whatever else was going on in Dev's head just stayed there. It seemed to work.

"Do you want some *kolacz*?" he asked, and sighed.

"What's that?" I said. "Beer?"

"Cheese."

"No thanks."

And an hour later my phone beep-beeped. And I blinked at it, surprised, and carried it into the living room for Dev to see.

"It is mysterious if a baboon falls from a tree."

—Traditional Shona Tribe proverb, Zimbabwe

I don't know what this baboon thing means. It was on a website with the others, my vague attempt to theme these blogs and keep all eight of you interested.

Having said that, it's probably pointless me trying to somehow relate to you a story from my recent life that involves a baboon falling out of a tree because if I'd met a baboon and it had fallen out of a tree I'd definitely have told you already by now. I'd have been straight on Twitter, too. Just seen baboon fall from tree. It was so mysterious! *So I'll tell you something else instead: today I wondered if he'd tried to get in touch. I changed my number when it all crashed and burned. I actually ended up with a better calling plan, so maybe everything happens for a reason.*

The strange thing is, I knew all along that it would end that way, because really, what was I expecting? For him to do anything else at all? Or for him to do what he's always done? I guess it's not mysterious if a baboon stays in a tree. Because people are predictable.

I feel quite clever now.

So there are eight of you reading these things these days. Eight! I wonder if we've ever passed each other on the street. I wonder if you'd know me if you saw me? My dad used to say he thought people could know each other with just a glance.

There are seven million strangers in this city, and I'll smile at some of them today, just in case one of them is looking for me.

It would be an embarrassing thing indeed if none of them was.

Sx

TWELVE

Or "Don't Leave Me Alone with Her"

Well, this was embarrassing.

I hadn't known where to suggest to meet Abbey when she texted. I'd been thrown. She wasn't supposed to call. Dev had convinced me. He'd said it had all been about the review, and I'd reluctantly, and in the sober light of day, conceded that, yes, it probably was. She was younger than me—cooler than me. And yet she'd texted, not once mentioning anything about The Kicks, and said she'd be in town at the end of the week for a friend's birthday and did I fancy grabbing a bite, or something.

I'd replied quickly, worried the offer was somehow as permanent as dust on a window ledge, here one second, swirling and moving and gone the next.

How about Charlotte Street? I'd said.

Yeah, so there were reasons I favored Charlotte Street. But I figured Charlotte Street gave the right impression, too. It was adaptable. You can go either way with Charlotte Street. You can impress someone. Buy them a double-figure cocktail from the Charlotte Street Hotel if they're that way inclined. Buy them a pie from the boozer round the back if they're not. But you need to start somewhere in the middle, so you know which way to head once you get the lay of the land. Something halfway between a pie and a cocktail.

Something midrange.

"Welcome to Abrizzi's!" said the lady on reception. "A magical slice of pizza heaven!"

I was a little early, and mildly distracted by this, but even so, her words seemed very familiar, though I struggled to place them.

"Have you booked?" she said.

"Um, yeah," I said. "Table for two. Priestley."

She started to scan her list, but then paused, and for the briefest of moments I thought I saw something explode behind her eyes. Her eyes flicked toward me.

"*Jason* Priestley?"

"Just so pleased you're here," said Gino, the manager, a wiry man with a watch too big for him. "Really—*welcome* back."

He had one hand on my shoulder and he kept trying to shake my hand with his other.

"Not at all," I said, staring straight ahead.

"Just, please, enjoy your meal, and let me arrange something special for you, too."

"Okay . . . ," I said, willing him away, and it worked, because he went.

This was horrible.

"A magical slice of pizza heaven" had, of course, been my official opinion on Abrizzi's, in my dashed-out and only-out-of-guilt review. But it looked like they'd taken it seriously. Really very seriously indeed. Because "a magical slice of pizza heaven" now seemed to be their official slogan. It was on napkins. It was on menus. It was on the T-shirts and shirts of each and every member of staff.

And not just that. But underneath every single one of them: my name.

"Jason Priestley, London Now!"

They'd even added an exclamation mark, so deeply excited and inspired were they by my talk of magic.

Again: this was *horrible*.

When Abbey came in—all ripped Bowie T-shirt and skinny jeans and electric-blue eyeliner—she would see me, Jason Priestley, surrounded by dozens of people carrying bits of paper or wearing bits of cloth with my name on. She would see a menu full of pizzas, with my name on every page, assuring her that whatever she chose, she was guaranteed a magical slice of pizza heaven. She would see balloons and notepads and one woman in a baseball cap—all proclaiming she was about to have the night of her life in what was—and this is what the quote *should* have been—one of London's most average restaurants.

And worse, it would look like I was proud of this. I could hardly claim it as a mistake, or a weird coincidence. I could hardly say, "Actually, I'm not much of a fan of this place." I am clearly a massive fan of this place. And denying it would not only harm my journalistic credibility, but make her wonder why I'd brought her here if it's so dreadful. It's not like I could say, "I didn't know if you were a pie girl or a cocktail girl, so I split the difference and thought I'd just lob pizzas at you."

So I'd just have to sit here and wait for her to walk in and pray she didn't notice. Because maybe she wouldn't notice. That was possible.

That was possible, right?

* * *

That was not at all possible.

"Well, this is unusual," she said, sitting down and placing on the table the flyer she'd been given outside, which had my name in eighteen-point Palatino right across the top.

I'd hoped maybe she was talking about the fact that two people, strangers just a week before, could meet up and share a magical slice of pizza heaven, but no: now she was pointing at a waiter in what I will now refer to as a matching Jason Priestley T-shirt and baseball cap set and she was looking concerned.

"I suppose it is a bit unusual," I said, before, adding quite urgently: "I didn't bring you here to impress you. I'm not trying to impress you."

"Well, that's nice to know."

"No, I mean, if I wanted to impress you, this isn't the way I would impress you."

"Your name is *everywhere*," she said, looking at the menu.

"I know," I said. "I know."

"Look. They've taken other quotes and put them under the relevant dishes. The Margherita is 'a delight!'"

I grabbed the menu and looked at it.

"I guess it *must* be," I said, shaking my head, "which is strange, because I'm not usually a fan. Look, do you want to get out of here? Maybe you'd prefer a cocktail, or a pie?"

She wrinkled her nose at me. People don't do that much.

"Hello, sir. Hello, madam!"

It was the manager. He was back. And he was bearing gifts.

"With our compliments!" he said, packed with pride and full of goodwill.

Two giant glasses, filled with prawns and lettuce, slathered in a bright pink sauce, and surrounded by little cocktail-stick Abrizzi flags with tiny Jason Priestley quotes on them.

Why? Why hadn't I put more effort into that quote?

Hemingway had hundreds, all brilliant. Wilde spat them out like pips. What if this is the only thing people remember me for when I'm gone? What if this is my legacy?

"Oh, thank you, that's . . . ," I began, and as I looked up, I could see the manager willing me to say something else, something nice, something they could get printed up on a flyer, or perhaps attach to the back of a plane and have flown around central London. "That's a *lovely* big glass of prawns."

The manager semi-smiled, going through the quote in his head, rolling it over and over, but knowing he probably couldn't use "that's a lovely big glass of prawns" very effectively in his next marketing blitz. He backed away, never once taking his eyes off our prawns, just to make sure they were just right, still *perfect*, and we waited for him to disappear.

"I think pie," said Abbey.

We were over the road from Percy Passage and I was secretly pleased Abbey was a pie girl and not a cocktail one. You find me a pie girl and I'll show you a girl who knows about life. Find me a cocktail one, and I'll compliment her shoes, because all I know is, they get very funny with you if you don't.

"So what's the official verdict on this place?" she said, looking around the pub, fork in hand. "Is someone going to come out wearing a full Jason Priestley bodysuit, and then start singing the Jason Priestley song, all about quality pies at low, low prices?"

I laughed, embarrassed.

"What kind of quote did you give *these* guys?" she said.

"I swear to God, I had no idea Abrizzi's were launching some kind of elaborate Jason Priestley campaign. If I had, it would literally have been the last place in London I would've taken you."

"Sure," she said. "Sure sure."

And she smiled.

I liked the fact that she'd called me. Out of the blue. I was flattered she'd want to hang out. And pleased that there'd been no mention of The Kicks or their review. It was refreshing to meet someone and be free of subtext or implications. Yeah, so now, in the cold light of day, our differences were clearer. She was young and cool and hot and I was a man who'd lent his name to bad baseball caps in an average restaurant. But this was just a meeting of two people who liked each other, pure and simple.

"So I wanted to ask you a favor."

Forget everything I just said.

"Shoot," I said, nodding vigorously, to show that yes, of course she did, I never thought this was just about hanging out with someone who seemed to like me, but she must've seen my face fall.

"Oh, God, that's not why I wanted to meet up," she said. "I didn't arrange this so that I could ask you a favor. Is that what you think?"

"Well, I mean, I didn't expect to hear from you at all, really. Or if I did, maybe not until the review came out."

She looked at me very seriously.

"Jason, I'm not after you for your reviews. I'm not even after *you*."

She finished her last bite of pie and I tried not to look disappointed.

"I just think you're bruised."

"I'm not bruised," I said, a little too quickly and before I'd really had time to consider what she'd meant.

"Of course you're bruised. The other night I asked you to tell me something about yourself and what was the first thing you told me?"

"The camera thing?" I tried.

She smiled, and sat back in her seat. A gap opened up—an awkward, yawning pause she didn't seem in a rush to fill.

"Okay," I said. "Yes, I'm a bit bruised."

"Most guys would've tried to impress me," she said. "If I'd said, 'Tell me something about yourself,' they'd've said, 'I once saved a life,' or 'I love animals,' or 'My greatest fault is sometimes I'm just too kind.' But you decided to show me how bruised you are."

"What favor do you need?" I said, trying to move things on.

"Jason . . ."

"Come on, anything. What favor do you need?"

"I want to have a child."

She sat back in her chair and stared at me, hard. The music seemed to get louder, the place more confusing.

"I . . . what?"

"I know it's weird, but listen: do you want children?"

Oh, terrific. A nutjob. She was a nutjob.

"Well, I, eventually," I stumbled, nodding, trying to pretend that almost everyone else in this pub was probably having a very similar conversation. "You know, but . . . not tonight."

"It wouldn't be tonight," she said. "It takes nine months. Bloody NHS. So when do you want children? Narrow it down for a girl."

"Well . . . I want them. I want them eventually. I . . . I've thought about it sometimes, I won't lie, but—"

I shrugged and waved my hands a bit. It was the absolute best I could do.

"And that's your final answer, is it?"

I just need to finish this drink and I could be home in twenty minutes.

"I think so, yes."

She thought about it. A frosty moment. And then a snigger.

"Jason, I don't really want to have a child, I'm about three hundred years younger than you with my whole life ahead of me."

And the relief and the joy on my face must have been obvious, because she laughed and said, "I'm messing with you! You looked *terrified*! I do not want your child!"

And while I struggled to find a response without the word "hallelujah" in it, she took a sip of her pint and said, "I just want you to talk to me."

I took a moment, studied her face.

Why would someone who was not interested be so interested? I thought, despite myself.

And then:

"Jason," said a voice, a stern one, breaking the silence.

I'm not keen on stern voices, piercing silences. They don't generally bring great news. I looked up.

Anna.

Anna? What was Anna...?

Words whizzed through my head.

"I just think you need to take a long, hard look at yourself and maybe rein in the drinking because it's not healthy, all this drinking, Jason."

My grip on the pint glass tightened.

"A pint does not solve anything, and you also need to let Sarah and Gareth live their lives because you had your chance and you need to be a grown-up about it."

"Hello, *Anna*," I said, and if I'd been in a cartoon, it would've been through gritted teeth. Anna had a way of talking to me that made me feel like I'd somehow been caught doing something I shouldn't, and here it was happening again: a quick flush of embarrassment rushed through me. Anna was Sarah's best friend. At least until I'd been on the scene. She hadn't taken to me particularly well, nowhere near as well as she'd apparently taken to Gary, I'd been told. Gary and his stupid man'd face.

Now Sarah was rid of me, Anna had been doing her level best to get back in with Sarah. Sarah and Gary. And I'd always suspected that was through badmouthing me. Never again would she let Sarah go. Anna thrived on information. By which I mean gossip. You give Anna some gossip, Anna will use it well and make it last.

I suppose if I was still a teacher, I'd mark her like this:

Appearance: Thin mouth, thin eyebrows, thin nose, thin body, thin skin. Pockets stuffed full of Kleenex. Perpetual cold and perpetually cold.
Conversation: Overuses the phrase "I'm only being honest!" as if this is some kind of get-out for rudeness and we should all in fact applaud her wonderfully open attitude because she's only being honest. Does not like it when other people are honest with her, and gets very honest with them if they are.
Overall: Avoid. Avoid avoid avoid. What? I'm only being honest.

"How *are* you?" I said, faux beaming, knowing I just had to brave this out, give nothing away, and she'd be gone soon.

Anna made a *tsk* sound and extended her arm to Abbey, using it as an excuse to take her in, study her, steal a glance at her ripped Bowie T-shirt and electric-blue eyeliner and all the other things that really didn't seem very me at all.

"Sorry, he's so *rude*, isn't he?" She laughed, lightly, but what she really meant by that was that I'm rude. "I'm Anna. I'm a friend of Sarah's?"

She put a question mark on the end of that. She didn't need to. It was a fact, not a question. She was fishing; trying to get Abbey's reaction; trying to work out who she was by what she knew. Did she know about Sarah? wondered Anna. Had I told her the full story?

"*Svetlana*," said a voice immediately to my left, in a deep and heavy Russian accent. Which was odd, because Abbey was immediately to my left, and her accent was not deep, or heavy, and it was British, and what's more, I was pretty sure there was no one called Svetlana here.

"Oh!" said Anna, seemingly impressed.

"I am Russian prostitute."

I turned and stared, shocked.

"Jason visit me often, but sometime he just want to meet up and cry."

Anna's eyes widened slightly.

"Today is just lot of crying. Crying and pie. I call these night a Jason Priestley night. Just crying and pie. CryPie."

Anna took a moment, nodded, grinned at her shoes, looked up and looked annoyed.

"Seems you've met someone your own age, then," she said. "I'll leave you to it. Enjoy your pie."

I watched her leave, wondering if she'd perhaps forget this, and Sarah might never hear about it.

"And crying, too!" shouted Abbey, after her. "Pie *and* cry!"

I turned back to her, speechless.

"I thought that was your ex," she said, stifling a giggle.

"So you thought you'd say you were a prostitute I visit so I can cry a lot?"

"Yeah, man!" she said. "Girls love that shit!"

"Do they?"

"Not many of them. She didn't look your type anyway. She'd been shopping at Crabtree & Evelyn. The minute you start buying anything that smells of lavender you might as well book your Saga trip, too."

I smiled, shook my head.

"Hey, let's go out!" she said.

I was confused.

"We *are* out."

"Then let's go *further* out."

I didn't know if I was "with" Abbey or not tonight, but I guessed I probably wasn't, because at one point she greeted another man by kissing him full on the lips.

We were at the Good Mixer, in Camden, surrounded by snake-hipped hipsters. Already, we'd visited an Indian takeaway on Castlehaven Road because they gave away free Bombay Mix, plus we'd popped into the Hawley Arms, where we'd seen Nick Grimshaw hunched in a corner animatedly squabbling with a tall man in a silly hat.

There is something that sounds young, and exciting, and cool about heading to Camden on a whim. In reality, it makes me very uncomfortable. Safeguards are needed. A sturdy pair of shoes, to navigate through the cricks and cracks of discarded chicken bones underfoot. A look of polite but steely determination to get past the men offering you drugs every six or seven feet, like helpers at a marathon offering cups of water.

"Hashish, mate?" says the first man.

"Hashish?" says the second.

"Hash?" says the third, just in case in the last twelve feet you've reconsidered, radically rethought your life, and suddenly developed quite a craving.

"Why?" you want to shout. "What makes yours better than his? At least put some effort in! You will never make it onto *Dragons' Den* with a pitch like that!"

I was tired already, and it was only 11:45.

I knew it was "only" 11:45, because Abbey kept using the word "only" whenever whatever time it was was mentioned. It could "only" be Judgment Day and Abbey would find one last bar for us to go to before we hit the Pearly Gates Arms.

This, of course, was why I liked her. She reminded me of the way things had been. Before Sarah, even. Time was, I could do all-nighters like Abbey. I kept it going, too, for longer into my twenties than might necessarily have been healthy. It was a way of being footloose, of being fancy-free, in a way the city's so practiced at encouraging.

So anyway, the guy that Abbey kissed—*briefly*, I kept telling myself; it was very *brief*—turned out to be in a band, too, and that was when I realized that Abbey probably mainly hung out with boys in bands. I decided to be supercool. I started to use the word "man" again.

"Can I getcha a drink, man?" I said. In my head, saying "getcha" was cool, but I'd forgotten that the next word was "a," so saying "getcha a" was pretty cumbersome and made me sound like perhaps I had an impediment of some kind.

"I'm cool," said the boy, and that was annoying, because he was right.

"Back in a mo," said Abbey.

I looked around and once more felt very old indeed. There were skinny jeans and skinny ties and tight-fitting tees and military boots and porkpie hats and lots of swaying and stumbling and slurring around the dimly lit pool table. With Abbey gone, I was hit by a wave of self-consciousness. I thought about what I was wearing. Jeans, so that was okay, but they weren't jeans like these people were wearing. I wouldn't know where to buy jeans like these people were wearing. I had a shirt I'd seen someone in *GQ* put on, and some Converse, but here I stuck out like a sore thumb. How old were these people? Twenty? Twenty-one? Any one of these people could have been my pupils. Any one of them might right now have been thinking: is that sir? Is that sir-in-his-thirties *sir*? Here in the *Good Mixer*? Walking *among* us?

"What's the name of your band?" I asked the boy, and he barely looked at me, maybe in case he caught whatever it was I'd caught that made you old, and he mumbled, "Bearpit Liars."

"Good name," I said, and he just nodded, then wandered off.

And then:

"Ta-dah!"

It was Abbey. She was back. But she wasn't wearing her Bowie T-shirt anymore.

"Where did you get *that*?" I asked, shocked.

"Stole it," she said.

"You stole that T-shirt? When?"

"When I went to the toilet at the restaurant. I think it makes me look very professional."

I read the T-shirt again.

A magical slice of pizza heaven! —Jason Priestley, London Now!

"Well, it makes you look professional in the sense that it makes you look like you work at Abrizzi's."

"Well, I have heard *excellent* things about their pizzas," she said. "Hey, where did Jay go?"

"Jay? Jay who you . . . kissed?"

Ah, Jay. You win. Looks like I'll be leaving soon.

"Relax," she said. "I'll probably kiss *you* at some point."

Or maybe I'll stay a little longer.

"Shall we go for a walk?" she said.

* * *

I don't know who goes for walks after midnight in Camden. Literally no one in the history of Camden or its neighboring boroughs has thought going for a walk after midnight down by the lock is a good idea. Plus, I feel I have made my own thoughts on walking around Camden at night quite clear, but obviously I hadn't made them clear enough to Abbey, because she seemed dead set on walking, not just through Camden, but right down by the houseboats, lit by candles and decorated by cans, under blinking, jittery, not-at-all-reliable streetlights.

But when a girl has said she might at some point kiss you, you sort of agree to a lot of things. Even if they *are* by a canal.

We walked a little farther, past two dark shapes I was certain were muggers but turned out to be a nervous man and a little dog.

"So what kind was it?" asked Abbey. "The camera you found?"

I smiled. The camera again. Maybe she had a thing for cameras.

"It was a disposable."

"Cooool," said Abbey. "So old-school. Something about them, though. It's like instant nostalgia. Like, those photos *mean* something because they were thought about, *then* taken. Not like the billion you end up with after a night out on your phone or whatever. Those photos are just wallpaper. Disposable is permanent."

"You should meet my flatmate. You'd get on."

"And the girl? What's happening with her?"

I frowned.

"How did you know there was a girl?"

"Well, when you said she was pregnant I kind of assumed."

"Oh. *That* girl. The *ex* girl."

"You're getting over her."

"How do you know?"

"Because she wasn't the first girl you thought of. She was the *second* girl you thought of. One day she'll be the third and then you won't even think of her at all."

I kicked at some leaves.

"Yeah, it's just . . . you know. When we broke up, it—"

"*How* did you break up?"

And as we sat down on a bench, I started to tell Abbey about it, and she stared out at the canal, and made the appropriate noises, and asked the right questions, and then I prepared myself to tell her the one thing that I've been avoiding telling you up until now.

Because we've been getting on, I feel, you and me. We had a rocky start where maybe I was a bit grumpy, but you know I had my reasons, and a lot of the time that was down to the *jezynowka*, and now, just as we're starting to properly click, I end up on a bench with an exciting girl and I get to the bit where I know you're not going to like me anymore.

And when I told her, she looked at me with pity in her eyes, but it was just so hard to tell who that pity was for.

THIRTEEN

Or "Who Said the World Was Fair?"

"Jesus, Jason, what's wrong?"

I hadn't known where to go so I'd come here.

"In, come in," she says, and I push past her in the narrow, dim doorway of the flat on Blackstock Road it'd taken so long to find in the dark.

"Where's your flatmate?" I say, noticing the Vietnamese for one, the single wineglass, the TV tuned to the news at ten.

"I don't have one?" she says, like a question, and for some reason I'm impressed, like she's grown up without me noticing, but we're both in our thirties and this is really the least we can expect by now.

"Do you want wine?" she says, as I lean away from her, suddenly paranoid she'll smell the liquor on my breath. "What's wrong with you?"

My eyes are glassy, maybe from the booze or the cold or the crying and I'm shaking slightly from the injustice of it all, the anger, and the sleet.

"You're freezing," she says. "What's going on?"

"I think I'm breaking down," I say, as honestly as I can, my smile a fake and my eyes welling up, and this has been a day of honesty all round. "I think I'm breaking down and I don't know how to cope."

And then it all comes out, and I can tell there are heavy, jagged, heaving sobs just below the surface, and she can tell, too, because she treats me with kid gloves and asks me if I want a baked potato or something, and this small kindness so innocently put near brings me to my knees.

I want the world back to where it was, before all this kicked off, before all the gin and whatever the opposite of a tonic is, but also I want to be treated like this, like she's treating me, not told I have to grow up or get past it or sort my life out.

Because that wasn't fair. I didn't ask for this to happen, I don't know why it's affected me the way it has, but it has, and why am I the only one who gets it?

But I'm not, am I? Because she gets it. Maybe because it's new, maybe because she doesn't have to deal with it day in and day out, but finally I feel I'm talking to someone who cares, someone who can see a different future for me, away from St. John's and Dylan and despair.

You cared, Sarah, but why did that have to stop so suddenly? Who turned that tap off? Who's ever been told they have to grow up and get on with their life and not felt patronized and misunderstood?

And I grab a tumbler and pour myself a giant glass of wine and she turns the heating up just for me, which again breaks my heart it's so nice, and I tell all, and she gets it, and soon it's past midnight and she finds the whiskey she forgot to give her dad for Christmas, and this is all so warming, so nourishing, so nurturing, and then my hand finds that it's nearer her leg than it should be and quietly I realize what a beautiful person she's always been, what a great friend, how right this all seems.

I leaned against the kitchen counter and immediately jolted away. I thought I'd just crushed a fly under the palm of my hand but it was only one of Dev's Sugar Puffs.

I laid it on the side of the sink, knowing he'd probably come looking for it later.

It had been a long night, and as the kettle clicked off and I reached for the teabags I thought about it some more.

It had been good to talk. She was a good listener.

And then I realized *I* was a *terrible* listener, as I'd forgotten whether she wanted sugar or not.

"No, ta!" she called out, from the bedroom, and perhaps a fifth of a nanosecond later Dev's door shot open and his head popped out, like a meerkat who might just have heard a lion.

"What was that?" he mouthed.

"That was Abbey," I mouthed back, and once the shock had dissipated he padded over to me in his pants.

"That is terrific news," he said, quietly. "Well done."

"Nothing happened," I said, and he made the face that implied he wished I hadn't told him that.

And nothing *had* happened. There had been no kiss. I got the feeling lots of boys hadn't kissed Abbey.

"We going out for breakfast, your treat?" he said. "Because I've got something to tell you if we are."

In the bedroom, my pillow folded and folded again behind her, and wearing a T-shirt she'd found on my floor, Abbey tapped about on the laptop.

"Your Facebook was still open," she said, sympathetically, pointing at the screen. "Do you want to know?"

"Know what?" I said, laying her tea down on the floor.

" 'Sarah is . . . ,' " she said, willing me to finish the status update myself. I shrugged.

" '. . . trying on dresses.' "

I didn't know what to say, so I just shrugged again.

Wedding dresses? Maternity dresses? Her status updates gave me information I didn't want and questions I couldn't answer.

For some reason I thought of Mum. She took our breakup badly. She'd have loved to be helping Sarah now, advising on a wedding dress, or helping select maternity dresses, planning for the day she became a mother-in-law and a grandmother again. Stephen had married Amy, and they Skyped when they could, but I knew Mum had had plans for me, too.

I guess parents are the hidden victims of a breakup. They watch their futures canceled, their wedding speeches disappear, their walks in the parks with the buggy to feed the ducks or have a picnic slide away thanks to one argument, or one misdeed, or one selfish act. And then they're forced to reset, and hope that in another month or another year or whenever you can, you'll meet someone and they can start to secretly hope and plan again. In the meantime, they stick by your side, because you're on their team, but the hope they had is gone, replaced by *Billy Elliot* or awkward dinners for three.

"Oh, Jason," my mum had said, sadly, on the phone, the night I told her. "What now? What happens now?"

It was all thanks to that stupid thing, just a stupid thing, but a thing nevertheless. And if I were a smaller man, I would blame it on the kid, a thuggish, bullish, angry kid at school. Racist, of course, but with no idea why, and angry at the world, but essentially nothing more than another mugger-in-waiting. And I sound bitter here, and I sound snobby again, but I ask you, how could I not, when Dylan did what he did? And when he did, I had to get out. I didn't do this lightly, and no matter what Sarah will tell you, I didn't take this decision quickly. She didn't get it. I couldn't believe it. This girl I'd been with for so long, she just didn't get it.

One day Dylan decided he wanted to kill a teacher.

I know—it sounds dramatic. But I know this because that's what the police reports said. He didn't plan to; he'd never seemed to want to before; he just *decided*. And so he'd gone home one lunchtime, to the estate opposite St. John's, over-looking the courtyard, and with his mate Spencer Gray he'd loaded up his brother's air rifle and taken aim at the classroom nearest the front, where I happened to be teaching year nine what a spinning jenny was.

It was just a flash at first. Just a tiny something that caught my eye, and the lightest of cracks. I'd carried on, but there it was again, like a firefly or the smallest, fastest shooting star across the room, in front of the posters about crop rotation and fallow fields.

I glanced at the window, saw the hole—small and round and perfect—and at first I remember thinking someone must've had a peashooter, but peas don't go through glass, and kids haven't used peashooters since the *Beano*, and then, though I couldn't quite believe it, I started to realize what was happening.

Forty policemen had turned up in the end. The kids had loved it, their faces pressed up against the glass, checking out the guns and body armor like it was *News 24* they were watch-ing, not real life on a gray North London afternoon. I'd managed to get everyone out, quietly and sensibly, and really, he'd never had any chance of hurting anyone, not with an air rifle that size, but nevertheless it was the intent, the thought, the sadness, the fury, and the hate that had the effect on me, and I went home that night and after I'd had my Findus Crispy Pancakes and a bottle of Rioja it hit me. And I cried. And not just cried, but bawled like a baby, until I shook, and spluttered, and couldn't catch my breath again.

Sarah had been so sympathetic at first, and full of warmth. She'd arranged the rest of the week off work, and I took a few days, too, but the shock ate up the hours before I knew where they'd gone. I became guarded and suspicious and nervous. I wanted to stay in, safe, soothed by the sounds of *Come Dine with Me* or *Watchdog* or anything that represented normality. After a while, perhaps naturally, Sarah became less sympathetic.

"For God's sake, he's just a kid," she'd said one evening, as we prepared to argue for the third or fourth or fifth time that day. "He didn't know what he was doing! It was just some tiny air rifle!"

I can see her frustrations now. I couldn't at the time. I was so engulfed in myself, in me the victim. And maybe she was just trying to do what her mother was always suggesting: get me to snap out of it. But you can't just snap out of something like that. I was in charge that day. I was the teacher Dylan had chosen. Yes, only because I happened to be in that room opposite that estate at that time, but it was precisely the randomness that scared me so, and proved the world to be more dangerous than I'd thought.

And I was angry. I was angry at Dylan, angry at the world, angry at Sarah for her disappointment in me as a man, whether that was true or not. The fact is, my life changed when Dylan cocked that rifle. I guess in some ways, he *did* kill a teacher that day. He certainly killed a relationship.

But no.

No, I'll take the blame for that one.

"So," said Abbey, interrupting my thoughts, "I deleted her."

"Hmm?" I said.

"I deleted her. It's not fair of her. She knows you can read this stuff and it must hurt, so I deleted her from your whole social network."

I smiled, thinking she was joking, because she did those little finger quotes when she said "social network," but she just took a sip of her tea and carried on clicking around.

"You ... sorry, you did what?"

She looked up at me, innocently, and shrugged.

"It's for the best. Trust me."

Trust her? I hardly *knew* her.

"Abbey, why the hell would you do that?"

I was angry now.

"You know *nothing* about me, not *really*. How can I trust you on this? You never met Sarah, you don't know what you're on about, and now you come round and you delete her? She'll know! She'll *see* I've deleted her!"

I couldn't believe this.

"Do you have any idea how this looks? You can't just mess about with someone's life like this. You can't just come in here and use my computer and make me look like a moron. I was just making things *okay* with her again, and now this."

I'm a polite man, even when riled, and it's horrible to make someone feel horrible, but right now Abbey needed to know she was out of line. What, so we have a couple of nice meet-ups, and now she feels she can meddle? Now she feels she can fucking *meddle*?

"You need to be told, Abbey, and—"

"Jason. You don't need this."

I stopped in my tracks. She stared at me.

You don't need this. Four such easy words, for her.

"You need to let go. You messed it up, but if you don't let go, you'll never be able to do anything good again. You're a catch, in your own way, Jason, but you're damaged goods. And you can't let that one thing define you. You can't have these constant reminders. 'Sarah is married, Sarah's having fun, Sarah doesn't need you anymore.' You need to reset, and recharge, and then you can have her in your life again maybe, but you'll have changed to what you need to be."

I don't know if it was what she was saying, or just the way she was saying it, but she was making sense, and though my eyes revealed nothing, I was calming. Maybe I just needed someone else to make this decision for me. It's possible sometimes you just do.

And then, the strangest thing: Abbey leaned close to me. So close I felt her breath on my face and could smell her shampoo and feel her hand graze my leg and it was the single sexiest thing in the world, this girl right next to me, in my T-shirt, so close and so lovely and so here.

And she kissed me. Tenderly and quietly, she kissed me.

She leaned back, brushed her fringe away, smiled at the window, then back at me.

"I just want to be friends," she said.

I blinked.

"Eh?"

"I'm not what you need."

"But you kissed me. Or, we kissed. But you kissed me."

"I just wanted to get that out of the way because otherwise we'd both have been thinking about it and it's not the way ahead for either of us."

I blinked again.

"Eh?"

"It's muuuch better this way," she said, grabbing a pillow and cuddling it, creating a barrier. "And anyway, I didn't actually delete her." She smiled.

"Sorry, what?"

"I didn't actually delete her. That'd be mental. You can't just go round people's houses deleting stuff for them."

"That's what *I* said!"

"Well, it's a bit insulting that you'd think I would. But now you've realized that you *can*, that it's allowed, that it's actually possible, well, you *should*."

I looked at the laptop.

"So!" said Dev, at the café down the road. "I've cracked it!"

We'd taken Abbey out for Saturday morning breakfast. I was still confused. I'd never met someone whose mind could move so quickly from one thing to the other. People I knew dwelled on things. They sat on them and nurtured their thoughts, and thought "impulsive" was a deodorant. But it was invigorating, somehow.

Matt was on his way over on his bike. Dev wanted to offer him some part-time work at the shop, partly, he'd said, getting ready to go out, "because I feel I can inspire Matt into fulfilling his potential." I was impressed. I hadn't realized the shop was in a position to take people on. Or that Dev was a man who could inspire, considering I knew for a fact he was wearing his *Pokémon* pants today.

"You've cracked what?" said Abbey, and we all fell silent as Pamela the waitress brought our food out. I caught Dev's eye as he studiously avoided looking at her, but what was that I caught? Had she looked at him for just a second longer than she needed to? Did she have a smile ready, just in case he said another stock Polish phrase to try out? Dev pretended to wipe a difficult mark off the table, while Pamela placed our cutlery on the table and glided off.

"I'm playing the long game," said Dev, conspiratorially. "Make her miss me."

"It will definitely work," said Abbey. "So what's this thing? What've you cracked?"

"The code. The theme. We're looking for a theme within the chaos of those photos."

"I'm not," I said. "I'm just looking for The Girl. So I can give her her photos back and have achieved something with my year."

"Is that what this is about?" said Abbey, smiling. "Some men climb mountains to make their mark, others swim the seas, but Jason Priestley hands in lost property."

"So what's the theme?" I asked. "What unites this woman's photos? And remember, this better lead me straight to her. I imagine, like your Pamela strategy, this proposal will be foolproof."

Dev took a deep breath, then looked to Abbey.

"Can this odd woman be trusted?" he said, pointing at her.

"No," I said.

"Then I shall tell you anyway. The girl in the photos is a vampire."

He sat back in his chair, in a there-I-said-it way. I stuck my bottom lip out and nodded, as if yes, I'd had my suspicions, too.

"Or not a *vampire*, exactly, but an obsessive. Some kind of gothic obsessive. They're dangerous, the gothic obsessives."

I held one of the pictures up. Dev had brought them out with us for his big announcement.

"She doesn't look like that much of a gothic obsessive," I said, pointing out her happy smile and blond hair and summery dress and total lack of gothic obsession.

"Well, that's the typical reaction she's probably used to from a 'Daywalker.'"

"Why do you think she's a vampire, Dev?" said Abbey, very seriously.

"The theme that's developing. Think about it. She goes to graveyards."

"She goes to *graveyards*?"

"Highgate Cemetery," I said, defensively, as if I knew her. "It's a tourist destination."

"Yes, but a tourist destination known for its vampires. The Vampire King himself lives there—you told me! Plus, they reckon Bram Stoker wrote *Dracula* after a visit to Highgate."

"Yeah, but I'm not sure we can take that as—"

"Whitby. Then there's *Whitby*."

"What about Whitby?"

"That's where Bram Stoker *set* Dracula! Don't you see? She's a Dracula nut! A *Dracunut*!"

"So how do you explain the scallops?" I said. "Did Dracula eat scallops?"

" 'Scallop' sounds a bit like 'scalp'?" offered Abbey.

"Dracula didn't scalp people. And he didn't club seals either, before you mention that factory."

"I dunno, Jase," said Dev. "Vampires are obsessed with death, whether human or aquatic."

"Look," I said, quite sternly now, because I was pretty sure this girl, my girl, The Girl, was not a vampire, "these are just random photos, taken at random times. They're not going to lead me right to The Girl, just as they're not going to give us some deep insight into her life. And I've done what I can with them. But Abbey taught me something good today. About fresh starts, and wiping the slate clean. And maybe that's what I need to do here. Just forget about it. Concentrate on my work."

But no one was listening, because Abbey looked lost in concentration. She held up a photo.

"Hey," she said. "*Hey!*"

We were outside the Rio Cinema in Dalston.

"I bet you it's bloody *Dracula* season!" Dev had kept saying, as the three of us rode the bus.

In actual fact, it was Algerian cinema season, so the tall red letters slotted into the sign said, and outside, a roadsweeper clattered a tin can down the street with his brush, oblivious, as we stood and stared.

"You know," said Abbey, a light wind whipping her fringe, "the only thing saving you from being a couple of oddball loons illegally stalking a girl is the fact that one of you is *in* one of the photos. If you weren't, I wouldn't be here. Even though I insisted we come."

"It's fate," said Dev, trying to look all mysterious, like a poet.

"It *is* fate, isn't it?" she said. "Except that, of course, fate doesn't exist. Reasons exist. And reasons are what move us to act. You've got reasons to find this girl. But there's nothing to say you will."

"How do you mean?"

"You like her. You had that moment. You thought there was something there. You found yourself in one of her snaps. All good reasons to find her. And you've got an excuse, too, because you're just being a good Samaritan. On the other hand, you've got reasons not to find her."

"And they are?"

"You're a mess. You lost the girl you hoped would be The One because you suspected she might not be The One, then she turned out to be someone else's one. He snagged her, knocked her up, and you're now living next to a brothel with Dev, totally Oneless. No offense, Dev."

"It's not a brothel," said Dev, quietly.

"So which reasons do you follow up? Because fate doesn't exist; not predetermined fate, anyway. Though I suppose if you do nothing, your fate will be just to sit in your little brothel-flat, in your pants, for ever and ever amen, and that'll be your fault. You *choose* which reasons to follow."

"At least you don't think it's weird."

"Oh, it's totally weird. No, I mean it's borderline stalking, and also, developing someone else's camera film must be illegal somehow, mustn't it? But these are your choices, and I reserve judgment until I find out what happens."

I looked at Dev, gave him a told-you-so. He wandered up to one of the posters to have a look.

There had been an auctioneer's shop here on Kingsland Road in the old days. In the seventies or eighties the Art Deco cinema that took its place became the Rio, in the way that I suppose a lot of places became known as the Rio around then, when Rio was at the height of its cool, dancing on the Seine. It stuck with the fad, though, as others don't. Millennium Cabs down the road was already changing its name to Hackney Comfort Cabs now that the buzz of partying like it wasn't 1999 anymore had faded slightly. Millennium Fried Chicken stood derelict and ashamed to its right, like an ugly friend on a night out with a WAG. My heart had sunk when I saw it—the cinema, not the chicken shop—because this, well, this was undeniably a *date* venue.

Where had I taken Sarah, when I'd last taken her to the cinema? What had we seen? I think it was *Iron Man 2*. We'd had an argument on the way there, and I'd annoyed her by complaining about the popcorn being nearly as much as the tickets, and we'd sat, barely speaking, in a Nando's afterward, hardly able to muster up the enthusiasm to comment when a drunk outside kicked a police van and was wrestled to the ground.

It wouldn't have been like that for The Girl. This was the glorious Rio, for a start—not the one-size-fits-all Vue in the N1 Centre just above HMV. This was classy. Classic. He—the man, Chunk, or whatever his name is—probably picked her up in that car of his—what was it again? A Vegas?—and brought elaborate cocktails with him in an antique silver hipflask, and arranged a special screening of his favorite Algerian film, and had the whole place just for them, and laid out a picnic blanket in the rich blue family tartan so they could lie down and watch it together, lit by neon. He'd have taken her out afterward, to a laid-back underground bar, probably French, probably members-only, where the good-looking barstaff would have cheered when he walked in, and the jazz trio in the corner started up a song in his honor. Bright, attractive women would have waved at him, in a way that was impressive but non-threatening to her, and he would have explained that they ran the New York gallery that's trying to get him to showcase his work there, or that they were merely tenants in his portfolio of Thames-side loft apartments with views of Big Ben, or that he met them during his time in Haiti treating children with Médecins Sans Frontières. And after telling her any one of those three specific things, he would have stared off into the middle distance looking tortured and intense and unreachable, his finger circling the rim of his beautifully chosen devil-red Romanée Conte, and The Girl would have fallen even more deeply in love with him.

Click.

I turned to see Abbey with my disposable.

"Good shot," she said, wrinkling her nose. "You looked moody."

She wound the film forward. How many was that we'd taken now? Four? Five?

"Did I look intense? Tortured?"

"Just a bit bad-tempered."

"Yeah, but girls love that."

She laughed, then frowned.

"Hey," she said. "I tried to match the shot, yeah? Make yours look like hers. And I got that poster in the background."

I looked over.

"So?"

"So where's *her* photo?"

I got it out, handed it over. Abbey smiled.

"See there? Over her shoulder? That film poster? If we can find out when that poster was up, we can find out when she was here . . ."

Before I knew what was happening, she'd dashed off, through the blue double doors of the Rio. Dev sidled up to me.

"Witch."

"What?"

"She's a witch. Been checking the posters. One of them's about a witch. Witches and vampires probably mix. The woman's obsessed. Where's Abbey?"

"Just checking something," I said.

Dev's phoned beeped.

Where the hell are you two? read the text.

We looked at each other.

"Probably should've told Matt we were here," said Dev.

"A month!" said Abbey, sizing up the pins. "You're only a month behind. You're close enough to *touch* her."

She scuttled forward, the bowling ball swinging wildly in her hand, and dropped it heavily in front of her.

"Unlucky!" said Dev, watching it thunk into the gutter.

"Just one month," she said, again. "It's as if these photos are like a vapor trail. She's left these memories behind and you're finding them just in time, just as they fade. You know? She thinks they're gone, these memories, but you found the camera. You're keeping them alive!"

"Fate!" said Dev, picking up his ball. "Fate."

It was quite tiring hanging out with Abbey. We were at

Bloomsbury Bowl, in the basement of the Tavistock Hotel, a stone's throw from the museums that Abbey had decided she wanted to go and see but, once there, decided she didn't. The same museums we'd traveled across town to see after she'd taken us to Spitalfields to buy a dress from an up-and-coming designer that, once she'd actually seen it, she decided was "too waxy" and didn't want.

"And that's just the cinema one that was a month ago. Any of the pictures taken *after* that were more recent. It's like they were all leading up to the picture *you're* in."

I tried to make an unimpressed face, like I just wasn't that bothered, but the way Abbey talked about it excited me. This was a girl's point of view. More crucially, it wasn't Dev's.

"Plus," she said, quickly, "that was *not* a date movie he took her to. It was about Vietnamese death camps. Why would he take her on a date to learn about Vietnamese death camps?"

To our left, a hen party gearing up for a big night spilled, giggling, from a karaoke booth, pushing one another's shoulders, flushed from Pinot and laughter.

"Maybe they were seeing another film," I said, though why I wanted this to be the case I'm not sure.

"If indeed it was *him* that took her there!" said Abbey. "You can only see her in the picture."

"It was him," I said. "Someone had to have taken it. And the only other person who ever features in the photos is him."

"No," said Abbey. "*You* feature. The only other people who feature are him . . . and *you*."

She held up her hands.

"The past . . . and the future."

Dev sat down sheepishly. We looked up to see his ball moving very slowly down the gutter.

"Unlucky," said Abbey.

Dev's phone beeped again.

"Shit," he said. "Forgot to tell Matt we'd moved on."

"Well, cheers, boys," said Matt, "for a cracking tour of London. I saw the café, the market, the outside of some bloody great museum, and now this place, fifty bloody feet from the café."

He pointed around. We were back in Power Up! Dev had left Pawel in charge of the shop that morning, and fully expected to come back to find packs of Saturday afternoon traffic.

"Nobody!" said Pawel. "Nobody want your little games."

"They're not little games, Pawel. The last *Call of Duty* had a multimillion-dollar budget and Kiefer Sutherland attached as voice talent, so—lesson learned, I think."

"Whatevs," said Pawel, which I can only assume he'd learned from the 4 p.m. school crowd that filled up his shop for ten minutes every day and cost him hundreds a year in nicked Twixes and lifted Lilts. Dev opened his paper and bit into a *krokiety* bap.

"So what's the story with that girl?" asked Matt.

Abbey had run off, down the road, in search of a cigar.

"Abbey?"

"Why's she getting a cigar for a start?"

"She just said she fancied a cigar and that we should all have a cigar. She's—you know—an art student."

Matt nodded a nod of understanding and rolled the words "art student" around in his mouth.

"Yeah, I see them sometimes, art students. Wearing big glasses. Saw a bunch of them recently down the Wimpy all wearing false mustaches. Dunno why. So why's she hanging around with you two?"

"Why wouldn't she?" I said, a little defensively, but then: "Aside from the fact that she's ten years younger than us and infinitely cooler. I mean, you're *both* those things, too, apart from the second one."

Matt laughed. It was good when Matt laughed. We were on the way to becoming proper friends. There was still that slight frost between us whenever we'd first meet; things needed to thaw before he forgot I wasn't his teacher and he'd stopped being my pupil. But laughing was good.

"All I'm saying," he said, trying to choose his words carefully, but failing, "is are you, like, going out with her?"

"No," I said, quickly, and embarrassed. "No, we're just friends."

The door opened. A customer walked in. We turned to stare at him and he faltered slightly as he wondered whether he'd interrupted something. Dev lowered his *Daily Star* in surprise. The customer closed the door gently behind him as he left.

"'We Just Clicked!'" said Dev, and Matt and I turned round.

"There's a story here," he said, "about a bloke who found a camera."

This piqued my interest.

"He found a camera, a digital one, when he was on holiday, and he looked at the photos and he put them on Facebook. The bloke whose camera it was got recognized by some friend-of-a-friend and he got his camera back. Nice."

"Six degrees of separation," I said, feeling clever.

"Six what?" said Matt.

"Everyone's connected to everyone," I said.

The bell above the door tinkled again, but I didn't bother looking round this time, because this sometimes happened with Dev; he was an intimidating force on the North London videogames scene, so customers often had to take a run-up at walking in.

"You can pick anyone in the world, and I'll know someone who'll know someone who knows someone, until eventually you find them. They say you can do it in six little steps. I've never tried it, because why would I, but it's a thought, isn't it?"

But Dev wasn't looking at me in a way that suggested he was impressed. Dev was looking at me in a way that suggested he was scared of what was about to happen next.

"Hello, Jason."

I turned around.

"Hi, Sarah," I heard myself say.

It was the first time I'd seen her in . . . God, how long had it been? She was wearing clothes I hadn't seen before. Still tanned and healthy from the Andorra. There it was. The ring. A sign of her permanent commitment to Gary, the wild man of Stevenage. My eyes flicked to her belly: not showing yet, not quite. Oh. She'd bought a new watchstrap. Funny, the things you take in when you see an ex.

"Who are you trying to find?" she said, making it sound light and airy and like maybe she could help.

"Nobody," I said. "You know. Somebody. A customer. Of Dev's."

"You're lying," she said, smiling.

"I'm *not* lying," I said, churlishly, not understanding why she always thought I was lying these days, even though I was. And then, maybe because I was so used to feeling that way, the shame came pouring back; the embarrassment and the *shame*. The shame was the worst. The guilt, strangely, was second, but always there, always locked at the back of my throat and deep in my chest for all the days I hadn't told her, but the shame second, all-encompassing and rich and thorough.

Because the thing I hadn't wanted to tell you—the thing I think you already know—is that about one month after Dylan and his air rifle, after about one month of near-constant support from Sarah, of hugs and tea, and tears and blackness from me, I repaid her for the one time she fell down, the one time she told me off, the one time she thought I should snap out of it, by getting angry and getting drunk and going out and sleeping with someone else. Sleeping, in fact, with Zoe.

Yeah.

You see?

It's worse now it's Zoe.

We stood, staring at each other, not quite sure what to say next, when in walked Abbey, beaming, and holding four cigars.

"Oh," said Sarah. "And you must be the Russian prostitute."

FOURTEEN

Or "Southeast City Window"

I think there's something nice about not knowing. There's plenty of stuff I don't know. And plenty of stuff I do that I'd rather I didn't. But not knowing—and not knowing you don't know—is something else. It frees up the mind. It means you can project.

That's what I'd been doing with The Girl, of course. This projecting. Finding meaning where perhaps there was none, basing it all on so little: a whip-quick half-smile on a dark night on Charlotte Street. But that was better than reality. Because this, right now, sitting in stony silence outside the café down the road with Sarah, her fiddling with a spoon, me waiting for our coffees to arrive: *this* was reality.

The guys had fallen into silence, too, when Sarah had walked into the shop. They'd exchanged pleasantries, Dev had given her a hug, but they knew this wasn't a social visit. This was an antisocial visit.

"So . . . ," she said, and then Pamela was upon us, splashing the coffees down next to a silver pot in which a thousand packets of sugar were suffocating each other for space.

"Do you think we could get some extra sugar?" I said, deadpan, and Sarah smiled.

"Yes," said Pamela. "No friend today?"

Dev would be thrilled. The long game was working!

"No, he's actually busy with some humanitarian work right now," I said.

I made a mental note to tell him he was now a humanitarian. He'd pretended to be harder things in the past. A priest. A commercial airline pilot. An Indian prince. Pamela shrugged and walked off.

"Dev's latest crush?" said Sarah, when Pamela was out of earshot.

"Pamela."

"He likes girls in uniform."

"Is a pinny a uniform?"

Inside the café, Pamela's boss was shouting at her. We paused for a microsecond, then continued nonplussed.

"Remember the time he was after that other girl?"

"You're going to have to be more specific than that," I said, raising my eyebrows. "*Much* more specific."

I guess talking about Dev was easier than talking about us, but then so was talking about anything else, including the rise of national socialism, or swingball.

"You know the one," she said, pointing her spoon at me. "The one he said was The One."

Oh. Well, that was different. There'd only ever been one The One. They'd met at an indie night at the Garage on High-bury Corner, when we could still go to indie nights at the Garage without looking like we were someone's dad waiting to pick them up. Dev had wooed her, pined for her, missed her when she wasn't around, picked her dry cleaning up for her, dropped her dry cleaning off for her, learned to cook her favorite dish in case she ever popped round, though she never would, and then after three weeks it turned out she still didn't even know his surname. He was crushed. I think that's why he had the business cards printed.

Sarah smiled as she remembered something.

"I always remember the night after, he said—"

"Yes. That was amazing. 'You can say what you like about love, but you can't say it's good.'"

"And we spent the whole evening giving him examples of people who'd disagree. Operas written in the name of love, paintings painted, mountains climbed, countries conquered."

"The defining works of Phil Collins, Elvis Costello, and Billy Joel, little-bitty-insects named things in Latin for love, the whole point of Heart FM."

"And still he was like, 'Okay, leave it with me, I'll think on.'"

A chuckle and a comfortable pause. The type Sarah used to say she liked best. These pauses weren't ours anymore, though. They were there just to be filled.

"And how's Gary?" I said, skirting around.

"Gary is great."

"That's great."

"He's great."

"Great."

"He's out looking for a new car."

"That's terrific news."

"The Golf started to play up, and I can't drive his Lexus, and—"

"People carrier. You'll need a people carrier soon."

I pointed at her belly. She bit her lip and nodded.

"Why are you here, Sarah? I've said sorry, and I talked to Gary, and—"

"I wanted to see you face-to-face. I don't know why you're acting the way you've been acting. The drunk messages on our photos I'm starting to understand, because I should have told you first, or not first, exactly, but at the same time. But this isn't my fault. This is your fault."

I stared at my coffee.

"We both have new beginnings. Let's be grateful for that. And who knows how long we'd have lasted anyway?"

She smiled and sipped her coffee, but all I could think was, What? *What?!*

"What do you mean, who knows how long we'd have lasted? I made a mistake, I was in a horrible place you didn't understand. You *know* this."

"It was stale anyway, Jason. Sometimes things just go stale. I used to annoy the hell out of you, and you certainly annoyed the hell out of me."

"You didn't," I said. "You were perfect."

"You hated the way I always wanted to be early for things. You hated the way I had to lock and unlock and lock the door whenever we left the house, just so I knew it was locked."

"These are so trivial!" I said, but really I wanted to shout it. There was the flip between sadness and anger in my stomach, and I didn't know which would win. "You don't give up on someone because they make sure the house is locked!"

"They're tiny things, but they mean something bigger. You're only remembering the positives. You doing what you did was something we needed. It was a great clarifier, Jase."

"I didn't want anything clarified, though," I said.

"It took you betraying me to realize there was nothing much there for either of us to betray anymore."

"Don't rewrite the past, Sarah," I said, because this was horrible; this was like her revenge. At least let me think I'd messed up something good; don't make me think there was never anything there.

"The problem with you, Jase, is that you're in love with the *idea* of being in love."

"Oh, you got that from a film. That's just something people say. And what's wrong with that anyway? A little romance in life?"

"It's fine, but you also need structure. You need reliability. You were always talking about leaving your job and doing God knows what. You never talked about marriage, or kids, or—"

"That's such a cliché! We're not those people—those people are on TV! You're being the sensible woman and making me out to be the childish man! This isn't *Doc Martin*! I'm not Gary or Tony and you're not Deborah or the one who lived upstairs!"

Annoyingly, I was kind of proving her point.

"Life isn't a series of Martin Clunes references," she said, sitting back, and that would have made me laugh ordinarily, but this was just too important.

"Look, all I mean is, you're completely making this sound like something it wasn't. And I suppose kids and marriage is what Gary opened up with on your very first date, is it? Great tactic. At the Hilton or Wagamama or wherever it was? No moonlit walk for you two, then? No *story* to look back on?"

"The last thing a relationship needs is a story. A story is just a story. Who cares how people met? Literally no one."

"I care."

"Literally just *you*, then. We'd been together four years when we split, Jase. I was thirty. My priorities changed. Haven't yours?"

I thought about it. What were my priorities? I racked my brains. I must have some. But all I could think of was that I needed to get some bread and a pint of milk, plus the bath could really do with some new sealant round the tiles.

"Then when I saw you'd . . . 'deleted me,' " said Sarah.

She made little finger quotes. I frowned.

"What do you mean?"

"It's such a childish thing. Me, I mean; I'm being childish. We're not teenagers. We're not going to argue about MySpace or Facebook or any of that. You're free to delete or unfollow whoever you want, and—"

Abbey. Abbey must've done it. She must've left it up to me and then when I finally chickened out and made an excuse about making a toastie, she must've deleted her from my account.

"Thing is, I actually respect you for doing it. One of us needed to. You need space; you need to do what I did and start again. It's just . . . it hurt a bit. Like you were shutting me out."

Good, I thought.

I'm pleased that it hurt.

And I felt cheered. Even though it was the most selfish thing in the world, it felt good to have hurt her, to have made some progress, to have chipped away at something, because it meant that she cared, somewhere; that I still mattered. I had hurt her once already in our relationship, and done it badly. And now here I was celebrating having done it again, celebrating the most minute and childish victory.

And that was when I realized that this is not how someone should behave. And that this selfish victory was pathetic, and hollow, and meaningless.

"I didn't delete you," I said, smally. "My friend did. The Russian prostitute."

She brightened, ever so slightly, but I noticed, because I always noticed the smallest things about Sarah.

"I'd thought about it," I admitted. "Not out of spite, but because it's hard to watch you starting again, when I'm living with Dev above a shop."

A council lorry ground by. We held the rims of our cups to the table as the ground shook and the air turned to diesel.

"But I couldn't. And I wouldn't. We share a history, and I'm all about looking forward, that's what I've decided to do. But what's the point in abandoning the past? It'd be a waste, no?"

She smiled.

Opened her handbag.

Got out an envelope and slid it across the table.

"I'd love it if you'd consider this," she said, her smile half hope, half apology.

Pamela strode out and dropped another thousand packets of sugar on the table.

Dev and I dropped Abbey off at Victoria to catch the six o'clock to Brighton.

"What are you guys doing next Friday?" she said.

"Dunno," I said.

"I'll call you," she said, kissing us both on the cheeks and backing away, saluting us with an unlit cigar.

"She is totally hot for us," said Dev, watching her go. "By the way, I told her I have a degree in sculpture. If you could remember that, that would really help me out."

"Right. To Charlotte Street," I said. But not for why you think.

"You came!" said Clem, clutching his beer tightly. He'd scratched off the label almost entirely, his nerves having taken full control of his fingers.

"It was pick of the day in *London Now*," I said. "We *had* to come."

"Don't judge me too harshly," he said, winking. "It's only my third giggle."

Clem had started calling his comedy gigs "giggles." I hoped it wasn't typical of his set, but I had a feeling it might be.

"This is Dev, my flatmate," I said.

"What's Dev short for?" said Clem, and Dev was about to tell him, but then Clem said, "Because he's got little legs!"

Dev stared at him. Clem tried to explain.

"What's Dev short for? He's got little legs."

He burst out laughing and made a whoosh sound to imply it'd gone over Dev's head, which I suppose, if he were that short, it would've.

We stood at the back of Chucklehead, in a part-time disco maybe sixty feet from Percy Passage, and took in the scene. A hen party in the front row, already drunk and rowdy at just gone half seven, the bride-to-be at the center of a mass of pink wings and halos. A group of foreign students behind them, victims of a last-minute flyering campaign, lured in by promises of the night of their lives and a genuine London experience. A middle-aged couple behind them, possibly fooled by badly photocopied photos of Jimmy Carr and Michael McIntyre, neither of whom, I would wager, had ever turned up to ply his trade at the Chucklehead, when Wembley or the O2 at least had a backstage area and free water.

By the bar, Clem was ingratiating himself with the other comics, trying to talk about the skill and craft of joke writing while they attempted to get into the right headspace to get the night started and over with as soon as possible, not 100 percent keen on taking advice from this middle-aged two-gig open spot.

"So what do you think the story is with Abbey?" said Dev, nudging me.

"How do you mean?"

"Why's she so keen to spend her Friday and Saturday with us? Why does she want to meet up next week?"

"I think she finds us charming."

Dev laughed.

It *was* a little ludicrous, I thought.

"She'll get bored," Dev said. "They always do. She seems like a free spirit, and they flit about a lot, don't they? They sort of collect friends and stick them into groups: 'These are my music friends. These are my arty friends. These are my thirtysomething lady-challenged should-really-have-settled-down-by-now friends from gritty North London. *They* eat in *cafés*!'"

"I dunno. She helped. She sort of helped with Sarah. Forced the issue, made us talk openly about things."

"And is she—"

"I don't know if she has a boyfriend. You should ask her."

"If I ask her, she'll say yes. It's better not to know. That way you're always in with a chance. Even if they're with their husbands, and you've just watched them take their vows, *never* ask them if they're married. *Totally* ruins your chances."

And then the compère was on the stage to introduce the giggle, and Clem started to scratch off his second label of the night.

"Ohhh, yes," said Clem, pushing through the double doors of the club and out onto the street, cleverly trying to be the dog from that advert. "Ohhh, *yes*."

He half-punched the air as Dev and I followed him outside, wondering what to say.

"You certainly seemed to be having fun up there," said Dev, and I was annoyed, because that was precisely the level of non-commitment I wanted to have. "How do *you* feel it went?"

"Me? Three words: *Worst* Great Western! You heard the response!"

We just smiled. We *had* heard it, but mainly we had heard it as a shuffle, or cough.

"I need a drink!" said Clem, waving his hands in front of himself like he'd had simply the most *unbelievable* evening.

"Thing about the travelcard stuff," said Clem, as we sat, staring at our cocktails, "is that it's *just* inclusive enough. Everyone's seen a travelcard; everyone's bought a travelcard. So when I say, 'This travelcard says I can get to King's Cross by "any route permitted,"' and then I say, 'so I can go via the *moon*, can I?,' it gets a big laugh, because everyone's seen a travelcard, but no one's thought of going to the moon with one."

We were ten minutes into Clem's dissection of a five-minute set, and we were still on the first joke. Dev had zoned out the second Clem had started speaking, staring around the bar of the Charlotte Street Hotel: Clem's little treat to thank us for our support. I don't think he'd realized that his little treat would cost him about £30 a drink. He'd tried haggling with the barman but that hadn't worked, so now he was going to make us work for our cocktails.

"If you had to pinpoint a favorite moment," he said, "what would that be? I'm just interested."

"Um . . ." I said, pretending to think. The windows were open and, outside, the pavements filled with tables and chatter and wine. An elegantly dressed doorman fiddled with his cuffs, pretending he wasn't waiting for the end of his shift, while Dev stared at a group of girls, all straightened hair and Louboutin shoes, their BlackBerry Pearls forming a caravan around three Sauv Blancs and two vodka limes, as if to say, "Yes, we are high-powered and successful and work-oriented, but here on Charlotte Street we play hard, too."

"Because my favorite moment," said Clem, oblivious to the fact that no one had replied, "was probably that ad-lib, where the guy dropped the glass, and I said, 'Careful, now!'"

"That *was* a good bit," I said, encouragingly, and Dev seemed surprised that someone else was talking.

"Oh, what am I doing?" said Clem, mock-slapping his forehead. "Tonight's not all about me. What were *your* favorite bits?"

"You just asked that, didn't you?" said Dev.

"But you didn't answer," said Clem.

"I liked the ad-lib," said Dev.

"But that's what I said," said Clem.

"Well, there you go," said Dev, and Clem looked grumpy.

"I should head off anyway," said Clem. "Need to work on my material. Big giggle at the Smile High Club next week. Need to nail it. Then the aim is corporates. That's where the money is."

He drained his cocktail and banged the glass down on the table.

" 'Cocktail' is a funny word, isn't it, considering it contains neither?"

I forced a laugh and he smiled, broadly.

"Well, *that's* going in the set!" he said, and then, as I worked out what my reaction should be, he seemed to have spotted someone at the bar.

"Oh, was your brother at the giggle?" he said. "Kept that quiet!"

"Who?" I said.

"Your brother. Isn't that your brother at the bar?"

"Jase hasn't got a brother," said Dev.

I turned to look.

"I never forget a face," said Clem. "Or a watch. Or a *watch*face!"

The man he meant was deciding which beer to go for. He was asking questions and tapping the pumps. And then he half turned, and . . . *oh* . . .

"Not that I can see his watch now, of course," said Clem. "But I could in that photo you had."

I froze.

People sometimes say they froze, but they don't mean it like I mean it. I froze, good and proper, because it was him. He was here. He was here in this bar.

"What does he do again?" asked Clem. "What does he do, your brother?"

"Yes," said Dev, now realizing, now recognizing, now smiling. "What does your brother do?"

"Chiropractor," I said, quietly reaching for the memory of whatever I'd told Clem that day.

"I thought he was an orthodontist?"

"He dabbles."

"And his wife has yellow hair?"

"All over her head."

"Right. Well, anyway," said Clem, as I stared on, and he started to say something about getting his things together and wondering if he should get the bus or the tube or maybe splash out on a taxi, but I'd stopped listening, because here he was— the man, Chunk, the chunky watch man, and maybe that meant that *she* would be here, too.

I suppose it made sense I'd bump into him here. They both must work around Charlotte Street. He's well-to-do, with his Alaska flat and his watch and his tan and his special-edition car. Makes sense he'd be schmoozing at the Charlotte Street Hotel, where you can either buy a drink or pay your rent. He's probably wooing a client, sealing a deal.

My eyes scanned the room again. Was she here? Was she here, too?

And then something strange happened. I began to wish that she wouldn't be. It swept over me and stayed there, this feeling of absolutely not wanting her to be here. I would *hate* it if she were here, in fact.

I didn't feel ready, for one thing, though my eyes scanned the room, just in case. I hadn't had a haircut, and I didn't like what I was wearing, and I felt like a self-conscious teenage girl dressed for church and surprised by the news she might be about to meet that guy from a boyband who happens to be a friend-of-a-friend of her parents.

Second: if she *was* here, in this ground-floor bar on Charlotte Street, in among the BlackBerry Pearls and the shiny hair and the Louboutins, that meant she was here with *him*. And if she was here with him, there's no way she could ever be here with me.

And third (God, there was a *third*!): if she was here with him, and not here with me, that would be it. It would be over. The romance and mystery and intrigue of stealing a girl's photographs and then using them to try to stalk her—that classic Mills & Boon plotline—would be over for good.

I studied the man for as long as I could without feeling like I might be noticed. Well-cut classic navy-blue suit, light blue shirt, silk tie. Shiny shoes, but with silver buckles. I felt glad about that. I'm not sure I could love any girl that loved a guy with buckles on his shoes. He was built well, which makes me feel better than saying he was well built, and his hair was longer at the back than it looked on the photos.

He was wearing no wedding ring.

"You should go up and talk to him," said Dev. "Find something out about him. Ask him if he's got a girlfriend."

"You think I should walk up to this stranger in a bar and ask him if he's got a girlfriend?"

"Not straightaway, no. Ask him what football team he supports, something manly, and *then* ask him if he's got a girlfriend."

"So I should walk up to a man in a bar, ask him what team he supports, and then say, 'Do you have a girlfriend?'"

"You are deliberately trying to make this sound like a gay thing."

I looked over at him again, drinking his half of Peroni, and laughing with another man. Colleague? Friend? Whoever he was, he was leaning up against the bar, like he belonged here, like the Charlotte Street Hotel was his, and this was his party, full of strangers he'd allowed to drop by.

Our plan had been to drink these and then slope off to the Newman Arms for a couple among our own kind, but now Dev looked excited.

"I'm going to go up if you don't," he said. "He must work round here, and either she was visiting him when you kept seeing her, or she works here, too. They might just be colleagues."

"Do not go up," I said, fixing him with a very serious look indeed. "This is not about him, it's about her, and she's not here."

But what I was really afraid of was Dev striking up a conversation with the man, explaining the photos, saying what a terrific coincidence this is, and then somehow agreeing to hand them over to him. Because then I would be robbed. Robbed of the chance. Robbed of the moment. The moment I craved. The moment I hadn't told him I felt could be the start of something. The beginning of a story. The kind of thing Sarah, now older, now more cynical, jaded by life and jaded by me, would laugh at, but which I never would. The kind of thing men aren't supposed to want, or crave, or admit to, because it's far easier to say only women want these things, and all *we* want is to watch *Top Gear* in our *Top Gear* T-shirts and have silent, bowed women bring us our *Top Gear* magazines.

And as I was about to explain that to Dev, he stood up and marched straight over to the bar.

FIFTEEN

Or "Man on a Mission"

"Well, it thrills me to say," said Dev, minutes later, outside the Fitzroy Tavern and shaking slightly with delight, "that now we know you're definitely in with a shot. I think you're definitely in with a shot."

We stood, pints in hand, relieved to be back among our own, staring through the window of the dimly lit bar. Dev had used the moment and was now reveling in the information he had brought back from the front.

"And why do I think that? Because that man in there"—he pointed, and I batted his hand down in case we were seen— "has absolutely no sense of humor. And you have the beginnings of one, so you're winning."

I looked to the glass again. The man's friend must just have said something funny, because the man slapped him on his arm and reared his head back in laughter. From a distance, the man *seemed* to have a sense of humor, but I was willing to believe Dev on this one.

"It's always topping lists, isn't it, sense of humor?" he said, looking ponderous. "It's always right up there, so I don't know what he's got going for him, other than money and looks and possibly charm. But you—you have nearly a sense of humor."

"Do you think Pamela will like your sense of humor? When she learns English, I mean, and memorizes everything about videogames?"

Dev made a Dev face. I continued, with what I really wanted to talk about: "So what did you say to him? How did you start it?"

"I went blank," said Dev. "So I got out my travelcard and I said, 'Isn't it weird it says "any route permitted" on my train ticket? Does that mean I can go via the *moon*?' And he laughed."

"He laughed?"

"He laughed. I followed that up with 'Cocktail's a weird name considering it contains neither.'"

"Did he laugh again?"

"No, he didn't like that. I think he thought it was a little bawdy. But I was in."

I had watched Dev talking to the man for a couple of minutes while he waited to get served (he'd ordered a tap water, and the barman hadn't looked best pleased). I'd been nervous. I felt like at any second I was going to be rumbled or caught. As if the police were going to turn up and demand the immediate return of the photos or march me straight to Belmarsh. My stomach had flipped as Dev squeezed in between the two men, and tapped the beer pumps just as he'd seen the man do.

At one point, when it got too nerve-racking, I started to come up with excuses I could make if somehow we were found out. I had got the disposable film mixed up with my own disposable film—that's why we developed it. Or perhaps I could say that Dev was care in the community, and he'd done all this when I—his carer—had had my drink spiked by a jealous rival at the home. But as I looked over once more, I saw what everyone else in this room could see: just three men, standing at a bar, smiling and nodding and talking to one another.

And then—one of them had reached into his pocket and brought out a business card.

"So who is he?" I said. "And why did you ask for his business card?"

"I asked them what line of business they were in."

"And?"

"They're restaurateurs. They even said it without the 'n.' Or, at least, they've invested in one. So I said my dad owns restaurants on Brick Lane, and boom—one business card."

He handed it to me. I read it. Just a name and a number, nothing more.

Dev had tried to convince me this was fate again. But again, I'd had to remind him that this was not fate: this was Charlotte Street. And people who work around Charlotte Street are likely to be found around Charlotte Street most days. Finding someone who works on Charlotte Street, still on Charlotte Street when their work on Charlotte Street has ended might be seen as lucky, but fate?

Fact was, I wasn't that bothered by whatever it was. Luck, chance, circumstance, the name didn't matter; what mattered was how it was making me feel.

I woke, the next morning, to hear Dev and his dad shouting at each other downstairs in Urdu. About once a month, recently, Dev's dad had come round to shout at him in Urdu. Only recently had Dev started to shout back.

"Family stuff," he'd tell me, sullenly, as he'd switch on *The Wright Stuff*, or make a coffee, and I'd let it slide, because that's what you do when people say "family stuff."

As I listened to them, I stared at the ceiling and tried to think of other things. There was Sarah, of course, but if there was Sarah then there was also Gary, so I passed on that. And there was last night. The man. And his business card.

"Tell 'em, then!" said Clem, delighted. "Tell 'em!"

"Clem was magnificent," I lied, and Zoe cocked her head, and smiled; an excellent move to show Clem her delight but me her disbelief.

"There was a great moment," said Clem, spinning around in his office chair, trying to be casual, "where someone dropped their pint glass, and I thought, 'Right, I'd better ad-lib here' . . ."

I nodded and smiled my way through the rest, wondering when a good time to turn back to my computer and hit Google might be. My hand was in my pocket, my fingers around one side of the business card.

I hadn't noticed how down and dour Zoe was looking this morning. I didn't notice until long after Clem stopped speaking—which wasn't for a while—when Sam took me to one side, and said, "What's going on? Have you heard anything?"

"Nothing," I'd said. "Heard anything about what?"

Truth be told, I was finding it hard to look at Zoe at the moment. Since seeing Sarah again, it was tough. Because every time I looked at Zoe I was reminded of the kind of man I could be. I forced it all out of my mind again, and felt my pocket for the card again.

Damien Anders Laskin.

What would we find out about Damien Anders Laskin?

Here is what I thought I'd find out about Damien Anders Laskin:

I thought I'd find out he was very, very rich.

I thought I'd find out much of this money came from his

father, a wealthy aristo-industrialist, a man who'd turn out still to be around and who continued to push poor Damien further into the family business, which was probably called Laskin's, and had something to do with vineyards and went back hundreds of years and had probably changed its name once or twice to hide its early involvement with slavery.

I thought I'd find out he went to Eton, clearly, and that he'd probably met some crown prince of an African country there, who was now only too pleased to grant him various weapons contracts, which he'd pursued in an effort to overshadow his father's comparatively paltry wine-based ambitions, but had faltered when a military coup had somehow toppled his friend.

I thought I'd find out he had been married, once, to an Eastern European model he'd met while setting up Laskin's of Prague, a mission given to him by his father but which would ultimately fail because Damien's heart just wasn't in Laskin's Wines & Spirits and never would be, but they'd never had a child, because she was too worried about her figure and the contract she was hoping to renew with Clinique and it's just so hard when you hit thirty and your husband only cares about his business and his mistress.

I thought he was probably good at tennis, having trained personally with Pat Cash or Ivan Lendl, whom he would've met on a celebrity golfing weekend in Maine, which Laskin's had started in the name of charity, but probably only for tax purposes and *OK* magazine kudos. I thought he could handle a sports car, and would say things like "I handle my sports cars like I handle my women" and then finish by saying something witty that I couldn't quite come up with just now, but which would've made Clarkson spit out his roast hog and clap his hands together at a bloated Cotswolds banquet.

And here's what I thought about Damien Anders Laskin: I

thought that wherever he went, people laughed with grace and volume at the things he said whether they were worth it or not, and when he walked into a room they would cut off their conversations just to nod at him in the hope he *might* nod back, and women wished he'd marry them, and men wished he'd piss off so the women they were with would stop wishing he would marry them, and that whatever hand life dealt him, he would always be okay, because Damien Anders Laskin had hope handed to him on a plate.

It all seemed so much. So different, and so much to contend with, so much to battle against. If, ultimately, I wasn't enough for Sarah, if things had been "stale" even when I'd ...

"Well?" said Clem, interrupting.

And we're back in the room.

Blank stares. Raised eyebrows. I had been asked for my opinion. But on what?

"Well ... I agree," I said, authoritatively, and with a flourish.

There was a hush.

"Unless," I said, "you were talking about the man who shouted, 'You're appalling,' halfway through your set last night."

Clem turned his back on me. Turns out they were.

It takes a man of enormous confidence simply to have a business card with his name and number on.

Dev's business card took things even further, of course, and just had his name on, but that was because he knew the girls he gave them to would never call him, and that takes a man of very little confidence indeed.

Who, though, now, can escape the Internet? Who can stave off Google? A mention on a social networking site, a brief whisper on an industry news sheet, a vox pop in a local paper about bike racks or planning consent.

Sure enough, Damien Anders Laskin yielded results.

Plenty of them.

Which you'd expect, seeing as he was in PR.

There was a lengthy profile on him in *Marketing Week*. A few *Telegraph* Diary entries, where he'd been spotted eating canapés at product launches with sparkling, glossy women called Camilla or Claudetta or Collette. A mention in the *Observer Food Monthly* about his restaurant investments. The *Guardian* called him "former PR wunderkind, now *wunderdult* Damien Laskin."

He was self-made: working-class roots; won a scholarship to university. Taken on by a fledgling publicity firm in Bradford in the early '90s; four years later he opened their Dean Street offices. Four years after that, Avenue of the Americas. Then he went solo. Now he was the CEO or MD or VP of Forest Laskin PR. It was all very impressive. I could find little reason to dislike him.

And then I read:

"The word 'forest,'" opines Laskin, 42, "implies natural growth, and natural growth is what we shoot for, quarter on quarter, year on year, and what ultimately we have achieved since day dot."

It's not day dot. It's day one. And who "opines"? Sounds like something yodelers do.

I scanned his list of clients. Hopefully it'd be all bingo halls and chutney.

Mercedes-Benz spring/summer campaign.

Oh.

D&G pop-up shop initiatives, Soho/Deansgate/The Lanes.

Swarovski.

Grey Goose.

Breitling.

The watch. His watch was a Breitling.

Bang & Olufsen.

Lexus.

I've been hearing some very good things about Lexus lately.

And something inside me snapped.

I Googled Forest Laskin Publicity.

Found an address.

Called Dev.

It's funny how finding a challenger can focus a man.

Of *course* Forest Laskin was on Charlotte Street.

There they were, yards from Saatchi & Saatchi, pretty much opposite Café Roma, where I'd unwittingly had my picture taken by The Girl that night.

Dev and I sat in the Nissan Cherry, our feet covered by a blanket of Walkers packets and Calippo tubes, on a single yellow line not far away.

It was after 6:30. Parking attendants all over London were already on the tube home. And people on Charlotte Street were knocking off for the night. Dev was engrossed in a months-old copy of *GamePro*. I found XFM and stared out the window.

It's a pretty street, Charlotte Street, I now realized. At this end, though, it was a little more corporate, a little less quirky. Huge trees reached above us, branches arching over the road where they'd mingle with others and wave away the sun or rain or sleet.

It's a street that people feel they're part of, too; a street people want to put their name to.

There's Jamie's Bar, where I imagine Damien Anders Laskin would sink a midnight whiskey waiting for Tokyo or Sydney to get back to him each night.

There's Elena's, timeless and named after the legendary Elena herself, scuttling about, putting people at ease, the ninety-year-old Frenchwoman as comfortable making a post-junket De

Niro as welcome with a coq au vin as she was the bloke who used to sell the *Standard* by the station.

There's Andrea's, which is really called Andreas, but which everyone calls Andrea's, because it seems to fit in more.

There's Josephine's, too, the Filipino Restaurant, and Siam Central, Palms of Goa, Niko Niko, Curryleaf, that Greek dancing place . . .

"All the world's on Charlotte Street," said Dev, stealing my thoughts. "So what's the plan?"

"We follow him."

"We follow him?"

"We follow him. Why not? Let's follow him."

"And then what?"

"Then we'll see."

"We'll see what?"

"What we do. If he's with The Girl, or he leads us to her, well . . . then I guess it's over. Because he's with her."

I patted my jacket pocket. Dev shot me a quiet glance.

"I have the photos with me," I said, not wanting to meet his eye. "And I'll post them through the door of wherever they are and we'll leg it."

Dev turned to me.

"Just like that? I thought this was your big move."

"This is the closest we've come. What was I going to do, just keep finding places she'd been and taking my own photos there? Invent less and less popular features to slot into *London Now*? It wasn't working."

"But don't you want to talk to her?" he said. "You know— closure?"

I'd thought about it. And I'd decided that, no, I didn't. Because, again, sometimes it's better not to know. I mean, what if she was perfect? What if all that stuff in my head was true?

The girl I wanted to know, with her shabby chic furniture and her healthy glow and her undying optimism? Imagine if I'd never written that letter to Emily Pye at school. Yeah, I wouldn't have closure, but at least the closure I did get wouldn't have been so brutal. I think you can trace most of my failures with women back to Emily Pye and the day I posted that letter and took that chance.

So no. Better not to know on this one. Maybe better to think it could've happened, than find out it absolutely wouldn't. Better that she'd remain just a girl in a photo, than a girl I'd met and felt I knew.

Of course, I didn't know if Damien Anders Laskin would lead us to her. I didn't know for sure they were even together. But even though I was playing it straight and grown-up with Dev, that was kind of what made it so exciting. A bit of blind poker with a whole bunch of new emotions for a heart that had felt deadened and battered and bruised. What is it self-harmers say? That they self-harm just to feel? Well, I wasn't that bad. But once in a while it felt enlivening just to take a risk. To use that moment.

Plus, I had nothing to lose. Not really. Just an idea. Just a little bit of hope. And then at least I'd be able to move on.

"I bet it turns out he's gay," said Dev. "That's what would happen in a film. There'd be a series of hilarious clues, all of which point one way, and then you'd confront him or something, and he'd say, 'Let me introduce you to my partner,' and we'd all be expecting The Girl and then we'd all be shocked when some bloke walked in."

Dev started laughing, and slapped the steering wheel.

"And we'd be in a gay bar and the bloke would have to have some kind of name that would've added to the confusion, like Pat, or Joe without an 'e'!"

He calmed down, and said, "*Man*, I wish life was like a film sometimes."

I looked at him.

"We're sitting in a Nissan Cherry in the middle of what is essentially a sting operation," I said.

His eyes lit right up.

And then I heard something familiar. I turned the radio up.

"The Kicks," I said, delighted.

"Who?"

"That band. We're friends. Well, we've met. They're Abbey's mates."

I turned it up further. It was "Uh-Oh." Then the DJ, the one who's going out with the Sugababe I think, said, "*Brighton's brightest, The Kicks, on XFM...*"

"That's my line!" I said, delighted.

"*So says their press release, and who am I to argue...They'll be at Scala in King's Cross this Friday night, alongside Play&Record, Neighbours From Hell, and—*"

"That's when Abbey's in town," said Dev. "Friday night."

And, as the DJ moved to ads, we looked up, and we saw Damien Anders Laskin leaving his offices and crossing to the other side of Charlotte Street.

"*Activate the Cherry!*" yelled Dev, turning the ignition, and doing just that.

As it panned out, we didn't have far to go.

We tried creeping after him, but following a man who's on foot is difficult when the cars behind you are insistent you at least try to come close to the 30 mph limit. They never did that in *Starsky & Hutch*.

Plus, Laskin wasn't going far. He wasn't going far at all.

"*Really?*" I said, staring up at the sign.

* * *

We left it five or six minutes before walking inside.

"Table for two, please," said Dev, as I scanned the room.

There he was, sitting by the window, no one in the seat opposite him.

Maybe he was waiting for her. Maybe all this would start and end at Abrizzi's.

"What shall we do?" asked Dev.

"Observe," I said.

But there was something odd about this. Why Abrizzi's? Why would he eat at Abrizzi's? Not that there was anything hugely wrong with the place. But Roka was just down the street. Men like Damien eat at places like Roka. And that's where they'd take girls like The Girl. They'd order mojitos to start, and they'd shun the tasting menu because they eat there all the time, so they'd take charge and fill the table with softshell crab and black cod and osetra caviar.

"Let's sit next to him," whispered Dev.

"Let's *not* sit next to him," I whispered back, but then the waitress was there, wearing her matching Jason Priestley hat and T-shirt set, and Dev pointed and asked, "Is by the window okay?"

Damien Anders Laskin smelled *good*.

I suppose if I were still a teacher, I would mark him like this:

Appearance: Damien has a look about him that says "I am very busy and my mind is very far away," even when just nibbling on a breadstick or casting a disinterested eye over a laminated menu in a restaurant that doesn't suit him. Up close, he reminds you of a man from an advert, who probably has a huge stainless steel fridge with bok choy in it. Conversation: "Thanks," he said to a waiter, as we sat

down, but not once did he look up at him, as his sparkling
water was poured for him, like he was a little prince.
Overall: I liked the fact that he didn't look up, that he
didn't acknowledge the server, because it meant we weren't
the same.

Though didn't that also disappoint me?

We were now sitting just inches from this man, and the strange thing was he had no idea what it meant.

I mean, he was sort of a celebrity in our house, this guy. I don't mean to say we were obsessed by him, or huge fans or anything, but we knew things about him. Like if you find yourself sitting in Starbucks next to Jean-Luc Picard. There's that thrill. You want to let them know that you know who they are. As if you've discovered their secret somehow. But you don't. You ignore them. Because that's what they want, and also, you don't want them to think you want them to know you know. You know?

I knew Dev felt the same. So we quietly studied our menus and tapped our chins and . . . *hang-about-what-the-hell-was-Dev-doing?*

"S'cuse me?" he said, suddenly, leaning in toward Laskin.

"Dev?" I said, as if I had a question about the pizzas. "Hey, Dev—"

"Sorry to be a pain . . ."

Damien Anders Laskin looked up from his iPhone and looked at us both . . . and what was that? A flicker of recognition? A split second of have-we-met? But what was Dev doing?

"I was just wondering," Dev said, as I watched, wide-eyed, "if you could take a photo of us."

He smiled, broadly, and held up a disposable camera.

My disposable camera.

Damien Anders Laskin stared at it for just a second, and smiled.

"Of course," he said. "I know how to use one of these."

"Heeey," said Dev, suddenly feigning a memory. "It's *Damien*, right?"

Click.

"Just so weird bumping into you again," said Dev, between mouthfuls of pepperoni, and for what must've been the fourth time. "Here of all places!"

"Well, I only work down the road," said Damien.

I had been keeping very quiet indeed, despite Dev's constant attempts to include me in the conversation.

"If you don't mind me asking," said Dev. "Is this the place you invested in?"

Damien smirked, put his fork down, and wiped his mouth with a serviette.

"No, no. Mine's in Shoreditch. Hustle&Jive. A kind of speakeasy-jazz diner with an edge."

We both nodded as if we knew exactly what that meant.

"No, this place isn't *quite* me"—and there was that smirk again—"but we just won the pitch to PR it. Small fry, really, but they're opening up in Manchester soon, plans for Glasgow six months later, so why not get in on the ground floor? Good account for a junior to have . . . and in a recession, it all adds up."

I looked at his watch, his suit. I couldn't imagine the recession had hit him *particularly* hard.

"What was it you said you did, Dev? Restaurants?"

"I have restaurant interests, yes," said Dev. "Brick Lane, mainly. But also, I'm in engineering. Videogame engineering. Pretty specific stuff we probably shouldn't go into."

"And you, Jason?"

"Journalist," I said, trying to keep things light.

"Last name?"

"Priestley," I said, and he laughed, but this time not for the usual reason.

He held up a napkin.

"'*A magical slice of pizza heaven!*'" read Damien, delighted. "That was you?"

"It was," I said, embarrassed. This man had a website, an empire. I had my name on a napkin.

"You know that's what helped convince them to spend on London PR? If I wasn't eating for free, I'd pay for your dinner!"

"You still can," said Dev, but Damien ignored this.

"So...*London Now*," he said, suddenly very interested, but then a look approaching concern shot across his face. "Tough times."

"Are they?"

"How are things there? How's morale?"

Morale? Morale was fine.

"Oh, you know," I said.

"Well, I think you'll be fine. I mean, you hear things. I don't mean to speak out of place."

"No, I mean, I'm freelance, so they don't tend to fill me in on—"

"Jason is reviews editor," said Dev.

"Acting reviews editor," I corrected. "Just while someone's away."

"Well, you've helped us out already," said Damien, and I shrugged it away. "Are you on our list? We have a list. Special friends. We hold events and suchlike. I'll put you on our list. What's your e-mail?"

And he tapped it into his phone.

* * *

Maybe ten minutes later, Damien said, "Okay," and stood up.

He looked around Abrizzi's and winked, conspiratorially.

"Well, at least I don't have to do that again," he said. "But it shows an interest—means the world to the client."

Dev and I stood, and awkwardly shook his hand. One after the other I mean, not at once.

"*Auf Wiedersehen*, boys," he said. "Jason, we'll be in touch."

"Oh!" said Dev, giving me a wink. "One last thing."

Damien spun round and raised his eyebrows in anticipation.

"Are you a single man, Damien?"

Nice, Dev. Subtle. I sat back down and pretended I'd had a text.

"What I mean is, are you attached? Currently?"

Dev couldn't help but glance at me. *Look what I'm doing!* his eyes seemed to say.

"Flattered," said Damien, half-smiling, his eyes darting nervously between us. "But I'm in a relationship, yes."

And as he turned and walked away, Dev realized what Damien had thought he meant.

"No, not for *me*!" he shouted after him, panicking. "Oi, Damien! Not for me!"

He pointed to where I was sitting.

"For *him*!"

But I didn't really mind. Because I knew how big Forest Laskin was—what they did.

And I knew that however this worked out, I'd just been added to The List. I felt a strange warmth toward Damien Laskin.

"Where there is the woman you love you will expend all effort, even to death, to get there."

—Traditional Shona Tribe proverb, Zimbabwe

Thank you for your comments on my blog. There are ten of you now, and while I'm sorry I'm being cryptic, I'm also trying to be honest.

Martin: no, I can't tell you his name, but your nickname fits quite well.

Maureen: I think I would quite like to have seen the photos in the camera, yes. But I think that's how this blog sort of started for me. As a way of remembering those moments I've got no proof of. So maybe I can learn from them.

Like, when we were in his flat the first time, a flat I'll simply say was as big as Alaska itself, I told him I had this list.

Here it is: all the places I've ever sent a postcard from, and to who. It's a potted history of me. Benchmarks, as much about who they went to as who they didn't.

Aberystwyth—geography field trip (to Mum and Dad, Nana)

Dieppe—school exchange trip (to Mum and Dad, Nana)

Glasgow—Take That, "The Pops" tour at the SECC (Mum, Nana)

Stirling—first week at uni (Mum and Dad, Nana)

London—job interview (Mum, Nana)

Whitby—to visit Dad's grave. He always said he wanted to finish where he'd started. I took his car, but saved the postcard for Mum.

And I guess that's where he got the idea, this ideas man. Maybe I gave him an easy in with that one.

And much as I wish it hadn't, it means I can't give anyone an easy in again.

Which is why, to answer your question Captain Stinkjet, it's good for me to remain anonymous for now.

Sx

SIXTEEN

Or "Goodnight & Goodmorning"

I suppose if I were still some anonymous teacher, perhaps one who covered the odd science lesson when Mr. Dodd was taking one of his sick days (if you wanted to find him at lunchtime to hand him a get-well card and some flowers, he would be happy to receive them at his corner in Ladbrokes), I would describe my current situation thus:

> *Objective: I can't be.*
> *Method: The courts might say stalking.*
> *Result: That'd be nice.*
> *Conclusion: One step at a time. But the list's a nice move.*

See, I knew all about lists like Damien's.

To be on the list, it meant you were a Chosen One. Someone regarded as valuable. Someone the PRs would call a "journalist friend," not just a "journalist." You were in the inner circle, invited to lavish events, days out, plied with food and drink, privy to the slaggings-off of other, lesser journalists, who are "not like you."

It's a great place to be. You can network. You have access. And I could use this. Thinking beyond *London Now*, to *GQ*, or

Esquire, or *ShortList*, or any number of other mags or papers keen to employ someone more on their level.

Being on Forest Laskin's list meant I'd soon be on other lists, too.

"We should head down Hustle&Jive next," Dev had said, on the way home. "See if we can bump into him again. And also, work out what a speakeasy-jazz diner thing is."

I explained we wouldn't have to. Being on the list more or less guaranteed hanging out with Damien more. So I could get to know him. And through him, find out more about The Girl. And when Dev realized he'd more than likely be my plus one he found it hard to sleep.

"We'll be invited to the Grand Prix!" he said, the next morning, back at the flat. He was playing *Nazi Zombies* and grinning. "Or Wimbledon! And they've probably bought up a load of Olympics tickets! There'll be a private box and canapés! I'm your plus one, yeah? You promise me now!"

"You're my plus one," I said, and he reloaded his carbine and blew away another Nazi Zombie in celebration.

Suddenly he looked at his watch.

"Shouldn't you be gone already?"

I know it seems ridiculous, thinking being on a list might change anything at all. But like I say, it was a sign of acceptance—of having been recognized. Sure, you might say it was really just another unknown name on a mailout for whichever blank-eyed and underappreciated intern was going to have to type it in, but I was weirdly grateful to Dev for pushing me into that situation.

He'd been doing that a lot, lately. That was the good thing about him. He was impulsive; he always had a plan. Even when that plan was a terrible plan, it was a plan fueled by optimism.

He likes to get involved, and there's something incredibly life-enhancing about being around someone who just wants to get involved. The fact that he was doing this to help me get past everything that had happened with Sarah meant a lot. The fact that together we were using the moment—as we'd always said we should and could and would—was great, too. After all, it wasn't us that had started this. Not really. It was The Girl, forgetting her camera, in that moment I hoped was a moment we'd shared.

So what was she to Damien? I wondered. He was in a relationship; he'd said so. Was it with her? Was she the girlfriend? Was he married and she the mistress? Did she know, if she was? Was it a brief fling? Ongoing? Or did she not have anything to do with him at all?

Maybe she was a colleague, I reasoned. One of his PR team. They work closely, those PR teams. They go to events. Eat out in restaurants. Work hard, play hard, swap sexually charged banter over sushi on the company AmEx. You see them sometimes, these teams of people, work suits on, united under one letterhead, all bawdy backslapping, then back to Foxtons. Be easy to mistake them for more than colleagues. Maybe that explained the seemingly intimate pictures of a happy girl. Or maybe Damien had only appeared in the first few shots because they were the only ones he was involved in . . . maybe someone *else* had taken the others. Maybe The Girl meant nothing to him whatsoever; perhaps he had only a fleeting memory of this girl he'd met at a party, once—a girl he thinks he might have had his photo taken with but wouldn't ever be able to tell you for sure. "You know what these events are like," he'd probably say. "Everyone wants a photo of everything."

Or what if . . .

What if she was on The List, too? What if she was a journalist, or an editor, or a sub, maybe for *Grazia* or *T2*? Invited out to restaurant soft launches or premieres, taking her beloved camera to record her memories in the way others would use their Nokia? What if those photos were just taken at jollies, hence, well, why she looked so jolly?

There was a chance she was just like me and that Damien just represented the same to her as to me.

Hey, is that hope, there? Is that excitement—that little bubble of something rising through me—as I stride from the underground to the office?

And then, just outside Pret, I remembered the car.

Of course. The car.

She'd been in a photo with that car, outside the Alaska Building.

I didn't know much about Damien, but I did know that out of everyone I'd ever met in my life so far, absolutely no one was more likely to drive a limited-edition car or keep a parquet-floored penthouse in a building marked Alaska than him.

Wedding photo first, Alaska Building second. A story of a relationship in two seconds and a flat.

And that, of course, meant there was more to it than just a chance encounter at somebody else's wedding. It meant there was history. Meet-ups by day and by night. Maybe professional, but more than likely personal. It also meant that these photos were probably as much Damien's as they were The Girl's.

Still, though, I thought. The List can't hurt.

"Hey, so I met Damien Laskin last night," I said, casually, and Zoe looked up from her screen, eyebrows raised.

"Did you?" she said. "Where?"

"Oh, you know . . . Abrizzi's."

"Abrizzi's? You know they're starting a radio campaign

using your quote? What were you doing there? What was *Laskin* doing there?"

"I think they're starting some kind of PR account for that place. Anyway, he said he'd sort me out with some invites to things. Put me on his list."

I shrugged, like this was nothing.

"Yeah, I'm on that list," said Zoe.

"Yes, but you're in charge, so that makes sense. I'm just saying."

"I'm on that list, too," said Clem.

"You?" I said. "You're on the list? I'm talking about the special list, not the general list."

"I'm on all the lists. Hate it. 'Oh, come down to the Trocadero and meet Flippy, the new face of Fiat.' Then they give you a plastic bag with a Flippy keyring in it and a calendar that's already half useless because it's July."

"I don't know who Flippy is," I said. "And Forest Laskin don't do that kind of stuff, anyway, do they? They handle big accounts, big-name deals. Mercedes, Sony, that sort of thing."

"Yeah. Big names. And tell me: how *was* your Abrizzi's?" asked Clem.

The only reason I'd raised Damien was to somehow work out what his story was. Not his business story, not the story of his successes and failures, but the story of who he actually was, when he was at home, reclining on his Eames chair peering out over South London from Alaska. I knew Zoe was bound to know. She'd been around long enough, she'd done her time. She had contacts, and contacts eventually become work friends, and work friends soon swap work-talk for gossip.

"Do you know anyone at Forest Laskin?" I asked, again very casually.

"Yeah, loads," said Zoe, barely casting me a glance.

"Like who?"

"Most of them are called Jo," she said. "There are lots of Hannahs, too, but mainly there are Jos."

"What about Damien? Do you know him?"

"Hmm?"

"I was just asking if you know Damien particularly well. He seems like a nice guy. Quite grounded and settled. Like a sort of family man, I guess?"

"Ha!" said Zoe.

"What?"

She just shook her head and kept typing.

Just after midday, when I'd already liaised with some lesser, non-special-list-promising PRs and arranged delivery of various packages and various invites to various freelancers (it still felt good, being the sender, the arranger, the *liaison*), I was thrilled to see that things were already under way. Things Had Begun To Happen.

> *From: Emily@ForestLaskin*
> *To: UndisclosedRecipients*
> *Subject: Final Reminder: Special Event, VIP Entry, Thursday @ 8 p.m.*

I didn't even need to read it to know I'd be going.

And that week, the invites came thick and fast.

I suppose in a bigger operation, the responsibility for attending might have been shared out. Please remember this was not a big operation.

Events I attended solo: late invite to lunchtime soft launch of fashion label Nabarro (I received one pair of soft leather gloves in return), Nando's Very-Peri-Peri "hot sauce celebration" (I received one case of Very-Peri-Peri in return, which I gave to Clem, who interestingly had *not* been invited, and I met a man named Martin whose job it is to drink hot sauce).

Events I attended with Dev: New Zealand tourist board Marlborough region wine tasting in Vinopolis with whiskey bar after-party at New Zealand House.

Events I had agreed to attend but had not yet attended, with Dev or without: Silverstone track day, champagne and hot-air ballooning to celebrate new Pixar hot-air ballooning–based animation, Paul Weller intimate gig at the Buffalo Bar, Journalists vs. SAS paintballing day at "Pow Pow," Southend-on-Sea.

I felt like Boyd Hilton.

Each time I'd looked around for Damien. Each time I'd looked around for The Girl. Each time I'd been disappointed.

At one point, I'd taken a Jo or a Hannah to one side, and asked, "So where's Damien? Does he not come to these things?" and she'd said, conspiratorially, in case her clients could hear, all the while looking around her, "Oh, no, his office sends out his *own* invites. He tends to mainly show up at the *big* things, to do with people he *knows*..."

All of which made my new soft leather gloves feel that little bit less attractive.

Fine, though. I would just have to wait. For Damien.

I knew going out Friday would be a bad idea.

For a start, Saturday follows Friday, and if you've agreed to go to your ex-girlfriend's engagement party on a Saturday, you'd best behave yourself the Friday before.

When she'd slid that invite across the table to me at the café, I, of course, had said yes. She had just told me I was mature and grown-up, and the childish thing about being called mature or grown-up is that for a moment or two you actually believe it. So naturally I had made a mature face and read the invite in a grown-up way and nodded, in a way that was both mature and grown-up, to confirm my attendance.

Which was stupid, because I really didn't want to go.

My feelings were thus: fine. Go off and get married. I'm fed up of being embarrassed by my actions; fed up of looking to the past. I'm not going to stop you. I wish things could've been different but they're not, so go, walk out the door, don't turn around now, 'cause I'm clearly not *actually* all that welcome anymore. But I had to pretend I was mature.

So yes. I knew going out Friday would be a bad idea. I knew it now more than ever because it was ten to ten on Friday night and Dev and I were still sitting indoors, with the telly flickering away against bare walls, waiting for Abbey to arrive.

Ordinarily, we'd have been thinking about coming home about this time, maybe stopping by the Cally Food & Wine for a bad pizza we could burn if we weren't feeling flush enough for a man on a Flying Lotus moped.

"This is the problem with young, cool women," said Dev, shaking his head. "They've always got about nine stops to make on their way to meet you. 'I've just got to stop by Marble Arch'; 'I've just got to pick something up from a mate on Old Street'; 'Hey, I can't make it. I've ended up in Marseilles.' It makes going out with old, uncool women a very serviceable idea indeed. Has she got a boyfriend in Brighton?"

"Not that I know of."

"Not that you *know* of?"

"I thought she was single. That first night she was definitely single. She'd have mentioned it, if that had changed. And there's no way of asking if she is or not without it looking like I want to be her boyfriend."

"Don't you?"

I showed him my watch. It was five to ten. Enough had been said.

Ding-dong.

"You sure you're cool coming?" said Abbey, all glitter and fringe. "We're on the guest list."

The Kicks were clearly going places. They'd been spotted, Abbey said, by a man who knew a man who knew the man who looked after Play&Record. And they were last year's going-places band, who really had gone places. Cover of the *NME*, XFM sessions, a smaller stage at Latitude.

"Scala, please," she said to the cabbie from Marvin's, and he, being the deaf one with the bifocals, seemed to think she'd asked for Scarborough.

"Scala's a pretty big venue," I said, impressed.

"Well, they're going to be a pretty big band."

"Hey, maybe I should do an interview with the boys. You know, a follow-up to my review."

"They *loved* that review, by the way," she said, "Mikey said it was his favorite."

I felt flattered, which was worrying, because an easily flattered reviewer is a reviewer who reviews easily.

Ah, sod it. I was never going to be one of those hard-hitters. Far better to have a nice time, get on lists, enjoy vast cases of Very-Peri-Peri.

"How's your dad, Dev?" asked Abbey, as we passed the garage by Orkney House. Scala was only a few minutes away, just opposite King's Cross.

"Dev's dad? When did you meet Dev's dad?"

"Last time. Just after Sarah turned up at the shop," she said. "Seemed angry."

"Abbey," said Dev, suddenly. "We were wondering: do you have a boyfriend?"

"I'm in a relationship," she said, quickly, but I still wanted to know why Dev's dad had turned up that day.

"What does that mean, when people say 'in a relationship'?" said Dev. "Why not just 'I'm married' or 'I have a boyfriend'?"

"Sometimes I think it means they're noncommittal," she replied, eyes out the window.

"Are *you* noncommittal?" asked Dev.

"I'm committal. Committed. Though sometimes I *should* be committed."

A pause as we tried to work out whether she meant that. It sounded like a moment where people would laugh, but no one did.

"So anyway, do you want to go out with me?" asked Dev.

"We're here," said the cabbie, brakes down. "Scarborough."

Inside, it became very apparent very quickly that The Kicks weren't really "supporting" Play&Record. Or, they were, technically, but *only* technically. They were one of six bands chosen to warm up the crowd for a long evening building up to the big boys. And we'd missed them by about two hours.

We'd made it to the upstairs bar, slack yellow wristbands on, while men who were clearly in bands or worked with bands or used to be in bands held plastic cups and played with their hats.

"Hi!" said Abbey, flinging her arms around one of them, and I nudged Dev to show him this was my moment to shine. It was important Dev realized I know how to hang out with rock and rollers like The Kicks.

"How've you been, man?" I said, hugging the same guy. "Not seen you since the Phoenix! Things are going well! Heard you on the radio!"

"Jason," said Abbey. "This is Paul. He's not in The Kicks."

"That's right!" I bluffed. "I thought that. That's what I thought."

"He's a puppeteer."

"Terrific," I said, and I caught Dev smiling at me, enjoying the moment I went from nearly cool to not-even-nearly cool. "I love puppets."

"What puppets do you love?" asked Paul, a little coldly, which you don't really expect from puppeteers.

"I love all puppets. I used to have one, as a child. A fox."

Paul considered me. I have never been made to feel so small by someone who plays with puppets.

"Paul is"—a micropause, a split second of something—"my boyfriend."

"Oh!" I said, trying to look delighted for them both.

"Oh," said Dev.

"Yeah," said Paul. "On-again, off-again, on-again."

Delightful.

"Jason's a journalist," she said, with just a hint of dismissal in her voice. "Jason Priestley."

"Ha ha!" said Paul. "Fallen on hard times since *90210*?"

"Ha ha!" I generously ha-ha'd.

"He's been covering the band. Wants to do an interview, I think?"

She flashed me an apologetic smile and Paul matched it with one of boredom. There was something not right about Paul. Good-looking, yes. Stylish, too, I suppose. He looked like he fitted in, here, in his skinny jeans and Topman checkout trinkets. But he also looked like he could quite easily grow a goatee and a ponytail. He sounded like a goatee-and-ponytail man. That they were not there was perhaps the most unsettling thing about him.

"Journos," he said. "You like flashy things. Shiny things with lights and mics. Not so big in my world. But then I'm not so big in yours."

"Aren't you?"

"When've you seen a puppeteer on the cover of *Time Out*?" he said, and I realized his eyes were hooded and bored.

"That's a good point," I said, trying to be friendly.

"Suppose it's not a bad job actually, journalist," he said. "You get to look important at something like this and then you look important when you write it and it comes out but you're not actually making anything, are you?"

This puppeteer was starting to grate. I started to want to grate this puppeteer. He smiled, pleased with himself, probably proud of being one of those people who think they tell it like it is, that if you're offended it's your problem, that they're "only being honest, that's just me, I'd rather say it to your face." Of course you would. Because that's what makes *you* feel important.

The amount of people he must've belittled, sitting cross-legged on ethnic throws at basement-squat dinner parties, who'd seen that very same, thin only-being-honest smile.

"But you go ahead and do what you do," he said. "Sell us the next big thing so that they can then sell us Carlsberg and Pepsi."

I couldn't help but notice he was drinking Carlsberg. I saw Abbey's eyes flick to his pint glass, too, but she bit her lip and looked back at me, apologetically.

I am pretty sure my face gave away exactly what I was thinking. Which was, "Are you kidding me, Abbey? This is your boyfriend? His stage name *better* be Captain Dickhead."

It was a face that said, "No longer will I accept relationship or life advice from someone wise-beyond-their-years sitting by canals in Camden or on buses through Bloomsbury or outside cafés near my flat. For you are going out with Britain's biggest tool!"

It was a face that was interrupted by Paul's monotonous barrage of hostile, unasked-for opinion.

"In a way I admire you for it," he said, and this is where I punched him to the ground, except I didn't, "but ha *ha*, tell you what, gents: I could never ever do what you do."

He shook his head and avoided our eyes, as if to say, "Yeah, I *did* just say that. End of story," and other smug, self-satisfied phrases. This wasn't entirely comfortable.

I stared out at the gig, silently, my fist choking the neck of my bottle.

"So, do many people come and watch you control your toys?" asked Dev, innocently, and Paul blinked hard in mock-shock. "Must be a great job. I'd love to just play all day. Must be a great stress relief. Unless one of the strings breaks. *That* must be stressful."

Paul immediately knew what Dev was doing.

"And what do you do?" he said.

"I work for the Ministry of Defence," said Dev. "Much more than that I can't say."

"You're implying you're a spy," he said, flatly, unimpressed. "Why do I imagine you're probably the receptionist?"

"Ha ha!" said Dev. "So are you doing any magic shows soon?"

"Theater," corrected Paul. "It's theater."

"Because I've got a four-year-old nephew who *loves* puppets. I got him started on the Muppet-puppets. He loves the Muppet-puppets!"

"They're just called the Muppets. Not the Muppet-puppets."

"Well, you're the expert. You must know all about puppet-muppets."

"The Muppets are not exactly my—"

"What first got you interested in the Muppets?"

I caught Abbey's eye. She was quietly enjoying this.

"I'm not sure four-year-olds really appreciate my approach."

"Why are you approaching four-year-olds?"

"Very funny."

"What's your best puppet? Have you got a monkey?"

"It must make you happy, making fun of me?" asked Paul, and this was Abbey's moment to step in, to say, "Come on, Paul, you were being a dick and needlessly patronizing. These are my friends," but instead she said, "Paul's got a point. Grow up, all of you."

"If that's her boyfriend, and he lives in London, why did she stay at ours that night?"

We were leaning over the balcony as the roadies tinkered with huge keyboards marked Play&Record.

"On-again, off-again. They must've been off-again. Plus, he's quirky and bad-tempered. Sometimes that works."

I don't know what I'd imagined Abbey's boyfriend to be like. I suppose I'd imagined that he was probably quite conventional. A little stuffy. That she'd have been attracted to the not-so-obvious, and would've reveled in the juxtaposition, the way you sometimes see supercool Japanese girls walking through Shoreditch arm in arm with cumbersome nerds.

And I was a little annoyed that he was suddenly here, in our group, unannounced. We'd gone from being a happy three to a frosty four, and all thanks to a chippy puppeteer.

It seemed like Abbey wanted us to meet him, but didn't want us to meet him. She wasn't seeking our approval. Perhaps she was seeking our disapproval.

Suddenly, from behind, a tap on the shoulder.

"All right?"

"Mikey!" I said, and then: "How ya doin'?"

I'd never said "ya" before. Mikey was on his own as far as the other Kicks were concerned, but there were plenty of people nearby, buzzing off him, eager to talk.

"Yeah, not bad, man," he said, and then, spotting Dev: "All right? Mikey."

"Dev," said Dev, with unexpected confidence. "I'm a musician, too."

Jesus.

"Yeah? What do you play?"

"Music."

Mikey did that thing people do where you nod your understanding but at the same time manage to imply you have not really understood at all. He turned back to me.

"Hey, we gotta thank you," he said.

"What? You haven't gotta thank me," I said, modestly, but pleased for whatever he was about to say.

"Nah, man, you're part of our story now, yeah? We stapled your review to about two hundred EPs, delivered 'em all over town by hand, one of them ended up in a pile on a man's desk. He chucked most of them out but your thing caught his eye so he stuck it in his bag, listened to it in his car, gave us a call that night . . ."

I smiled a big smile. He kind of had Abbey to thank for that review.

"We've got our first airplay, we're here with Play&Record, we've got journalists saying we're the new whatevers—"

"Who are the Whatevers?" asked Dev, but we ignored him because we're cool.

"It's all coming together, man! I was saying to Phil the other night, we should get Jason to be our official rock biographer.

You can tell it how it was, from the start! He said I might be getting ahead of myself."

Over his shoulder, I could see people observing our conversation. They were watching Mikey. He was becoming someone, and they could sense it.

"So, anyway, we *owe* you, yeah? Beer soon?" he said, backing away, a twenty-year-old with the world at his feet, pointing his bony fingers at me and smiling, like I was someone, too.

"Deffo!" I said. "Deffo, man."

We watched as Mikey was swallowed by the small crowd. Hipsters and girls younger than Abbey, with homemade Kicks shirts and bangles.

I turned to Dev, proud.

"Do you think he knows you listen mainly to Hall & Oates?" he said.

In the corner of my eye, I thought I saw Abbey push through some double doors, hiding her eyes.

We stayed to watch Play&Record. I composed my review in my head. Mikey had inspired me. I could make a difference! I could be a part of things! I might only be a cog in what Paul would probably disparagingly call "the machine" before smiling at his own originality, but I could make of my cogness what I liked. And maybe it'd mean Play&Record would like me, too. I must be a terrific music journalist, to have spotted The Kicks so early on, and to have played such a part in their story.

Play&Record, I decided, blended emphatic, anthemic powerhouse rock with downbeat trip-hop melodies. Also, that's what their publicity flyer said.

I cast my eye around the room, looking for Abbey. She was nowhere to be seen. Paul remained by the bar, arguing with a blond girl, probably about Proust and his influence on European puppetry. I really did not like Paul one bit.

In fact, I suppose if I were still a teacher, I would mark him like this:

Paul: is a knob.

And then I'd blame it on one of the kids.

"We should've got Matt out," said Dev. "He could've found a metal post and smashed all Paul's puppets. Did you call him?"

"I did," I said. "No answer."

"Why the hell is she going out with him?" he said, as we shifted our collars in the wind that buffets you up Pentonville Road. In six minutes, we could catch Oz before he closed and stuff our faces with chili sauce. "I mean, people are funny, aren't they?"

"Maybe she loves him."

"She can't love him. What's to love? He's like one of those tennis ball launchers, firing chippy opinions into your face from three feet away then looking over your shoulder. Every time he looks back at you it's just to fire another ball into your face."

"He's pretty tiring."

"He's worse than that. He's like . . . he's like something worse than that."

"Hey, why was your dad at the shop the other night?"

"My dad?"

"Yeah. Abbey said she saw him at the shop, and—"

We turned as we thought we heard someone shout something behind us, but quickened our pace. What was it? A fight? A mugging?

We saw Abbey padding up the road, her bag flinging itself around her as she ran.

"Can I stay at yours tonight?" she asked. "Paul's got to be up at five."

"Puppet emergency?" I said.

"Shut up." She laughed. "So can I stay at yours?"

I tried to see if she looked like she'd been crying, but the air was cold and we all did.

"Sure," I said.

"I brought treats!" she said, brightly, and patting her bag.

"We're off for a kebab," I said.

"Of course you are," she said, pushing into my arm, affectionately. "Of course you are."

Back at the flat, Abbey had laid out her treats on the table, next to mugs of milky, sugared tea.

We shared the sofa, but not the treats. Abbey jumped straight in.

"Spacecakes," she said, anticipating them, welcoming them, the way I'd say "Big Mac."

Not since university had I had a spacecake. They just didn't seem to figure in the real world of traffic jams and tube strikes and pay-as-you-go. I was tempted for just a second, just to remember that one night of staring, blank-eyed, at a Leicester University halls of residence doorknob, but declined. Dev looked frightened by them, as if Abbey had just revealed she was a heroin dealer and all her friends were coming round to stay. Abbey munched on, undeterred.

"So The Girl. What's happening with The Girl?"

"Not much," I said. "Nothing, really."

"Oh, come on," said Dev, excited. "We found the man. The man from the photos."

"Her man? Chunky watch man?"

She sat up, delighted.

"We don't know if he's her man. We just know he's a man."

"How did you find him?"

"Fate!" said Dev, finger in the air.

"But really?"

"He was on Charlotte Street. He works there. And then we followed him into a restaurant and started chatting to him."

"OhmyGod are-you-serious thatis*brilliant*," she said, breathlessly. "You followed him! What did you talk to him about?"

It was exciting, to see her excited.

"Did he mention The Girl?" she said, pressing on.

"Nope," said Dev. "But he will! We've been going to events where we think he'll be, only it turns out he doesn't go to them, but one day she'll be there and we'll *pounce*!"

We all pretended that didn't sound sinister.

Abbey smiled, then stifled a yawn. She sat back on the sofa, wriggled herself comfortable.

"That'd be amazing if that happened," she said. "I wish I had a dream to follow. Like, a practical one. Not just a dream dream, but a dream you can make come true."

"An ambition?" said Dev.

"That's a better word. Yeah, I wish I had an ambition. I just sort of drift. Or help other people with their ambitions. You know, Paul had never written a serious theater piece before I made him do it? Then I forced him to sit down and a week later *Osama Lovin'* was done. I'm a dream-facilitator without a dream of my own."

"That would be a terrific line in a musical," said Dev. "You should suggest it to Paul."

She yawned again.

"What are we doing tomorrow?" she said.

I shot Dev a look, a please-no look.

"It's Sarah's engagement party tomorrow," he said.

"Are you going?" said Abbey. "You should go. Are you invited? You should be invited."

"I'm invited. I'm going."

"He's bricking it," said Dev, finishing the last of his tea.

"I want to come with you," she said, her eyes closing. "Let's all go. I want to see what you're afraid of."

"I'm not afraid."

"You're *so* afraid of these people, because you can't control them. They control you. You shouldn't be controlled by people. You should be free. We should all be free."

I think the spacecakes had kicked in.

"Being free to do what you want is the important thing. That's why you should find The Girl. That's being in control. You should definitely find her, Jase. For me. No, for you."

And by the time I'd worked out how to respond, and tapped the rim of my mug in thought, Abbey was asleep on my shoulder.

Carefully, I moved away, gently lowering her head toward a cushion. I laid a Garfield blanket over her, moved her bag to where she'd find it in the morning, and paused a second.

Peeping out from a side pocket was a CD marked "Abbey's Songs."

SEVENTEEN

Or "And That's What Hurts"

I turned the page, and then turned straight back to read it again.

> *"I didn't think anything would happen when I placed the advert," says James Ward, who placed it in the Scottish listings magazine, the* List. *The subject of his advertisement was a young lady he spotted in a travel bookshop.*
>
> *"I'd always been dubious about love at first sight, but I think that must be what it was," says Mr. Ward, now a flow cytometry operator at the University of Edinburgh. "She was tall with short black hair, big blue eyes and a lovely smile."*
>
> *Mr. Ward's advert in the next week's edition of the* List *read:* You were reading a book on Perthshire, I was the man standing with two coffees. I wish I'd offered you one. Maybe now?
>
> *That was four and a half years ago. Now, he and Jenni Bale-Ward are married and have an eighteen-month-old son, Henry.*
>
> *"I have always thought that if you don't take your chances you'll end up with absolutely nothing," said Mr .Ward.*

* * *

"Breakfast!" shouted Abbey, loudly, from the living room.

I took the chance.

I'd lain in bed last night staring at the ceiling and thinking about what Abbey had said about ambition. She didn't seem the sort not to have any dreams. She seemed the sort to have a million. And I don't mean that she's flighty, or scatterbrained, although coincidentally she is both of those things. I just mean for someone so full of life, so full of joy, I found it hard to believe she could be so empty of dreams.

"Ambition" wasn't a word I was unfamiliar with. Sarah and I had had ambitions. At first, they were huge and vast and yet still felt oh-so achievable. We'd work as hard as we could for a year or two. I'd make head of department; she'd become a senior analyst. We'd save our money, Sarah would hit her targets, we'd only spend the bonuses on things we really wanted, like breaks in the Cotswolds or a weekend in New York. We'd buy the small house we were renting in Fulham for a steal, paint the whole thing white, retile the bathroom, and sell it on for sixty grand above its value. Then we'd take a year out, fly to Thailand, buy a rickety canary yellow VW camper, and live off rice throughout Southeast Asia for twelve tanned months.

Then: stage 2. We'd return to the UK rested and wise, and Sarah would be begged to return to work, where she'd be made some kind of senior partner and impart her newfound Eastern philosophies in front of shocked boards and impressed clients, and I would write up my notes from the road and secure a three-book publishing deal and a post as contributing editor to a travel magazine called something fancy and ethereal.

But you know what? Things got in the way. The car needed a new exhaust. One night the clanking we'd assumed was a burglar dragging his spanner across our railings was instead a thoughtful suicide note from an unhappy boiler. I got dragged into more and more meetings at work, my shoulders became heavier, my dreams fell further away before ever getting any closer; we'd weekend in Whitstable but never New York. It was like we were constantly waiting for the *Mad Men* finale to come on, but the announcer kept saying we had to watch yet another episode of *The One Show* first.

We decided to concentrate for a while on the achievable: the house. But then Mrs. Lampeter got sick, and her son took over her interests, and he convinced her to sell up, and must've seen the same episode of Sarah Beeny as us, because four months later the house had white walls and a retiled bathroom and laminated flooring and was on for sixty grand more than it was worth.

So we moved to North London, where Sarah didn't hit her targets and I failed to make head of department.

And then one day Sarah had a miscarriage.

I know.

I'm sorry.

I didn't mention it before. I didn't want it to cloud your judgment or tug on your heartstrings. I didn't want you to know what we'd lost, knowing what surrounded it. Because that's all you'd have thought about; all you'd have considered.

Does it make it worse, what I did to Sarah, when she'd had a miscarriage a year before? Yes. Yes, of course it does. So maybe, if we're being honest here, that's why I didn't tell you. And now that we're laying our cards on the table, now that we're going for it, here's the worst thing, the thing I still find hardest, the thing I hate: selfishly—unforgivably—some little part of me in there felt relief.

Horrible, I know. Horrible is how I feel even just putting that to paper. But honest and aboveboard, too, and I hope you'll at least take that into account, because that's got to count for something.

We hadn't planned it. We just found out one day that she was pregnant. A week of panic, of highs and lows; a week of planning then followed.

And another day later, as quickly as that: nothing.

For Sarah, it changed things irrevocably. Made her focus, realize what she wanted, what she nearly had, how selfishly we'd been living our lives. She was destroyed and distraught at first, and I was strangely jealous of her instant connection with something that never even was; that she could picture a future far better and more fulfilling than the lowly ambitions we'd carefully shared and nurtured since day one, all based on something that was there just a moment. And I imagined she hated me for not having that, too, not wanting it like she now did. But all I could think about was how life had nearly changed. How little control I actually had over my own destiny. How unhappy I was not . . . *doing* something.

Still.

Today was Sarah's engagement party. Sarah was going to where she wanted to be. She was on the way.

And all I had to do was turn up and wish her all the very best.

I could do that.

"What have you brought?" I asked, suspiciously. "It stinks!"

"Pamela recommended it," said Dev, holding it at arm's length. Whatever it was was wrapped tightly in a blue plastic bag, and I was happy about that. "It's some kind of cheese."

I smiled. "Pamela? You popped in to see Pamela, did you?"

"She has a boyfriend, Jason."

"They won't mind me coming, will they?" asked Abbey, struggling into the straps of her backpack as we stepped off the bus. "I just sort of invited myself last night, didn't I?"

"I'm pleased you're here," I said, which was true.

Sure, the adult thing would've been to go alone, make polite chitchat with semiacquaintances or never-before-met family members who'd feel awkward when they discovered who I was. "Oh, you're *that* Jason," they'd say, all rictus-grins and backing-aways. Far better for everyone concerned for me to have my own team.

The party was at the Queen & Artichoke, just off Great Portland Street, in the upstairs room.

There was Anna, straightaway, in my face, backlit by a harsh sun through the window, dust dancing all around her.

"It's very mature of you to come," she said, not quite making eye contact, "although I suppose it *is* in a pub."

"Nice to see you again, Anna."

"I see you've brought your prostitute with you."

Abbey was standing in the corner, staring at the ceiling like it was confusing her.

"She was joking about that," I said, a little unnecessarily. "I don't really eat pies and cry."

She looked me up and down.

"Well, I'm not sure about the pies," she said, smiling.

I let her have that.

"Brought some cheese," said Dev, shoving it straight in her hands, pleased to be rid of it. "You're welcome."

I scanned the room as Anna backed away. Oh, there was Ben. And Chloe. And a host of other people I hadn't seen in some time. I'd hidden away after Sarah and I broke up. Given up my friends so that she could have them. I'd just wanted it to be easy on her, and easier on me. And that meant never really confronting things. Why should it be so hard, seeing these people again? Was it just the shame, or was it that by seeing them again I was admitting my previous cowardice?

A waitress slipped by and I reached for a vol-au-vent. Anything to look busy.

"Nice spread," said Dev, chewing something. "Bet you can't get a prawn ring in an Aldi for *miles* around here!"

And then Gary was there.

"Jason Priestley!" he said, putting his hand on my shoulder and trying to make sure everyone could *see* he was putting his hand on my shoulder. "Not the one from the *Beverly Hills* program, of course! Good of you to come. Sarah told me she'd invited you. I said it was fine."

He spotted Abbey. She was taking a picture of a potted plant on her bright pink phone.

"Is that your . . . friend? I can't remember. You had a photo of her? Whitby and all that?"

"No, that's . . . another friend."

He winked at me.

"Good work."

"It's not like that," I said. "She is literally a friend."

He winked again.

"Understood," he said.

"No, I mean it."

"Course you do."

He winked a *third* time.

"So, how are things with—" I started, but Gary had a piece of paper out, and popped his finger to his lip.

"Speechwork," he said. "Better just work out what I'm going to say."

He sidled away, and in the corner of the room, there was Gary's fiancée, glowing, happy, blooming. She was surrounded by her friends, excitedly chattering away at her, but after a moment I guess she sensed she was being watched, because she turned her head slightly, took me in, smiled a welcome, and raised her glass at me.

Dev was suddenly by my side again, a plate of vol-au-vents in his hand, and two pints crushed up against his chest.

"Here y'go," he said, as I took one. "Where's Abs?"

We looked around. She was nowhere to be seen. She'd probably been distracted by a fly, and followed it outside, or something.

"Not exactly a rocking party, is it?" said Dev.

"It's only three o'clock. I'm not sure it's supposed to be rocking."

"What happens at these things then? We just sort of stand around, do we?"

"We do. We just sort of stand around. It's the being seen that counts. We're here to be seen, because when we're seen here, we're seen supporting."

"Oh," said Dev, disappointed. "So, there's no, like, brides-maids or anything?"

"Not at an engagement party, generally, no."

"So what is it, just like, vicars and shit, yeah?"

"If that helps you, yes."

Dev nodded, and looked around the room.

I guess I should've started mingling, but to be honest I didn't feel I'd earned the right. I could only be a minglee.

I could sense Anna in the corner of the room, already spreading whatever gossip she could, all plaintive nods and subtle glances. She'd already have told people about bumping into me with Abbey, how *young* she was, how immature that made me, how she'd always thought I'd had deeper problems, deeper issues, how lucky Sarah was to have met Gary, how there's always a silver lining. Some people mask negativity so well, just by coating it with a clingfilm-deep layer of concern.

"All right?" said Abbey, suddenly there, as another waitress slid by, carrying a pompous tray of tiny muffins.

"Where've you been?"

"Kitchen," she said. "What's been happening? Has anyone got off with anyone else yet?"

I checked my watch.

"*Five* past three now. You'd think it'd have happened."

Abbey giggled. She'd seen something. I followed her gaze but didn't get it.

"What?" I said.

"Nothing," she said, and giggled again.

"What is it?"

"Not yet," she said. "I had an idea. I'll tell you in a bit."

My God, Gary could talk.

"Taking Sarah to Florida next month," he said. "She was like, 'Save it for the honeymoon!,' but the world is there to be traveled, y'know? We'll just go somewhere better for the honeymoon."

I felt a childish need to compete.

"I'm going hot-air ballooning soon," I said. "And also to Silverstone. But first I'm going hot-air ballooning and we're going to drink champagne in the air."

Gary looked at me like I was mental.

"Also, I'm taking on the SAS soon at paintball."

He continued: "Thing about Florida is, you're never unsure what the weather's going to be like. My parents are moving out there soon, so we'll be able to stay with them every year, you know, with the little one."

I smiled. Rocked back on my heels, nodded. Gary paused a second and looked at me, sadly.

"You two never think about having kids?" he said.

Oh, Gary, don't, please.

"Nope," I said, as matter-of-factly as I could. "Never the right time."

Sarah hadn't told him. Why would she? It was history. Today was about the future.

"Oh, there's never a 'right time' for kids, Jason!" He laughed, like he'd coined the phrase, like he already had hundreds of children. "Until it happens. *Then* it's the right time."

"Yep."

"She's starting to show now," he said, wistfully, and we both looked over at happy, beautiful Sarah.

She *was* starting to show. And for just a second it was all too much.

The thing I'd never told her, what I always wished I had but now never could, was that I'd wanted it, too. Once I'd got over the shock, once I'd vanquished those confused, selfish thoughts, I'd wanted what she wanted. And when I'd messed it up, when Sarah had gone and left me and I'd been forced to just keep my head down and convince myself I was okay, that if I just plowed on I'd be fine . . . I felt like I'd lost *two* people, not just one. I felt like I'd lost a *family*, because a family is what we could've been and nearly once were.

I'd lost a whole other life.

"She looks amazing, Gary," I said, and then, not out of engagement-party banter but because I painfully, truthfully meant it: "You're a really lucky man."

Outside, by the bins, I sat and toyed with my phone.

I was fine, really. I just needed a moment. To be confronted with the truth of it all—that I'd stayed where I was when where I was wasn't all that great, while others had moved on—was hard enough. When they'd moved on so well, it was a quiet moment of torture.

And then Sarah came out and sat down next to me.

"It was good of you to come, Jason."

A pause. A silent nod from us both. I stared straight ahead while she clinked the ice around in her glass, the noise somehow louder than the buses and cars and bikes of London.

"I'm being a dick," I said, powerless to come up with anything more convincing than the truth. "I just needed a moment. It was hot in there and—"

"The thing you need to remember," she said, "is that you didn't want any of this. So don't mourn it."

"I'm not mourning it. I'm celebrating it, not mourning it."

Actually, I was mourning it. But that's what the selfish do. We mourn what we have, and we mourn what we lose when we realize that we're no longer the center of attention, or even just a part of things.

"We'll always sort of love each other," she said. "We were part of each other's lives. We still can be."

I faked a small smile. Was that true? I mean, really? Things had changed, and soon they'd change further.

"You know I always wanted kids one day," she said. "It's happening sooner than I'd thought, but you could always choose to be happy for me."

"I *am* happy for you," I said. "Honestly, Sarah."

"But you never wanted them."

"I never knew what I wanted. I'm only finding out that I do. And anyway, we never talked about it. How do you know what I wanted?"

"I could tell. Do you think someone can't tell if their boyfriend wants kids one day? Look...when we nearly had what we nearly had—"

This was how we'd always described it. The truth had always been too raw and too difficult to tackle head-on. *When we nearly had what we nearly had* was our way of couching it in something, creating some distance between the pain and the present.

"—well, it was pretty obvious, Jase. I could see how you felt. There was a coldness there."

"You never asked me."

"You never *told* me. You didn't need to. And then you did what you did and everything was clear."

And then you did what you did. Our other pain-limiting catchphrase. Do all couples develop these? These ways of dealing with the horror of it all?

"When I did what I did . . . it wasn't because of what we nearly had. I wanted what we nearly had, too. It just took me a little time to realize."

"But, Jason, you didn't *not* do what you did."

She was speaking tenderly now, like I was fragile, precious, breakable.

"You did what you did *despite* what we nearly had. You did it despite everything we *already* had. You did it. And it broke my heart. Not forever, but for a while, because, as obvious as it sounds, I loved you."

I looked at her for the first time. Her eyes were pricked with tears and something jolted in my heart and I just wanted to fling my arms around her. But how would that look? The evil ex-boyfriend making one last pass at someone else's pregnant fiancée? She knew, because she always knew, and she smiled a faint smile.

"I'm so sorry, Sar," I said, and then I could feel the tears, too.

When I walked back inside, Dev was on me in an instant, pouncing like a tiger.

"I've got a great name for a band!" he said. "Thought of it just now. Shall we start a band?"

"What? No," I said, looking over at Sarah, now back in the corner, laughing away like nothing had happened. We'd walked in separately, for obvious reasons, and I'd grabbed the first drink I could and all but skulled it. "Why? What's your great name for a band?"

"It's 'Great Name for a Band'! That way, we could shout, 'We've been Great Name for a Band,' and everyone would be, like, 'That's a *great* name for a band!'"

"Yeah, okay, sure, let's start a band."

"Who's starting a band?" said Abbey, suddenly there.

"Me and Jason," said Dev, proudly. "Do you want to be in it?"

"Me? God, no. I have little to no talent."

I blinked and remembered last night. The CD poking slyly out of her bag. *Abbey's Songs*.

"Where've you been?" asked Dev. "I was stuck here this whole time talking to that thin man."

"I was talking to Gary," she said, turning to me and smiling, broadly. "And also to Anna."

Her smile didn't leave her face. I wasn't sure what to say. But it was clear she wanted me to say something.

"And . . . was that nice?" I tried.

She just kept smiling.

So I looked over at Gary. Now *he* was talking to that thin man, and balancing a little paper plate on his wrist. So far so normal.

And then I went a little white.

"What the fuck did you do?" I said, quickly, and her smile only broadened, delighted I'd noticed. "Oh, God, Abbey, what?"

I broke away from them and started to pace toward Gary. I could see Sarah in the corner of my eye looking overconcerned, like she thought she'd dealt with me but now here I was, determined to cause a scene. I slowed down, instinctively, but as I got closer . . .

"Now that's a cake," said Gary. "Wotcha, Jason."

"Wotcha," I said, which I won't be trying again. "What, um . . . so, what are you eating there?"

Over his shoulder I saw Anna. She had one, too. She was staring at hers like she didn't like it much, but was munching it down nevertheless.

I felt a little tug on the back of my shirt and I turned to look at Abbey, shocked.

She was smiling in anticipation, her eyes sparkling like she was getting ready to cry laughing, Dev next to her, looking confused.

I turned back, slowly.

"Teacake, I think," said Gary. "Bit dry. But *delicious*, too."

Oh dear God.

I grabbed Abbey, moved her to one side, as Gary asked Dev how "the good ship Nissan Cherry" was doing.

"What have you *done*?" I said, and that was when she cracked. And a second after she cracked, the dam burst.

She laughed, and laughed, and she had to grab a six-foot dragon plant to steady herself, but when that rocked about, she just laughed even more.

I moved her into the hallway.

"Are you *high*?" I said, my teacher voice suddenly back in play from who knows where.

"No!" she spluttered, and laughed even more.

"What the fuck have you done?" I asked, and she might as well have exploded at that point. "Do you know how dangerous that is? Do you realize how *irresponsible* you've been?"

"Come on!" she said, between breaths. "This is funny. This is funny. You're at your ex's engagement party with some of the most boring and sullen people on earth, one of whom thinks you have a drink problem and the other who just patronizes you all the time. How else were you going to enjoy it?"

"I didn't come here to enjoy it! I came here to show how mature I am! And now you've given Gary and Anna some spacecakes."

Abbey took that in. Thought again of what had happened and who they'd blame, and exploded again.

"Jason, if you and Svetlana are ready," said a stern Anna, leaning through the doorway, all judgment and scorn, "we'd like to begin the speeches. But take your time. This is your day, after all."

I looked again at Abbey, shook my head the way I'd done countless times as a teacher, took a breath, and strode back into the room.

Oh, God, this was horrible.

This was like a time bomb. A really formal time bomb where you're not allowed to mention the time bomb.

Twenty minutes later, I was standing between Dev and Abbey in this crowd of maybe forty people and my nerves were racked.

Please let it have been weak stuff, I kept thinking. Please don't let there be any noticeable effects. Please let Abbey have been terribly ripped off, or incapable of basic cookery, or just plain wrong.

I was sweating. Dev was oblivious. Abbey kept shaking slightly as she stifled her laughter, and leaning into me to steady herself.

I felt sick.

Sarah was up first. Start the speeches, I kept thinking. Or cancel them! Cancel the speeches!

I looked over at Gary, but all I could see was the top of his head, and Anna was leaning against a wall. Is that what people do? I thought, panicked. Is leaning against a wall the first sign of spacecakes?

"Just to say, thanks so much for coming," said Sarah. "It means the world to both Gary and myself. God, I should start calling him my fiancé!"

Polite, well-meaning laughter. That was my chance to look around.

Anna was on her third cake.

"Anna's had *three*," I hissed, desperately, and Abbey burst out laughing. "How many did you give her?"

"Three. Don't worry, that's it now. I said my nan made them. She said, 'How lovely,' but then looked at me like I couldn't afford Waitrose ones or something, so I felt like giving her more."

"*DON'T!*" I said, as loudly as you'd imagine. I made an apologetic face to the dozen or so people who turned to stare at us. Sarah carried on.

"Christ, Abbey," I whispered. "I'm all for free spirits, so long as there are sensible limits in place. There need to be *rules* for free spirits."

"It also means the world that not only do we have some of our newer friends here—friends we made as a couple—but that there are people here who've been part of our lives for considerably longer..."

That was me. Sarah was talking about me. I felt my face flush.

"...like our families..."

Oh.

"...and others."

She glanced over, gave me a half-smile, long enough to mean it but short enough not to be disrespectful to Gary.

"Often in life, we move on. It's natural. But you can't delete a real friend."

Someone in the crowd said "aw."

"And on that note, over to my fiancé!"

Everyone started clapping. I took my chance to whisper, "We

could go now, we should go now," but Dev said, "Speeches are the best bit!," and stayed put.

The clapping petered out, and there were more good-natured chuckles, as Gary was nowhere to be seen. Oh, *fuck*. Sarah stepped back to the center of the room.

"Er, I'll do that again! Over to my fiancé!"

More chuckles. But still no Gary.

Then, from someone at the back: "Gary! You're on!"

Gary emerged carrying a small plate stacked with food. It was like he was trying to play Jenga with it.

"Fooood!" he said. "Dig in! Dig in! Food is, yes, lots of it."

He put the plate down on the table next to him, and then picked it up again.

"So! Absolutely. Let me see."

He tried to get his piece of paper out of his pocket but seemed unwilling to put his plate down.

I looked at Abbey. She was watching, open-mouthed, wide-eyed, loving it.

"So!" he said, again, trying to unfold the paper, putting his plate down, failing to unfold it again, picking his plate up, abandoning the paper, and saying instead, "I'll just speak from the heart."

This is not good. This is *not good*.

"Friends!" he started. "Are like flowers!"

That same woman said "aw" again.

"You must water flowers! But also give them sunshine!"

I am not overusing the exclamation marks here. He was doing a lot of exclaiming.

"You are our flowers! And we are watering you."

"Here, here!" yelled a bawdy man, raising his pint glass. His wife shushed him and made him put his hand down again.

"Ahaha!" said Gary. "Here, here, indeed. Here . . . here, there and everywhere. Are friends!"

He seemed finished. One lady, who seemed to think this was some kind of haiku, attempted to start the applause. But Gary was far from finished.

"He's quite poetic, Gary. Isn't he?" whispered Dev, as I stared, blankly, ahead of me.

Abbey kept nudging me. I could feel her shaking. I looked around the room. Most people seemed confused. One or two seemed to be getting really into it. I caught sight of Sarah, studying her feet, her hand covering her eyes.

And then I saw Anna.

Anna was grinning and clicking her fingers, trying to find the rhythm in Gary's words.

"It might be time to go," I said, snapping out of it.

"This is all very unusual," said Dev.

Abbey wiped the tears from her eyes.

We snuck away, as Gary moved on to reason two of six of why he chose the Lexus over the Porsche Cayenne.

"What just happened?" asked Dev, as Abbey broke down into fits outside. "What just happened there?"

"Jason, you don't need those people," said Abbey, calming down. "You've got nothing to prove to them. I don't know why you were so nervous. When I walked in, I thought, These? *These* are the people he's scared of? Who *cares* what they think?"

"We could literally go to prison, Abbey," I said, but as I looked at her, there was that glint of cheekiness, of impishness, the life-affirming, soul-enhancing *who-cares?* of it all, and though I wanted to be stern and prim and teacherly, I just couldn't anymore. She caught the faintest glimpse of a smirk.

And that was when she really lost it. Howlingly, tearfully lost it.

And that was when I gave up and let the laughter in, too.

I laughed, because laughing was so much easier than crying, and out it all came, all the emotion, the turmoil, the nerves, the anger, the loneliness, the despair, the sweet relief that it was over.

And when the laughter subsided, and we collapsed on a bench, drained and in pain, tears dried on our cheeks, Dev held out the disposable at arm's length and said, "Smile!"

Only an hour later, with guilt still many miles away, did I think to look at my phone. I'd had an e-mail.

"This could be the chance!" said Abbey, a little later still, at the coach station. "You're narrowing down the odds! Achieving your ambition!"

"Maybe," I said. "Maybe."

"Just got to get me some now!"

I hugged her good-bye and thought about what I had to do next.

Number 1: What to do at Damien's own Forest Laskin PR launch next week.

Number 2: Get my iPod out of my pocket and listen to the tracks I'd secretly imported from a recordable CD I'd nabbed from a backpack late last night. That would bring its own fun.

Life was good!

It wouldn't be for much longer.

EIGHTEEN

Or "You Burn Me Up, I'm a Cigarette"

I had never seen Dev so absolutely insistent that he have a full English breakfast.

"I heard a rumor," he said, conspiratorially. "Pawel said Tomasz said Marcin told him."

"Who's Marcin?"

"Marcin. Marcin with the ankles."

"I'm not sure what that means."

"It means there's a *chance*!"

We sat outside the café, as his head bobbed and weaved, trying to catch sight of where Pamela might be. I was sure if Pamela could see him do this she would fall instantly in love with him, providing she was looking for love with a meerkat.

But Pamela wasn't here. It was her boss working a shift, instead.

He was a hard-looking man we'd see every now and again, reading a Polish newspaper in the corner, scratching a strange blue tattoo he didn't seem to want anymore. He had the air about him of the drunk in the pub who walked that wide-eyed tightrope between telling you you were all right and slamming your head into the table. We tended not to talk to him too much for this and maybe six other reasons.

But today Dev felt different.

"Um . . . where is Pamela?" he asked.

"Ha ha ha," said the man, who I'm not convinced understood the question. He slid our plates onto the table. The eggs now covered the bacon, slopping over it, shimmying in the sun.

"The girl?" said Dev. "Uh . . . Pam-*eh*-lah?"

"Ah!" said the manager. "Yeh! Pamela. Yeh."

He made a grumpy face and put his hands on his hips, hitting a new low in international mime.

"She here?" asked Dev, pointing at the café. "*Où est* Pamela?"

"No," said the manager. Then he rubbed his eyes and pretended to cry for a second.

Then: "Ha ha ha!"

He turned and walked off.

"That was odd," I said.

"Was he saying I was sad, or she was?" asked Dev. "Because if he was saying she was sad, the rumors could be true!"

"Maybe he was saying you were both a little sad, but in different ways."

He nodded, a little lost.

"So what's the invite?" he asked, because that morning, quite unexpectedly, I'd received an envelope in the post, all cream and embossed and linen, like my gas bill's pompous cousin.

"Sarah's wedding," I replied, patting my pocket to make sure it was still there. "I obviously passed the grown-up test. They're just cracking on. Gary wants to be married by the time their kid pops out."

"Yeah, not that invite. I saw that invite. *The* invite. The *exciting* invite."

Aha. *The* invite.

The e-mail had been marked "Tropicana—Urgent" and as such I nearly ignored it (because really, unless there's a Tropicana Monster, how urgent can anything about Tropicana really be?) until I'd looked once more and finally taken in whom it was actually from.

"Say it's a Grand Prix or something. Or a premiere! Or the launch of a new vodka. That'd have models at it, I bet, all dressed in silver and handing out vodka. Or the Golden Joysticks! Let it be silver models or the Golden Joysticks!"

Dev has always wanted to go to the Golden Joystick Awards. He says he thinks it's probably magical. I think it's probably in the basement of a Hilton.

"It's like the Oscars of the videogames world. Everyone's there. All the big names."

"Like who?"

"You wouldn't have heard of them. These are not that type of big name."

"Well, it's not the Golden Joysticks. It is in fact"—I showed him the e-mail and made a little *ta-dah* noise—"the launch of the new Tropicana Acai Berry range!"

He nodded at me, willing it to be better news than it was.

"Tropicana," he said, taking it in.

"Apparently acai berries contain ninety percent more anti-oxidants than previously thought," I said.

"Well, I suppose that's good news."

"It's at a manor house in the countryside. I imagine there'll be models dressed as berries."

Dev suddenly looked very interested indeed.

"Guess who's about to win his first major comedy competition?" said Clem, beaming, pointing at himself with both hands.

"Is it you, Clem?"

"It is indeed, sir! Yes, sir! Well, I say 'win,' I mean 'enter,' really, but I've got a veeery good feeling about it."

Clem seemed to be one of those people who could remain entirely oblivious to the mood of the room around them. I wasn't. I pick up on these things—take my mood from whatever's going on in the room. And right now, unlike a booming Clem, I was quiet.

Zoe wasn't in this morning. Sam said she thought Zoe was on a course, but people who work at *London Now* don't get sent on courses. Someone else thought she was meeting with Daryl Channing, the swaggering, one-of-the-boys owner of *Manchester Now*, *London Now*, and, until he closed it just before Christmas, *Glasgow Nights*.

Clem stared at his flyer for the Chuckle Cabin's New Act of the Year award, perhaps imagining himself holding the novelty plastic banana they hand out to whichever comedian goes best on the night and making a funny speech.

I put my feet up and leafed through the latest edition of *London Now*. I found the right page and smiled to myself.

She was going to *love* this.

Indeed, that night, *I can't believe you did that!* was the text I got from Abbey.

Ha! I replied, and waited for her to text something else.

But nothing came, so I wrote again.

Did you like the picture? It was off Dev's phone!

Again, nothing. Nothing for hours and hours.

So I pottered about, attended to my business. I wrote a review of the Scala gig, and put new batteries in the TV remote control. I fixed myself a sandwich, took the bins out, bought fresh milk. And started to wonder why I still hadn't heard from Abbey.

So I looked once more at her text. And realized I'd made a mistake.

It didn't say, *I can't believe you did that!*

It said, *I can't believe you did that.* Flat, and with no exclamation mark.

ABBEY'S SONGS—ABBEY GRANT
Lightness of touch meets soulful seaside splendor

Brighton's doing well at the moment, musically. At the beginning of the year The Kicks burst onto the scene—and now please welcome the soulful grace of up-and-coming singer/songwriter Abbey Grant...

That was how it began, this five-star review of an album no one could possibly hear yet. No one but Abbey and me. This was supposed to be a gift. A nod of understanding to a girl who claimed she had no dream but clearly did. Because this was her dream, surely, and the best thing was: she was good at it. It was achievable! Okay, so the recording left something to be desired, and there was no production to speak of, just real-time recordings of her with an acoustic guitar or sometimes a mate with an accordion or something . . . but that just made it better, for me. More real, and more live, and more like life.

Abbey had kept this quiet, this CD of songs and hope and love, but why? It seemed ridiculous. She had the power to go places, and I didn't understand why she didn't grab it. Was she just scared? In my head, this review—my generous intervention—was all she needed. Outside acknowledgment. A friend telling her she was good, making it okay to take the next step, and I would be that friend. But I would do it in a spectacular way. I would do it in the pages of *London Now*, and give her her first press quotes, something to cut out and stick on the front of CDs, just like The Kicks had done. Force her to take this further.

That had been the plan.

The plan did not appear to be working.

"You've *embarrassed* me," she said, that night, on the phone, hurt, angry.

"I didn't mean to," I said, and I was desperate for her to believe me. I spoke urgently and with care. "It was supposed to be a *nice* thing. I swear I thought it'd—"

"You go in my bag, you steal my songs—"

"I didn't steal them, I just listened . . ."

"You stole them. You made copies. You stole them because they were mine and now they're not."

"What? Yes, they are!"

"You took my diary, basically, and you read it and you made copies of it and you wrote about it in your paper."

"Abbey, no, look—I saw the CD and—"

"That stuff you wrote—about my relationship with Paul . . ."

"I didn't write about it. I just said that there was one song in there about being trapped, and—"

"I'm not trapped! And it's not about Paul. You were clearly implying it was about Paul."

I kept schtum. I *had* thought it was about Paul.

"Paul read it. He got angry; he wanted to know what was wrong with me. He didn't know about the songs. Now I've had to show him. Do you know how embarrassing that was for me? You took something from me. I don't know why. You're so self-ish. Why would you do that? You were taking *massive* liberties!"

"Well, where do you think I learned to do that, Abbey? Who was it that walked into my flat and deleted my ex-girlfriend? 'Oh, you don't need this,' you said. Maybe I thought this was something you *did* need!"

"You're just another one of those people, Jason."

"What people?"

"You're just another face in the crowd, aren't you?"

"Abbey, I'm your mate, I'm—"

And I listened, as the receiver clattered against something—the table, I guess—and was picked up, and placed heavily back on the phone.

I kicked myself for what I'd done. Of course she'd be angry. If she'd wanted people to know about her songs, she'd . . . well . . . she'd have sung them. Something about that night—the way the CD had been poking out of her bag, willing itself seen, and all right after we'd talked of life, and ambition and dreams—had made me feel like what I was doing was undeniably right.

And, sod it, it was, wasn't it? This was the kind of over-reaction you'd expect from girls like Abbey. I'm not saying she's flighty, or ditzy, because she's actually one of the most together people I've met, but she's emotional, isn't she? Led by her heart. Actually, that should mean she'd *get* me doing something like this. This was for her. All completely from the right place, straight from the heart, and if anything she should be grateful she's got someone looking out for her like this. I mean, yeah, maybe I should've left Paul out of things, I accept that now as I did then. I hadn't named him, of course; I'd just mentioned somewhere in the review that Abbey's sly, light lyrics showed a woman who'd lived or was living within a relationship that might not be entirely good for her. That may have given things away, as far as Paul was concerned.

That, and the fact that I said it was a song about not living your life as someone else's puppet.

I didn't know what to do. The review was out. Right there, in a hundred thousand copies of a freesheet, swirling around the capital, on benches, in bars, on buses, with five stars and a black-and-white picture taken on a phone.

So I picked up my mobile and I sent a text.

I'm really sorry is all I could say.

And I sat by my phone and waited for a reply.

Three days later, and Mackenzie Hall was a full-on Tropicana celebration.

I have no idea where the money comes from for events like this. Or how you go about planning it. My list would, I imagine, start at balloons and end at cake, like I was planning a toddler's birthday party. But these people were pros.

There were the Tropicana girls for a start. A dozen or so students/models in white catsuits and capes—capes!—holding trays of spiked juices.

Dev suddenly became a huge fan of Tropicana.

"You need to slow down," I said, as he plucked another boozie smoothie from a moving silver tray.

"They're free and I'm nervous. There are women in capes here. Do you know how that makes me feel? That makes me feel like I'm around superheroes."

"They're models, not cat lady."

"Cat *Woman*. It's Cat *Woman*. Do you think I'd be nervous if they looked like cat *ladies*?"

Forest Laskin had arranged a fleet of luxury cars—all Audi R8s and walnut dashboards and black leather bucket seats—and invited us to drive around the grounds, imagining a life that'd never be ours. Some of the more important journalists had been picked up from Bath in blacked-out alloyed-up Range Rovers, allowed for an hour to picture themselves as bona fide VIPs, rather than the people who write the RDA! section of *Good Food*, or the picture captions in the Sainsbury's magazine.

A few announcements had been made already, by the girl who does the entertainment reports on *Wake Up Call*. You

292 · CHARLOTTE STREET

know the one. She's in Cannes one week, then suddenly on a jet ski with Gary Barlow the next. Came third on *Strictly*. Anyway, she was a big fan of the new Tropicana range, luckily, "because Tropicana has sixty years' experience in blending fruit, so perhaps it's the knowledge that goes into every carton that makes Tropicana taste so good!" I liked that about her. Professional. On message. She'd be around later for a Q&A and on another note has a new fitness DVD out in the autumn, which was news to Dev, who likes to keep his eye on these things.

Ocean Colour Scene would be playing tonight in the marquee. Someone stood the chance to win business-class flights to New York in the raffle. There was a small bottle of champagne in every room (forty-two, since you ask—thirty-three in the main and coach house, six family holiday rooms for the big hitters, and three in the lodge, for Laskin and Co.). Some people seemed excited by the free spa treatments in the Cowshed Sanctuary; the others muttered they'd make do with the mixologists in the library.

I drank my juice and looked around. This was what it was all about. This, right here. Forget Pulitzers, forget front-page splashes or toppling governments. Journalists who had never once in their lives written anything about—or even mentioned in casual conversation—their love of quality, healthful fruit juice, wandered around with press packs and T-shirts, ready to get the presentation out of the way, thrilled to have been given room and board for the night, already planning what from their goodie bags they could legitimately give to family members this Christmas.

And over there in the corner, talking to a couple of girls with headsets and clipboards, was the man who'd put it all together. Damien Anders Laskin.

The flights, the cars, the treatments, the DVD, I began to realize, all from clients of the mighty Forest Laskin.

I tried to catch his eye. To raise my eyebrow in a friendly manner, a thank-you manner, a nice-to-see-you-again manner, but everyone else was trying to do that, too, and in the hierarchy of things, a *Grazia* nod is worth five from *London Now*.

And anyway, that wasn't why I was here.

"I don't see her," said Dev. "She's not one of the Tropicana girls."

"Stop looking at the Tropicana girls," I said.

"Why *are* they wearing capes?" he said.

Part of me had been sure The Girl would be a journalist, but more and more, looking at the people Damien surrounded himself with, the people he employed, I was starting to think she was part of his team.

Presentation is half of PR. You need to be presentable; you need a presentable team.

Damien had, let's say, an eye for presentation.

And when I looked over once more, he had his arm round a very presentable wife, who was holding their very presentable son.

"Hmm," said Dev.

"So would you say you'd always had an interest in fruit juice?"

It was my turn interviewing the girl from *Wake Up Call*. I remembered her name, now: Estonia Marsh. There it was, in bright, gold, embossed letters across the top of her new DVD: *Fit Needn't Be Harsh . . . with Estonia Marsh.* Dev seemed to be quietly tracing the shape of her leg with his finger. He'd seemed like a little lost lamb when the Forest Laskin girl had come to fetch me for my face-to-face with Estonia. He's not good in crowds. Falls apart in busy places. I guess that's why he's so relaxed in Power Up!

"Don't leave me out here," he'd said, eyes pleading. "The men all look like they know about football. You know what happened last time you left me with men who know about football. I panicked. I said I had a season ticket for Arsenal versus Brazil. I wasn't making sense on any level."

The PRs hadn't minded. I'd said he was our intern, and now Estonia Marsh was answering my questions with speed and professionalism as Dev sipped away on a fresh glass.

"Eating healthily is important to me and I treat Tropicana like it's one of my five-a-day!"

"And . . . what is it about *this* fruit juice in particular that you like so much?"

"It's important to me to keep a well-stocked fridge, particularly when it comes to vitamins, and the new EasyPour system the guys at Tropicana have introduced has made it easier than ever for me to get a quick vitamin fix!"

I nodded, and pretended to take notes.

There was a pause. I wasn't really sure where to take this next. I'd already asked her whether she liked fruit juice in two different ways and I wasn't certain there was a third.

"And . . . do you have any funny stories about fruit juice?" I tried.

She looked flummoxed. Her eyes darted nervously to the PR in the corner.

"Um . . ."

"Or not *funny*, exactly. But true? Or even just stories?"

"Stories about fruit juice . . . ," she said slowly, searching her back catalog, but coming up blank.

And then Dev piped up.

"My friend Jason is trying to find a girl whose camera he found. He thinks she might be The One."

"Okay, Dev . . . ," I said, quickly, eyes wide and moving to his empty glass.

"Are you?" she said, flashing me a smile, then sharing it with Dev. "What do you mean?"

"He found a camera. Well, not found. She accidentally left it with him when they met for about three seconds on Charlotte Street one night. He developed the film, and—"

"Um, well, you developed it, Dev, and—"

"However it happened, the film ended up developed, and now he's properly into her because she's properly fit."

"Aw," said the PR in the corner, but I do think he could have put it more romantically.

"So my question to you, as a lady, is: what would your advice be?"

It turns out Estonia Marsh wasn't particularly big on advice, though she did say, "I think you should follow your heart!," and nodded, encouragingly. "Grab life by the horns," she'd said, "and ride it like a bull!"

I hadn't really planned on discussing all this with the entertainments reporter from *Wake Up Call*, so I just blushed and said I would.

Dev had then said, "Have you ever been truly in love, Estonia? Like, *truly*?," and it was then that I decided he should absolutely stop drinking the special Tropicanas for a bit, because the special Tropicanas seemed to be making him wistful and romantic.

"Oh, you know . . . ," she'd replied, raising her eyebrows and looking at the PR in the corner, who jolted into action, and said, "Maybe if we could keep the questions about how fruit juice is advantageous to a healthy lifestyle, especially when used as part of a sensible diet and fitness plan, that would be—"

"Yes!" I'd said. "Absolutely."

"But good luck finding her," said Estonia, smiling.

* * *

"She was terrific," said Dev, outside, by the marquee, where a barbershop quartet was singing the theme tune from *Home & Away*. "Do you think if I relaunched Power Up!, she'd come and open the shop? Should I ask her? Because it would be really good to get a celebrity to reopen the shop."

"Why do you want to reopen the shop? The shop's not closed. It's open."

"I'm just saying, if a relaunch might raise awareness. You know. We could do canapés from Waitrose. Little sausages. Or maybe some of Abbey's special cakes."

"I think you would definitely raise awareness then," I said. "Local paper, police force, that kind of thing."

We fell silent as we looked around. New people had arrived, people too important to have traveled in the morning just for a Q&A with Estonia.

But not one of them was who I wanted them to be.

"She's not going to be here," I said, deflated. "She's just not."

"She might. And then you can say hello."

"What then?"

"Tell her your story."

"And claim this is just coincidence?"

"You've already got coincidence on your side. You're in one of the photos. Or you could not tell her about it, and one day tell your grandchildren you met at the launch of the new Tropicana Acai Berry range."

"There is . . . another thing I could do."

Dev looked at me, quizzically.

I looked across the room, nodded my meaning.

Dev got it.

"No, mate. No, that's a bad idea."

"Why?"

"What we did already is one thing. This is another thing

entirely. Because what we've done so far has just been fun. A fun thing to do. The boys! But that . . . that would make it serious."

"What's the point if it's not serious? You've always been trying to make this more serious!"

"No, but . . . you don't know what you could be doing. Just stumbling into someone's life like that."

The words hit home. I thought of Abbey. I thought of my stumbling. But that had been for her. This was for me. I could grab life by the horns. *Ride it like a bull.*

I looked again across the room, at Damien Anders Laskin, laughing with a girl in a headset, putting his arm around her and pulling her close, and I thought:

Why not just ask him?

"Ladies and gents, the raffle will begin in five minutes," said a man with more pens in his pocket than any human could possibly need. "If you'd like to adjourn to the main hall, please?"

Dev had spent the last fifteen minutes actively discouraging me from what I intended to do. He outlined five or six possible scenarios, and each of them ended up with me getting a black eye, the sack, or another black eye.

"He won't see it the way we see it," he said. "You can tell strangers, like Estonia, but you can't tell Damien. He's something to do with it. He'll care."

"I'm going to do it," I said, and Dev looked terrified.

"He's married, he's got a family, and—"

"Look, I'm not going to accuse him of anything. Remember, I know almost nothing, and I'll tell him that. I'll handle this."

"No, mate, wait," he said. "Wait—"

"For what? This could end it right here. Then I'll know. I'll have an answer!"

"This isn't the way."

"This is the only way. That's the point. We're two degrees away. He knows her. I know him. I can ask."

Dev paused. *"How* are you going to ask?"

Damien smiled at me.

"Having fun?" he said. "I see you brought your friend with you . . ."

"Dev? Yeah! He's doing some intern work with us, and—"

"*Course* he is. No, why not. I'd do the same."

"And thank you again for inviting me. Us."

There was one of those moments. One of those moments where you know you have to shift gears but you just don't know how.

I moved an inch closer, dropped my voice.

"Could I have a word, Damien? It's about something personal."

He looked at me.

"Are you all right?"

"Yes, but maybe we could just step out?"

He frowned, like I'd actually just told him I'd like to cradle his bottom.

Outside the coach house, we stood in the afternoon sun. The fields around us waved and shushed in the breeze, offering advice I ignored.

"Raffle in a minute," said Damien, opening up a box of Marlboros, pulling one out, tapping it on the lid. "I'm supposed to hand out the flights."

"Ah, yes," I said. "New York."

"Do you go much?"

"No. I . . . had plans to. In another life. But no."

"I'm taking Annie and James next weekend. All about the perks, isn't it? They wouldn't normally come to these things, but sod it, why not, a weekend at Mackenzie Hall. She's a sucker for spas and they lay on a nanny for Jim."

He took another drag on his fag and looked at me.

"So what's going on?"

"Well," I started, in as friendly a way as I could. "This will sound very strange. I don't quite know how to explain it."

"So just explain it."

"This thing happened . . ."

"Great start."

"I bumped into a girl one night on the street. I didn't know her. And then, I . . . well . . ."

And then what? I could see Damien was confused, wondering why I was telling him this, what it could possibly have to do with him. What do I say?

Do I say, "And then I realized I had her camera film so I developed it and then tried to follow her footsteps because there was something about her and everything lacking in my life, and I thought maybe this would lead somewhere, somewhere better, and then I saw you in a photo with her and I was weirdly jealous and when I saw you in that bar one night I decided to follow you into a restaurant where we got chatting and you put your trust in me and now here we are!"?

No.

So I reached into my pocket, and I pulled out the one photo I had with me.

The one where she was smiling at someone or something off-camera, her cheeks flushed, hair whipped by the wind, my *favorite* photo.

"It was *this* girl."

This was a risk. It was my big play. It had to work.

And Damien took it, glanced at it, looked back at me.

There was an awkward moment. I half-smiled.

And then Damien blew a plume of smoke to his right and said, very slowly, very purposefully, "Who the *fuck* are you?"

I blinked.

"No, Damien, it's—" but he wasn't listening; he was folding the photo, stuffing it into his pocket, looking around to see who could possibly have seen.

"Who the fuck *are* you?"

"I'm just me!" I said, and then, unnecessarily: "Jason."

"What are you trying to do?" he said, coldly. "What is this, a sting? Who the fuck are you?"

He glanced at the bushes, at the far wall, at the trees, and I realized he was looking for photographers. He was proper PR.

"I'm . . . no one's taking your picture. This is not about your family."

"My family? Why are you talking about my family?"

He was getting close now, I could feel his breath, smell the nicotine, and his arms had tensed like he was preparing for something, a sudden surge of something.

"Damien, this is just about the girl in the picture, I swear, and—"

"Who the fuck *are* you? What do you want? You're here as my guest. You *know* my family is here. Who sent you?"

"No one sent us."

"Us?"

"Me and Dev. We're here for the Tropicana launch."

It sounded absolutely ludicrous in this situation. The word "Tropicana" is not one often used in outdoor confrontations. I felt like pointing that out, like it might puncture the tension, might make this okay again.

"You and your friend need to leave."

"Listen—"

"You need to leave. Right fucking now."

I grabbed Dev.

"We need to leave," I said. "Right fucking now."

"Did it go okay?"

"Not exactly."

"Surprising, that," he said. "Walking up to a man who's here with his family, his friends, and his colleagues and then showing him a picture of a girl he's been having an affair with."

"We don't know that's the case."

"Did he react like it might be the case?"

"Right fucking now," I said, and I forced his glass to the table, and we left.

Outside, we waited for the cab that'd take us to Bath Spa, the train, and our escape. I thought of Damien. He'd invited us here. Now I'd done this.

"Well, I don't blame him," said Dev, which was the last thing I wanted to hear. "How can you blame him?"

"Shut up," I hissed, though I didn't mean to be harsh; I just didn't want to deal with this. I knew I'd been stupid and didn't need it pointed out to me.

"What?" said Dev. "Think about it. You just blew it. You just blew loads of stuff."

"That's enough."

"Now he knows what we did. He knows we stalked him. How do you think *London Now* are going to react? He'll tell them. He'll say you did this. This'll impact on your career."

"Yeah, well, at least I've got one."

Boom. I'd moved straight for the kill.

"Oh, my little shop not good enough, no? You think I don't

know you think that anyway? You think I'm not told that every bloody day?"

"By who? Pawel?"

"By everyone *but* Pawel. At least I'm doing something— at least I love it. Do you love interviewing girls from TV about fruit? And what, you think you and Damien are so different?"

"We *are* different."

"You big up this problem you have with him. That he's here with his family when you reckon he was also with this girl. So he's a cheat. Remind you of anyone?"

"Piss off, that was *different*. You know that was my mistake, but it wasn't calculated. It just happened."

"You know nothing about this man except he has a watch and a car and a flat and you confront him with the 'evidence' of something you know nothing about."

"How was I supposed to find out what it was evidence of if I didn't?"

"That was stupid, what you did. Don't act mental over this."

"Me? You've been on at me from the start to do this!"

"A general search, yes! Something to make your life exciting, yes! To cheer you up and give you hope. But nothing odd."

"*You* made us go to *Whitby*."

Dev smiled, shook his head, looked away.

"What?" I said. "What's that look supposed to mean?"

"It means I had my reasons for Whitby."

"What? What reasons?"

"Here's our cab."

I seethed. I seethed all the way to Bath, I seethed on platform two as I stared at the city, and I seethed all the way back to Paddington after that.

*   *   *

"How was it?" asked Zoe, coldly, as I walked into the office. I'd made it back by six. I hadn't talked to Dev most of the way home and right now I wanted to be anywhere but with him. He was an idiot and I didn't care anymore. Who was he to give me advice?

"Fine," I said, slinging my bag down on my desk. "If you like the new Tropicana Acai Berry range. Anyway, thought I'd come in, stay late. Got a pile of stuff to wade through. Need to knuckle down."

"What happened there?" she said, and Clem immediately stood up and left the room.

I watched him leave, then looked at Zoe. She didn't seem overly happy.

"How do you mean?"

"I had an e-mail from Andrea Sparrow. Not sure if you know who that is?"

"I know who that is."

I didn't know who that was.

"She says that due to your behavior at the launch, you are no longer welcome at any future Forest Laskin events."

Oh, God. That was quick. Even for a number two or three at a big PR outfit, that was quick.

"Fine."

"No, not fine, Jason. Bad. Bad for us. What did you do?"

"Come on. It's one company. They need us more than we need them."

"Oh, is that right? Do you have any idea what we're doing here? Running a tinpot freesheet, miles behind our competition, scrabbling stuff together, and not because we love it, but because we have to because we need jobs?"

"I'm sorry!" I said. "Were we at all likely to run an exclusive story about the new Tropicana Acai Berry range? Are our readers expecting more Tropicana-based insights? Was there a focus group I missed?"

"I let you go because it was a jolly. But it's also good PR for us. It's good PR with the PRs. You just pissed off quite a big name. God knows how. What did you do? Were you drunk?"

"No. Look, I'm sorry, but there are a ton of PRs out there. Ones that are more relevant to what we do. I'll be back on it now, I promise, I've got some good stuff lined up that is totally without mention of fruit juice."

She sighed, put her hand on her hip.

"I can't let you."

"What?"

"I can't let you. You can still write for us. But you can't be reviews ed. I'm sorry, Jase. It was never official; you were only filling in anyway. Rob's feeling better, he'll be back in soon, and we'll make do in the meantime."

"You . . . you've been waiting for this."

"Oh. Yeah. Course. The world's against you."

"Seems that way today."

"Sure. Even though I gave you a chance."

"This is because of us."

"Oh, come *on*, grow up. Really? That was a *lifetime* ago. I moved on. And this is about work. You had a chance to do something with that little section, you know? We have no money. I dunno if you noticed, but we're on a sinking ship. Do you *read* the trades? I gave you that section and you could've made it your own while it lasted. When all that stuff happened between us, you told me that was your aim in life: to have something and shape it as your own; that Sarah didn't understand, but it was what you wanted. Well, maybe it was guilt, but I helped, didn't I? Not because I still liked you, not because I wanted to be with you, but because I was *guilty*."

You know when people tell you you need to hear a few home truths? It's terrific when that happens.

"But instead, what do you do? You review your mate's songs and give them five stars."

She threw down the page with Abbey's review on it.

Abbey's Songs—Abbey Grant. Soulful, powerful, light. Let Abbey show you the way.

"Who is she? Because she's not signed to anyone. She's not on the Internet. There's no MySpace page. No one here's heard of her. The album's not available. You know how I know? Because I wanted to listen to it. That's the sad thing. You made me want to listen to her."

"You'd like her, and it's undiscovered talent. That's valid—"

"You idiot. You can't do that. You can't use the paper to plug your unsigned mates. Five stars, for God's sake. What if someone found out?"

"She's really bloody good, Zo."

"Let's talk about what else you've done while you were here. You copied press releases and pretended you went to see exhibitions you did not go and see."

"I went to gigs! I discovered that band!"

"Everything you've written has been blandly positive. That's not reviewing. That's not being a critic."

"I'm in a good place. And criticism can be—"

"You made sure our name was all over London's most average pizzas."

"They're nice!"

"Did they pay you?"

"What? No!"

"There is an Internet forum currently dedicated to your Abrizzi's review, did you know that? Thirty-one posts. Someone asking who they need to pay to get good reviews."

"Probably rival chains," I said, smally. "It's good buzz—"

"You suggested *terrible* features for elsewhere. Hidden London? Did you ever even reveal where it was?"

"Highgate Cemetery."

"Well, you should go there again," she said. "Visit your career."

That hurt. She could see that. I thought of Dev—what I'd said to him.

"Oh, and the I Saw You thing?" she continued. " 'Get in touch if you want me to give it to you'? Just a bit sad."

Clem. *Bloody* Clem. His revenge. He'd found out that day, hadn't he? Seen what I'd done on his computer. And he'd told the whole office. The final humiliation. How often had that been an in-joke behind my back? What nickname had they come up with for me? Something suitably funny, if Clem was involved, methinks.

"Look, I'm sorry," she said. "You know I'm in an impossible situation here. But pissing Laskin off was just a step too far. Go home, have a drink. We'll go back to how we were. I'll mail you some stuff later in the week. Or if you have any feature ideas, we can look at perhaps—"

But I was already out the door.

Dev was nowhere to be seen when I got in. How things change. I needed him now. If there was one thing Dev was normally fantastic at, it was taking your side. Friendship means the world to Dev. If he'd been at uni with Hitler he'd have probably made him look on the bright side as the seconds ticked away in the bunker.

He hadn't done that today, of course, with the whole Damien thing, but I reasoned that was a blip. He'd take my side now. He had to. I needed him to. He spent his life as an underdog—with girls, with his family. I'd always thought that was maybe why he'd disappear into games. You were always an underdog in a videogame, but always guaranteed to win if you just kept plugging away, learned the moves, knew when to Save and when to Quit. That's what he'd done with Pamela the waitress, wasn't it? Saved his progress. Quit the game. Ready to play another day.

I got my mobile out and tried him. It went straight to answerphone.

"Dev, it's Jase. I think I've been fired. Or not fired exactly. But demoted. Even though it was never official. They'll still let me freelance, but . . . give me a call, yeah?"

I hung up and stared out the window. You could almost see the evening smell of chips on the Caledonian Road, hanging there like an invisible fog, coating people as they shuffled by, processed meats and variety packs weighing down their Iceland bags. A man stood in the doorway of the Ethiopian restaurant, hopping from foot to foot, shaking a worn lighter, trying to coax one last, low flame.

I tried to switch the TV on, but it was pointless because I knew I needed a drink, but I didn't want to drink alone, here on the Cally. Some streets you can do that fine. Charlotte Street, for example. But drinking alone on the Cally would never lead to anything good.

I opened the fridge but that was pointless, too, because the beers we put in there were always that night's beers, just momentary houseguests, always gone the next morning without even a note. I slammed it shut again and out of instinct flicked on the kettle, but lost interest the second I did because I remembered the *jezynowka* Dev kept buying from Pawel. There was always *jezynowka*. Even when you'd had as much of it as you could take, there was always just a little bit left at the bottom.

I flipped open cupboards, moved chipped and cracked porcelain around, even checked behind the Breville in that cupboard at the bottom I don't think I'd ever opened before. No *jezynowka*.

Dev's room.

I knocked, even though I knew he wasn't in there, because that's what I hoped other people might do if ever they walked into my room, and I waited just a second in case anyone replied.

Inside, Dev had left his radio quietly burbling away and his blind half-down. I padded through a minefield of games carts and trainers, over to the bedside table where the bottle sat on a pile of papers, guarded by mugs.

"Hello," I said, because I think I've seen people on TV do that to inanimate objects they're pleased to see, and I picked it up by its sticky neck. The bottom clung to a beermat Dev had picked up somewhere, and I prized it off and dropped it back on the table, but not before something had caught my eye.

Maybe it was the big purple ring that caught it, maybe it was the keywords highlighted by dried blackberry liqueur, or perhaps I'm just a bargain hunter and these words will always mean the world to me.

But there, right at the top of the stapled pack of paper, above pictures of my room, with my stuff in it, and Dev's room, with his stuff in it, and next to pictures of the shop under the flat that was next to that place that everybody *thought* was a brothel, but wasn't . . . the words "For Sale. Offers Invited. No Chain."

I couldn't take my eyes off them.

For Sale.

Well, this was an unusual end to my day.

I went and drank on the Cally on my own.

NINETEEN

Or "At Tension"

Dev and I had met the day we both arrived at the University of Leicester.

You know the type of friend you make where you just think, It's you and me! We'll be friends forever! We should get a flat together in our second year! And then move in together when we leave university! And you want to introduce them to all your old schoolpals—this new, exciting, vibrant character in the screenplay of your new, exciting, vibrant life?

It was nothing like that for me and Dev.

I'd thought he was an oddball. He was wearing a Sega Power T-shirt, for a start, and he had a wispy mustache and a mullet. He introduced himself as Alexander, until his mum rounded a corner carrying a potted plant and told him he wasn't called Alexander, he was called Devdatta, and I smiled, because here was a boy trying to reinvent himself before his mum had even left. He said he was a big fan of the Manic Street Preachers, and when I asked him what his favorite album was, he looked pale and uncertain and mumbled something about not learning all the names. He said he was working on his first videogame idea—*Basteroids!*—and while he was doing his BSc in computing with management it was going to make him rich.

And then he unpacked his N64 and we sat in his halls room and played *GoldenEye*, just as we would do for years to come. Like we'd have done tonight, if all had been well.

So, no—I never, in those early days, thought here is a friend I will have for life. But slowly, surely, he became part of it anyway. And if you'd asked me an hour before I found those papers, I never thought it could be any other way.

Because we had history now. The history that close friends write so quickly. We'd been through breakups, and stared mournfully at the wallpaper of whatever pub we happened to be in that time, until the don't-want-to-talk-about-its became here's-*another*-reason-why-you're-better-offs. I'd been to his brother's wedding, I'd advised him on life, jobs, and girls, and on one long, sad Sunday morning, I'd spoken at his mother's funeral, as he'd clenched his teeth and stared at the ground and tried not to let his dad see him cry.

He'd been there for me, too, through Sarah . . . and if ever I'd told him about the miscarriage, he'd have been there for me then, too.

But in all that time, as far as I knew, he'd never done anything like this to me. And maybe, as I look back on it, it's not important. Maybe I should have been cool. I mean, he must've had his reasons, and so what, it was just one secret. But right then, with everything surrounding it, with the year I'd had, and as I sat in the Den and I gripped my glass, I felt betrayed.

I closed the door a little too heavily and found Dev in the living room.

"Hello, maaaate," he said, not looking up. He was chasing a smuggler in *Brotherhood*.

"Sorry about today," I said, affecting a matey tone. Oh, yeah, I thought, I know *just* how to handle this.

"It's okay. Me, too," he said, and put the controller down. "Where you been? I got your message. What happened?"

"Damien had his people inform the paper I was no longer welcome at events."

Dev didn't say I-told-you-so, but he thought it.

"So one thing led to another and Zoe told me all about the other misdemeanors I'd done, too."

"Oh," he said. "Well, she'd probably been waiting to do that, eh?"

There was the support.

"You a bit drunk?" he asked, which he didn't need to, seeing as I'd slurred my way through words like "misdemeanors."

"A little," I said, and then, as sincerely as I could: "And maybe it's the booze, but I just want to thank you."

"Thank me?"

"You were honest with me today."

What was that I saw? A flash of guilt?

"I shouldn't have gone up to Damien like that. If I hadn't, I wouldn't have been at the Den tonight drowning my sorrows with that old man with the blue bag who used to work in drainage. How about you? Where were you this evening?"

He turned back to the screen, picked up his controller.

"Had to see Dad about something, down on Brick Lane."

"You're there a lot lately."

"Yeah, well, you know. Family."

I sat down on the sofa, facing him.

"How is your dad?"

"Fine."

"How are his businesse—"

"All fine."

A pause. He pretended there was a problem with his control pad.

"Also," I said, like a cat about to bat a mouse, "I want to thank you for letting me live here."

"Whatever. You pay rent when you can. You help out in the shop. It's no bother."

"Yes, but it's my one constant. And I'm grateful for that. It's *great* living here with you."

He turned to face me. I could see him wondering if I knew something. He decided I didn't and turned back. I was annoyed. That had been his in. I'd given him an in. He could've come clean. He chose not to.

"Do you fancy a nightcap?" he said. "There's a bottle of *jezynowka* in my—"

"I finished that. Unless you mean another bottle? The bottle I'm talking about was next to your bed, on some papers."

"You went in my room?"

"I went in your room, yes."

"So…"

"The papers."

"You looked at the papers?" He was trying his best to quickly build to outrage, but I was there first.

"How come you didn't tell me?" I asked, straining for calm. "You're selling up, Dev! I know it's your place, but the least you could've done was tell me! What, it's not important to you, this whole homelessness thing?"

"Don't be so dramatic," he said, and I laughed. "What? You're right! This is my place! Or Dad's anyway! There was never a good time to tell you! I tried once or twice but there was the Sarah stuff, or there was your work, or—"

"Well, Sarah's done. My work is laughable. So what else? And when did you try?"

"I tried, dude, I tried to bring it up once or tw—"

"When did you get the pictures of the flat done? How long's this been going on?"

"Not long."

"Since before the night we said we'd go to Whitby?"

Dev took a moment. I'd already worked it out. But I wanted his confirmation.

"We never said we'd go to Whitby," he said. "I just said you had and said we had to go."

I'd gone over it already in my head tonight. It explained his hurry to leave, his enthusiasm for something I now knew he didn't care about. He didn't give a damn about the girl in the photo, or me, or any of it. He was just covering his tracks because he didn't want to face up to things. His dad. The shop. Anything.

"You tricked me," I said, and even as I said the words they shocked me as I heard them. "You used The Girl to trick me?"

"I thought it might help you, as well, and—"

"You said you wanted me to do this because it got me out of the flat," I said, furious. "You weren't kidding. So all those times you wanted to do something? Like afternoon pints or developing shots or hey-let's-all-go-to-Whitby? That was just to distract me so you could get away with this? So your dad could come round and take measurements or show the premises or take photos or—"

"You're saying it like I wanted this to happen! And Whitby was for me, too. I needed it. A break. Dad had called, said he was on his way round, I needed to go somewhere and I needed a mate. This is a lot worse for me, Jason. This is my dream, this place."

"And you're letting it go so easily?"

"*You* try growing up with an IQ you can't live up to. *You* try proving your dad right every time you try to prove him wrong. He already thinks I'm a fuckup. You think I wanted my best mate to know it, too?"

"What did you keep telling me? That I should develop the pictures, follow this girl, use the moment?"

"I wanted you to have hope, Jason."

Hope. That word again.

"And what about you?" I said. "Where's your hope?"

"Oh, come on. I said this was my dream. Dad gave me a chance and he proved it: dreams are unrealistic and that's why they're dreams. This place had about as much chance of working as . . . well . . ."

"As me finding that girl."

"Yeah!" he said, suddenly more angry now. "Yeah, if you like. But that doesn't mean you don't try, does it? But this dream is over, Jase, because I did try. Dad gave me a year to give it a go. Yesterday, do you know how much I brought in? £1.50 for a used *Sonic 2*. People want new games. They don't come to me; they go to GAME or HMV or somewhere they think has a good chance of still being there next week. I had a niche, I thought, but as Dad has taken great pleasure in telling me time and bloody time again, niches don't work too well in a recession. His stuff's been going well on Brick Lane, he wants to concentrate on that, and there's not an accountant in the country who wouldn't agree."

"So that's it? It's all signed off?"

"It's his place. His money. There was never a question. But look, someone might not take this place for months, or years. That old pet shop round the corner's been on the market *forever*, so there's still the flat! I didn't want to worry you. You're my best mate, Jase. We could be here ages."

I had little savings, I had little prospects, and now I had even less hope. It was one thing me believing something good could come out of that night on Charlotte Street. But it was quite another knowing that even Dev had thought it was stupid all along. I felt ridiculous, tricked, hopeless.

I looked around the flat, knowing we *wouldn't* be here ages. I wouldn't, at any rate. So I went out, angry, and I drank, angrily, and when I didn't want to go home but I didn't know where else to go I made a phone call and she answered and she said, "Come round. Now."

And The Girl?

The Girl was just a dream, and in the words of my great friend Devdatta Patel, dreams are unrealistic.

> "What can be expected to be dropped is held in the hands, but what is in the heart I shall die with."
>
> —Traditional Shona Tribe proverb, Zimbabwe

Hello. Seventeen of you, eh? That's enough for a party. We could get drunk and not speak to one another, then go home and blog about it.

Martin in Malaysia: I know you'll like this. On the tube this morning, at Goodge Street, I remembered an advert I saw in one of the free papers recently where a man professed his love for a stranger.

I don't usually look, because I get far too embarrassed. And I worry one day I'll see one that I convince myself is for me and that will be it; I will have to marry whoever it is out of sheer gratefulness.

Mind you, you can make anything sound like it's for you. Girl in a red top. I saw you from the window of the VD clinic. I'd been given bad news but you brightened my day. You'd be so thrilled all day, you'd be asking your friends, "What do you wear if you're meeting someone with VD?"

Anyway, the one I saw said this:

I saw you. You don't use overhead handles on the train. Hoped it would jolt and you would fall to me. But no.

At first I smiled and turned the page because you do get quite used to things like this in those papers. Like reading about people who meet in weird ways whose write-ups always end with the sentence "the pair recently announced their engagement," or words along those lines.

But I wonder if that man felt he was taking a risk, the day he wrote about the girl with no overhead handles. I wonder if his heart beat faster at the possibilities he was hoping to open up.

Because isn't to be pursued, to be thought of as special, to be needed by someone somewhere, whether we know them yet or not, all any of us actually wants? To have our story end in a sentence exactly like "the pair recently announced their engagement"?

Maybe I'm having a weak moment. I'm pretty sure we're all going to end up having to get cats to keep us company anyway.

And I fucking hate cats.

Sx

TWENTY

Or "Cold Dark and Yesterday"

One month and one day passed by with little incident.

I'd done nothing, really. Nothing except find myself a little flat on Blackstock Road. It had been easy enough to move out. Nine boxes, a telly, a laptop, and a rolled-up duvet. Not much to show for a life lived, but you don't really mind when it all fits into the back of an Addison Lee.

My savings had dwindled, of course. They'd always been good dwindlers, my savings. Naturally adept at dwindling. Seems the less you're paid the more proactive your savings become, dwindle-wise.

But I'm procrastinating. Because like I say, a month had passed with only a few events to distinguish it or set it apart. Though I suppose, if pressed, there were two in particular.

The first was the phone call.

"Jason?" it began, the voice familiar. "It's Estonia Marsh."

"Oh," I'd said, and that was the best I could do.

"I'm so sorry to call you like this. I got your number from *London Now*. Are you not there anymore?"

"I've . . . I still freelance, but no, not really."

"Listen," she said.

Turns out Estonia had been having dinner with her producers, and they'd started talking about how they met their partners, and Estonia said, "Oh, I met this guy recently..." and now her producers on *Wake Up Call* wanted to get me in to the studios on the South Bank to help me with the search.

"It'd be fantastic!" she said. "A million viewers, you've got a photo, someone will know her, and we'll get you together on the show!"

"Oh!" I said, stalling. "Well, that's an interesting—"

"Because your friend had said you'd already put an ad in the paper, and tried to find her by different means, so this would just be stepping it up a level, wouldn't it? It'd be great fun!"

"Yeah. Yeah. I'm not sure, though."

"There'd probably be a few quid in it, too—sometimes we hook up with the papers or the weekly mags and they get the contributor to write their story up. I'm sure we could fix you a commission with the *Mail*, or someone?"

"I...can I think about it?" I'd said.

"Sure! Yes. Of course," she said, clearly disappointed I hadn't been as effusive as they'd clearly been after three bottles of Pinot Noir. "I mean, personally speaking, I really think you should do it. Because here's the thing: you don't know how your story ends yet!"

And though I toyed with the idea—though I thought maybe my life might yet end up as one of those stories you read in the tabloids that end with a wonderfully cheesy final line—I knew toying was all I was doing.

Because just hours later, as the day wound down and just minding my own business at the bottom of Poland Street, the universe had sent me a warning shot. A *no-you-don't*.

There, up ahead, leaving the NCP...the unmistakable rear lights of a light green Facel Vega, exhaust humming away, condensation clouding the back window, hiding me from Damien, and Damien from me.

I kept my head down nevertheless, nipped down D'Arblay, and quickly made my way to the tube.

Back to this morning.

There was another one in the tabloids today.

> *It was love at first sight for Interflora deliveryman Jon Bindham, when he delivered a romantic bouquet of flowers to office worker Laura Davis.*
>
> *So much so that the very next day he returned with ANOTHER huge bouquet of flowers—this time from HIM!*
>
> *Today they will tie the knot in Limpley Stoke, Wiltshire.*
>
> *"I took a chance!" says Jon, 30.*
>
> *What he didn't know was that the original flowers were **not** from a prospective suitor—but from Laura's dad, congratulating her on passing her driving test!*
>
> *"I suppose it proves sometimes you should say it with flowers!" jokes Jon.*

Love those last lines. I wonder if people actually say them.

I took a mug from the cupboard and realized it was one of Dev's.

I hadn't seen him since I moved out, partly because I had so much to sort out, but partly because I was embarrassed. Embarrassed at how I'd behaved, embarrassed because in all the time he was going through that stuff with his dad I'd never once thought to ask how things were going, was he okay, how was the shop? Embarrassed, too, because I'd been tricked, and only tricked because I'd been starting to mildly obsess over a girl I'd never met and now never would and how stupid that made me feel.

But maybe a drink would be nice, maybe offer an apology, for running out on him like that, maybe end up at the Den, for old time's sake.

Not today, though.

The Kicks were on *T4*. Though my portable fizzed and crackled, I could tell Rick Edwards really seemed to love them.

"Brighton's brightest," he called them.

Things were going pretty well for the boys. I know I'd only met them a couple of times, and I know they'd met a hundred journalists since, from proper papers, too, like *The Times* and the *Guardian*, who adored these rock and roll upstarts (*Uh-oh! Move Over Arctics!* screamed the *NME*; *Things are about to Kick off*, warned *Q*), but I'd always feel a little linked to them. And I kept looking to the sides of the screen, just in case I could see Abbey, or a hint of electric-blue shoe.

I hadn't spoken to Abbey since that night. I'd tried, but I'd failed. It had taken me a while, but I'd realized, slowly and grimly, what I'd done. What right had I had to do what I did? Not a day had gone by that I hadn't kicked myself for it. Of course she'd be angry with me. If she'd wanted people to know about her songs, she'd . . . well . . . she'd have sung them. Something about that night—the way the CD had been poking out of her bag, willing itself seen, and all right after we'd talked of life, and ambition and dreams . . . it made me feel like what I was doing was undeniably right. A favor.

Now I could see that it wasn't. I could see now that I'd stumbled into someone's private life, and . . . no, not stumbled. Stumbled implies something accidental. No, I'd broken in. I'd kicked the door down; like a burglar, I'd rifled through her secrets, and then I'd taken them, and worse . . . I'd shown them to the world. That wasn't fair.

So, after a few unanswered texts and a couple of unpicked-up calls, I took to keeping myself to myself. In some ways, it was nice. I was reading more. Eating Iceland meals-for-one and mindlessly reading the ingredients while Radio 4's *Play for Today* was on. Things were calm, I guess, and I was resigned to life. Because once again, I'd seen where hope could get me. Better to live without it, I reasoned. Better to be surprised when something good happens, than to try to make it happen yourself and fail.

I turned the telly off. For the first time in days, I had somewhere to be.

"So," said the man. "You've been out of the business how long?"

"About eighteen months."

"Not gone well?"

"It's gone fine. I'm ready for a new challenge."

"How do you approach a challenge?"

"Well, I'm a team player, though I'm equally suited to working alone."

"And you worked here, at St. John's?"

"I did."

"You decided to leave, why?"

"It should all be there, in my file."

"Ah, yes." A pause. "Weaknesses?"

"Chocolate."

"Ha ha! Lovely sense of humor!"

"Thank you. But seriously, I'm a perfectionist, that's probably my main weakness."

"Terrific." The man looked at me. "So how are you fixed the week after next?"

I was going to be a supply teacher.

There was nothing wrong with that, I know. I had the form, the qualifications, the experience, and people weren't exactly lining up to spend more time at St. John's. Yeah, so it was a bit of a step back, seeing as I'd been deputy head of department, and it was a step in a different direction from the one I'd always told myself I wanted to be going, but it was work. Work I could do, too.

And being back in St. John's had reminded me of someone.

Not Dylan Bale either, which had been my fear. How embarrassing a meltdown would have been. How embarrassing to have to flinch every time I passed a window, and all thanks to a kid and an air rifle.

No. I was thinking of Matt.

Where had he gone? I'd texted him a few times, followed it up with a call, but his number had been disconnected and I didn't know what to do. Had I done something? Let him down, too?

I wanted to talk to him, though. The stuff with Dev, the stuff with Abbey . . . well, he knew them. He might have advice.

And then, on the way back from St. John's, I found myself either by accident or by design at the Sainsbury's by Angel tube, browsing the falafel, and I realized just how close I was to Chapel Market.

It was 10 a.m. and men in England tops were drinking pints under a George cross outside the Alma with their dogs.

I knew where the garage was: just beyond the DIY shops

and chicken cottages of Chapel Market, tucked down a side street with a giant hand-painted MOT'S & REPAIR'S on its wall.

As soon as I got there, I instantly felt that creeping feeling of uncertainty and unease that washes over me, sickeningly, when surrounded by men. Not men in general. Not men in pubs or men in suits or men like your dad or mine. Real men, with black-bruised nails from car doors or hammers, and swallows on their wrists, and chain-link gold swaddling thick leather necks.

I prepared to drop my aitches.

"All right?" I said, to the main one, as he watched over the others, the one I should probably call the "gaffer" or something.

He put down a tool I couldn't identify and wiped his hand on the side of his overalls. He looked exactly the way a child would draw a mechanic.

"Matt around?" I said, attempting to seem disinterested, or at the very least distracted by a car they had up on that machine that makes cars go up that I've only ever seen in places like this.

"Matt?" he said.

"Fowler?" I said, grateful he had a surname out of *East-Enders*. "Matt Fowler?"

"Matt Fowler?" he said. "You know him?"

This, I realized, would be one of those conversations that go better if dealt with exclusively in questions.

"Is he about?" I said, hoping we'd soon start dealing in facts.

"Warren?" shouted the man, turning. "Is Matt about?"

I looked over at Warren, who started laughing.

"Dean?" he shouted, to another man, fiddling with a radio at the back. "Where's Matt?"

Dean started laughing and nodding.

"He's with his university chums!" he said, and they all started laughing together.

"He's where?" I said.

"Matt hasn't been here in about a month. He had an epiphany!"

They all started laughing again. Warren got back to work, shaking his head and smiling at the word "epiphany."

"Do you know where he is?" I said.

"I imagine he's gone boating," said the man. "Or, whatch-acall it . . . scrumping. No, not scrumping. Cramming. For his 'finals'!"

I wasn't sure if they were taking the piss, and if they were, out of who? Matt? Or me? Me, with my clean clothes and deli-cate little never-done-a-day's-work grease-free hands.

"Is Matt . . . at university?" I asked.

How? You don't just go to university. You study, you do exams, you get A-Levels, you apply. You sit down and go through prospectuses and when you realize you have no idea what you're doing you end up doing geography at Cardiff.

"He has, if you count a room above a chippie as a university," said the man, and he cleaned his fingers, and smiled at me.

This would be the end of our conversation.

I trudged back to Blackstock Road.

When I told you a minute ago I'd found myself a little flat on Blackstock Road, I mean I found myself living in a little flat on Blackstock Road.

And it was with someone.

It's not something I'd have bet on happening, post-Tropicana. But I needed a friend and now she was the closest I had.

I'd stormed round that night, a beacon of rage and injustice and disappointment, lost and sad and alone.

"Jesus, Jason, what's going on?" she'd said, answering the door, and I'd pushed past her, into the dim and narrow hallway in this flat it'd taken so long to find in the dark, just as it had taken once before, when all this started.

Zoe and I talked long and hard that night. She apologized for what she'd said about my career and whether or not I should look for it in Highgate Cemetery. She'd been under a lot of pressure, she said, and the last thing she needed was what happened today, and *London Now* was in pretty deep trouble, might only have a few months left, plus Rob the reviews ed had been on at her about coming back, and *blah blah blah blah blah*.

I knew what she'd done because I'd done it myself. Sometimes you hurt someone who's hurt you, because it's like a tiny victory. Your own little PS on an event that still stings.

So we talked about that day. But also, slowly, we talked about what had happened that night, in that other life.

"We were friends who sort of took advantage of each other," she said, and while once the guilt would have flashed through me in an instant, now there was a dull ache of resignation.

"It was my fault," I'd said.

"It was mine, too. I just didn't know what to do. I loved you once, as a friend, I mean. It hurt to see you in pain. I mean it almost physically hurt. I was trying to make you see that everything would be okay. Like, if you left your job, I could throw some work your way, maybe you could find what you wanted to do. But there was never any question of what you should do with Sarah. I never said anything about that but then you kissed me and I don't know how it didn't stop there but it didn't."

Part of me had always wondered what would have happened if Zoe and I had got together afterward. But what I wanted was Sarah. It would never have worked, the two of us, the shame and the recriminations; the soul-slashing guilt was just too claustrophobic. It wouldn't have been honest. It wasn't the plan. We couldn't just improvise our way into it.

But what about now? I thought, looking at her.

I'd given Zoe most of whatever I had in my account at the time to cover things. This wasn't a permanent thing, of course; it was just until I found my feet again. I just hadn't known what else to do when I'd moved out of Dev's and craved something familiar, something warm. I needed to tell Sarah I was moving, but how could I tell her where I'd ended up? And when I decided just to play it vague, this happened:

Me: "Hey, so I'm just checking in, I got the invite, I meant to RSVP, and—"

Sarah: "Wow! It's you. You've got a nerve, I'll give you that."

Me: "Eh?"

Sarah: "You think I'm stupid? I was waiting to see if you'd call, and here you are. Thing that bugs me most is you know I thought you'd grown up. And you could have told me you hadn't. But you came along and just pretended like you had. You didn't come clean, you didn't admit it; you just let me down again."

Me: "Are you talking about—"

Sarah: "Drugging my guests? Yes. Yes, I am talking about you and your odd little friends turning up at my engagement do like a mental bunch of Chuckle Brothers and feeding my guests drugs. It was Anna who worked it out. Thought she had food poisoning so had some tests done. Nearly lost her job."

Me: "That was all a misunderstanding, that was—"

Sarah: "Gary vomited all the way home. I had to drive the Lexus. We need all new foot carpets."

Me: "Please tell Gary I will pay for—"

Sarah: "Anna tried to take a lamppost on the bus with her."

Me: [laughing] "I'm . . . did Anna—"

Sarah: "Great. You find it as funny now as you did then. Have you ever seen someone try to get a lamppost onto a bus? It is not dignified, okay, and she didn't deserve that. I'm getting married in eight weeks, Jason, and it's a shame we will never speak again. Because we will never, ever speak again. Good luck growing up. It's as likely to happen as any of your other pathetic little dreams. Oh, and give *Zoe* my love."

Click.

So she knew. Dev, maybe? I suppose if I were still a teacher, I'd . . .

Oh. I am.

Anyway, when Zoe got back from work the next day, we'd met up at the Bank of Friendship.

We'd met every night since, in the kitchen, at about seven thirty.

Things had been frosty at first, like this had been inevitable from that first drunken time, like it had been prophesied. That didn't make us comfortable. We hadn't chosen this. It had just happened. Nothing *else* had happened, not yet, which I put down to the pressure of Something Possibly Happening; we were essentially just strange, weary flatmates trying to make a tawdry history something respectable. But then one night, with *Who Wants to Be a Millionaire?* in the background, she said, "This is good. Me and you, in this flat, together."

I put my spoon down in my soup, and looked at her. This felt like the chat I didn't want to have. The one about the future, where this is going, are we an "us"? Mentally, I started preparing. I still had those nine boxes, packed flat under the bed. I still had Addison Lee's number for another people carrier. I wasn't sure about this. I didn't think this was our deal.

Thing was, I still sort of needed her. I had no Dev. I'd re-angered Sarah. I hadn't seen Abbey, and Matt had disappeared off the face of the earth.

I steeled myself.

"Because," she said, "it means there's no more guessing. Sometimes I'd wonder what would it have been like if we'd ended up together after you and Sarah. I was doing you a favor at *London Now* but also I was seeing who you were. I hoped I wouldn't like you. But also I know that sometimes it's better not to know."

I was still just looking at her. She was pretending to be casual, like she was reading this out of the paper.

"Luckily, with you, I do know now. And so do you, which is important, especially after what you lost. And there can never be any of that longing, or anything. Because I think, to be clear: we both know we're not right for each other in almost any single way."

I laughed and picked up my spoon again. You hear about people falling into things; you hear about them staying there forever because they don't have the strength to pull themselves out. That could've been what happened on Blackstock Road. This could've been the end of the story. This could all have been about how I ended up moving from a flat above a videogame shop next to a place everyone thought was a brothel, but wasn't, to another, smaller flat with a cracked back window and a lamp that hung too low over the table, and all because I was weak, and tired, and beaten.

"I mean, we'd be terrible together," she said, looking up at me at last. "Look how you hold a spoon. I could not be with a man, long term, who holds a spoon like that. Plus there's your pretentious films, which I know you don't watch, because you've still not taken the Jim Jarmusch box set out of the wrapper. And you never got rid of those boxes under the bed, which also shows the level of commitment you're offering."

I smiled. We were two unhappy people, living with each other for a while, knowing there was someone else to be around for a while, happy with that. Now we could stop going through the motions. Now I could take the sofa at nights; she could stop pretending she was asleep when I stumbled in.

She was no Dev. But I had a friend again.

"Shall we go out?" I said.

Zoe snorted spritzer through her nose.

"'Stupid Man'd face'!" she exclaimed, and someone at the next table turned to look at her. "This is a fantastic insult. Once you've worked out it's an insult, it's a fantastic one."

"I'm pleased you approve."

"And what was her reaction? No, forget that. What was *Gary's* reaction?"

She seemed delighted by all this.

"He called me 'buddy' a lot and tried to bond."

"The best revenge!" she said. "He's a pro. Totally proves to Sarah what a man he is and what a child you are. Genius."

This was nice. It could have been awkward, talking about the aftermath of an event in which Zoe played no small part. But it was nice. Saying it all out loud somehow rid it of its awfulness and punctured my pomposity. It felt like I'd gained something back in my life. An old friend, someone who knew me, someone who used to revel in my inadequacies over student union Snakebite and rain-spattered rollies and apparently hadn't changed.

The strain had gone. I had missed her.

"So then what?" she was saying, leaning forward, eager for more.

"Then I deleted her from my Facebook friends," I said. "Except I didn't; Abbey did, but weirdly it seemed to make her think I was a grown-up handling the situation with aplomb."

"Very twenty-first century. Very mature of you. What then?"

"Then I ended up going to her engagement party and Abbey handed out narcotics to the various guests and it all kind of went downhill from there again because her best friend Anna tried to take a lamppost on a bus and Gary was sick on some foot carpets."

Zoe slapped the table and shouted, "Ha!"

"Oh, we should've done a feature on this, Jason," she said. " 'How to Take a Breakup Like a Man.' "

I smiled and took a sip of my drink.

"They'll be married soon and I'm sure it'll all be forgotten."

"How long now?"

"A month. They want to move quickly so that when the baby is born Gary can introduce himself formally as Sarah's husband."

She laughed. "And this Abbey . . . this singer. She's the girl? The one you left the message in the paper for? Because secretly, I thought that was sweet. I didn't want to say anything because . . . well, I guess it went nowhere. Or went wrong. Hence you crashing on Blackstock Road instead of with her—"

"Abbey's not The Girl. Abbey's a girl but not *The* Girl."

"So who's 'The Girl'?"

I laughed. This was nice. It was like clearing the air, some-how. No awkwardness, no regret, just friendship.

"I don't know who she is," I said.

She scrunched up her nose and theatrically clicked her finger to alert the barman she'd need another drink for this. He ignored her and continued wiping down a glass.

"You don't know? You don't know who 'The Girl' is? Are you being metaphorical? Like, you know her, but you'll never know the real her? Are you being daytime drama about this?"

"I am being literal. I literally don't know who she is. And yet in a way I kind of mean the opposite."

"You *are* being daytime drama!"

She turned to the barman, annoyed, as if to say I've-asked-you-*once*, but he remained resolutely adhered to the you-need-to-actually-*ask* rule on which barmen seem so keen.

I got up to get her that drink, and to work out how to tell the story. And when I sat back down and I'd finished, she looked me in the eye, and said, "You always said a relationship needed a beginning. You've got that. So what are you going to do about the end? Because this—me and you sitting in this dank Highbury pub before traipsing back to a grim Highbury flat—this *can't* be how it ends."

"And yet," I said, my hands in the air, my mind made up. "And yet it is."

"*Dank?*" said the barman.

There was a time and a place for The Girl.

I had to take the hints life was throwing at me. No Dev, no Abbey, no Sarah. No *London Now*, no prospects, no hope.

I was starting to think it might be me.

Sometimes life isn't magical, you see. Sometimes life is everyday. It's a trip to a keycutters in a rushed lunch break. It's the light, high rattle of a lightbulb's broken filament. It's your neighbor coming round to tell you you've left your car lights on.

Yes, rarely it's something other. Maybe it's the glance of a girl on Charlotte Street, for example. But how long before a glance runs out? How long can you keep coasting on a look?

DANNY WALLACE • 333

If I was going to sort myself out, I had to prioritize the practical. There are too many tramps out there who had big dreams.

And there were things to sort out. My friendships. My own flat. My job.

Zoe's interest had been nice, but it was the interest of someone just wanting to hear the end of a story. She didn't have to get out there and make it happen. Making it happen was hard. It took effort, and time, and . . . well . . . I had a job now. Places to be and things to do. And plans, I had plans.

I'll be honest, I felt a little empty. Like an ambition had been thwarted or a dream left unrealized. Like I'd been close, somehow, but close to what? Looking at it, I'd been no closer to her yesterday than I had been when this all started. I mean, sure, I'd found her ex-boyfriend, but what had that cost me, that little discovery? And how wonderfully had I messed it up? My life, which had been getting steadily worse, if that was in any way possible, had been made just that little bit more awful by that little jaunt. But still the emptiness was there. The ache of giving up on something you hoped might be magical.

The magical could wait.

It was time for the everyday.

Day Three at St. John's. "Oh, you're *back*," said Jane Woollacombe, head of maths, in that way people do when they've heard you're back from somewhere but didn't actually notice you'd gone. We were in the hallway of the maths block, all green lino and peach walls, like we'd pressed a button marked 1970s to see what'd happen.

"And how was . . . where did you go exactly, in the end? Traveling or something?"

"Nope, not traveling."

She fiddled with her butterfly brooch, nervously.

"Career break, then?"

"Not that I'd intended."

She looked at me blankly.

"I tried something," I said, as casually as I could. "It didn't work out. I was living on peanuts, moving very slowly, so I decided to cut my losses."

"Oh," she said, her face falling. "Well, you didn't fail. Because you tried."

"Didn't say I failed," I said.

"And how's...um..."

"Sarah and I split up. A while ago."

"Well, relationships...you know. That's not failing either."

"I didn't say any of this was failing."

"Well, good, because you didn't. Some people just use that word, don't they, and they shouldn't, so you tell them that trying is what counts."

"Who's been saying the word 'fail'?"

"Doesn't matter. No one. People who do aren't worth talking to anyway."

She eyed Mr. Willis, suspiciously, through the squared glass of the door next to us, and raised her wild eyebrows.

"And it's not like *he's* ever done anything with his life, is it? Collecting car horn noises, or whatever his hobby is? You tell him that."

She lifted herself up onto the balls of her feet, turned, and scooted away.

I looked once more at Mr. Willis. He smiled at me and waved.

Room 3Gc was the one I wasn't looking forward to sitting in again.

Room 3Gc was overlooked by the estate.

I walked in, a few minutes before my class would arrive, and paused for a second.

Just there, in the window—tiny, imperceptible, probably unrecognizable to anyone but me—a crack and a hurried repair job.

The only evidence that it had ever happened at all.

My eyes flicked up toward the estate. Which window had it been?

And then the bell rang, and I jolted.

And I told myself to deal with it.

"Oi, sir!" said a kid, by the gates.

There'd been a fight here a day or two before between someone from St. John's and a group of kids from the technical college near Stokey. Mr. Willis and myself were supposed to be acting as some kind of barrier to this happening again, even though the closest I'd come to a fight was that night in Whitby where I'd had to be rescued by a former pupil, and Mr. Willis increasingly looked like exactly the type of man who'd collect car horn noises, actually.

I looked at the kid. Maybe fourteen or so. Holding a half-massacred Chomp. He'd done that thing to his tie to make it incredibly short. I don't know how they do that. I imagine they just buy toddler-size. "You're Mr. Priestley, yeah?"

"I'm Mr. Priestley, yeah."

"You know my brother," he said, as my eyes flicked over his shoulder. A kid pushed another kid into a wall, then they both looked at me, guilty, and laughed loudly to show they were friends. "Matt Fowler?"

Matt's brother?

"I do," I said. "But I haven't seen him in ages. How is he?"

"Busy," he said.

"At the garage?" Maybe those guys had been taking the mickey the other day. He could've been anywhere. Tea run. Sick. The Arcades.

"Nah," he continued. "He's busy with work and that."

A thought struck me. Tony is a really weird name for a fourteen-year-old. I ignored it.

"Yeah, but work where? I was near Chapel Market the other day—I didn't see him about."

"He don't work there no more."

"*Doesn't* work there *any*more. No, I heard. Where's he now?"

"Burger King, innit."

"*Isn't it.* And saying 'isn't it' after Burger King doesn't really work. Why's he working at Burger King? What happened at the garage?"

The kid shrugged and sniffed.

"Didn't want to do it no more. Couldn't do that and his course. So he does Burger King four nights, then works down the Queen's Head rest of it."

"You need to work on your grammar, Tony," I said. "And what do you mean, his course?"

I got it.

I now got it.

The thing that had always concerned me about Matt was his rage. It was a rage I'd seen at school, of course, the day he'd nearly blinded a kid with a compass...though that depends on whom you choose to believe, of course. The school board had gone with the kid. Unprovoked attack, he'd said. As soon as Matt could get out of there, he was gone. I'd thought perhaps there'd been a mistake, that Matt had been treated unfairly and lost his faith in the system. But then, that night in Whitby, when he'd saved our skins with a show of might . . . I'd been unnerved as well as grateful. Because I'd seen his rage close-up. The roar, the anger, all served up neatly with a length of pipe and a phonebox.

But now I got it. It wasn't rage. It was *frustration*.

Matt Fowler had left his job at the garage near Chapel Market in order to better himself. That's how I'd chosen to phrase it, until I realized he wasn't someone out of a Jane Austen novel. He'd left to Do Something. He'd had the epiphany his mates had found so funny. And that led him to a part-time diploma course. Tuesday and Thursday evenings between seven and ten. Saturdays between ten and five. It cost £4,500 in deposits, but with something to show for it at the end. He'd sold his bike, his PlayStation, his phone, whatever else he could, and he'd given his notice at the garage. He was working all hours to make up for it, but this was it, this was Doing Something. More specifically, a sound engineering and music production foundation course, just off Denmark Street.

I thought back to Whitby. "I wanna *make* something," he'd said. I thought he meant *of* himself. Turns out he meant both.

I looked it all up when I got home and felt excited for him. There were only five people per course. He'd learn about mixing, patching, signal flow, multitrack, compression, noise gates, digital delays, DAW sequencing, VCOs, VCFs, VCAs, and a million other things I couldn't tell you the first thing about.

At the end of it all he could expect to make tea for grumpy engineers for six months or so, get some on-the-job training in return for being a dogsbody, but sooner or later he'd catch that break that'd one day make him a studio engineer himself. I found myself weirdly jealous while absolutely delighted.

He'd found his thing.

* * *

Zoe was still taking great pleasure in teasing me about The Girl.

"You've got to go for it," she said, stirring the pot. We were having hot dog stew—the only thing we could put together from the vegetables in the fridge and the lone tin in the cupboard. It could have been 1997, in a Leicester flat with Dev. "I completely think you should ring Estonia Marsh back and tell her you want to do that *Wake Up Call* thing."

"Nah," I said. "From now on, I'll let fate deal with my life. Dev was always on about fate."

"You're talking like he's passed away. He's on Caledonian Road."

"Brick Lane, now, actually," I said. "I saw on Facebook. He's made the move. Going to be looking after one of his dad's restaurants. So no more Power Up! Officially shuts down next week."

"Funny, things like Facebook, or Twitter. Just seeing a second of someone else's life. Almost means you don't have to see them again. You're just drip-fed their moments. You lose all the other stuff in between. It's *efficient* friendship."

I played with my spoon. Maybe I didn't want efficient friendship. I suddenly wanted our old, inefficient, slow-moving friendship.

I should see Dev. With Abbey it was kind of her choice; she'd have to warm to me again, and given how long we'd known each other I couldn't count on that happening. Sarah had made her feelings perfectly clear, and pillow talk with Gary meant they weren't in any danger of changing.

But with Dev . . . well, that was down to me.

I'd build up to that, I decided. No sense rushing things. Maybe I could swing by Brick Lane, have a curry. Actually, I'd had an idea for Dev. Something great. Something to warm things up between us. I'd asked Zoe if she could sort it, and she'd put in a few calls, and I'd been promised a yes.

First, though, there was someone else I wanted to see. And as I thought about the how and whens, my pocket started vibrating.

"Unrecognized number," I said, staring at my phone. "It is undoubtedly another glamorous woman from breakfast television, urging me to unleash my romantic dreams upon the nation."

I hit ACCEPT.

"Hello!"

"Jason?"

"Yes, it is!"

A pause. Then: "This is Damien Laskin."

TWENTY-ONE

Or "Go Solo"

"Hi," I said, both hands on my phone, in the corridor outside the flat, with its stained blue carpet tiles and cracked back window. "Hi, Damien."

"Listen, I'll be brief about this," he said. "We should meet."

I must've stalled for a second, because very quickly he followed up with, "Look, I jumped down your throat that day because I wasn't sure what you wanted. I'm still not sure what you want, but I'm fairly sure it's not to hurt me. Would you agree with that?"

"Yes."

"Say it."

"I do not want to hurt you."

"Or my family."

"Or your family, of *course*! Look, Damien, it's a strange thing, and—"

"No, no, we'll meet and talk, okay? Monday, five-ish. Suggest a place."

I did as he asked, but then felt inexplicably nervous. What did he want? And why now? And also . . .

"How, um, how did you get my number?"

"I could have got your number in myriad different ways,

Jason. In actual fact—and to be honest, this is what prompted me to phone today—I got your number from the window of my local *fucking* kebab house."

He laughed, and then hung up.

I told Zoe and she nearly choked on her hot dog. She slapped the table and all the forks fell to the floor.

The Old Queen's Head is on Essex Road, a former gay pub now serving up leather sofas and imported French table football tables for the middle classes, halfway between the quirky antique shops with their stuffed bears and brass lamps and the more chichi chain restaurants where friendly foreigners tie balloons to toddlers' high chairs on command.

I stood outside for a bit as the closing-time crowd thinned, heading for buses or a last can from the Tesco Express on the corner. I could see him inside, dressed in black, leaning on the bar as an old soak with rolling tobacco prepared his little kiss good night.

I pushed through the doors, trying to look busy and distracted, ready to feign surprise when I spotted him, though it was him that spotted me, straightaway.

"Hey," he said.

"Matt!" I said, trying not to make my double take too cartoony. "What are *you* doing here?"

I made the appropriate confused face as he dropped another glass into its plastic crate for the night.

He smiled to himself for just a second.

"My little brother told you, yeah?" he said.

"He did, yeah," I said. "Your brother's the one with the tiny tie, yeah?"

He smiled. "That's him."

"So how are you? What's going on?"

"I'm all right, yeah," he said, nodding, and I was a little taken aback. Not because he was all right. But because he'd said he was. I don't think I'd ever heard him say he was all right before. I guess for the first time I realized how sad he'd always seemed by comparison. But then, maybe that's what I wanted.

"What time does your shift end?" I asked.

He pointed at the now-empty pub.

"I was surprised when I heard what you were back doing, man," said Matt, fiddling with his cuffs. We sat at our table in McDonald's by the roundabout, me with a flat Fanta, him with a Filet-O-Fish and a shake.

"Why?" I said.

"Didn't think you'd go back to that," he said, wiping sauce from his mouth. "You were always on about moving forward."

I thought back. Was I?

"When?"

"Well, you left St. John's, didn't you? You made a change. But like, also, when you was a teacher. You told us we could all do it, too. You said that in life you can make things happen."

I nodded, but had I? I didn't remember that. I remembered coffee breath and waiting for the break and bluffing through questions and 9 a.m. Nurofen, but no, according to Matt, I was like the bloke out of *Dead Poets Society*.

"But you said that to make them happen, you had to *make them happen*."

Oh, hang on. This sounded familiar. The one assembly I'd not managed to wriggle out of, so fearful was I of the complete lack of reaction from a bored and listless mass of lost causes.

Mr. Ashcroft, the old head, had been insistent, though. He'd thought it important that we absolutely take turns to speak in front of the kids. "Inspire them. Come at them with words of motivation and positivity! Show them the world they *could* have!"

I'd called mine "Making It Happen!," and some of it I'd actually written myself. The rest I'd found on an Anthony Robbins quote page I'd Googled. But there were parts I remember being quite proud of.

Never, at any point, though, did I think anyone was *listening*.

"You said that even standing still was going backward, because if you stand still the world passes you by, and that's the same thing."

"And . . . you took that on board, yeah?"

"The words stuck with me, yeah. But I still thought you were full of shit. Mr. Ashcroft used to make all you lot do that once a month, innit, to 'inspire' us. Mr. Cole just used to do his about Arsenal."

He started laughing.

"We all used to do impressions of you after. 'Making it happen! Ooh! Look at me, I'm making it happen!'"

He laughed again.

"But then I met you again, right. And you'd done it. You'd actually done it. Most of those teachers: they're still there. They're teaching my little brother now."

"Little Tony."

"Yeah! Ha. Little Tony, exactly. They'll probably end up teaching *my* kid. 'Cause they're not ever gonna leave."

"It's a good job. And baby Elgar would be lucky to have them."

"Yeah, but if your heart isn't in it, you need to be where your heart *is*."

"Well put."

He raised his eyebrows, put his Filet-O-Fish down.

"*You* put it that way. Jesus, do you even remember *any* of this?"

I shrugged, caught out.

"Because actually, it doesn't matter if you don't. You got up, you left your cozy little job, you put things at risk, you made it happen. You wanted to be a journalist or whatever, so you did it, yeah? And when we were in Whitby that night you said I should do a course or something and I remembered what you were on about that day at school and I looked at you and I thought, Maybe he meant it after all."

Wow.

"But maybe you didn't."

"I did. I did mean it, Matt. Definitely."

"So why are you back there?"

"Sometimes . . . you know, sometimes life gets in the way. Like, you might want to go traveling for a year, but then your boiler explodes or your car needs a new exhaust and everything changes."

"There's always an excuse. That's what you said, too, in your little speech or whatever."

"Christ, look, okay, I was making all that up, Matt. I'd never taken a risk. I'd never made it happen."

"But then one day you did. And *that's* what inspired me. Not what you said, but what you *did*."

I looked at him, realized he'd used the word "inspired," realized I'd never had that before, and remembered a time when perhaps that's all I'd needed to hear.

"Turns out you're a good teacher," he said, smiling. "But maybe teaching's not your thing."

I got in late, that night. Late but happy.

My chat with Matt had reminded me of all sorts of things. How my career at St. John's had started. How I'd been. How slowly that had ebbed away. How I'd lost my mojo. But to lose it, you had to have had it. If ever I'd had it, I now wanted it back. Not necessarily for teaching. A week in, and I knew that boat had sailed. But for life. For *something*.

I knew I'd always be Matt's old teacher first, his friend second. But that was kind of *okay* with me. Because as it turned out, I hadn't been that bad a teacher. Even when I was just his friend.

And now, whether on purpose or by accident, he'd helped me, too.

Zoe was already in bed when I'd crept in, but the TV was on low. Some panel game. I plumped my pillow, made my little bed on the sofa, and fired up my laptop.

It felt like time to sort myself out, at last. Find a place of my own. Take responsibility.

Next to my pillow had been a small golden envelope, marked *Jase*.

I'd opened it, and smiled. Zoe had done well.

If I ever got round to seeing him again, Dev would absolutely *adore* me for this.

Not yet, though. Not while I'd given up and gone back to St. John's. I'd be ready to see Dev soon. But I had some things to sort out first.

Top of the list was my life.

Monday, 5:15 p.m. So here I was, back in Postman's Park. I hadn't known where else to suggest and I thought a paranoid Damien would appreciate its secluded-yet-public nature. What were we? Spies?

It was a gray day, one of those days where everything's out of focus, and I was maybe fifteen minutes early. I have a crushing fear of lateness. I would rather be an hour early than cause someone a minute's wait. Dev would always say, "We're not late until we're *late*." I knew what he meant and it was technically true, but it never worked for me. Knowing I'll *be* late is always bad enough. The least I can do is get the worrying in early.

I kicked a can so it was nearer a wall. I just did; no one had asked me to. I suppose I should've picked it up and put it in a bin, but kicking it a few feet to one side seemed to demonstrate enough effort. I puffed out some air, interested to see whether I could see my own breath yet.

I realized I was nervous about seeing Damien again.

I stopped, looked up at the Memorial to Heroic Self-Sacrifice.

WILLIAM GOODRUM
Signalman, aged 60
Lost his life at Kingsland Road Bridge in saving a workman
from death under the approaching train from Kew.
February 28 1880

I must've read that one a hundred times.

"Jason?"

I turned. Damien was standing by the grass, and nodded when our eyes met. He was wearing one of those three-quarter-length jackets you see men in magazines wear, standing next to classic Jags on windy days on airstrips while silent blond women in sunglasses and headscarves pretend to light fags in the passenger seat. There was a hint of crisp light blue shirt at the collar, most of it hidden by a scarf I guess I'd say was probably cashmere.

"How are you?" he said, though coldly, and if I'm right, without a question mark.

"I'm fine, yeah," I said, low-key. "Thanks for coming."

Thanks for coming? He'd summoned me.

"Cold day," I said. "Did you drive, or . . . ?"

"I don't drive," he snapped, so quickly and so full of snip I was shocked. "Look, I suggest you ask me your question again and I will tell you what you want to know but that is all I will do. I will not entertain a barrage of questions, I will not enter into some huge conversation. I just, for the sake of my own peace of mind, want this resolved."

I nodded my understanding.

"So go on, then," he said. "Ask me your question."

I shifted, uncomfortably, from one foot to the other.

"It doesn't really matter anymore," I said. "I'm moving on."

"Moving on from what?"

"From whatever it was. I was in a weird place. There was a lot going on. To do with my past. To do with my present not quite living up to what I'd wanted. To do with the future looking the same."

"Ask me your question."

"We don't have to do this—"

"I want to talk about it."

I looked at him. He looked at his shoes. It seemed like he needed me for something, for this, whatever "this" is.

Sod it. Why not.

"So who's the girl?" I asked.

"I met her at a wedding," he said, as we both leaned back onto the bench, pretending it wasn't weird we weren't looking at each other. "She was a bridesmaid, wearing the worst dress I had ever seen in my life. Generally bridesmaids' dresses are quite nice, but she was like something out of an Anne Hathaway film. Some things are just *too* green, y'know? We were seated on the same table and I inveigled my way round to the seat next to hers."

Inveigled. He could use the word "inveigled."

"Whose wedding was it?" I asked, almost involuntarily and

just to show friendly interest, but now Damien shot me a withering glance.

"What did I just say? I'm not going to enter into some grand dialogue about this. I'll tell you what you asked, I want to do that, but I won't tell you everything you ask. What does it matter whose wedding it was? Why would that matter at all?"

"Carry on," I said, avoiding his eye, finding a bin to look at. "Sorry."

"It was a friend's wedding, okay? In Berkshire. Well, this friend is also a client. She put me at that table, and she winked at me when she did. She knew we'd get on."

"You and the girl?"

"Me and . . . the girl, yes. I'd had a bit to drink, I was probably a bit too friendly, I don't wear a wedding ring, and she was in the mood for romance."

He said all that liked he'd practiced it. Like he'd rehearsed the reasons at home until he could say them with no passion so that maybe they'd lose their meaning. Or maybe this was his story, the one he'd decided on, and he was sticking to it. I turned my head to look at him but still he stared straight ahead.

"There were these cameras on the tables, these . . ."

"Disposables?"

"Disposables, yes. The idea was we'd all take pictures of each other and hand them in at the end. Nice way of letting the photographer go home early and saving a few quid. Anyway, I grabbed it and took a photo of us together. And then she wanted to dance. Some AC/DC thing came on; she said it was the best song ever written or something."

I smiled.

" 'Back in Black'?"

He looked at me, askance.

"I'm really not sure. I told her I hated it but she made me

get up. And then later she looked at me and, I don't know, it just felt right."

God. I'd been looking at the photos. At the moments. I'd ignored the moments *after* each one—the moments I couldn't see. Now I resented them, slightly: partly because they'd surprised me and partly because those moments belonged to Damien and not me.

"So that was the beginning. That was how it started. Two people at a wedding."

"What did you chat about?" I asked, and Damien stared at me.

"Did you follow me that day?" he said. "Did you follow me into the restaurant?"

"I did."

"And you think that's acceptable?"

I imagine I looked a little ashamed here. It's hard to justify following someone. Difficult to admit everything started on a lie, or that trust was misplaced and abused.

We took a second; Damien reset.

"I have a place in Bermondsey," he said. "We were there our first weekend together. It's in an old factory, and—"

He paused.

"But then you know all this."

I smiled, embarrassed.

"So anyway, we got talking about the world. I'd just been to Sarajevo for the film festival; she said she'd always wanted to go. She'd never really traveled. Grew up on a farm."

A farm!

"I told her about Bosnia . . . Croatia. She said they sounded incredible. I said maybe one day I'd take her to places like that. You know? Said I'd show her the world. We talked about that a lot."

"Sounds . . . like something people say," I said, and I shook my head. This seemed to jar with Damien, and I could understand why. He wasn't used to his own weaknesses, exposed.

Quickly, he continued: "Then, we talked for a couple more hours, we kissed, I texted her, we met up, met up a *lot*, I broke her heart, I'm a dick, and that's that."

He clapped his hands to his knees and stood.

"So there you go," he said. "That was your question answered, with a couple of juicy extras thrown in for free."

"It was big of you to meet with me," I said, and he nodded a no-thanks-necessary.

As he wrapped his possibly cashmere scarf round his neck again, he stopped and looked me in the eye.

"So now you tell *me* something . . ."

In a flash it was clear this was why he'd come. He was curious, just like me.

"Why did you want to do this? I mean, I thought maybe you were her brother, or a jealous ex, or perhaps her new bloke intent on, I dunno, revenge or extortion or blackmail or something?"

"I met her one night on Charlotte Street," I said. "I found her camera afterward. And I want to give it back to her."

Damien looked up at the sky, laughed.

"So you just fancy her?"

He laughed again. A colder laugh this time.

"It's . . . it's difficult to explain . . . it's . . ."

"That's sweet. It's deliciously sad and pathetic and, if you don't mind my saying so, odd, too, but it's sweet. Why can't you just go to a bar? Or a wedding? Better still, a wedding she's at. She seems up for it at weddings."

I didn't like this. He was trying to ruin it. Ruin her. He saw that I could see what he was doing.

"Look, we didn't end on good terms. For obvious reasons. And she changed her number, otherwise—"

He shrugged.

"E-mail?" I tried.

He shook his head and brought something out from his pocket.

"Can I keep this?" he said. It was the photo he'd taken from me that day.

Of course, I kept thinking. She was yours. And you took the shot!

But instead, I said, "It's not really mine to give."

Damien held the photo. He seemed to be considering what to do: whether to hand it over or just shove it back in his pocket.

"Pub in Finchley," he said. "The Adelaide. That's where this was taken. That was kind of our thing."

"Pubs?"

He handed it back, shook off whatever he was about to say, and looked at me with disdain.

"No, not pubs."

I shrugged. I didn't get it.

"There's something about you," he said, "that makes this acceptable. But you're on thin ice here, you know that, right?"

I didn't know what to say. So I said, "I like beginnings. I like the way things start. Because if they start well enough they can see you through to the end."

"But *everything* ends," said Damien.

Then, as he collected himself together, got ready to go: "Why wouldn't you give me the photo?"

"I told you—it's not mine to give."

"You didn't give it back because this isn't over for you," he said. "You're not moving on. You haven't."

I could've watched him as he left, now, assured this had been dealt with, it was finished, it would not come back to haunt him. But there was something else—one little thing—that had been bothering me. And as he turned away and looked at the ground it just came out.

"You said you don't drive," I blurted, clumsily, "but in one of the pictures, there's this car, and I sort of assumed—"

"Facel Vega." He smiled. "Not mine. *Really* not mine. Slightly insulted you might think it was mine, actually."

"It's a good car," I tried, but as you know, my experience is mainly limited to a Nissan Cherry covered in Calippos, plus no one on *Top Gear* ever calls anything "good"; you have to compare cars to horses, or tits.

"No, I'm afraid I've been off the road for a little while. I was a little 'happy' in my driving. Tried pleading exceptional hardship, but even with four PRCAs I couldn't manage it."

I pretended to know what that meant.

"That big old thing is hers. It was her dad's. She couldn't let it go. She said it would be like letting him go."

Now Damien did walk off, showing me his back, striding toward the edge of the park. But by the gates, he stopped, and thought for a second. I watched as he did, unsure of what I was supposed to do, suddenly aware I had no idea what to do with my arms, and then he turned, and cupped his hands around his mouth.

"Jason!" he called out. "Her name's *Shona*!"

And then, with a nod, he returned to his world, and I remained in mine. And that would be the last time I would ever see Damien Anders Laskin.

"The chakata fruit on the ground belongs to all, but the one on the tree is for she who can climb."

—Traditional Shona Tribe proverb, Zimbabwe

The last time I ever saw him, I had this idea.

It's one that won't go away. I've resisted telling you, because I fear it makes me sound pathetic and weedy. I watched that Julia Roberts film where she eats, prays, and loves (I forget its name) and I'm a little terrified of turning into her.

At first I thought all it might take is a change in career. A teacher, maybe. That's a job. That was Dad's job.

Then I thought maybe I need to make my mark somehow and do something even more out of the ordinary. Have you heard of Phyllis Pearsall? She was very brilliant. In the 1920s and '30s she used to get up every day at 5 a.m. and go for an eighteen-mile walk through the streets of London, taking precise notes of where everything was and then stashing 23,000 individual street names in a shoebox under her bed.

I realize that you're probably thinking she sounds mentally ill.

But that was the first London A–Z, and even though everyone she approached completely refused to publish it, she used to walk around with a wheelbarrow delivering *copies to all the WH Smiths. She only died in 1996, by which time she'd sold millions of editions and become pretty much my favorite Londoner ever. Do you ever feel like you're not really using your life, the way someone like Phyllis Pearsall did? Like the everyday is too everyday and it's time for the magic?*

All of which has made me think: I want to make the thing that nearly happened happen.

For myself this time.

I don't want to just rely on someone else to make it happen for me, because really, that's how I got into this mess.

And I honestly think I can make this work.

I was thinking about it all last night and I woke up this morning thinking about it. All day I've thought about it and there comes a time when really, you should stop thinking about it, because really, you could be hit by a bus tomorrow. Instead, you should start making it happen.

Perhaps the first step is just deciding to.

Sx

TWENTY-TWO

Or "Adult Education"

I walked into the staff room and there he was, Mr. Willis, holding court with his favorite red mug.

I had formed a childish insistence on calling everyone by their teacher names. It was rebellion by formality.

"Course, it was a breakdown, you see," he was saying. "Couldn't deal with it, but you know, this is an *inner-city school*. There was a *Panorama* on . . ."

I caught Mrs. Woollacombe's eye and instinctively she went for her butterfly brooch, running her fingers over its wings for comfort. Her eyes darted nervously around to see who else had noticed me standing self-consciously in the doorway.

"Everyone thinks we can do something better, but of course, when it came to it, he—"

"Jason!" said Miss Pitt (BSc) loudly and obviously, and I could see the others—the lab technician whose name I could never remember, and Mr. Peterson, fresh from Loughborough and eager to revolutionize the world of barely funded PE—trying to work out how they were going to get out of this one.

"It wasn't a breakdown," I said, in as friendly way as I could, although it was, of course, it undeniably was. "It was just a shock to the system. Which I needed, I think."

"Jason, no," said Mr. Willis, spinning around, guilty and anxious. "I was just saying how hard it must be to—"

"Yes, how hard it must be," said Mrs. Woollacombe. "Particularly when you set out to do something and you failed at that, too. I mean, not failed, because you didn't 'fail,' but—"

"It's fine, everyone. It's all fine."

I sat down on the sofa, surrounded by years of coffee rings and sandwich stains. If the police ever did a DNA test on this sofa it would be 90 percent disappointment.

"So what else is going on?" I said, lightly.

"Gary's sick again."

"Mr. Dodd? Have you tried Ladbrokes?"

Good-natured laughter.

See? I could make jokes. I wasn't going to have another breakdown, everyone! Because that's where that conversation had been heading, hadn't it? I'm a fully functioning member of the team!

"Well, it just means we've got to draw straws, you see," said Mrs. Woollacombe, rolling her eyes.

"Straws for what?" I said.

"Friday."

"What's Friday?"

Here's an interesting fact to share with your friends. I found it on the Internet, while Googling furiously the second I got home from Postman's Park.

Shona is a Scottish form of Joan.

Okay, fair enough, not interesting exactly. But true.

So maybe she was Scottish. Maybe she grew up on a Scottish farm in Scotland, with Scottish people and a Scottish name.

Shona is also the name of a people and a language of Zimbabwe, but it seemed less likely she was Zimbabwean.

There's the island of Eilean Shona, too, just off the west coast of Scotland, with a population of just two, making it either the most romantic or the most depressing place possible.

And these were talking points, after all, in case I should bump into her one night. I nearly had, after all.

The Facel Vega. The night I saw it leaving the NCP on Poland Street and ducked out of the way. If I'd looked closer, if I'd *been braver*...

Anyway, "Hey, isn't Shona the name of a Zimbabwean people and language?" I could finally say, if I did see her again, tapping the tobacco out of my pipe and looking urbane and sophisticated as I sat down beside her, sliding her Tango out of my way, uninvited but clearly welcome.

"Yes," she would purr, in her soft Scottish brogue, perhaps blushing (nearly) imperceptibly at the confidence of a very slightly older man with a pipe, avoiding my eyes lest she give too much away. "Indeed it is the language and name of the proud Shona folk, with whom I studied during my gap year and came to know as a wise and gracious people, as we fought side by side to vanquish the Western developers intent on their destruction."

I would look unimpressed.

"Does it not also mean 'sweet' in the language of the Bengal?" I would add, staring into the middle distance, aloof, unattainable, *fascinating*, and she would lean forward, her chin on her hands, and say, "I did not know that..."

And then I'd tell her about my many cats, and she'd squeal, because she fucking *loves* cats.

It was weird, knowing her name. I mean, I always knew she'd probably have one. I don't know anybody who doesn't, and even if I did, I wouldn't be able to name them.

But now that I knew what it was...she'd become real to me. Not just a girl in a moment. But a girl who right *this* moment *was* somewhere, *doing* something.

Damien had talked about her with affection and regret. Two things you wouldn't do if she'd been a horrible person, or selfish, short-tempered, angry, arrogant, belligerent, willful, or cold. He'd talked about her like the one who'd got away, or the one he'd always regret; the one he'd never mean harm to.

And she was out there.

And though I told myself I'd given up, though I'd convinced myself that this particular beginning had already ended, part of me was pleased that now I could decide the ending for myself.

Whether that ending was trying . . . or whether it was stopping.

At least I was in control.

"POWER UP! IS POWERING DOWN," said the Facebook invite. "COME AND SAY GOOD-BYE TO A LEGEND."

I checked to see who else had been invited. A couple of regulars. Someone I didn't know but had seen in the shop. Pawel, who didn't really understand social networking and was yet to figure out how to reply to things. And me.

The plan seemed to be to have a short eulogy in the shop before retiring to the Den for the evening. A typically ambitious night from Dev.

I was sure it'd be fun.

I looked at the RSVP options.

Are you attending? Yes, No, or Maybe.

And I clicked *No*.

It wasn't just that I was ashamed of showing Dev I'd taken a giant step backward when all we'd really talked about was moving forward. It was that in some ways, not attending was moving forward. Because what's moving forward if not *not* looking backward?

This is how confusing things get when you're trying to convince yourself that all is well. You bend logic to your will.

But anyway. It wasn't like I hadn't made an effort with Dev. I'd sent him the golden envelope I'd managed to get from Zoe. He'd loved it. He'd sent me a text with a little kiss on the end. So there was time for me and Dev to get close again.

But first I had to sort myself out.

I would be moving out of Blackstock Road in a month.

I'd found myself a nice little studio flat in Canonbury Square, so small I'd constantly smell of kitchen, but with a desk by the window that filled the place with light. The rent was high, but I reasoned this was good for me. It would force me to work. I couldn't just rely on supply teaching that way; I'd have to freelance, find ideas, write, maybe even progress.

Zoe was pretty down. *London Now* was finally on its way out.

"Could be any day," she said. "They could literally just shut us down at any time they like."

She'd started making calls already and thought she'd made a few inroads with a couple of papers, but budgets were tight these days, she said. We'd still spend our evenings cooking together, then finding our way to the Bank of Friendship, and it was there, this night, that she slid an envelope across the table to me.

"What's this?" I said.

My name was still on a few out-of-date PR lists, and every now and again she'd bring home an invitation to interview the star of a bad new musical, or a heavily packaged new pie from Ginsters, and I'd read the release or try the pie, but both would inevitably find the bin. This one, though, was different.

"Arrived this morning," she said. "It looked personal, so I didn't open it. Although that was also what made me *want* to open it."

It had a stamp, for one thing, rather than the red splotch of a hurried in-house franking machine. And the address was in ink, in a small and spidery hand. I looked at the postmark.

Brighton.

I opened it, and inside was no note, no explanation—just a colorful flyer, with a guitar, and a rainbow, and a soft photo of a girl with a fringe and electric-blue eyeliner sitting by the shore.

Abbey Grant
"Lightness of touch meets soulful seaside splendor"
    —London Now
The Open House & Performer Bar
Thursday, 9 p.m.

I was thrilled. And I beamed. She was doing it.

Then, inspired, using the moment, I got home, I opened up the only two boxes I'd yet packed, and I riffled around, pulling out the file I'd hung on to from my last time at St. John's, hoping I hadn't chucked out the one stapled-together document I actually never thought I'd need again.

Brighton's Open House & Performer Bar is all Chesterfield sofas and rough wooden tables, red walls and Jim Morrison pop art, and really needs a catchier name.

There's a student crowd, but locals, too, and on this Thursday night at half past eight I found myself somewhere near the back of the room and quietly pretended to read a discarded *Argus*.

I hadn't told Abbey I was coming. I know she'd sent me the flyer, but there was no note, nothing to indicate she wanted me there. I got the sense it was out of politeness. Something to say, Look, I'm doing this, I'm trying it, wish me luck, all the best.

I'd stared at the flyer on the train down, played Abbey's songs on my iPod as the city sun faded into a countryside night. They were beautiful. Not perfect, but they were *her*. They were fragile, but full of life, so delicate and breakable, but so hopeful, too. I hadn't been lying when I'd written that review. I was, in fact, I *think*, being more honest than I'd ever been. My gift to Abbey would have been my gift whether I knew her or not, but somehow that had been devalued and lost.

Ha. My "gift." Like five stars from a mildly disgraced half-sacked acting reviews editor was a gift. But those five stars weren't my gift, not really. I guess my gift was just belief. The only thing I had to give.

Then the crowd settled as the lights dimmed, and Abbey walked out, eyes down and self-conscious, plugged in her guitar, and started to play.

And I felt so happy, so thrilled, so *full*.

"I wasn't sure you'd come," said Abbey, afterward.

"I wasn't sure you wanted me here," I said.

"I wasn't either."

"You were brilliant, Abbey. It was—"

"Jase, I'm sorry about reacting the way I did."

"It's my fault. I messed up. If it's any consolation, it was one of at least nine things that lost me my job as acting reviews editor. So we're even. Although you *did* drug my ex-girlfriend's fiancé and friend, so actually, I think you still owe *me* one because now she's not talking to me and my wedding invite was revoked."

She giggled, guiltily.

"God, I don't know what I was thinking. Escapism, I suppose. Guess we *are* even."

"That's not what I said. I said you still owed me one. And afterward, after that gig, I just got excited when I realized that you did have an ambition. You were lying, before, or—"

"I wasn't lying," she said, rolling her eyes, and I was quick to get this back on track.

"No, I mean not lying exactly, obviously. Just wrong. Because you clearly did."

I'd wondered about Abbey, when I first met her. Why was she always following The Kicks about? Or the other bands she seemed to know and trail and traipse after? I'd wondered if maybe she was some kind of groupie, taking senior position among the other girls, because she was "with" the band, knew them to talk to and drink with. But that wasn't her at all. Now I realized she hung around with those people simply because they were doing what *she* wanted to do. She loved the music, not the band, and she loved the universe of it all. She wanted to watch, quietly, from the side of the stage, as others gave it a shot, because maybe she just wasn't brave enough to walk out there herself and tell the world what she was thinking.

Yet.

"You're doing it," I said. "Going for it."

"Just a few gigs. It's *hard* to get gigs. But the response has been good. Well, from nearly everyone."

"Tough crowds?"

"The crowds have been good. Polite, anyway. No, I mean Paul."

"Puppeteer Paul? What about Puppeteer Paul?"

"Puppeteer Paul wasn't quite as keen. Said we had to decide who the creative one was. Says it never works out when there are two people trying to crack the same world."

"He's a *puppeteer*!"

She broke into a smile, and put her hand to her cheek.

"Actually, he'd prefer it if you refer to him as a *political* puppeteer."

"Where was he tonight, then? The UN? Or did they parachute him into Gaza with a sock and two Ping-Pong balls?"

Her smile fell, but only very slightly, and only for a second.

"We're not together anymore, Paul and me. If you could say we were *ever* together, I don't know."

Oh, God. This was my fault. That review—my little gift— had kick-started this. The catalyst that enraged a political puppeteer. I should say sorry. I knew that. I should apologize unreservedly for a relationship ruined.

But then I remembered that night at Scala. The disparaging remarks. The cynicism masquerading as wit. The way he seemed to be with her. My childish mental report card (*Yes, Mr. and Mrs. Anderson, from my notes this term, it appears that Paul is a knob*).

"Why did you go out with him in the first place, Ab?" I said, like I was a disappointed older brother, or something.

"I dunno. Structure? I know he liked his puppets, but he was the most organized person I knew, puppets or not. And I think I thought, well, you need limits, don't you? You need rules. I feel like I'm just wafting along most of the time, it was nice to feel there was only so far I could waft. Though the thing is . . . I think I really *like* wafting."

A pause.

"People don't use the word 'waft' enough, do they?" she said.

"Sod that political puppeteer," I said. "Sod *all* political puppeteers. May their puppets rise up against them in fury."

Abbey laughed.

"Sod him," she said.

I raised my glass.

"To making it happen," I said.

"You're using that phrase a lot at the moment." She smiled.

I blushed. I was.

"How's Dev?" she said, lightly.

"Haven't really seen him much," I said. "I seem to have developed a habit for not seeing people much."

She tapped the table and took a sip of her drink.

"When I first met you," she said, "do you know what I thought?"

I shook my head.

"I thought, He's like me."

"A small girl who hangs around with bands?"

"No. A bit broken."

"*Bruised*, you said."

"But fixable, maybe. I'm trying to fix things, and yes, it's kind of thanks to your idiotics, so thank you, I guess. And when we were hanging out, it seemed like, more and more, you were, too."

She clinked my glass.

"Don't stop," she said.

We sat together for a second, just two mates in a pub. I noticed her guitar again.

"Listen, I might be able to waft a gig your way, if you're interested?"

The next morning. Friday. The day Mrs. Woollacombe had been dreading. The one Mr. Willis had prepared a short straw for, probably cursing Gary Dodd and Ladbrokes as he did so.

I pulled out the document I'd found in my boxes that night. I'd read it on the train home last night to remind myself, to see if it still stood up, but I'd suddenly found myself furiously rewriting it, reworking it, *renaming* it.

Making It Happen! it read. *A Mr. Priestley Assembly!*

The others had all but jumped with glee when I'd said I'd be happy to take that week's assembly. They tried to give me outs—said supply teachers weren't expected to pile in with the others, said they could always cancel and just have a study period instead. But I said no, I'd be grateful for the chance. "Be good to connect with the kids!"

Everyone had looked at me like I was mental.

It wasn't just that they wanted to avoid a ten-minute speech. It wasn't just that they didn't fancy the prep, or the angst, or the listless feeling they'd get halfway through when they realized their words were falling on permanently disinterested ears.

"There's an inspector in," Mrs. Woollacombe had told me, finally, as we'd walked toward the hall. "They'll be *inspecting*!"

She made a sorry-I-should-have-mentioned-it face, but I waved it away. I'd been looking forward to this, by and large. The thought excited me. Maybe I need this, I thought. Get back on the horse. Do it properly. Do it right. Inspector or not. And all thanks to Matt.

I glanced up from my little red plastic chair on the stage. Mrs. Abercrombie, the new head, was waxing lyrical about the importance of covering textbooks in brown paper, and if you didn't have brown paper, you could use wallpaper, or just wrapping paper, but ideally brown paper or sticky back plastic. She had been making this point for quite some time. The kids were glassy-eyed, their skin dull, the room just a yawn, early-morning hair gel yet to set, a bored sea of tiny ties and scuffed-up Golas. I could see Michael Baxter in the second row, his collar upturned, chewing and snapping his gum, loudly, a ten-pack of fags and a lighter outlined in his too-tight trousers. Teresa May had snuck her phone in, and little Tony couldn't stop scratching.

". . . which actually brings us to the theme of today's assembly," said Mrs. Abercrombie, suddenly, and I jolted. Michael Baxter noticed and smirked.

"So, Mr. Priestley . . . ?"

I stood.

"Thanks, Mrs. Abercrombie," I said, looking out at my audience, my kids, my young minds to mold.

Somewhere, someone burped.

"Making It Happen," I started, and my eyes scanned the room, for someone, anyone, who had about them the look of a Matthew Fowler. Because if I saw one, I would do this, and do it properly, and crucially, I would do it for *them*. "How do you 'make it happen'? And what does 'making it happen' even mean?"

Another burp, this one followed by a giggle.

But I ignored it. Because actually, I had stuff to say.

And so I went for it.

I talked, and I talked, and I talked some more. I made some jokes, and two of them got small laughs, and as I looked around the room, among the bored faces, the glum faces, the distant faces, I saw the odd, all-but-imperceptible pocket of something. Small sparks of interest; the odd head tilt. Maybe only two, three kids. But two, three kids nevertheless.

It felt good. I felt different.

And as I turned the pages, and moved closer to my final point—about dreams, and about how dreams are supposed to be unrealistic, but about how some dreams *can* come true—I felt like I was the inspirational teacher in the closing scenes of a Disney movie. I never once thought I'd have that. I'd never once had it before. This was not my ideal job. I was not overly brilliant at it. But then, I would not be here forever. I knew that, because I intended to be true to my word and Make It Happen, so that out there, in this school hall, I would not disappoint any budding Matthew Fowlers when they watched me do precisely nothing for five more years. *That* was teaching. *Showing*. And that was my plan, vague and small and naive as it was.

And then something strange happened.

The woman who works in the head's office—Sheila?—pushes through the double doors at the back of the hall and then holds her hands up apologetically. I look at the head, and the head raises her eyebrows at Sheila, and Sheila makes a phone call mime. So Mrs. Abercrombie stands up, but that's not what Sheila meant; she points at me.

Me? I now mime.

Yes, she mimes back. And then: *Quickly.*

"Jason?" said the voice. A female voice with a heavy accent.

Sheila was hovering around, full of concern, popping her hand on my shoulder and patting me a lot, but I was pretty sure I knew who this was.

"Um . . . Svetlana?" I said back. "This is not really the best time to be talking about pies and crying. I was onstage, inspiring the youth of today."

I rolled my eyes at Sheila in a what-can-you-do? kind of way, and she stopped patting me.

Silence on the other end of the line.

"Abbey?" I said.

"It is not Abbey. This is *Pamela*," said the voice.

Pamela?

She sounded fraught, shocked, frightened.

Instantly I was afraid. Amazing how you can catch a fear before you know what to be afraid of.

"Please, Jason. You come now!"

"What? Where? What's going on?"

"It's Dev."

Shit.

"What's wrong?" I said, a low panic rising in my voice. "What *about* Dev?"

TWENTY-THREE

Or "Do What You Want, Be What You Are"

Devdatta Ranjit Sandananda Patel was a hero.

A hero among men.

A hero facing down robots, and Nazis, and aliens.

A man who knew his way around a gun, around nunchakus, around a Hadouken punch.

A man who'd saved damsels, freed animals, bumped off end-of-level baddie after end-of-level baddie, and always, *always* lived to tell the tale.

But in real life, Devdatta Patel had never done anything heroic.

That's what had bothered him more than anything.

"We've never *done* anything," he'd tell me, on another lunchtime in Postman's Park. "What have we ever done?"

I remember one time in particular. We were standing, staring at the tile that said:

William Freer Lucas
MRCS LLD, at Middlesex Hospital
Risked poison for himself rather than lessen any chance of
saving a child's life and died.
Oct 8th 1893

This one, more than almost any other, had always been Dev's favorite.

"It's a legacy!" he'd say. "He *did* something, and here we are, a hundred and whatever years later, and maybe it's just you and me, but *we know* the name William Freer Lucas. We're on this planet for the blink of an eye but some of us live longer, even when they die young."

That was all I could think about in the taxi. Staring out the window at the gray shops and streets and malls, noticing every siren, every ambulance that screamed by.

So no. Dev had never been a hero.

Until today.

The taxi ride had been sickening.

I knew nothing. Just that he'd been rushed to hospital, that from the catch and the fear in Pamela's voice it sounded bad. Maybe very bad.

She'd been jittery at the end of the call, right when I'd said I'd be there as soon as I could, like she'd passed the news on and could allow herself a brief emotional collapse.

Christ, Dev, what did you do? Are you okay?

I leaned against the window of the cab, my fists tight, and for the first time in my life I prayed for my friend.

"We were going to the place," said Pamela, gripping her tea.

"Which place?" I said. "What happened?"

"Hilton Hotel," she said. "In Mayfair."

Oh, no. Of course. The Golden Joysticks. That was today.

That was my big surprise. My olive branch. Zoe had had to make a few phone calls, but two tickets to the videogames bash of the year had been secured.

He'd been excited in his text: *Thank you thank you thank you! The Golden Joysticks! A reference to its early days as part of the GamesMaster franchise! Guess who I'll ask ... you never know! x*

"We were walking to the tube station," said Pamela, her eyes on mine, "and Dev, he saw a girl, maybe fourteen years, she cycles on her bike, but she was ... um ..."

She gestured with her hands.

"Swaying?" I tried.

"One way then the other," she said, nodding. "She was *swaying*, she had bags on her bicycle, from shops ..."

I sat her down on two blue plastic chairs. I could feel her arms shaking.

"And she fell, bad fall, I heard her bell ring when she fall, and she made a noise," she said. "And her bags go everywhere but her leg is under her bike and she ... um ..."

"Panics?"

She nodded, and I was starting to sweat, feeling the pressure of the moment.

"And a car comes, quickly, very quickly, and I grab Dev's arm, but he starts to run ... he pulls her away from her bicycle, but the car, it comes quick, and Dev is there and ..."

She clipped her hands together.

"He spins," she said. "Hit! His leg is rip open, Jason, a lot blood, I saw the bone and it—"

She couldn't find the words, but her hands did the work. I think she wanted to say "twist" or "twists"; his bone, the femur or the tibula or the shin, twisted in among flaps of skin and blood and car and jeans, ligaments stretched and torn, and he'd lain there, my Dev, a bloodied and useless, desperate heap.

She looked at me, full of disbelief, that this could happen, that a car could hit a man she knew.

"How is he?" I said, my hand now shaking.

* * *

There are moments in life—days, even—that can block out the others in an instant. They're like pinpricks. Sharp and painful and dominating, turning the moments either side into a pointless haze.

I'd never considered what it might be like to lose a friend. To lose Dev. That it could be possible at all seemed unreal, impossible. Or it did until today.

Dev was alive, I knew that. But what sliver of chance would it have taken to change that? A mile-per-hour more, a split second later on the brakes, an inch or two to the right or left? But the overriding thought and the feeling I just couldn't get away from . . . was admiration.

"He's lost blood," said the doctor, about my age but worn and beaten and not up for a role in *Holby City* anytime soon. "It was a nasty hit."

How nasty? I wanted to say, but he wasn't finished and in situations like this you want to delay the bad news as much as you can. Let the doctor say his piece: he's done this before; he knows what he's doing.

"His leg pretty much buckled," he said. "There are lacerations, multiple fractures, some muscle damage . . ."

I began to feel ill. The doctor's voice was soft even as the words became harder.

"His hamstring has torn, I'm afraid. We had to—"

I began to feel faint.

Enough.

"Is he okay?" I said. "Is Dev okay?"

Four hours later. Pamela had popped out to get KFC but I couldn't touch mine. Too many bones. Too much loose fat, so warm and oily.

Pamela sucked at the bones until she caught sight of me, as gray as the tea in my hand.

Then the bang of the door.

"*Wise fwom your gwaaave!*" was the first thing I heard as Dev was wheeled into the room by a man he proudly told us was Charles, his new best friend. I could see from Charles's badge his name was Phil.

Dev's leg was in plaster, his face swollen and bloodied, but he seemed strangely happy.

"I've got a very badly broken leg!" he said, waving his keyring about. "And some other stuff."

"Dev," I said. "Do you know what you *did*?"

"If you can't save a little life once in a while, what *can* you do?"

"But you did!" I said. "You saved a life! You're a hero!"

"I would not use that word," he said, graciously, "but you must always feel free to. Hello, Pamela."

"Dev," she said. "*Thank* you."

We didn't quite know what she was thanking him for but we went along with it, because it sounded pretty positive.

"Bloody car," he said. "A Vectra! Bloke was on his phone. Didn't see me till the last second. He managed to swerve, but he caught me right on the ... um. The ... um—"

"The leg," said Pamela, helpfully.

"Yes. The leg. *This* one."

He pointed at his plaster.

"*And* we missed the bloody Golden Joysticks," he said, shaking his head. "That's the tragedy no one here is talking about. The nurses don't seem to care. Bloody NHS."

"We'll go next year," I said.

"Could probably still hit the after-party?"

"You've broken your leg, mate," I said. "And I'm pretty sure you're on quite a lot of morphine."

"I *am*, actually!" he said, nodding. "It's given me a remarkable sense of well-being. We should get some for the flat. Abbey could make omelets out of it. I wonder what's number one on the charts."

I weighed up the situation.

"I should probably let you rest," I said, and Charles nodded, like I was a medical genius and could expect my PhD by special delivery in the morning. "Do you need a lift anywhere, Pamela?"

"I stay," she said, and Dev tried to give me a subtle wink, which was so very subtle I'm fairly sure people in Germany saw it.

At the door, exhausted, happy, relieved, I turned.

"Do you know what this means, Dev?"

"I do, sir. I will need round-the-clock care!"

"It means you *did* something, Dev."

He cocked his head.

"There was a moment, and you *used* it."

I got home that night shattered. I could've lost Dev, was all I could think.

The people around you *are* you. They share your history. They can even write it with you. And when you lose one, there's no doubt you lose some of yourself, however they're lost.

So I sat down at my computer. I tried to work out an e-mail. I tried to put into words what I was feeling. I wanted to say sorry, *unreservedly* sorry, sorry for *everything*, and make promises, and just be cool again, and have her back in my life even just as a pal.

But there was too much to say.

So I thought for a second, then went to Facebook, where I sent Sarah a friend request.

And those two words, I hoped, said it all.

"The cook does not have to be a beautiful woman."

—Traditional Shona Tribe proverb, Zimbabwe

Your comments have been very funny.

I know I don't tell you very much. Place names, events, yes; names not so much. And I'm sorry I can't tell you yet what my big plan is.

But maybe if you've been following this blog since the start you might have guessed.

I was sitting on the bus this morning thinking about it all. There'd been some accident up ahead, somewhere— ambulance, police, someone on a motorbike, I think, the awful rubberneckers craning to catch a glimpse of whatever. I'd been slowly coming to the conclusion that I should stop hankering after moments that have gone and start using the ones that are here.

Is that what you'd say? "Using" them? It sounds weird but I don't know what else to put.

On that note, a man tried to pick me up today by sitting very close to me on the bus and accidentally brushing his hand against mine so that he could apologize and then say, "Wow, did you feel that? The electricity!," but maybe it's a testament to my current state of mind that my first thought was, "I hope I don't get a rash."

I think the face I made must have made him stop short of his next conversational gambit because then he kept himself to himself and weirdly I felt a bit sad about that.

So I've had another chat with HR, about the idea. Apparently there are "ways and means." Mum always praises my practical side; it was Dad who liked the risks I took. But with the year I've had ... with Dad, with "him" ...

I hold no grudges against "him," by the way. Because really, now that I think about it, maybe it's made me stronger. I wouldn't now be wondering whether I should do something, or get out there, without having the year I'd never have chosen.

You can buckle, in life, I think, or you can bend.

*I thought about my camera again this morning as I got off the bus near Charlotte Street. Would I have developed that film or those memories? Yes. In a moment of weakness. But I like to think maybe I'd have been strong and made the **choice** not to.*

It's the year of choosing for myself. But: will I?

Maybe I'm just in a weekend vibe, but if I do, I promise to be far more open with you. Yeah? You deserve that. And I'll share one embarrassing secret as penance for my secrecy in a selfless act of friendship toward you.

I might even tell you my name.

Sx

TWENTY-FOUR

Or "Children Go Where I Send Thee"

The weekend was over and I was weighed down by books as I trudged down the corridor toward room 3Gc again. There was the odd snigger as I did.

"Oi, sir, you makin' it happen?" called out Trey Stoddard.

"Piss off!" I said, because I'm a supply teacher, and no one told me I couldn't.

Trey slapped his hand to his thigh and laughed, then ran off to tell his mates.

"Jason," said a voice behind me, scuttling closer. It was Mrs. Woollacombe. "Laura's looking for you."

Laura? Mrs. Abercrombie? What for? To offer me more work? Or to tell me my work here was done? I had a contract with St. John's, but there'd never been any hint that it was rolling. I sighed to myself. If the work here dried up, it'd be other inner-city schools for me, other faces, longer journeys, shorter nights.

"I'll pop in to see her at break," I said.

The kids were being good today. I liked to think maybe I'd calmed them with my wisdom during that assembly, but more likely, they were knackered from PE. They were attentive, though, and when I asked them to open their books, they did so without protest or sigh, and now we sat quietly, and I listened to them read.

Then, without warning and out of nowhere, some noise outside. I jolted, quickly recomposed.

It had been loud and fast. A car backfire, maybe, or bin lid slamming, or some other kind of crack or bang. A couple of kids looked outside, stretched their necks to look up or down the street, but my eyes were scanning the windows of the estate.

Nothing.

I looked back at the class, who were already back in their books.

I got back to work, too.

"Basically, you were a hit," said Mrs. Abercrombie. "A huge, massive hit. So well done and thank you."

"What do you mean?" I said, genuinely confused.

Perhaps the kids had had a vote and decided I was terrific.

"The inspector," she said. "Loved your assembly. Said you were inspirational. Said you had a keen grasp on the language of the kids, and you used it to motivate. Said she was impressed you'd put the time in, that most people would have just printed something off the Internet and read it out."

"Well, I mean, it sort of started that way, but I added to it, you know. Put in some personal experience. Made it a bit anecdotal."

"Mr. Cole just used to do his about Arsenal."

"I heard."

"I should thank Mr. Willis, too. He said it was his idea to get you to do it."

"Oh."

"And Deepa Dristi, you know her?"

I nodded. She was a senior student.

"She told the inspector that moments like that gave her hope."

Bloody hell. I knew how she'd have done it, too. With doe-eyed drama. She was always on about auditioning for *Hollyoaks* if university didn't work out. She'd have made me look good, albeit in a *Hollyoaks* way.

"Tanya Myers is the inspector's name. She wanted to mention to you that there is actually an actor who shares your name."

"Is there? I had no idea."

"And she wanted to speak to you afterward but you'd gone . . ."

"Well, my best mate got run over."

"Oh," said Mrs. Abercrombie. She hadn't been expecting that. To be fair, I should probably have been a little more gentle, but all this was a bit surprising. She was probably wondering how to deal with it.

"Anyway," she said, which was as good a way as any, "give her a call, please."

She handed me a card.

A few nights later, outside the Den, the traffic swooshed through a wet and dismal Cally. A few kids were leaning over one of the balconies of the council flats opposite, trying to catch the rain in cupped hands to flick at their mates.

Pamela had wheeled Dev down so that we could say our own little good-bye to Power Up! It felt right. Dev made a roll-up, pressed against the side of the pub for protection, and looked at me.

"I know we're not here to say sorry, mate," he said. "But sorry. I just wanted the shop to keep going because I thought it was my dream, but one day I looked at it, and I realized that you can adapt what you want, you know? I should've told you, but I was just thinking about myself, and I thought, Well, whatever happens, we'll just go somewhere else. But that was stupid and selfish. I sort of forgot it was your home. I felt like a parent or something, making sure their kid didn't worry at night."

"It's okay," I said. "I needed a kick up the arse. I needed to move on. I probably never would've otherwise. We'd have been flatmates forever."

"That would've been nice."

"That would've been weird."

"No, but . . . the other stuff I said, too. The stuff about The Girl—"

"Shona?"

He looked blank.

"What's that mean? What's Shona mean?"

"Shona is a Scottish form of Joan," I said, "and also the name of a people and a language of Zimbabwe. But go on. What about The Girl?"

"Well, I'm just saying, I was a bit thoughtless when I . . . hang on, what are you saying, with this Shona stuff?"

"Her name is Shona."

I raised my eyebrows, nodded, shrugged. It took him a second, but then he broke into a huge Dev-smile, and tried to slap me on the shoulder, though that was fairly hard from a wheelchair.

"You found out her name? How did you find out her *name*?"

"And guess what she drives."

"No!" he said, in disbelief.

"I actually saw it one night, on Poland Street."

"You saw her?! Dude, that's fate again!"

I laughed.

"Let's get a drink," I said.

"No! Jase! Come on! Look at the evidence!"

"Dev," I said. "I think what I should do is work on what I already have. Not chase what I don't. That's what I want to make happen. Does that make sense?"

He thought about it. I know he wanted to talk about it more, chase me to act. But I also know we'd turned a corner.

"We should go," I said. "We'll be late."

We could see the chalkboard sign outside the Old Queen's Head the second we turned the corner.

Live Music Tonight.

Abbey Grant.

And underneath it: *"One to watch"* —*Brighton Argus.*

Nice one, Abbey.

Matt had cleared everything with his boss, Jerry, but it was a Thursday and Matt was panicked.

"He only let me do it because it's a Thursday and Thursdays are quiet... everyone goes to Brown's down the road. I got a PA from college and lights and that but what if nobody comes?"

But they came. I'd made sure they'd come. I'd called, I'd texted, I'd harassed the hell out of Facebook. I was a gig promoter for one night only.

Me and Dev, of course, joining Pamela and a couple of her mates at a table in the corner.

Then Pawel, and Tomasz, and Marcin with the ankles.

Zoe came down, with an "At last I can see if she's worth the five stars!," followed by Clem, and Jo, and Sam. They'd just found out *London Now* would be shut down at the end of the month. But they'd been given assurances, could coast for a few weeks, been promised other jobs within the company.

"A pretty good deal, really," said Clem. "Little holiday."

"How's the comedy?" I asked.

"I'm knocking it on the head," he said. "There was an incident to do with what I perceived as a heinous conspiracy within the judging panel at the 'Ha-hamageddon' New Act of the Year competition."

I didn't ask.

And then: the kicker.

Through the door, holding hands: Sarah and Gary.

"I can't believe you came," I said.

"I wasn't going to," said Sarah, and I noticed Gary squeezing her hand. "*We* weren't going to. But then I realized: all our meetings have been pretty high pressure. You know? Like we're always trying to say the unsaid. Just thought it'd be nice to do something...normal. See a gig, or something. Like friends. And you seem pretty sold on this girl, from the sheer volume of reminders you sent everyone. Who is she?"

She'd made me wait, had Sarah. Left it a day or two. I knew she was always online. I knew she'd have got the alert as soon as it had been sent.

Jason Priestley has sent you a friend request...

And then she'd said yes. Forgiveness in a click.

"Hello, buddy," said Gary, coldly, and I snapped out of it. "Nice little stunt you pulled."

"Gary, I..."

"No, no, I get it, I get it. Student japes. You wanted to liven up a square party. I get it. Are you on drugs now?"

"I am not on drugs. I am never on drugs."

"This better not be psychedelic music tonight."

"It's not, I promise. Look, let me get you a drink."

"Orange juice for me," said Sarah, and I looked at her bump, and I felt so happy for her in that moment in a way that months before I just could not have been.

"Absolutely," I said, and I went to the bar.

"Well, this is awkward," said Zoe, staring at her drink. "I should go."

"Don't go," I said. "What happened was my fault. Sarah knows that. And she knows you've helped me out, helped me get back on my feet. She thinks everything happens for a reason, and—"

And quickly—far too quickly—Sarah was there.

"I can guess what you two are probably talking about," she said. "I knew you'd be here, Zoe."

"Hi, Sarah. Look, I can go, and—"

"I don't blame you for what happened. I wish life didn't happen the way it happens sometimes, but we're adults, and I'm pregnant and about to get married and I'm just exactly where I want to be. So let's all just act like the world is a wonderful place, even if it's just for one night. Because I'm in a good place now. And it's a really good one."

And I looked at Sarah, and I wondered if I would ever be as grown-up or practical as her.

The applause for Abbey when she walked out was rapturous.

From nearly everyone.

"Are you kidding me?" asked Sarah, her face like thunder, leaning over to me as Gary looked on aghast. "Are you *kidding* me!? *Her*!?"

I'd made sure Abbey would have a roomful of friends, whether she knew them all or not. It was like we'd all decided in that moment that she belonged to us. I'd sort of forgotten in my enthusiasm that perhaps Sarah and Gary might remember her with something other than fondness.

"Look, hey, that wasn't her fault, that was mine," I whispered, urgently. "Let's all just act like the world is a wonderful place, and . . ."

But Abbey did the rest for me.

"I would've dedicated this first song to someone who means a lot to me, despite my meddling. I mean, he meddles as well. Don't get me wrong, I wouldn't be standing here if he didn't, but I meddle the most. And with that in mind, I think it would actually be better if I dedicated it to a very lovely and lucky couple who are getting married soon, and whose engagement party I managed to solely and *royally* fuck up. It's about true love, and not pressing charges."

And she started to play. And a few minutes later, I looked over, and Gary was stroking Sarah's bump, and she was squeezing his hand.

Later, I found myself at the head of a long table at the Talk of India.

Dev was on the other side, barking orders at the waiters in Urdu like he'd spent his whole life barking orders, as Pamela looked on, proud. Turns out as a shop manager, Dev is lost. But as a *people* manager, he is, to put it kindly, unusually proactive.

I cast my eye around the room.

Pawel was stuffing his face, Abbey and Matt were clinking glasses, and I broke bread with Sarah and Gary. Just as they'd wanted. As friends, on a normal night out.

"You must be excited," I said. "Wedding next week."

"Yeah, about that," said Sarah, and Gary rubbed her back, gently, adoringly. "Are you still free?"

Oh.

"I'm . . . yes, I'm—"

"Because if you're free you should come. It's been hard, this year, with you. But I think you should come because if you don't it'll be like a full stop. An end to things. And let's not make it a full stop. Let's make it . . . a comma."

"Or an *ellipsis*," said Gary, enjoying the word.

"How are you with that, Gary?"

"Not particularly overjoyed," he said. "I had to buy all new carpets for the footwells, as you know. But I take Sarah's point. No sense running away. Things change. *People* change."

He made a wise face. I'd actually never heard that said in real life before.

"And also," said Sarah, sensing what I was thinking and managing not to giggle. "Look, I know it's been hard, watching me get on with things. And I said some harsh stuff to you. Which I meant. Totally meant. And which I stand by!"

I smiled.

"But which I regret. You know, that stuff about the keywords to your life."

"Oh, yeah!" I said. "Tap 'failure,' 'regret,' 'selfishness,' and 'arrogance' into Google and you'll find me!"

She smiled, embarrassed.

"I don't—"

"I'll be there," I said.

"Good!" said Sarah, grateful to be moving on. "If nothing else, you'll be able to watch a disaster even greater than the engagement party."

I laughed.

"I'm not joking," she said. "Our wedding band has canceled."

"Abba-solutely," said Gary. "They got a gig on a cruise ship."

"Add to that our caterers seemed to be under the impression we were getting married next year, not next week."

"Not guilty!" said Gary. "I'll take the former, but not the latter. That one's Anna's."

I slapped the table with joy.

"Anna messed up?"

Oh, this was terrific! Even Gary gave me a knowing glance.

"Anyway, I have it in hand," he said.

"We're not using Greggs," said Sarah. "I am not having my wedding catered by Greggs."

"It's good grub!"

Over their shoulder, as they bickered, I noticed Dev smiling at me. He raised his glass to me, and I nodded and looked back at Sarah.

"Listen," I said. "I know you've no reason to, but do you think you could trust me just one last time?"

"So have you recorded your stuff?" asked Matt, as I walked back into the restaurant. I'd been outside, on my phone, making a few inquiries. Pretty much everyone had gone by now, though Pawel was still wordlessly munching his way through the leftover naan.

"Just, you know, in my bedroom," said Abbey, one hand on her glass, the other brushing her fringe from her eyes.

"I'm off, guys," I said, but it was like I hadn't said anything at all.

"Only I'm doing a course. And, like, we need to find people to record for our final project."

"Oh."

"So, like, if you need a producer, I'm here," he said. "I mean, I've only just started, but—"

He was blushing.

"I'll see you soon, yeah?" I said.

"We've got studios and that," said Matt. "We could get other musicians in. Or it could be just you and your guitar."

"I'd love that," said Abbey. "Yes."

I made a little coughing sound, like they do on TV programs or in films, to subtly make myself known.

"Like, a natural sound. Not forced. So you can hear the room, if you know what I mean. Like tonight."

"Yeah," she said, excited, "because the room is part of it. The whole world is!"

And I smiled, and left them to talk, and I was pleased as I saw that they hardly even noticed me leave.

And this might have been the end of the story: me, walking out of a restaurant, having made up with Sarah, having come up with a plan to really help them out, having watched my friend Dev—a *hero*!—take control of a new business and maybe even a new life, Matt and Abbey not knowing they were just hours away from a kiss, surrounded by friends I'd helped and who I knew for certain would always help me. In control of things. Concentrating on what I had, not chasing what I didn't.

And it would have been a nice end, of friendship, and curry, and maybe even a glimmer of the hope I'd always told myself to avoid. That maybe—actually—I just thought I didn't deserve.

So yeah. It might well have been the end.

If it hadn't been for one last thing.

TWENTY-FIVE

Or "Sometimes a Mind Changes"

Sarah Jennifer Bennett became Sarah Jennifer Temple on Saturday, November 26, at 2 p.m. precisely, and I suppose the bump in her tummy changed surnames at around the same time.

She looked radiant.

Yeah, I know. An obvious word to pick and certainly overused, but look, you weren't there; it's the most accurate, and it's a word I'm glad to say I can use with the generosity and comfort of a now completely nonjealous ex.

She'd allowed me a guest, and so obviously I'd asked Dev. Who better to ask to a wedding than a socially awkward man with a broken leg you can then spend all day looking after?

But someone else had also helped with the arrangements today, too, and gained a free pass.

"They're ready!" said Abbey, and I noticed Matt was here, too, standing just behind her, sheepishly. Her hand reached for his and he stared at the ground. Wow. He was officially a plus one.

"Hello, mate," I said, and I half thought he was going to say "hello, sir" back.

They looked good together.

I took Abbey's cue.

The DJ was belting out Chumbawamba, which Gary's rugby friends were enjoying a little too much, and I gave him the nod to fade.

"Ladies and gentlemen!" I shouted into the mic, and people spun round, a few of them drunkenly shouting hello back. "Um . . . my name is Jason Priestley . . ."

A woman laughed at this.

". . . and I am Sarah's ex-boyfriend!"

A few mock boos and gasps.

"You're too late!" shouted the priest, who was getting gently sozzled in the corner, and everyone laughed.

"*Stupid Man'd face!*" shouted someone else with great jollity, and the response was more muted. I tried to make out who it was, in case I could reply with something witty. It was Michael Fish, the weatherman.

I moved quickly on.

"So I hope you're enjoying the rather odd buffet tonight . . . a unique Italian-Indian dining experience laid on at very short notice by our friends at Abrizzi's—for that *magical* slice of pizza heaven—and Brick Lane's own Talk of India."

I hadn't meant to, but I'd inadvertently stared straight at Anna when I said this. She avoided my eye, embarrassed.

"It's all *perfect!*" yelled Sarah, starting the applause. Dev raised his hands to try to take some of it, but as he was sitting in his wheelchair, no one could see him, so he stopped again. One of his waiters pointed at him and laughed.

"And as a last special gift . . . well, we were *supposed* to be enjoying the strains of Gary's favorite band, Abba-solutely—"

I could see Gary's bawdy rugby mates pushing his arm and laughing at him, like he was a little Abba-loving lady.

"—but sadly they're on a seven-night P&O cruise to Lisbon this week. So instead, all the way from Brighton—"

I looked at Abbey. She smiled. But tonight, it wouldn't be her that'd be performing. Because from behind her, they started to walk onstage. A young girl near the front gasped.

"—gearing up to release their first album—"

Someone got close and took a picture, then looked round their camera to make sure it was really them.

"You may have seen them on *Wake Up Call* this morning when Estonia Marsh *proposed* to them."

Mikey gave me a little hug. I looked *cool*.

"Sarah and Gary, the happy couple, present to you... *The Kicks!*"

And the crowd went wild.

Even the people who had literally no idea who these young men were—and I'll be honest, despite my impressive buildup, that was most of them—well, they went wild, too.

And moments later, on the dance floor, as "Uh-Oh" filled the room, Abbey was there, and she dragged Matt out... and I turned around, and Pamela was here, spinning Dev round in his chair and laughing.

And I reached for the camera one last time, and looked at it. One shot left.

Was this the one? The moment to capture?

The Girl's camera roll had begun at a wedding. I guess it was fitting that mine might end at one.

"Dance, Jase!" shouted Abbey. "Life is *good*!"

Click.

"A nice thing you did, my friend," said Dev, on the terrace outside. He was having trouble lighting a cigar but pretending he wasn't. "A nice thing indeed. Seems like you're heading for Level Two."

"Level Two?"

"The next level. The future. Moving into your new flat in a couple of weeks, that's Level Two. And Level One's the present. The way I see it, whenever you've got stuff to deal with—unfinished business like Sarah and Gary, or like The Girl—you're stuck on Level One. It's rare to be on Level Two because there's always stuff going on, always overlaps, always some evil end-of-level boss to stop you . . . but *you*, my friend . . . you might just level up!"

I smiled.

"Nicely put."

He stared out into the darkness.

"Like, in a videogame—" he said.

"I understand that you're comparing life to a video-game, yes."

"No, hang on, because you might have to replay a level to make sure you've done everything you need to do. Or in *Call of Duty*, when you move to Prestige Level, there's always—"

"I don't think you should stretch the videogames metaphor any more than you have. I think you should Quit and Save. But I take your point. Level up. I guess that's the terrific beauty of losing your flat and your job and your girlfriend."

"That's exactly it," said Dev, oblivious. "Exactly."

"So they've asked me to speak at a local teachers' conference," I said, shyly.

"Who have?"

"The teaching gods. This inspector heard my assembly and called it 'inspirational.'"

"That's great news, mate! Well done!"

"And I've started to send some stuff off to the mags. Ideas for features, and stuff, you know? And a column."

"A column? A column needs a good name."

"I have a good name: And Another Thing!"

"That's a good name, though I'm worried you'll put an exclamation mark on the end."

"Point is, I didn't feel brave enough before. It's taken me till now to start to feel like myself again. But I just thought: Take the bull by the horns. That's how stuff happens, isn't it? That's how you got Pamela, isn't it?"

Dev made a slightly awkward face.

"What? What's that face?"

"Yeah, me and Pamela. I'm not sure it's going to work out with me and Pamela."

"What? Why?! You put in all that legwork!"

Actually, looking at him, sitting there, he'd probably put in a bit too *much* legwork. Dev dropped his voice to a half whisper.

"She's absolutely lovely, right, but when you get properly talking to her, it turns out she is actually a very boring woman."

"Oh."

"Pawel was right."

"I see."

"Plus she's got a boyfriend."

"Ah."

"But they were on a break."

"I see."

"But I've suggested she doesn't stay on a break very much longer. It's a long and complicated story. But I think we're better off as just friends."

Wow. Friends. That was mature. Maybe Dev had found a little of Level Two as well.

Well, I thought. That's that, then. We got away with it. The wedding had gone well. And Dev was right. It was time to move on.

But then: "One other thing. There *is* one other thing, isn't there?"

"And what's that?"

"Oh, come on," he said, and then he broached it. "Is there anything else at all to sort out on Level One before you move forward?"

"Jason's totally given up on that thing he was doing," said Dev to Pamela, and she sat down, intrigued.

"Why have you given up?" she said.

"It was to do with hope," I said, trying not to sound pompous but failing. "And I realized that actually, the best way to live your life isn't just to hope. It's like Sarah says: you look at what's practical and do that instead."

"Make the best of things?" said Matt, tapping out a Silk Cut.

"Yes! Exactly. Make the best of things."

"Not 'make it happen,' then?"

Caught out.

"Well, you can make it happen by making the best of things."

"Dev told me about the camera girl," said Pamela. "This is the same thing?"

"It is, Pamela," I said, hoping to move things on now.

"And this is camera?" she said, picking up the disposable from the table.

"Nah," said Dev, "I got him that one. To record his little journey. What's on there, do you reckon? When are you gonna develop them?"

"I'm not sure I will," I said. "I'm not sure there's any point."

"What?" he said. "The memories! You and me and a pizza in an Italian restaurant, taken by a man who'd had an affair with her! *That* was lovely! And there was you standing looking all awkward in Whitby."

"There was those blokes running off after I smashed up

that phonebox," said Matt, and Abbey scrunched her nose at him, confused.

"The cinema," said Abbey. "That was a nice day."

"That posh restaurant," said Dev, "with those scallops. I think they're still in my system, to be honest."

"Didn't you take one in a cemetery, as well?" asked Abbey, and everyone laughed, but I wasn't listening anymore, because a strange and unusual thought had struck me.

"The cemetery is the weird one," said Dev. "Otherwise, it's nice pubs, nice restaurants, a nice little film night—"

A strange thought.

But one that caught me like a slap in the face or a stamp on the foot and a thought that now wouldn't let me go.

I ran through it again in my head.

"What was the name of that cinema again?" he asked.

Jesus.

Jesus, hang about . . .

"You always said the photos were themed," I said to Dev, trying not to let the urgency in my voice show. "What did you mean by that?"

"I dunno," he said. "It's . . . it's like all the photos in a disposable belong together, because they're all locked up inside. They're a group. They need each other."

"You're drunk!" said Pamela, playfully.

"No, I mean it," he said. "They mean more in a group. They're a collection. Why?"

I shrugged. I didn't want to say. Not yet.

Because now, suddenly and without warning, there were images flashing at me like the flashes of the disposable.

Trips we'd taken, things we'd seen, things we'd said.

Some made sense, some didn't, but everything was coming at me at once.

The scallops in the restaurant, they came at me.

Damien, in a park, all cashmere scarf and: "Said I'd show her the world. We talked about that a lot."

Shona. Population: two.

The car outside the big white building, the seal fur factory by the pub . . .

Dev in his Nissan Cherry, XFM on the stereo, me looking round: "All the world's on Charlotte Street . . ."

It all hit me and hit me fast.

God.

I'd been looking for clues in the photos. But the clues *were* the photos.

Dev had been *right*.

I was suddenly, inescapably excited. For the first time in forever, there was that feeling in the pit of the stomach, the hope I'd been so used to fighting, the feeling that something might be *starting* rather than just another thing ending.

But how to go about it? How to use these images, these moments, these flashes?

And then I wanted to laugh. Because I *knew* how. We'd discussed it, me and Sarah, just a few nights before.

In fact, it was Sarah that had shown me how.

If you were to type "failure," "regret," "selfishness," and "arrogance" into Google, you'd find a picture of me, my ex-girlfriend had told me, angrily, not long before she married. "Those are the keywords to your life."

I guess we all have keywords. I guess we all have a unique set of characteristics: the DNA we wear on the outside and put on show to the world.

I couldn't disagree with Sarah's assessment of me, based as it was on the me she thought she knew. The mildly grumpy ex, down on his luck, beaten up by life, now not even living in a room above a shop next to a place everyone thought was a brothel, but wasn't.

But I also knew that maybe my keywords had changed.

Changed thanks to Matt, thanks to Abbey, thanks to Dev. Maybe I'd needed Sarah to meet Gary, too, and for all that to happen the way it did. To make the past a thing of the past. Somewhere you can't ever revisit, somewhere you can only move on from, like taking a bad picture on an old camera and just winding the film on.

I'd always been suspicious of hope. But now I could see that hopelessness wasn't the way forward either. It's nice to be surprised by good things, of course. An out-of-the-blue phone call. An unexpected win in life. But how nice it is also to try to make good things happen.

And that's what I was now hoping to do.

So, yes, we all have keywords. But your keywords can change.

Things change. *People* change. And I promise I will never say that again.

But it's only if we're lucky. And it's usually thanks to other people. There's no self-help better than the self-help that comes from someone else. The small group around me had proved that much. They proved we can go from frustration and rage, the bottled-up, pent-up, seemingly unventable fury that soon becomes focus when channeled the right way.

The scared can become brave. The hopeless hopeful.

I'd Googled Shona before, of course I had, and you're silly for asking.

I'd Googled *Shona London*.

Shona London girl.

Shona London I have lost my camera I probably ride an old bike with a basket on girl.

But nothing, obviously, other than the heart-sinking sight of 2.4 million results in 0.06 seconds.

Shona, as it turns out, is not the rarest name in a city of seven million.

But now . . . now I had some of her DNA. I had some of her story. Some of her life. The clues were focused and useful, now no longer just pictures.

Now, they were *words*.

This had all been staring me in the face for so long. The connection I hadn't been able to make until thinking about the reasons for my own photographs: my *own* story.

So, at home, that night, the wedding done and dusted and an old life now finally behind me, I headed for Google and started to type.

The first three words came easy.

ALASKA.

As in the building.

RIO.

As in the cinema.

OSLO.

As in the restaurant.

I thought of the walkway in Highgate Cemetery—the Egyptian walkway—so . . .

EGYPT.

I thought of the pub Damien had mentioned he'd taken her to, the moment captured perfectly in my *favorite* photo, her hair whipped by the wind, her cheeks flushed and warmed, the photo I wished *I'd* been in . . .

ADELAIDE.

And then, as my head began to spin at the link, as the diamonds began to sparkle in the ground as I found my inner fish, and just as I was about to press search, a thought struck me—and I laughed, and I shook my head, and I remembered the sausage and the sweet tea and the streak of a yellow taxi light against the black of a back window and the surprise of finding that *I* had been there *too*.

ROMA.

As in the café.

And finally, to fill the box, to complete the journey...

SHONA.

And *click*.

"A new thing does not come to she who sits, but to she who travels."

—Traditional Shona Tribe proverb, Zimbabwe

Hello.

My name is Shona McAllister.

I am twenty-nine years old.

I grew up in the village of Kilspindie, in Perth and Kinross.

My favorite color is yellow.

My favorite thing is my bike.

And my something-embarrassing is my guilty pleasure. The complete back catalog of Hall & Oates. Can't help it. I was born that way, though I realize I am on my own on this one. ("London, Luck, and Love" is where it all began . . . Thank you, Dad. x)

And with that dreadful confession made, here's another, but on a more positive note: I have decided.

I'm going to do it.

I'm starting to feel like myself again.

Shona
x

TWENTY-SIX

Or "Make You Stay"

He'd promised to show her the world.

That's what I remembered Damien saying.

And so the story of the camera—playing out shot by shot in a 35mm disposable—had been the story of their short relationship. A trip from Alaska to Rio and back again. A story documented in short bursts on the newly bookmarked *MyLifeInProverbs* blog. A whirlwind, *world tour* of London.

Damien was an ideas man, of course. I wonder if he treated the whole thing like a PR strategy. Each date themed around a different place, each photo adding to the story. The perfect set of dates captured as a collection in the same disposable they'd picked up when they first met. The story of a meeting and a split in twelve frames or less.

The more I'd read of her blog, the more bruised she'd seemed to be. There was no mention of what she did for a living (just "work," though I still liked the idea of something with books, maybe, or a university), nor did she make mention of anyone new in her life, aside from a bloke on a bus she was scared she'd catch a rash from.

But the story of her and Damien was there, for all to see, anonymous but familiar.

She was an optimist, but she'd been hurt. I'd stop short of calling her a romantic. She was a realist. An optimistic realist.

There was mention of the night she lost her camera, too, which prickled my skin and made my heart beat faster. I was referred to as both "a guy" and "the guy" in that order. She'd been back to Snappy Snaps the day after, the day I'd seen her while eating my magical pizza in Abrizzi's, and she'd sat in the café once more that night, too, drowning her sorrows in sweet white tea while I avoided mine a hundred meters away.

And she seemed lovely.

And I knew it could never work.

Because The Girl—I could only call her Shona if I knew her, I decided—had made a decision. If someone wouldn't show her the world—if she couldn't see the world *with* someone—then she would see it alone.

She had sold her dad's car, the Facel Vega from her childhood, the one he'd driven her to Glasgow to see Take That in, the one she'd taken on as her own when he'd passed, and she'd raised the money. She'd given up her flat, alerted HR.

So what chance did I stand now? What chance does anyone stand, when the other person doesn't even know he exists?

The Girl would be leaving Saturday morning from King's Cross.

Alone, because like me, she prefers hellos to good-byes.

Maybe if I'd been in a film, I'd have found out the very morning she was going. I could've blamed impulse and urgency and following my heart, for flinging open the door of my flat or leaving an important meeting halfway through or exiting my ex-girlfriend's wedding or a million other tiny sacrifices. But I had all week to wait, and all week to think about it, to change my mind, to decide against turning up, to fantasize about what might happen if I did.

And then one night, Friday turned to Saturday, and the morning was soon upon me.

"No."

"You gotta do it."

"I don't."

"Level Two. You do."

"I don't, Dev."

"You do, Jase."

"I don't, Abbey."

"You should, though."

"I can't, though."

"You should Make It Happen, Mr. Priestley."

I sat in the kitchen, my packed boxes around me, ready for the move, ready for Level Two, and I watched the kettle boil again and again to the tick of the clock.

I'd woken early. Done everything I could to distract myself. I'd opened my laptop, clicked around, found my way to Facebook, and I'd laughed as I'd seen those same, seven words again.

. . . is having the time of her life.

But now they didn't hurt. They cheered me.

I clicked on the pictures.

Sarah. Happy. Tanning. Her hand across her bump. Gary's arm around her, adoringly. I smiled.

Sitting in the winter sun, I saw the postman come and go, heard the dog next door bark its welcome.

And as slowly I left the house, and I walked up Blackstock Road, toward Upper Street, and the Caledonian Road, past Power Up!, and heading for King's Cross, I knew I'd just committed myself to something.

I'd always known I would.

* * *

At the station I checked the platforms.

Nothing for a while. Cleaners, stewards, men with briefcases and papers.

I felt calm. The person I was looking for didn't know what I looked like. The people around me would assume I was waiting for a train. For maybe the first time in my life, self-consciousness didn't come into it. I felt . . . calm. I was in control.

And then . . . like I was drawn to the colors . . .

I stopped for a second, leaned against a pillar, nervously felt for the photos in my pocket, as I'd done all the way from home.

The blue coat. Red shoes. Backpack and bags.

I wanted to run away for a second. To change my mind and turn around. What exactly did I stand to gain here? What was I risking I would lose? What would Dev tell me to do? Well, he'd tell me to Use the Moment, to know that at least something had ended, even if nothing had started, but the thing about—

"I know you," said the voice.

She'd spun around, flashed me a quick smile. *That* smile.

"Hi," I said.

"*Do* I know you?"

I was already closer to her than I'd thought. I pretended to look up at a departures screen, but it was broken, so I looked back again.

This was it.

I had it all practiced, I realized. I knew exactly what to say and how to handle this, because despite myself I'd rehearsed this, and not just once. The best course of action was to be forthright, I'd told myself. Be practical and sensible; approach this like it's the most normal thing in the world. But that all started to crumble now, here, in her presence, around her voice.

"Well," I said. "Here's the thing..."

She tilted her head at me, smiled...Was she remembering Charlotte Street, the taxi, the bags, the driver and his fag? Or maybe she'd noticed me in the café that night? Or maybe it was just because I was here, looking at her, like someone she knew.

A moment's silence, mine to fill. But I couldn't find the words. So I reached into my pocket, and I handed over the packet, now creased and crumpled and torn, and looking as tired and apologetic as I did.

It took a second for her to realize what had happened. That these were hers. That I'd developed them. That I'd seen something of her. Me—a stranger.

She could have done anything now. Shouted, or run.

But she didn't. She opened the packet, started to flick through, a half-smile welcoming home some old and sad memories.

"Obviously...to find you, I mean to give these back to you, because they're *yours*, I had to...you know..."

I indicated the packet. She bit her lip, nodded. I couldn't work out what she was thinking.

"Thanks," she said, looking up. Her next question should have been, "How?"

But she said nothing. Like she'd been expecting me.

I cast my eyes around. Bags. Purse. Eurostar ticket in hand.

There was no time for anything other than this.

Well, this and maybe one more thing.

"Listen, um...in case you ever feel like saying hello...," I said, and I handed something else to her.

My disposable camera. Twelve moments of my own.

She took it, and smiled like she understood, then looked at me once more. It was a look of recognition, something slowly dawning on her, my face meaning more to her than it had.

"I *knew* I knew you," she said.

"I think I knew I knew you, too," I said.

And then I backed away, and left her, to her bags and her train and her future, and I walked away, out of King's Cross, to go and find Dev, and Pamela, and Abbey, and Matt, and tell them all about it, tell them that I'd found her but I'd let her go.

And then we'd drink and be merry, and I'd start the rest of my life, from this day forth.

TWENTY-SEVEN

Or "Halfway There"

"So?" I said, beaming. "What do you think?"

"Amazing!" said Dev, shaking his head, lost in the moment. "Just *amazing*!"

It was an hour since King's Cross and we were in Postman's Park one more time.

Pamela, Abbey, and Matt had wheeled Dev there under the pretense of visiting an unusual Nando's, but in reality they'd brought everything we needed: Pamela had made *krokiety* baps, I picked up a six-pack of Lech, and the grand unveiling—with a little blue curtain St. John's had kept from when Princess Anne had opened the science block in the eighties—had gone well.

A new tile on the wall.

DEVDATTA PATEL, restaurateur and videogame enthusiast

Risked his life on the Caledonian Road to save a stricken cyclist, did not actually die, but with scant regard for personal safety he hurt his leg a bit.

Dev stared at it, proudly.

"I'm gonna bring people to see this, y'know," he said. "I'll be all, like, 'Gosh, is that still there?'"

"Yes, you'll have to act embarrassed and humble," said Abbey, and Matt made a noise like she'd just said whales wear little hats.

I gave the tile a quick polish. It was a little away from the others, this one, and I'd had to sneak in pretty late last night with the contraband adhesive, but there it was, resplendent in the lunchtime sun.

I felt like Banksy. How long until someone noticed? How long until it mysteriously disappeared? It didn't matter. It was all about today. Though I liked to think that maybe it might sneak by forever.

"Here—Pamela . . . would you mind?" I said.

From my pocket I fished something out.

She looked at it. It was bright blue with a flash of red text.

Single-Use 35mm Disposable Camera.

"Is new one?" she said, and I nodded.

"Brand new."

I gave Dev a wheelie to the wall. I spun him round, put my arm on his shoulder, and Abbey and Matt squeezed in either side.

Click.

It's funny. Dev had always said that disposables were different. That what they contained was more special because you couldn't instantly see inside. You had to wait. You had to invest in the moment and then wait to see what you got. And those moments had to be the right moments. You had to be sure you wanted this moment when you pressed the button, because time was always running out, you were always one click closer to the end. That's what it felt like here. But that's what made it exciting.

I looked at the tiny number at the top of the wheel.

1.

Eleven more clicks.

What would they be? Who'd be in them? What story would they tell?

I shoved the camera in my pocket, and looked up at my friends.

I was ready for Level Two.

We had to wheel Dev out of the park backward when we left. He wanted to keep staring at his tile. I could tell what he was thinking. He was thinking, At *last*.

And so was I.

One year later

It was love at first sight for smitten Jason Priestley when a girl he saw on Charlotte Street one night left her disposable camera behind!

Lovestruck Jason, 32, developed the film and discovered to his dismay that the mystery girl already had a boyfriend!

But he persevered and tracked her down to King's Cross train station in London, where he handed over her photos as she left the country to travel round the world—for six whole months!

Shona McAllister, who is 30 and works for a book publisher, was intrigued, and managed to track down Jason's phone number—thanks to a cheeky note his best mate had secretly hidden in the photo packet!

Jason, a part-time teacher who also writes the And Another Thing . . . column for style magazine Man Up, *says: "I have always believed in making it happen!"*

And of finding love thanks to a camera, he says, "I suppose you could say we just clicked!"

The pair recently announced their engagement.

ACKNOWLEDGMENTS

My biggest thanks must go to Greta for her never-ending support, to Mum and Dad for theirs, and to Elliot, who makes life such fun.

Thanks so much to Dave Cobbett for advising me so brilliantly on the life of a London teacher.

Thanks to Jake Lingwood for saying I should write a novel and for his invaluable advice throughout. Thanks to Simon Trewin at United Agents for the same, and to Jago Irwin for the fun that comes after. Thanks to Gillian Green for her attention to detail and excellent ideas, to Ed Griffiths in advance, and to everyone else at Ebury for all the incredible work they have put into my books over the years. Thanks to the estate of the much-missed Richard McFarlane—aka Hovis Presley—for allowing me to include his lovely poem.

And thanks to you for reading.